I0549121

Some magical force had taken slices of cities from our world and reassembled them into a bizarre mosaic in an alternate reality. Dash is a private detective who works in this patchwork of cities and who discovers that there is a sinister connection among some of his current cases.

MANAGANSETT PRESS

MULTIPLICITY

Don D'Ammassa

This book is a work of fiction. Names, places, and events are not based on real people or places. Any resemblance is purely coincidental.

Copyright ©2015 by Don D'Ammassa. All rights reserved. If you would like to use material from this book other than brief excerpts for review purposes, prior written permission must be received by contacting the author at dondammassa@cox.net.

Managansett Press Edition 2015

MULTIPLICITY

CHAPTER ONE

The sun was just creeping up above the roof of the Parthenon as I turned my Studebaker onto the on-ramp for the Golden Gate Bridge and left Brooklyn behind me. I could tell that a fire crew had been at work recently because the kudzu had been driven back again, clearing all lanes for travel in either direction. The tresses and uprights were still completely shrouded above the reach of the salamanders so it was like driving through a claustrophobic yellowish green cave, or down the throat of a sea serpent. Not that I've personally been inside a sea serpent, mind you, but I know a guy who has and he described it pretty graphically. Occasionally unseen things moved within the vines, or perhaps the kudzu itself was becoming more animated.

At the moment there were no other vehicles in sight. Traffic seemed to grow lighter every day; gas tank demons had been scarce all summer and every automotive thaumaturgist in the Cities had a waiting list. A few vehicles here and there have been modified to run on more conventional fuels, but since we don't have many oil fields to drain and we're already approaching the limits of how much hydroelectric power we can generate, the choices are limited and unattractive.

At the foot of the off ramp, I turned north, then detoured west to leave a respectful buffer around the Tuilleries, which sat in the middle of lower Manhattan like a boil waiting to burst. Whatever mysterious force had copied slices of cities from the Original World and reassembled them as the Cities had slipped up occasionally, which is why the Golden Gate Bridge links what's left of Brooklyn to Manhattan and the Taj Mahal sits on what should have been a soccer field in Athens. We live in a chaotic patchwork of cultures and architectural styles that snuggle against each other in patterns that bear no relationship to the geography from which they were taken, but within each slice the arrangement of buildings and physical features remains almost always unaltered. It is true that

Manhattan ends just north of Central Park, which abuts the southern borders of Washington and Moscow, but Fifth Avenue still runs north and south, and the Empire State Building is right where it is supposed to be. Similarly, Brooklyn has been truncated just a few blocks east of Prospect Park and the fragment that remains is a roughly triangular island joined to the mainland by two bridges and one tunnel, the only island we have, so far.

The one glaring exception is a roughly rectangular block overlaying Union Square Park, which contains a distorted but recognizable version of the Tuilleries Gardens, notably missing from our slice of Paris. The Tuilleries are a striking anomaly in a world filled with incongruities, and are acutely dangerous as well. The containment system is supposed to prevent anything from escaping that hellish place, but there were periodic budget cuts and the wards weren't always maintained adequately. From time to time the protective spells misfired and reacted to the aura of an innocent passerby, and the Cities would eventually pony up a cash settlement for the next of kin. Since I had no Uncle Lemuel to make wealthy in his dotage, I wouldn't even have the satisfaction of knowing my death had profited anyone.

The inhabitants of the Manhattan zone of the Cities were beginning to stir by the time I reached midtown, sidewalk vendors setting up their stalls, maintenance workers gathering the night's debris with recycling spells, homeless people and a few unpeople as well, staking out the best begging spots for the day to come. I even caught a glimpse of a tardy lattice weaver retreating up the side of a skyscraper to its nesting place on the roof. The lattice weavers did not come from the Original World, of course, nor did the handful of trolls and goblins who'd managed to integrate themselves into human society, but if any of them knew why we'd been brought here, they weren't telling.

Ditto for the human population. We were all copied along with everything else in the Cities and we assume that our originals continued with their lives, unaware of our existence. I don't even have the questionable satisfaction of knowing what my real name and situation might be back in the Original World, since I was just an infant when my chunk of Brooklyn manifested itself as an island off the coast of Manhattan and Paris. As our population ages, memories of the Original World are slowly fading from our collective consciousness and for the younger generation, the Cities are the real world. The occasional influx of newcomers when another piece of the jigsaw is added to our evolving puzzle is quickly diluted.

Some of the new arrivals retreat into themselves when faced with the reality of the Cities. Typically they refuse to leave their home segments and try to pretend that nothing has changed, really. But this is the only world I've ever known, and I've made a point of getting to know it. I live in Brooklyn and have an office in Manhattan, but I've been aboard one of the handful of offshore drilling platforms sprinkled across what we call the Gulf to the south, and I've been ice fishing in the Arctic Ocean to the north. I've visited every one of the Cities at least once and I can make myself understood in a dozen languages. I've eaten sushi in Kyoto, gotten drunk in Berlin, played darts in Dublin, and fell in and out of love in Venice, and on each occasion I drove home at the end of the day. The world is what it is. We are what we make of ourselves.

I was delayed for several minutes just south of Central Park. A work crew was gathering the scattered wreckage of a limousine into a dump truck so I guessed someone's restraint system had failed and a tank demon was on the loose. They would try to recapture it, of course, since they're a vanishing resource, but the odds weren't good. At that time of the morning, swarms of fishing boats were already working the Atlantic to our east and far to the west there was almost certainly a flotilla of junks making its way along the coast of one of the barren areas, preparing to set out toward the South China Sea to fish. We had named the waters surrounding the Cities as a matter of convenience, since as far as we could tell they stretched off forever into what some of us called the Big Empty. We don't have a panoramic horizon curve here in the Cities; it's just a straight level line which, I'm told by people who are smarter than I am, means that the greater world is flat. I'll take their word for it.

Land traffic had picked up by now, mostly cabs and pony carts, but I reached the autopark I favored without trouble, less than a block from the Museum of Natural History. The damage deposit had gone up again; I had barely enough cash to cover it. "What's going on, Hamish? This is the third hike this month."

Hamish looked up from the bowl of goatmeal he'd been messily devouring and scowled as only a troll can scowl, but I could tell that he wasn't really annoyed. There were only a few hundred trolls in the Cities, most of them concentrated in Rabat, but Hamish and his family had emigrated to Manhattan and bought themselves an autopark after choosing the wrong side during some kind of tribal rift. I'd helped out his wayward nephew a year earlier, and Hamish had been noticeably less unfriendly ever since. Of course with trolls, that still left him miles away from cordial or even neutral. "Another tank demon escaped yesterday. Tore up most of Level Three."

"You're insured, aren't you?"

"They raised my premiums again, Mr. Dash. Old model cars can't handle the higher level demons." He glanced at my ancient Studebaker and his eyes narrowed.

"I upgraded my containment just last year." It was true, but I had upgraded from a fifteen year old system to one only half as obsolete. On the other hand, I'd been using the same tank demon for almost ten years. If it hadn't escaped by now, it probably never would. The truth was that I couldn't afford a replacement. The wild ones had become progressively harder to handle because their less powerful and skillful brethren were captured before they could generate more of their kind. We had selectively bred them to the point where the next generation might see the end of most powered vehicular traffic within the Cities. Of course this was all a metaphor, since they're not really demons, or alive for that matter, but they function as though they are.

I walked from the autopark, approaching the Kremlin from the southeast. The Mayors hadn't finished their relocation from the Parliament Building, and the streets on the other three sides were congested with moving vans and their cargo. Two heavy set men were yelling at each other, one in French, the other in Arabic, while a handful of day laborers stood around looking bored or amused. A pair of young entrepreneurs were hawking falafel and cold drinks respectively, and doing a surprisingly brisk business. I showed my identification to the security guard and he waved me through with a flurry of incomprehensible Russian. There was very little signage inside; about half the doors had nameplates but there was no building directory and each corridor looked pretty much like the next. The entire complex had been guidespelled though, and I made my way without hesitation through a maze of intersections, even though I'd never been inside the building before.

Although each segment of the Cities was theoretically autonomous, it had quickly become obvious that there needed to be some consistent overriding authority to deal with trade and other issues that transcended borders. The Mayors – not all of whom technically held that title – were the supreme political figures in their respective home segments, some elected for specific terms, others self appointed for life or until the next assassination. Collectively they functioned as a kind of congress or parliament, electing officers from among themselves, passing laws that they could agree should be applied universally, and quarreling endlessly about many others. Every two years the seat of government shifted, and London's term had just expired so things were even more unsettled than usual as the Mayors and their staffs adjusted to their new circumstances.

Mayor Burford's name was on his office door, but it was hand lettered on a sheet of paper taped to the glass. As I raised my hand to knock, the door opened without human intervention. Obviously I was expected. The temptation to ignore the summons made its last appeal and I hesitated. Most of the Mayors were career politicians, which meant they were more or less corrupt. Usually more. This particular summons had come from Mayor Henry Burford, who represented the Boston segment, which included Boston Commons and the land east to Chinatown and southwest to include most of the South End. I was from Brooklyn and technically not subject to his authority, but it was not a good idea to piss off any of the Cities' leaders. The Minsk communists might not get along with their immediate neighbors, the Mecca Saudis and the Raj, but their respective Mayors had no trouble putting aside their differences when there was wealth or influence at stake. Mendacity was the glue that held our government together.

It was a small corner office on the outside, but Burford must have had considerable financial resources because an expansion spell was in place and you could have played soccer on the inside. I began to sweat the moment I saw it. I used to know a guy who got caught in one of these when it collapsed. The owner's credit chit had bounced and the spellcaster repossessed his charm. There was no way to separate out the remains so all twelve deceased were buried in a mass grave about the size of a grapefruit. There were half a dozen clerical workers in the front section of the office, each in his or her own cubbyhole, but none of them even glanced in my direction. Directly ahead was the receptionist's desk. A mildly pretty, businesslike woman greeted me by my name.

"Good morning, Mr. Dash. Go right in. He's expecting you." Her voice was professionally warm but her eyes were shuttered. I might have been just another piece of paper in her inbox. She pointed to a partitioned area in one corner. The door was unmarked and closed. "It's all right. He knows you're here. He takes a precognition pill with his morning coffee."

Henry Burford looked vaguely familiar, somewhat heavy set, rather jowly, hair so neat that it might have been painted onto his skull. He smiled insincerely without rising from his ornate desk and gestured to a chair that looked so fragile I was surprised when it supported my weight. Designed to make visitors less certain of themselves, I figured. I decided to let him speak first.

"Thank you for coming, Mr. Dash. Could I often you some coffee or other refreshment?"

It was obviously his standard greeting, all the words blurred together. "I'm good, thanks."

The social amenities disposed of, he switched from impersonal to attentive. "I imagine you must be wondering why you're here."

"I'm a private investigator, Mr. Mayor. I assume you have a problem which requires my services." I leaned forward and casually laid one hand on his desk, intruding into his territory. It was a deliberate act and I was glad to see that he blinked and pushed his chair back a fraction of an inch. Politicians are by their nature bullies and opportunists and I find it helpful to keep them just slightly off balance.

"More precisely, the Cities have a problem. As a representative of our community, I have the pleasure of enlisting your aid in finding a solution."

I didn't like the sound of that. "I appreciate the opportunity to serve, sir, but with all due respect, I have to pay my bills like everyone else." That actually wasn't literally true in our three communist boroughs, but he knew what I meant. "I understand some of the bigger agencies do pro bono work from time to time, but I'm a one man operation."

Burford's face was unreadable. "I'm aware of your situation. You'll get your standard daily rate, plus a personal bonus from me if, no, when you settle the matter."

"Which matter might be what?"

"There's been a murder."

That caught me by surprise. "So why call me? You could ask for help from the Gestapo, the KGB, or the LAPD to name a few." All of whom had seers and clairvoyants on their staffs. I couldn't compete with them, which is why I eked out a marginal existence working for people who couldn't afford the high priced talents, or whose problems involved things best concealed from the authorities. Fortunately, there was a lot of the latter.

"We've considered that, but the circumstances of this case are rather unusual. The official agencies have regrettably become perhaps slightly too dependent upon their special talents, talents which are decidedly inferior to your own in this particular case. You see, the murder took place at the Baker's Dozen."

This time it was my turn to blink. The Baker's Dozen is a hotel, but it's also an anomaly within the greater anomaly of the Cities. We have a few hybrid buildings here and there; the Vatican and Windsor Castle abutted each other thanks to the way Vatican City and London were sliced, and they now have a common wall. But that was built after the fact and the interiors of both buildings conform to their counterparts in the Original World. The Baker's Dozen is the only such building whose individual components technically never existed elsewhere.

The hotel consists of the thirteenth floors of thirteen separate hotels. None of which had thirteenth floors in the Original World. And magic doesn't work inside the building, although I suppose that's not entirely true since the building is itself magic. But you can't cast a spell or mix up a viable potion or set a ward or invoke a demon. Trolls and other inhumans can go in and out, but they don't stay long. Apparently it makes them ill. I'd driven by it a few times but had never been inside.

"Why is this particular case so important?"

The Mayor's face twitched but I couldn't read it. "Let's just say that it has the potential to generate rather embarrassing repercussions for the greater community. I understand you have a reputation for discretion."

I sighed, not entirely for effect. "Look, sir. I'm a businessman. Murder investigations are messy, time consuming, dangerous, and generally unprofitable. I don't have the personnel or resources, arcane or otherwise, to handle elaborate investigations. As much as I would like to help you out, I just don't see how it makes sense economically for me or practically for you."

Burford gave no sign that he'd even heard me, let alone recognized my objections. "I'll be paying you as special consultant to the city of Boston so I can't raise your fee above standard. It would violate local as well as Cities policy. On the other hand, as I said before, I'm a concerned private citizen and I would be willing to supplement that fee with a small bonus from my personal account." He mentioned a number so low that I wondered why he had bothered. I couldn't decide whether I should be insulted or amused.

"I appreciate your generosity," I said with just a hint of sarcasm. "But I still don't think I'm well suited for the job."

He nodded just perceptibly, an acknowledgement to himself rather than a sign to me. The Mayor was no fool. He had anticipated my reluctance and was about to play the card he'd been holding back. I wasn't being coy; I really didn't want this job. But I was curious to see what he was going to offer.

"There's going to be an official Public Appeal tomorrow, concerning a different matter. Since you're a licensed investigator, I imagine your office will be receiving notification sometime this morning."

That got my attention. "Is it the O'Brien case or that business in Baghdad?" A young woman had been killed in Dublin a few weeks earlier, rather messily. The case remained unsolved and a Cloak of Secrecy had kept further developments pretty much out of the public view ever since, although the word on the street was that the killer had struck again and that the Mayors were keeping a tight lid on the case. The Baghdad bombings were likely a local political problem, but Mayor Hussein insisted that outsiders were responsible and had demanded an all-Cities investigation. He had stayed in power for years by convincing his people that they were being targeted by outside agitators, and quietly killing those who weren't convinced. There had been talk of removing him, but the right of autonomy remained as an unspoken but very real barrier to concerted action. After all, if one Mayor could be removed from power by external forces, what would prevent the same principle being used again?

"I can't reveal any details before the Appeal is officially made." This was probably literally true; the Mayors would all have submitted to a compulsion spell preventing them from spilling the beans, by accident or by intent.

Like I said, I don't take on murder cases but if the Mayors issued a Public Appeal, it would mean that the Police were stumped and the Mayors were willing to pay a very large bonus to any private party who pulled their collective chestnuts out of the fire. It would likely be as much or more than I made in a year, before expenses. "So what are you offering? Once the Appeal has been issued, I'll have access to all of the information that's available, and so will every other investigator or interested party."

"All of whom will be considered temporary contractors for the Police Forces, who will naturally report all progress promptly to any of the Mayors who request that courtesy."

It was a legal fiction, but a convenient one. Respondents to a Public Appeal were assigned a liaison within the Police through whom they could channel queries and to whom they were supposed to report any progress. Because an Appeal was a competitive arrangement, contractor access was limited to information gathered by the Police Forces themselves. Respondents could choose to exchange information with one another voluntarily, but their communications with the authorities were kept strictly private. At least theoretically. We both knew the rules, so Burford had raised the point for a specific reason.

"Are you offering to tell me what the other investigators are doing, Mr. Mayor?" It was supposed to be impossible to cheat without getting caught by truth sensing spells, but it was an open secret that there were ways to beat the system. There are always ways to beat the system.

Burford managed to look distressed and amused simultaneously. "Of course not, Mr. Dash. I'm shocked that you would ask such a question. I would never share privileged information with anyone except my personal staff." Shocked or not, he was wearing a smile that said he was waiting for me to hear what he was really saying.

I blinked. Was he implying that one of his staff members would act as a conduit?

Burford sat back in his chair and folded his hands over his chest. "However, I think you should know that I believe in keeping everyone who works for me thoroughly briefed at all times. You do remember that I promised you a bonus, drawn from my personal account, when you clear up matters at the Baker's Dozen? I would be willing to consider advancing that as a retainer, contingent upon a successful outcome."

I caught on, finally. By offering to pay me out of his own funds, Burford was making me a de facto employee, to whom he could convey information which would otherwise be constrained by ethical considerations or magical compulsion, more likely the latter. I still wasn't sure I liked the situation, but the potential return was enticing. Even if this particular Appeal was beyond my reach, it couldn't hurt to have a connection with a Mayor. On the other hand, if I couldn't handle Burford's current little problem, he'd undoubtedly be disappointed. Refusing outright, unfortunately, was not going to improve things.

"All right, I'll go over to the Baker's Dozen and look at the crime scene. But this is only provisional, Mr. Mayor. I honestly don't think I'm the right person for this job."

"You come highly recommended, Mr. Dash. Your clients report a very high success rate."

"That's because I'm selective about the jobs I take."

Burford brushed aside my reservations. "I've been told that you are a very resourceful person. I have every confidence in you. They're expecting you at the hotel. Ask for Connors, the head of security. I can't give you official authority over the police, of course, but they've been instructed to cooperate."

I had arrived curious and was leaving with a sense of foreboding. Part of the trick of being successful in the investigating business is to know your strengths and limitations and skew things toward the former. Only one of my previous cases had involved a murder, and I hadn't known that when I took the job or I'd have lied and said my workload was too heavy to take on any additional clients. Most detective work is boring and I liked it that way.

I retrieved the Studebaker, which had developed a bang in the engine – probably the tank demon trying to hammer its way to freedom. In the distance, I could see that it was snowing in Washington and it looked like thunderstorms off toward Paris. I glanced at the weather chart on the back page of the morning paper and was pleased to see that the Commons area would be warm and sunny for the remainder of the day.

It was only a short drive to the Baker's Dozen, which sat in a little bubble of empty land just beyond the now truncated Beacon Street. There were three police cruisers parked in front but their flashers were off and there was no sign of a crowd of spectators or reporters. Either this was being handled very quietly indeed, or the mob had already come and gone. From the outside, the hotel looked like a very neat pile of rubble, the architecture varying dramatically from one floor to the next. The Black Cat Lounge was on the ground floor. An elaborately decorated stepladder straddled the entrance to play on the bad luck theme, although no luck charms – good or bad – would have any effect once you were inside the building proper.

The autopark attendant was human, but he was even more disagreeable than Hamish. When I identified myself and asked for Connors, he glared at me and complained that there weren't enough spaces for the guests, let alone visitors. I ignored him for the minute or two it took before the security chief showed up.

Connors turned out to be Sheri Connors, who wore her obsessively neat civilian clothing as though it was a uniform and who was obviously expecting me, but not pleased about it. Her hair was short and well disciplined, her eyes constantly moving to assess her surroundings, and she radiated controlled tension, a compressed spring waiting to release its kinetic energy. She didn't smile, which was a shame because I thought she might actually be pretty if she did, shook my hand perfunctorily, and didn't ask to see my identification, which was just as well because I'd forgotten it. Again. She was polite, not cordial, and I hoped we weren't about to engage in a turf war.

We entered through a rotating glass door. Facing us was a small lobby with the usual, a registration desk, plush chairs too hideous to describe, fake plants, and so forth. The far wall was interrupted by a single door marked "Private – Staff Only" and two elevator bays. A youngish man, also not uniformed but with a nametag on his pocket – Douglas – was holding one of the latter open and watching us expectantly. Connors nodded to him without speaking and punched for the thirteenth floor, not surprising since all but two of the buttons bore the same number. I wondered if you memorized which was which or if it didn't matter. Maybe the elevator just knew which destination you wanted.

Anyway, we got out on the thirteenth floor, having exchanged less than a dozen words, and Connors led the way to one of the suites, room 1313. Douglas wandered off but I'm sure he was within hailing distance. The door was closed and the man standing outside DID have a uniform on, a Boston cop. Only his eyes moved, giving us the once over as Connors turned the knob and we entered. I noticed that the chain lock had been ripped from the wall. "Forced entry," I said quietly.

"Very perceptive." There was no sarcasm in her voice, which only emphasized its presence in her mind.

"Just thinking out loud," I said defensively. I hate it when people make me defensive.

"The victim is in the bathroom." Connors pointed the way.

The victim was a woman, and she was very dead. Someone had driven a wooden stake through her heart. It was about as long as my forearm and roughly carved, obviously fashioned in a hurry and without the proper tools. We don't have vampires in the Cities. Or at least, we haven't up till now, although there were groups of vampire wannabes, mostly bored young adults looking for a new thrill who pretended to that lifestyle, complete with clan marks tattooed on the sides of their necks and faux blood cocktails. We have at least a couple of dozen major cultures and scores of lesser ones sprinkled across our world, but some people still have to create fantasies of their own.

The dead woman was lying on her back with one forearm across her face. "Can I move her?"

"The police already did," said Connors, who stood with her arms crossed, regarding the corpse without visible emotion. I'm not fey so I couldn't read her, but she seemed almost angry. I suppose I couldn't blame her; this wouldn't reflect well on her next performance review. "They needed to confirm the ID. We put her back the way she was so you could view the scene the way we found it. The coroner's team is waiting downstairs to take her away." And the sooner the better, no doubt, from her point of view.

I don't like dead bodies, even the ones that don't move around on their own. I reached down and caught the sleeve of her nightgown – she seemed to be naked underneath – and tentatively lifted the arm, half expecting to see fangs. Her mouth was slightly open and her teeth looked normal, but I gasped anyway.

"Recognize her?" Connors actually sounded amused and I realized she'd been waiting for me to react.

"It's Mayor Porter. What was she doing here?"

Bad tactics. My tone had suggested that the Mayor had been slumming. I'd impugned the Baker's Dozen and I could hear the irritation in Connors' voice. "This IS a five star hotel, you know. She told the desk clerk her apartment was being repainted. The Mayor has stayed with us occasionally in the past when she wanted to avoid company." She let a second pass, then reverted to her usual neutrality. "But I asked the same question for a different reason. This isn't Mayor Porter's room."

I stood up. "Say again?"

Her eyes flickered up to the ceiling, translucent panels slightly discolored by cigarette smoke. "She checked into Room 1313, one flight up."

"Then whose room is this?"

Connors shook her head. "It was vacant. A housemaid came up to freshen the linens and couldn't open the door because the deadbolt was engaged. One of my security people broke the lock and found the body." She glanced toward the tiny sitting room. "There's a broken chair in there. One of the legs is missing. It was made of wood."

"The stake?"

"Not officially confirmed yet but I'd say the probability was approaching certainty." A hint of sarcasm again.

"Probably not premeditated then." I looked around. There were no personal items in the bathroom, no sign that it had been used recently. Without speaking I went back into the bedroom. No luggage, nothing hanging in the closet, and there was no loose change or other personal items in sight. "Could she have gotten a key to this room?"

Connors was right behind me, as though she wanted to be certain that she saw everything I did. But I had the sense that she'd been watching me rather than the crime scene. Trying to take my measure, no doubt. "There are no pass keys missing that we know of. If she had one, it's gone now. We checked the pockets of her robe and searched the suite. Nothing. Her own room key is upstairs."

I crossed to the windows. They were locked from the inside. We appeared to be on the top floor of the hotel, but since all of the rooms were on the same floor, that didn't seem to make sense. My head started to hurt. "Then how did she get in here? Magic?"

"Magic doesn't work at the Baker's Dozen."

"I know that!" I snapped. "I was being ironic." Out of the corner of my eye, I saw just the faintest hint of a smile, or maybe a smirk, but it was gone like a firewraith in a thunderstorm. I glanced up at the ceiling over the bed. The panels there were of mirror glass. I wondered what kind of hotel this particular thirteenth floor hadn't existed in. "Let's check out her room upstairs."

Connors led the way. I was expecting a return to the elevator or maybe a staircase but she just led me through a disconcerting maze of corridors until we reached another Room 1313. There was a uniform standing outside the door, but not the same one.

"Weren't we just here?" But even as I said it, I knew we hadn't. The first Room 1313 had been in a dimly lit corridor with frantically busy flower patterned wallpaper. This was set in a brightly lit cul-de-sac with painted walls.

"Since all the floors are the thirteenth, they all interconnect. We only have to use the elevator to get to the roof or the garage and lobby."

But from the outside, the hotel was thirteen stories high. I shook my head, not wanting to think about it.

I spent almost an hour going through Mayor Porter's personal belongings. It was all pretty much what I expected to find – makeup and toiletries in the bathroom, a few assorted items of clothing in the closets and drawers, one large empty suitcase, and an attaché case. Enough for a weekend, or perhaps a bit longer. Everything was arranged perfectly, her blouses absolutely square in the drawers, the shoulders of her suit expertly draped over its hanger. Even her makeup was lined up like a row of soldiers with no drip marks around the caps. The bed was still made up, but very rumpled, as though someone had slept on top of the bedspread. Or perhaps they'd indulged in something more energetic than sleeping. An ice bucket was sitting on the night table, with two inches of tepid water.

"I don't think the Mayor was alone," I suggested. Connors didn't answer, but I could tell that she'd come to the same conclusion. Or maybe she'd known that from the outset. This looked like a carefully planned, discrete assignation. But something had gone wrong. A lover's quarrel? A jealous wife?

I glanced through the contents of the briefcase, similarly neat and orderly, but nothing stood out. Position papers on various bills before the Mayors' Council, yesterday's *Boston Herald*, a book of crossword puzzles, and the latest Nora Roberts romance. Roberts was abducted, or copied, along with the rest of us. Why couldn't it have been Stephen King or even J.K. Rowling?

I tried the less obvious places next, but there were no loose tiles in the ceiling, nothing under the mattress, no hidden pockets in the luggage, and no bottles of blood among the complimentary cocktails in the tiny refrigerator. I had just about run out of places to look when I noticed that one of the large area rugs was not lying properly square relative to the wall. A floor lamp anchored one corner, and it too seemed out of place. It was too far forward to have provided much light for anyone sitting in the adjacent chair. I thought about Mayor Porter's precisely arranged personal possessions and knew that this would have driven her crazy.

"Step back out of the way for a minute." Connors gave me an odd look as I lifted the lamp and set it down on the bare floor. I grabbed one corner of the rug and pulled it back.

Even thus exposed the anomaly was hard to spot but when I got down on my hands and knees I could see that a half meter square of the hardwood floor had been cut out and then set back in place, the work so meticulous that the seam was almost invisible. There were two well camouflaged finger holes at one end and when I tugged, I felt resistance, and shifted position for better leverage. Wood scraped against wood and the section of floor came up, revealing a clear glass plate. There was an unmade bed directly below us. Connors crouched down beside me.

"One way glass," I said quietly. Down on my knees, I tapped at it tentatively, then felt around the edge until I located the latch.

The near end gave way and the pane fell open, dangling from a pair of well concealed hinges.

Below us was Room 1313. The other Room 1313.

"Well, now we know how she got there," said Connors, whose immobile face concealed her reaction to my discovery.

"And how someone else got out."

"What's that?" I could see something metallic on the opposite side of the hatch, just visible where it peeked out from concealment. Connors shifted position, reached down and felt around between the floorboard and the drop ceiling. Her lips thinned as her fingers traced the shape of the hidden object. "Mini-camera," she said quietly. "Someone's been naughty."

Security at the Baker's Dozen was atypical. Most hotels, at least the good ones, have wards in place that deny entry to anyone who isn't a legitimate guest or visitor. Since magic doesn't work here, management had resorted to using cameras and live security personnel and, Connors admitted, coverage was far from complete.

"A lot of people come here to avoid being seen, so management obliges them and keeps surveillance to a minimum."

"So someone could have walked in off the street without being questioned and gone directly to Porter's suite?"

"Well, yes, if they were careful and knew what room she was in. We don't release that information without the guest's permission. The Mayor wouldn't have wanted her whereabouts to get out." She bit her lip. "Public figures need a refuge where they don't have to worry about slipping out of character. We try to shield them from intruders."

"So the Mayor didn't have to worry about being inundated with angry constituents." Porter was Mayor of Hollywood, in her first and now last term, although had she lived it is unlikely that she would have been re-elected. Even Schwarzennegger was ahead of her in the polls, and he had died a few weeks back. "Can we find out if she officially entertained any guests while she was here? Or would that be too indiscrete?"

Connors gave me a reproachful look. "We keep a log."

The desk clerk was very helpful, even though he had just come on duty. "All visitors and guests are logged in and out if they stop at the desk." He ran his finger down one page after another, stopping three times. "Mayor Porter checked in at 10:05 yesterday morning. She went out for lunch at 12:20 and returned almost exactly an hour later." He turned the page. "She ordered room service for her evening meal. Called the desk at 6:30 and told them to admit two guests."

"And they were...?"

"Deborah Lerner. Evan Garner. Lerner came at 6:45 and left at 7:20."

"She's Porter's executive assistant," explained Connors, her voice a degree or two warmer than it had been before I'd found the concealed hatch. "She lives in Hollywood. I can give you her address if you want."

"Garner arrived at 7:30 and left at 9:00."

"That's Evan Garner, the sculptor," Connors advised me. "He's also one of our regular guests."

"Do we have a time of death yet?"

"Tentatively 11:00 PM, but there's a two hour margin of error. The air conditioner was turned up full blast when we forced entry, so the body cooled down faster than usual." She ran her hands through her hair, a nervous gesture I'd noticed once or twice earlier. Behind the professional façade, a real person was tense and tired. "And no, the police couldn't raise her spirit and ask. They'll try again at the morgue during the scryopsy, but if you don't raise them during the first hour, it's usually hopeless."

"What's the line on Garner?"

Connors looked vaguely uncomfortable, perhaps reluctant to violate the privacy of a customer. "Rumor has it that he is, or was, her current boyfriend. I've seen no real evidence of it. He lives in Whitechapel, not far from London Bridge, but his studio is in Paris."

I was impressed. "Do you run background checks on all your guests?"

Connors shrugged but looked uncomfortable. "I take my job seriously, Mr. Dash."

"It's just Dash, no mister." I turned back to the desk clerk, who shrugged. "That's it, sir. There are no other entries concerning Mayor Porter."

"You said she ordered room service."

"That's right."

"What time was it delivered?"

The clerk frowned. "That's not in my log, sir." His face brightened. "I could call Food Services."

"No, that's all right." I turned to Connors. "Let's pay them a visit."

Food Services was in the basement, so we had to take the elevator again. Connors led me to a small, glass sided office where I shook hands with a nervous looking, acutely thin man named Bransky. His attenuated frame made a poor advertisement for the quality of the food served at the Baker's Dozen. He had a shamrock sewed into the lapel of his jacket.

"Mayor Porter was most explicit in her instructions," he said nervously, refusing to meet my eyes. "We've had the honor to see to her needs on previous occasions, and successfully I believe, but she has always been very demanding. She was very specific about the way her meat was cooked, for example."

"What time did you serve her yesterday?" I asked, cutting off what promised to be a detailed description of the late Mayor's culinary preferences.

"Let's see." He glanced at a sheet of paper on his desk. "That would have been at 7:40 give or take a minute or two."

So it had arrived while Garner was still with her. "And what time was it taken away?"

He turned the paper over and frowned. "Well, there was a bit of a mix-up about that. Mrs. Dorrance, that's Emily Dorrance in Room 1313." He frowned. "One of the other Room 1313s, you see. She called and requested retrieval and one of our busboys, he's new you understand, well, he went to the wrong room. It does take a while to get used to things here."

"So when were the Mayor's dinner things actually picked up?"

He shuffled the paper again. "The cart was returned here at 8:35 so it would have been perhaps ten minutes earlier."

Which placed it shortly before Garner had left. "Can we talk to the person who delivered the food?"

"Yes, of course." He consulted his paperwork once more. "It was Peter Robertson, and as it happens, he's on duty right now."

Peter was summoned to the office, where he sat nervously, apparently concerned that he'd done something wrong, or more likely that he'd been caught at it. Connors tried to reassure him but she was so stiff that she probably made things worse rather than better. I was starting to get a handle on her now. She was a small woman, almost petite, in a job that was usually reserved for macho, overbearing men. That meant she was good at her job, probably, but it also meant that she would be constantly on the defensive, would feel it necessary to prove herself at every opportunity. And that sometimes led to overcompensation, even bullying. I finally cut in before she scared him into clamming up completely.

"You're not in any trouble, Peter. We just need to know if you saw anything unusual when you made one of your deliveries last night. To Room 1313."

He seemed relieved to have a clear question to answer, then frowned. "Which Room 1313? I delivered to at least a dozen of them last night."

"The one Mayor Porter was staying in," I said impatiently.

He didn't look any more enlightened, but Bransky finally proved helpful. "The veal, Peter, with artichoke hearts, brazed chicken livers, and anchovy paste on the salad."

"Oh, that lady!" He brightened up. "I didn't know her name but I could hardly forget her. Came to the door half naked. Came on to me a little too," he laughed uncomfortably.

Bransky started to admonish him but I raised my hand. "So she was in a good mood?"

"I'll say. But it came out of the bottle, I'm sure. I've waited on her before and she's always been a real bitch." He glanced suddenly at the frowning Bransky. "I mean, I brought her dinner once a couple of weeks ago and she had quite a temper then, but last night she was very friendly, if you know what I mean."

"So she'd been drinking?"

"Yeah, I could see a couple of champagne bottles on the dresser. One of them was lying on its side, so it must've been empty. And there was a guy with her and he was holding a glass."

"Could you identify him if you saw him again?"

Robertson looked uncomfortable. "Maybe. I don't know. I only saw him for a minute and he wasn't looking in my direction. He was just a guy."

I turned to Connors. "Does the hotel have a bar?"

"Of course. But Porter didn't order anything from them. I checked."

"How about Garner? Could he have bought the champagne before going up to her room?"

Connors frowned, apparently annoyed with herself. "Give me a minute." She used Bransky's internal phone, asked a couple of questions, and hung up. "We don't have a name but someone picked up three bottles of expensive champagne at 7:20 last night. He also bought two wine glasses."

I nodded and turned back to Robertson. "Did either of them say anything to you that seemed unusual?"

"No, sir. He didn't say a word, and she just teased me a little, then lost interest when I didn't respond. She gave me a tip and I left."

I was trying to decide if there was anything else I need to ask when Douglas appeared at the door, apologizing insincerely. "There's a Summoning Sphere hovering outside the front entrance and it insists on seeing you, Mr. Dash."

CHAPTER TWO

If you've never been chased by a Summoning Sphere, you might not appreciate how effective they are. Once they've reached their target, they relay their message in increasingly strident tones until they're satisfied that you're going to comply. This one came from Moira, my secretary, and she used a spellcaster who was particularly skilled at fashioning them. Barred by its nature from entering the Baker's Dozen, it hovered directly in front of the main doors and began repeating its demand that I come to the office immediately. It had reached screaming level by the time I arrived and was getting ready to move on to shriek mode.

"All right, I'm going," I reassured it, but Moira knew me too well. The first few times she'd summoned me, I had broken my promises. Now the Sphere was waiting for some evidence of concrete action before it would desist.

"Someone wants you really badly," said Connors, implying that no one at the Baker's Dozen would fall into that category.

"I have to go," I said unnecessarily. "But I'll be back. Would you let me know when you or the Police contact Lerner or Garner?"

"All right, assuming the Police bother to keep me in the loop. Should I let them take her away now?"

"The body?" I thought about it and nodded. "I can't think of any reason why not. But I want to see the post-mortem report."

"I'll relay your request to the Police. I don't have any more authority over them than you have, probably less." She looked as though she was going to say more, but the Sphere began its prepared speech again and threw her off her game.

"I'll be in touch." I tried to make it sound friendly, but it came out terse and dismissive. I find it difficult to think clearly when there is a glowing object the size of a basketball screaming into my ear. "All right! Give me a break!"

It fell mercifully silent as soon as I stepped away from the hotel, but it followed me all the way to the Studebaker and hovered overhead during the drive back, threatening to resume its tirade if I took a wrong turn.

I live in Brooklyn, a little house on a hilltop that gives me a great view of the Eiffel Tower. I share the place with Darla, my cat, whom everyone assumes is a familiar even though she's actually just a very good mouser. My office, however, is in Manhattan, a half mile northwest of the Tuilleries, near the border with Pretoria. I took what should have been a shortcut through Berlin, but got delayed on the Danziger Strasse when a tank demon escaped its confinement and wrecked six vehicles including a small bus before vanishing. I sat for almost an hour, amusing myself by watching an angry young man hacking at a thick mass of webbing a lattice weaver had draped over his balcony. Several rickshaws passed while I was waiting and I had time to reflect on the possibility that this was the future of inner city transportation.

The Sphere correctly interpreted the situation as beyond my control and remained mercifully silent. It hovered directly overhead, however, and I attracted a small crowd of street kids who tossed pebbles for a while before losing interest. Some components of the Cities tried to restrict contact with outsiders, but the interface was porous and younger children in particular seemed to have an almost magical talent for evading detection. Judging by their clothing, the little crowd I attracted included kids from Rabat, the Raj, and either Peiping or Hong Kong, as well as locals.

Eventually the road ahead was cleared and an arched bridge took me back into Manhattan. I found a parking space on the street and a few minutes later entered my building. As I stepped through the doors, the Sphere silently imploded behind me, its duty done. The doorman was human – management couldn't afford a troll – and he had a marvelous gift for conveying his disapproval with minimal fuss – a lifted eyebrow, a slight adjustment of the edges of his mouth, a subtle change of posture. He'd replaced old Jacob, who'd finally retired a few weeks earlier, and I didn't know his name yet. He nodded disinterestedly as I passed, barely raising his eyes from the magazine he was reading. There was a sign on the elevator door. "Levitation Spell Failure. Please Use Stairs." So I did; I was only on the third floor.

I passed the law firm that had become my most recent neighbor and then skipped the door with my name on it, using my key to open the unmarked one just beyond. It was only a few steps down the inside corridor to my private office, and the rear entrance bypassed the waiting room. Moira would know I was in, of course; she was fey enough to pick me up anywhere in the building most days, and often managed to track me down even when I slipped out for a break.

Sure enough, the intercom light started to blink as soon as I reached my office. I caught my metaphorical breath, anticipating a cannonade of unpleasant news.

"Yes, Moira?"

Her voice was calm and businesslike, which didn't fool me one bit. She was mad at me again. Or still. "Mr. Pheng has called twice already this morning. He says you promised him a progress report today and he's very anxious to see it. The check finally arrived from Loing and Wartsoff; I put it in your inbox for you to endorse. Please note the amount. Your ten o'clock appointment has been here for over an hour and she looks about ready to jump out of her skin. Mrs. Croydon called to thank you again for clearing up her little problem and wants to know when you're going to keep your promise and come over for tea and biscuits. Mr. Delianides also called and insisted that you reconsider his offer if he agrees to pay for a minimum of ten days surveillance. Cities Revenue would like to know exactly when you will be filing your returns for last year, which are now three months delinquent, and I'm sure it slipped your mind but I still haven't been paid this month. And how are you this morning, boss?"

"If Mr. Pheng calls again, tell him the day isn't over yet, and if Mr. Delianides calls, inform him once again that I don't do divorce work. I'm looking at the check and it is not what we agreed upon. Please call Loing and Wartsoff and advise them that the amount is in error - again. Mrs. Croydon is very welcome but my social calendar is quite full just now, I've left my checkbook home but I'll be sure to bring it tomorrow, and I'm fine thank you. You can show the new client in as soon as you've brought me some coffee."

The door opened almost immediately and Moira was holding a steaming mug in one hand. She could be frighteningly efficient when she wanted to be, but she was careful not to spoil me by being consistent. The coffee was as good as always and I sipped it thankfully before glancing at her. She was wearing a plaid skirt this morning, incongruously mismatched with a ruffled blouse and a beaded shawl. Moira was a very attractive young woman but she had less clothing sense than a troll.

She stood in front of my desk, waiting patiently until the first hit of caffeine reached my bloodstream. Moira is not a small woman; I'm taller than most and the two of us see eye to eye even when we don't see eye to eye. "And where have you been all morning? This is late, even for you."

I repressed a sigh. "Long story. I'll fill you in later. Have you read the new client yet?"

"You could almost read her yourself. Her sister's missing. She's badly worried and it's not pretense. She's also actively afraid of something, but her emotions are muddled. It might not be related." Moira always evaluated new clients while they were waiting; she had just enough magic to pick up major emotions and even the occasional powerful thoughts. "I also think she's got a secret she doesn't want revealed and she's nervous about speaking to you. I'd be wary of this one. She doesn't mean you harm, but she wouldn't weep at your funeral either."

"We all have secrets," I said mildly.

Moira shook her head, suddenly serious. "It's more than that. There's nothing more important to her than keeping this hidden. She's even having doubts about whether she should be here, whether she's risking too much even to find her sister. There's danger there."

"All right, I'll be careful. Send her in." I rearranged myself behind my desk and tried to look competent and efficient. Image is important in this business, sometimes almost as important as results.

I sensed something wrong the moment she walked through the doors. I didn't need Moira's magic to tell me that Rachel Deacon was disturbed. She hesitated in the doorway until she'd scanned the office thoroughly, hesitated noticeably before taking one of the chairs facing my desk, and gripped her purse so tightly that I thought she'd dislocate her fingers. She appeared to be in her early twenties, good looking in a vaguely unapproachable way, expensively and tastefully dressed except for the ornate and slightly oversized amulet that hung from a gold chain around her neck. It was probably a protective charm of some sort, though unconventional in design and placement. Most people preferred not to advertise their use of magic because it implied that they were somehow inadequate in conventional terms. Charms and amulets were meant to be discrete, worn inside the clothing or with a minimal visual footprint. Only mundane jewelry was allowed to be gaudy and obvious. But this was too ugly to be ornamentation, and it clashed with her outfit.

"I need your help, Mr. Dash." She had a strong voice, deep and rich. Rachel Deacon would probably best be described as handsome rather than pretty, only slightly shorter than Moira but with a lot more flesh on her bones. Most of it in exactly the right places. I normally don't mash on the clients, but I hadn't had more than a casual date since Katrina broke things off and six months was a long time to grieve for a broken relationship, particularly when that relationship had been uneasy even in its best moments. The only jarring note was a hint of frostiness. It was in her voice, her posture, and her eyes.

"Well, I hope that I'll be able to help you. Would you like some coffee?" She shook her head, then glanced around the room again, her eyes jumping from one point to another rather than sliding. "I understand your sister is missing?"

"Yes. I haven't heard from her in three days. I've checked her apartment, and there's no sign of a struggle or anything like that."

"What about her workplace?"

"Ruth's a freelance photographer and photojournalist. She turned the spare bedroom into an office and works at home."

"Could she have gone off somewhere without telling you? Most missing person reports are just miscommunication, you know."

She shook her head vigorously. "That's not the case this time. Something is seriously wrong. The people at her apartment complex told me that she hasn't left the building since the last time she logged in, and their guardian confirms it. But she's not in her apartment and before you ask, no, she's not the type to shack up with a neighbor for a few days. I've already hired a professional scryer, a woman named Dussaud. She seems quite certain that my sister is not in the building or the immediate vicinity, but she couldn't pick up a departure trace either." She took a folder from her voluminous purse and set it on my desk. "I gathered all the background information I thought you might find useful."

The puzzle pricked my interest. Whether the doormen were troll or human, they were certainly fallible and probably amenable to bribery. On the other hand, if the apartment complex had a guardian spirit installed and it confirmed their story, then it was equally certain that Ruth Deacon had not left using conventional means. I knew Marie Dussaud personally as well as by reputation and she wasn't likely to have been fooled or mistaken. The contradiction was intriguing.

"Did my secretary explain how we charge?"

"Yes, that's not a problem," she said quickly, and I noticed an immediate change in her attitude. She had expected to be refused. I made an intuitive leap, which usually gets me into trouble.

"This isn't the first agency you've approached, is it?"

Her eyes dropped and she made some totally unnecessary adjustments to her clothing. "No, it's not." I let the silence prolong itself, and she eventually sighed and looked up at me. "You're the fourth. I'm sorry, but I have no experience with this kind of thing. I didn't know what to do."

"Who turned you down?" She hesitated, but I prodded her. "I'm not offended, Miss Deacon, and I have a reason for asking."

"All right. I went to Touche Anderson, Bagwell & Chandra, and Darke Inquiries. None of them were interested. They all claimed that they were too busy to take on new clients just now."

The names she had given were the first three in the rainbow pages; Dash Investigations was the fourth. Touche was brilliant but boring; his specialty was document analysis and ferreting out concealed financial transactions. Missing persons weren't his line at all. Darke Inquiries attracted a lot of clients with their flashy advertisements and their caseload might indeed have been too heavy for them to take on another case, although it sounded peculiar. But I'd had lunch with Maggie Chandra two days past and she'd been complaining about how slow business had been lately. This was exactly the kind of job she and Tina liked, but they'd turned it down. Why? Had Deacon told them something else that she'd concealed from me?

"I can't promise you anything, Miss Deacon, but I'll look into the situation on a preliminary basis for our minimum fee. If I decide that it would be useful to continue, I'll be in touch and we can negotiate further terms. My secretary will take your deposit and I'll get back to you in two or three days, sooner if something turns up. Is there a recent picture of your sister in the file?"

She looked momentarily confused. "No, I don't have one with me. No, wait." She fished around in her purse again and then handed me a flat, inanimate snapshot. A familiar looking woman stood in front of one of the finest restaurants in Tokyo, wearing a business suit and an oversized amulet on a chain around her neck.

I looked up at Rachel Deacon in confusion, and she answered before I could voice my question.

"Yes, that's a picture of me. Ruth and I are identical twins, Mr. Dash."

I stood up, spoke a few obligatory hopeful reassurances, then escorted Rachel Deacon to the door. Moira was waiting just outside, wearing her professional smile, but I sensed that she didn't care for our new client. You don't have to be fey to read Moira; you just have to know how she expresses her feelings.

The next thing I did was call Marie Dussard, who confirmed Rachel's account in every detail.

"It's beyond my talents, Dash," she admitted readily. "I checked everywhere within three blocks of her studio. It is my professional opinion that she never left without also returning. The tracks cancel each other out."

"Then she must still be somewhere in the building."

There was no response for a second or two. "While that might be the logical conclusion, I've never heard of a guardian being wrong before, and the building guardian says she's not within its walls."

I didn't like where this was leading. "If she's not in the building anymore and she never left, then she's dead, isn't she?"

"That seems the most likely explanation."

Even over the phone, I could hear the skepticism. "Then why don't you believe it?"

"Because her sister insists that she's alive."

"She wants to believe it. That doesn't mean it's true."

"Ordinarily, no, but they were bonded on their thirteenth birthday. Their souls are connected. If one dies, the other will follow, within days if not sooner."

Which Rachel Deacon had not told me and which might explain her obvious anxiety. I didn't know much about bonding, except that it was powerful, dangerous magic. "Could the link have been severed somehow? Maybe Ruth didn't relish the idea of being dependent on her sister's well being. The downside is obvious."

"I've never heard of such a thing. I don't think it's possible. The souls are not attached, Dash, they're merged. They feel each other's pain but they can also draw on each other's strength."

We talked a bit longer and I thanked her and hung up, not particularly pleased by what I'd learned. Ruth Deacon had entered the building where she lived and worked but had not come out. She wasn't there now and she was presumably still alive. All I had to do is find her. But if she wasn't inside the building, and hadn't left, then where was I supposed to start looking?

When Moira walked into my office a while later, I still didn't have a viable line of investigation, let alone an answer. "This just came for you." Her voice was marginally warmer now that Deacon was gone. She handed me an oversized envelope, sealed with wax. "Are you in trouble with the Mayors again?"

I shook my head. "Not that I know of. I think this is an invitation to a Public Appeal. I got a tip this morning."

Moira claims she can't read me, but sometimes I think she just says that to make me feel at ease. She gave me a sharp look now that told me she knew this was something out of the ordinary. I hate concealing things from Moira, even little things. For one thing, she knows when I'm being less than candid and resents it, even if I am the boss. For another, she almost always finds outs eventually, whether I tell her or not. "I thought you never paid attention to those things."

Ordinarily true. I didn't have the resources to compete with the bigger firms. But this time I had an advantage, or would have if things worked out right at the Baker's Dozen, no sure thing in itself. "It won't hurt to find out what they want." I tore open the envelope and unfolded the parchment. As expected, I was invited to participate in a Law Enforcement Posting. No further details, of course. The Mayors didn't like to advertise those cases where they were compelled to rely on outsiders to solve their problems.

She wasn't buying my act and we both knew it, but she pretended to be fooled. "Morris called while you were interviewing Miss Deacon. He wants you to stop by."

Morris was an old friend, my oldest friend in fact. I was just an infant when my neighborhood was joined into the Cities thirty years ago. Things were pretty chaotic back then, I guess. The Council of Mayors hadn't been formed and there was no one waiting to explain the situation to new arrivals. Not that we know a whole lot even now. There were riots and looting and general chaos before cooler heads were able to begin restoring order. Major battles were fought over food stores and medical supplies until it began to sink in that magic worked and that supplies were spontaneously regenerated, with a few peculiar exceptions. We no longer had cottage cheese, for example, or broccoli.

I was found lying in an alley beside a dying woman, who was presumed to be my mother. We were both taken to a makeshift field hospital and admitted together. The woman carried no identification and was listed as Jane Doe23. My entry followed, reading simply "baby" followed by a dash and a question mark.

Morris Ngambe was working as a volunteer and he was the one who began calling me Baby Dash. Jane Doe23 died without regaining consciousness and I was sent into foster care, but Morris continued to take an active interest in my welfare. As a teenager, I worked part time in the small coffee shop he opened on Bourbon Street, and later in his curio shop off Broadway. Morris had ambitious ideas back then and hoped to spread his influence throughout the Cities. A lot of the old barriers were down at first as people huddled together against the great unknown, but when the novelty began to wear off, the old ways returned. Plans for a central government foundered early and the Mayors remained as a cohesive force only because they avoided meddling in one another's affairs.

But for a while, it was like a frontier. A very crowded frontier. I worked in store fronts Morris opened in Addis Ababa, London, and New Delhi, and visited half a dozen other zones often enough to pick up a smattering of the local languages and cultures. Language turned out to be my strong point. I could make myself understood almost anywhere in the Cities now, though I'm sure my accent was painful. About ten years back, Morris reassessed the situation and decided to put all his marbles in one jar, Manhattan. It was the right choice for him, but my skills weren't as valuable there, so he loaned me the money to set myself up as a private investigator, and I'd paid him back right on schedule even when the telephone company was threatening to cut me off. I still owed him, but the debt that remained was not financial.

"This really isn't a good day for it. Can you call him back and tell him I'll try to come tomorrow?"

"He said it was important. I can't read someone over the phone, but he sounded upset."

I've never known Moira to misjudge the seriousness of a situation. I glanced at my watch. "All right, I'll go see him."

Morris had started as a street vendor working against the grain. He sold falafel in Dublin, used the proceeds to buy Irish stew and colcannon to peddle in New Orleans, then, Cajun food and beignets in Khartoum, and so on, working his way through the Cities, setting aside a little more cash after each stop. Sometimes he sold things that weren't on the menu. The existence of magic was not welcomed universally. In places like Baghdad and Berlin, where the local leaders were obsessed with personal power, the possibility that ordinary citizens might employ extraordinary remedies to their problems was a disconcerting concept and efforts were made to suppress the trade in amulets, charms, and potions. Predictably, this made smuggling a very profitable sideline for itinerant vendors.

There were no uniform currency exchange rates in those days and the banks weren't able to cope for a long time, so Morris converted most of his profit into real estate and durable goods. Within a couple of years he had six small shops scattered through the Cities, the biggest of which was the Lagos Castle in Manhattan, a cubbyhole in the warehouse district that had no inside seating but an enviable reputation. Morris had the foresight to liquidate most of his other sites when things began to settle down and decided to raise his profile in Manhattan.

The Lagos Castle no longer served people out of a window facing the sidewalk. It was a large, lavishly furnished restaurant three blocks south of Central Park that required reservations at least a day in advance for a sit down meal, although there was a more accessible lunch counter between the main dining area and the attached gift shop. Morris had also become one of the larger dealers in low level magic charms, potions, wards, and associated paraphernalia in the Cities, as well as a variety of other mismatched merchandise. He was the exclusive distributor for several well respected charm casters.

I took a cab this time to avoid the parking problem, ignoring the constant chatter from the cabbie, a Scot with an unusually heavy accent. He threaded his way through a throng of automobiles of various vintages, rickshaws, brougham carriages, motor scooters, and pedestrians. I even saw a couple of flying carpets and one set of litter bearers, which was odd because none of the Cities predated the 20th century. I used the restaurant entrance, avoiding a group of young beggars who had come up from the Raj wearing specially designed rags to shame the unwary into giving them a handout.

Lily was on hostess duty and she flashed her best smile, waving me past the stern faced greeter. "He's in his office, Mr. Dash. He said to send you right up when you arrived."

As usual, every table was occupied. I noticed a party of Arabs trying to look inconspicuous as they drank the wine they weren't allowed to touch at home, and the Mayor of Port Au Prince sat with his wife and two of his mistresses, all of whom seemed to be having a great time. I threaded my way through the crowd, avoiding the fast moving waiters and waitresses whose ability to avoid spilling their overflowing trays struck me as verging on magical, and found the nondescript door at the rear that led to Morris' inner sanctum. The doorknob turned into a snarling dragon's head when I reached for it.

It growled at me. "No admittance!"

"He's expecting me. I'm Dash."

The dragon's brow furrowed and then slowly morphed into a miniature replica of Morris Ngambe. The face grinned at me and the voice changed, assumed the familiar melodic tones of my friend. "Come on up, Dash." Then it was a doorknob again and felt perfectly normal as I turned it.

The office was at the top of a short flight of carpeted stairs. It was a large space, decorated with what Morris told me were authentic reproductions of artifacts and flowering plants from his homeland. Morris was Nigerian, a trade representative who happened to be in Brooklyn at just the wrong time. To date, no portions of Nigeria had been added to the Cities, although we had pieces of Nairobi, Addis Ababa, and Khartoum, a tiny sliver of Conakry, and most recently a segment of Pretoria.

Morris rarely used the oversized desk at the far end of the room and was waiting for me in a recessed alcove furnished with comfortable chairs and a small bar. "What can I get for you, my friend?" He gestured toward the array of liquor bottles.

"Just a beer. How have you been, Morris?" Morris is a very large man, well over six feet tall and heavily muscled, although in recent years the muscles have been slowly melting into fat. His close cropped hair was gray but just as thick as ever.

He handed me a glass of rich, dark beer, properly chilled, before answering. "Myself, I have been as good as always. But my business," he shrugged his shoulders. "It's been having some problems."

I sipped at the beer. It was just the right temperature. The glass was undoubtedly charmed to sustain that until I was finished. "You still seem to be packing them in downstairs."

"I have been able to contain the situation so far, but it's only a matter of time until it gets out of hand."

"What situation?"

He sighed. "It started perhaps a month ago. We began to have a few complaints in the restaurant. The first few cases might have been human error. The wrong ingredients, an error in procedure. I have excellent people working for me, but no one can be at the top of their game every day. I thought it was just a streak of bad luck at first and hoped to wait it out, but the incidents have become more serious recently, spoiled food, sour wine, inadequate hygiene. Someone substituted shrimp for chicken when Rabbi Yehzoud ordered fried rice, and two imams were served pork. Several of my customers have suffered food poisoning and I have been forced to invest in an expensive upgrade of our food preservation spells."

"I know it's unethical, but could one of your competitors be behind it? This sounds like more than just a prank. It wouldn't be cheap to get past your kitchen security charms."

Morris shrugged again. "It is possible, although I can think of no one I would accuse of such a thing. There is more than enough business for all of us at the moment."

"An old enemy?"

He shook his head wearily. "Perhaps, though I have outlived those whom I thought angry enough to do me actual harm."

"How about a disgruntled employee? Someone on the inside who knows how to get around your protective spells?"

He shook his head. "Again it is possible, but for what reason? I have had no serious problems with my staff for several years."

I considered possibilities. "Could you be using a flawed spell, or some combination which interacts adversely? You know, the spell that ages your wine quickly might be conflicting with the anti-spoiling charms."

"Not according to Tilden and Gerber. I had them in for a consult and they went through everything."

I dismissed that possibility. Mel Tilden and Edna Gerber were the best analysts in the Cities. If they hadn't found a glitch in Morris' magic system, then it wasn't there. "I sympathize, Morris, but I don't know how I can help. Magic's not my strong point and even if it was, I wouldn't be able to do any better than you have already."

"There is more." Morris let the words hang in the air for a few seconds. "When you have finished your drink, let us take a walk together."

There was a second exit from the office, this one opening on a narrow corridor that crossed over the main restaurant. One way glass let us look down on the crowd without being seen in turn. At the far end, the corridor turned to the left, eventually leading to the second floor of the elaborate gift shop that adjoined the Lagos Castle Restaurant. We stepped out into an array of clothing racks bearing shirts, sweaters, hats, and other paraphernalia all emblazoned with the distinct logo of the Lagos Cafe. The door closed behind us and immediately vanished, leaving behind only a narrow stretch of bare wall.

"This way." Morris led me to the charm shop, almost a store within a store. There were several hundred charms displayed on the walls and inside locked glass cases, arranged by function. There were love spells and protection spells, the two most common, but only a handful of each. The ones you could purchase from street vendors were almost as effective, unless you wanted something unusually powerful, and countercharms were sold in equal quantities. Obsessive love spells were illegal throughout the Cities, although they could be found if you were determined, and for industrial class protection spells, you went directly to the conjurer and had the conjuration tailored to your specific situation.

Most of the business done here was for less common applications. I saw charms related to health issues, particularly memory loss, and others that enabled the bearer to find a lost object, to sleep without dreaming or avoid sleep without adverse side effects. There were investment charms and good luck amulets and wards against allergies, accidents, and bad weather. Even as I watched, a teenaged girl approached the attendant, a woman about my own age, and bought a potion that held acne at bay.

"So what am I looking at, Morris?"

"You know where I get my merchandise, don't you?"

"Sure." Morris only dealt with established vendors. Everything he sold did exactly what it was advertised to do. Sometimes customers assumed too much, but Morris always stood behind his advertising.

"Three weeks ago a customer bought a good luck charm. She was knocked down by a bicycle messenger the moment she stepped out the door, suffering a broken arm." He let me digest that for a moment. "Two days after that, we were notified that a Miss Acosta was suing us for non-performance. She bought an anti-allergen bracelet and less than a day later she was hospitalized after being briefly exposed to peanut oil. Another young man bought a mild love potion and was savagely attacked by his girlfriend after she had taken the potion voluntarily to improve the intensity of their relationship. Since then we've received an average of one complaint a day. They've been relatively minor so far, but it can only be a matter of time until we face a serious charge."

"Have you contacted your suppliers?"

"Of course. Ori Kanazawa and Meg Ogden came in personally and audited their items. They each discovered that approximately one third of their merchandise had become corrupted. Some were ineffective, some distorted, and a few generated exactly the opposite effect to that which had been intended. Ori suggested that we'd been subjected to a polarization curse but such things apparently leave an arcane residue and the sweepers found no evidence of outside interference."

"So they were defective when you bought them?"

Morris shook his head. "I am the exclusive distributor for Ori, but Meg sells her work to several other outlets. None of them have experienced anything similar. We removed the defective items, but when Meg returned two days later, several more of her charms had become unsaleable." The last two browsers left the area and Morris waved to the attendant, beckoning for her to join us. She had long black hair and strikingly dark, recessed eyes. It was almost as if she was looking at us through a mask.

"This is Jessica Crane, one of my most valued employees." She smiled tentatively but her eyes were watching me intently. "This is that friend I was telling you about."

Her smile broadened. "Mr. Dash. I've heard a great deal about you."

I've never known how to respond to that gambit except with a cliché, so I ignored it and tried one of my own. "I'm charmed to meet you."

Both of them grimaced and I guessed that this must be an old joke. "Sorry. I couldn't resist. I understand you've been having some quality problems."

She glanced at Morris for approval before speaking and he gave it to her silently. "I just don't understand it. We've been selling some of these items for years and I've never had a complaint before. We hadn't made any changes to our security system for months before this started, and the upgrades we've made since don't seem to be having any effect. I hope you'll be able to help us."

My head was beginning to hurt. I owed Morris big time and I knew I'd do whatever I could, but this was another problem not in my area of expertise. Murder and magical corruption, both in the same day. Maybe I was the one who'd been cursed rather than Morris. "I'll do my best, Miss Crane."

"Jessica, or actually Jessie, please."

Morris looked marginally happier. "I just wanted to make sure you understood that Dash here has my full backing, Jessie. Anything he wants to know or see is all right with me. You don't have to wait for my confirmation."

"I'll be happy to do anything I can."

Morris put his hand on my arm. "We're not done yet. There's one more place we need to go."

He led me down a spiral, wrought iron staircase to the street level, which was filled with display cases. The merchandise here was primarily mundane, cut glass decanters, hand carved jewelry and figurines, other gifty and rather pricey items. Morris told me once that he couldn't sell less expensive giftware because his customers expected to feel the bite in their wallet. Since his business was obviously thriving, I couldn't quarrel with his assessment. Even the committee members who jointly served as Mayor of Communist Peiping were among his regular patrons. We swept past the displays and entered a narrow corridor that led to the rear of the shop, which betrayed its nature by the distinct smell of old books even before we were able to see them.

The selection presented for sale reflected the taste of the owner more than anything else in the building. There were a few copies of recent releases at the entrance – the latest Eve Dallas thriller, Paul Di Filippo's *Return to Salem's Lot*, a romance novel with a lurid cover – but beyond that the store was divided into three distinct sections. To the right, an array of cookbooks covered an entire wall and the first aisle adjoining it. Prominently featured were several titles bearing the Lagos Castle logo on their cover, supposedly revealing the secrets of Morris' highly trained chefs, actually a distillation of the best recipes he'd found while he'd been working his sales circuit as a young man. To the left, covering another wall and a somewhat shorter aisle were books about Nigeria and adjoining portions of Africa in the original world. Morris had an extensive collection of his own in his apartment, but he had gathered here virtually every other surviving volume in the Cities. They were priced so high and required such a specialized interest that he rarely sold any, but sometimes they were borrowed by interested scholars.

In the center, and extending up a short flight of stairs into a low loft, a selection of magical books, documents, and even scrolls filled the largest part of the store. Like myself, Morris had no magical abilities whatsoever, but that didn't prevent him from being very interested in the subject. He probably knew more about conjuration and simple spellcasting than most professional practitioners and he had even lectured from time to time at both the New School and the Sorbonne.

Everything looked perfectly normal to me and I glanced at my companion, waiting for him to explain. Morris stepped behind the counter where the cashier, a spindly young man with a Mohawk haircut, ignored him after a brief glance. There was a small safe under the counter, which Morris opened quickly. He took out two books, both of them quite delicate looking, the pages and even the covers threatening to disintegrate.

"Come look at these."

I joined him at the counter. He had opened one of the two, which appeared to be a parchment manuscript bound by having a leather cord wound through a series of holes at one edge of each page. I glanced down and read the page he indicated, which didn't take long because the words were scattered at odd intervals and most of the parchment was blank. The spelling seemed archaic and the words made no sense, as though they had been extracted at random from a more complete document.

"This is a copy of the diary of Nicholas Vail."

I knew that name. Vail was one of the first people to begin codifying the magical laws that prevailed in the Cities. He had been living in lower Manhattan when the area one block south of his location up through and including the lower half of Central Park suddenly found itself transformed into a smaller island surrounded by water, the first portion of the Cities to make the transition. Chunks of other metropolitan areas, at least one so small it contained only a single building, had been added ever since at the rate of about one every four months, although the pace of addition was apparently slowing.

"He wrote on parchment?" That made no sense. The additions to the Cities were as disparate in time as in location, which is why we had Nazis in Berlin, simple fishermen in Hong Kong, and advanced electronics in Boston, but the earliest segment was Kyoto from around 1900.

"No, he kept his journal in a set of three ring binders. This was a replica published in a limited edition several years ago, with a modern binding." Morris looked almost as though he was feeling pain. "This copy was perfectly all right ten days ago. Then the pages began to yellow and the binding fell apart. I locked it up for safekeeping and when I came back a few days later, it had deteriorated, and not just physically." He tapped the open manuscript with one finger. "The paper turned to parchment and the binding has changed completely. But what is even more disconcerting is that words have been disappearing from the text. What remains is almost unintelligible now." He turned to the other book and pushed it toward me. "Now look at this."

I picked it up. The binding was solid and the pages, though somewhat brittle with age, were paper. It was a hardcover but there was no dustjacket and no title was embossed on the cover. I opened it.

The book was *The Bonds of Enchantment* by Marilyn Soo. It was a layman's guide to love spells and it had been published within the last few weeks. But this copy felt as though it had been around for at least a hundred years.

CHAPTER THREE

I left Morris with a promise that I would look into his problems, but with little confidence that I could do much to help. Whatever was wrong involved magic, sophisticated magic, and if the experts he'd consulted already couldn't help, there was little chance that I would be more successful. The only angle I could think of was to find out who might have it in for my old friend. If I could figure out the who and the why, I might be able to proceed to the how and then to stopping it.

The day was pretty much gone and I almost welcomed the drive back through the kudzu to Brooklyn. I turned on the radio, listened half attentively to the news. They still hadn't been able to move the Bedouins out of Central Park, the Israelis and the Palestinians had both closed their borders again, Bollywood and Hollywood were proceeding with their joint ventures, easier now that their production lots were adjacent, the Raj wanted the Mayors to order Berlin to remove the offensive billboards facing in their direction, and the Vatican still hadn't decided on a new Pope. The Tokyo Tigers were heavily favored to win the Cities Series this year, but the Toreadors from Madrid had won the opener in a squeaker.

Over time, I make a decent living as an investigator, but it's a roller coaster ride. Sometimes I have had as many as three active cases, sometimes none at all. I've been months behind in the rent and once or twice a month or two ahead. On a few occasions I've hired people to work a case for me, particularly when there was lots of surveillance involved, but I mostly prefer to work alone. Surveillance is expensive and boring, which is why I don't take divorce work. Unless I'm desperate. Moira and I have a workable relationship, but I'm no better at being a boss than I am at being an employee.

But within a matter of hours I was facing three very difficult, perhaps unsolvable cases, and even if the Public Appeal tomorrow proved interesting, I wasn't sure I'd have time to deal with it. Mayor Porter's murder looked reasonably straightforward, and there was a good chance the police would solve it themselves. It was just a question now of finding out who had motive and opportunity. I was betting on the new boyfriend. The Deacon case was a real puzzler, although I had only the sister's secondhand account so far. It was possible that something would pop up and scream at me once I actually started poking around.

The problems at the Lagos Castle were probably out of my league, and I reluctantly decided that they were going to get the lowest priority. I would ask Moira to get in touch with a few people, try to find out if there were any rumors of bad blood, but I couldn't believe Morris had ever done anything to evoke this kind of animosity. The Porter case was problematic, but I'd have to at least appear to be working on it in order to satisfy Mayor Burford. Rachel Deacon hadn't been completely honest with me, which I resented, but given the possibility that her own life was at risk if her missing twin was in danger, I decided to give her the benefit of the doubt. Tomorrow I would call her and we'd visit the sister's apartment.

I reached home at dusk. The streetlights were off again but the magic lantern above the door recognized me and lit up in welcome. I opened the door carefully; Darla is a housecat but every once in a while she thinks otherwise and slips past me if I'm not careful. She was waiting for me, with that indignant posture that reminded me I'd forgotten to feed her. I rectified the situation – dry food today – and she began looking for the good bits.

The house is too big for me, technically. There are four bedrooms upstairs, but three of them are pretty small. I'd cleared the furniture out of one so that Katrina could turn it into an office – she's a freelance graphic designer – but she never got around to it. I think she knew our relationship was going to be short lived long before I did. I was surprised at how quickly and efficiently she'd moved out. It had been weeks now and I hadn't found a single reminder of her presence. Her favorite foods were gone from the pantry, there were no stray articles of clothing under the couch cushions, her post-it notes had vanished from the side of the refrigerator, and the toiletries in the bathroom were exclusively masculine.

I made myself a pair of bacon sandwiches – so crisp they were almost charcoal – and ate them at the narrow table in the kitchen. Katrina was a dining room type of person, but I always felt uncomfortable there. The furniture was all left over from the former tenant and I still felt like an intruder. I found one last bottle of beer in the back of the refrigerator and took it with me into the den, settled down in the overstuffed chair to review the day just past and plan the one to come.

As happens from time to time, I fell asleep there, and my dream sieve is in the bedroom. Marie Dussaud is always telling me that I should get rid of the sieve; she insists that we receive useful insights in our dreams and that I should let my subconscious participate in my thought processes. Maybe she's right, but what works for her doesn't seem to hold true for me. If I do a lot of dreaming, I don't get a lot of rest, and my mind becomes filled with images that persist through the day and interfere with my concentration. I like to sleep when I'm asleep. I charge by the hour and my conscience won't let me bill for time I spend unconscious, no matter how productive it might be.

That night, for example, I dreamed that I was back in room 1313, bending over Mayor Porter's corpse, except that the body was Rachel Deacon, or perhaps her sister. Her body had begun to disintegrate, but not like a rotting corpse. Instead, her skin was wrinkling up as if it was parchment and pieces of her were disappearing, an eyelash, a finger, a toe. Apparently my subconscious was having trouble keeping my three current cases separate. When I woke up in the middle of the night, the chaotic images were all vivid and jarring, and that just reinforced my conviction that Marie was full of it.

It wasn't the first time I'd been wrong.

Getting to the Kremlin the following morning was not easy. The Chinese Communists had been stirring up trouble among the other zones for a while now because Houston had a near monopoly on oil supplies. Technically that was true, but in fact the complex and ever changing Cities Trade Agreement artificially depressed the price of any relatively rare commodity in order to prevent any one municipality from becoming financially dominant. The Chinese knew this, of course, but they hoped to force Houston to grant them some territorial concessions and they had considerable influence in Sao Paolo, Baghdad, and Addis Ababa, enough to stage an impressive, multi-cultural protest march on the Kremlin. So I ended up parking way over near Polyanskiy and walking almost half a mile to get there.

I explained myself to a bored but not actively unfriendly security officer who provided a guidespell to lead me to a conference room on the fourth floor. Much to my surprise, I had trouble finding a seat even though I'd arrived nearly twenty minutes early. Rumor had it there was an unusually high bounty on this job, and every professional in the city was present, along with an even larger number of amateurs. There were six Mayors attending, which in itself suggested that this wasn't a routine referral. I recognized Kreizle and Ming, both accompanied by their translators, and Curtis and Walensky. The other two were strangers, but that was no surprise. There were a lot of Mayors, and the turnover rate was high, at least in those boroughs where they actually held regular elections or periodic coups. What did surprise me was the presence of Curtis, an up-and-comer who would probably be on the Executive Council by the end of the year. He'd appeared out of nowhere a few years back, had rocketed to prominence by becoming mayor of Toronto, and was reportedly very active and influential behind the scenes. It was unusual to see him in public other than during formal sessions.

I finally found a seat close to the front and squeezed in next to a woman I'd seen working as a bouncer at one of the new trendy saki clubs, and a skinny Sikh whom I'd met but whose name I couldn't remember. Given the turnout, I wondered if I was wasting my time even assuming that Burford's assistance was more than just nominal. On the other hand, I was curious.

Walensky called the meeting to order, banging a gavel on the podium. I didn't care for the man. He was pompous and opinionated and had an annoying habit of not looking at you during a conversation. Sure enough, he was staring up at the ceiling as he called us to order, pouting when the last murmurs of conversation and movement took almost a full minute to die away.

"Please settle down gentlemen. We can't spare you much time this morning." I estimated that a third of the audience was female, and wondered again how such a politically inept nebbish had ever managed to get elected as a Mayor. "This meeting has been called in recognition of and in conformity to the Unified Citizen Participation Protocol. I'm sure everyone knows how this works, so I won't waste any more of your time than necessary explaining it all again." He paused and wet his lips and I sensed that he really didn't want to talk about whatever it was that he was about to talk about.

"As some of you probably already know, there have been three particularly brutal unsolved crimes during the past few weeks which the Police Forces believe to be the work of a single criminal or group of criminals, and which are as yet unsolved. Although we have every confidence that the Police are capable of identifying and apprehending the guilty party or parties, the possibility of additional fatalities has convinced us to request civilian assistance in an effort to expedite that end. The purpose of this meeting is to formalize the terms and conditions of the warrant approved by the Mayors during their emergency session two nights ago."

The number "three" had given rise to some murmuring so I wasn't the only one taken by surprise. I knew about the O'Brien murder, of course, and I'd heard rumors of the second. There hadn't been a hint in any of the news services about an additional death. Unless they were talking about Mayor Porter.

Walensky could not completely avoid the necessary formalities but he rushed through them, obviously bored. I'd heard the litany of disclaimers often enough that I could almost have recited them myself, but what they amounted to was that if any of us undertook to pursue the matter, the Cities were not to be held liable for any expenses or physical injury incurred during that process. Further, we were enjoined from breaking any law or local regulation in the process of our investigation, were prohibited from representing ourselves in any way as agents of the Cities government in general or any of the Mayors singly or jointly, and were reminded that in the event that our efforts were successful, that the actual arrest should be consummated by members of whichever of the Police Forces had jurisdiction. Then he came to the good part.

"The Mayors have set aside an honorarium for any citizen who provides the critical information leading to a successful arrest and prosecution of the person, entity, or any combination thereof responsible for the following crimes."

The first named victim was, as I expected, Ashley O'Brien, a young woman in her mid-twenties, ostensibly a cocktail waitress working in Dublin although it was pretty well known that she supplemented her income by entertaining young men, and some not so young. She had been found dead in her own bedroom two weeks earlier, with a series of unusual symbols carved into her nude body. No word on whether they were post mortem or even kinkier. "We have no reason to believe at this point that there was any genuine magic involved," Walensky assured us. "Several experts have examined the evidence and none of them have uncovered any link between the symbols and any known magic system. The initial hypothesis was that they were a ruse designed to mislead us into investigating a blind alley. That still may be the case." The woman's murder had received little official interest because the victim had no surviving family and lived what we like to call a "dangerous lifestyle." Given her occupation there was a high probability that she had been killed by a disgruntled customer.

The second victim, Aram Gudanoff, had been found murdered in his luxurious suite near Gorky Park almost a week later. The name generated some muted whispers from several part of the room, but I had never heard of him. The details of his death closely resembled those surrounding the first victim. The Police Forces had suppressed the details of the case, but through the grapevine I'd heard from usually reliable sources that portions of his body had been consumed and that a werebeing of some variety was considered the most likely suspect. According to today's briefing, that was not the situation at all. "Disinformation was released initially in an effort to mislead the perpetrator into believing that the Police were not aware of the connections between the two incidents." Although Gudanoff's body had displayed very similar mutilations to those in the O'Brien case, they were relatively minor in both instances and there had been no missing parts. The compelling common factor was the pattern of arcane symbols. "They were virtually identical, both in form and location. There are photographs as well as the autopsy and scryopsy reports in the information folders which will be handed out before you leave. They indicate to the Police that the killings were connected, probably the work of the same person or persons, although the first attack was significantly more savage. It is also believed possible that O'Brien's death was an act of passion and the second a more cold blooded follow up, possibly to suggest that the victims were random when in fact O'Brien was the primary target from the outset." Or vice versa, I thought to myself.

The third incident had not even made it to the grapevine as far as I knew, although at least a few people in the audience clearly had some foreknowledge, probably those who could afford to consult a prescient. The third death had forced the Police to reconsider their original hypothesis. Walensky spoke with obvious distaste, as though it was beneath his dignity to deal with such a sordid matter, but after his first few words, I realized why the Mayors were making this a priority. Porter had not been mutilated in any way, but another of their own had been touched.

The most recent killing was actually the second. What I mean is, the third murder discovered was actually committed sometime between the other two. The victim this time was Steven Sandobhal, estranged son of a prominent financier from Sao Paolo, whose wife was currently serving as Mayor. Sandobhal lived in a cottage in the sliver of Hyannis that appended the South China Sea. "He hadn't spoken to his family in over a year, nor was he financially dependent upon them. Sandobhal worked as a commercial artist and made enough for a comfortable, perhaps even luxurious lifestyle." Sandobhal had been killed almost exactly midway in time between the other two, but his body had been dumped into a freezer in the basement of his expensive house and had not been discovered until a neighbor reported that he had not emptied his mail box for more than a week. The same mutilations had been inflicted, but with a slight difference. "Identical symbols were incised into the victim's body, but in this case the coroner believes that they were not the work of the same individual. They were less precise but more deeply incised. We have discounted the possibility of a copycat since the symbols are unique and none of the details have been made public, and our best guess now is that there are at least two perpetrators, probably acting together."

Several questions were shouted from the audience, but Walensky waved them off. "Most of what you're likely to want to know can be found in the handouts. Each of you who are interested can register with the Police on your way out. You will receive regular updates on anything new that turns up during our official investigation and you are, of course, encouraged to share information among yourself as well as with the authorities. You will each be assigned a contact person in one of the associated Police Forces to whom you can address any further questions and report your findings, if any." He then launched into a recap of the familiar warnings about not exceeding our authority and the limited liability of the Cities administration. "I must stress that you are not empowered to apprehend any suspects, and any use of force is subject to the usual civil and criminal constraints."

In other words, if one of us was fortunate enough to uncover the killer but unfortunate enough to be forced to kill him or her in self defense, we could find ourselves facing legal problems of our own. I shook my head and glanced around. Assuming that I was gauging the reaction of the rest of the audience accurately, Walensky's presentation hadn't generated as much interest as might have been expected. For the bigger firms, the announced reward was still pretty small in proportion to the amount of time that would have to be invested in even a cursory effort. If the killer knocked off a few more prominent figures and the price tag rose commensurately, it might be worth their while.

Walensky talked a little longer but didn't say anything useful or interesting and I tuned him out. People started leaving before he had finished, and he hurried through the end of his speech, obviously miffed. Half the crowd was gone when I finally stood up and walked over to the table where the handouts remained largely untouched. If I'd been more aware of my surroundings, I might not have been taken by surprise, but I was thinking about the Deacon case and didn't realize Goff was there until his big hand was clutching my right shoulder.

"Well if it isn't my old friend, Dash."

I shrugged out from under his hand and stepped backward, making no effort to conceal my repugnance. Goff was human, or at least that's what his citizenship card said, but he looked more trollish than some trolls I knew. He was well over two meters tall, heavy set, running just slightly to fat. His face was pockmarked and knobby, and his hair grew in patches, long black spikes that looked like torn wires. One eye was slightly higher than the other, his nose was crooked, and his teeth uneven. Theoretically he ran a detective agency just like mine, but in practice he was hired muscle. We'd crossed paths a couple of times in the past, with mixed results. Even when you beat someone like Goff, it doesn't feel like a victory.

"Were not friends, Goff. What are you doing here?" Ignoring me, he picked up one of the handouts and flipped it open. "I didn't know you could read."

The insult didn't bother him; he might not have recognized it as such. "I'm just hanging around waiting for a client. Supposed to meet me here but hasn't showed yet. Are you going after the big prize? Seems like it's out of your league."

"Just staying informed. Nice talking to you, Goff." I started to brush past him and he put his hand on my arm. I stopped immediately, turned to look at his hand, then trailed my eyes up the attached arm to his face. I think he was doing his best to appear serious and professional, but he hadn't had enough practice.

"I hear you're working for Morris Ngambe. That right?"

My first inclination was to brush him off, but then I began to wonder how he knew so much about my business. It had been less than a day since I'd learned of the problems at the Lagos Castle, and anyway, it was more of a personal favor than a job. "You have heard of client confidentiality, haven't you, Goff? You are still supposed to be a private detective, aren't you?"

His false smile faded a few degrees. "Some clients are more trouble than they're worth, don't you think?"

"So why the interest in Morris Ngambe? What is he, another dissatisfied customer?" It wasn't likely, but I wanted to provoke Goff into talking rashly. He had the brains of a kobold and was about as subtle as a goblin in heat, but if he knew that Morris had talked to me, then maybe he knew something else that might be useful.

Goff gave me a nasty look. "I never worked for him, and I don't have any dissatisfied customers. I'm just passing on a friendly bit of advice. Some jobs are just healthier than others. I wouldn't want to see you walk into a pile of trouble. Consider it a professional courtesy."

"You're neither professional nor courteous, Goff. Why don't you just tell me what's on your mind? Just between the two of us."

For a second or two, I thought it might work. But then his expression cleared and he smiled at me. "You're a detective," he said calmly. "You figure it out." And then he was gone.

I found a phone booth on the first floor and called my office. Moira picked up the receiver just before the first ring. "What do you want, Dash? I'm busy." She sounded out of sorts.

"What's my schedule for the day?"

"If you'd bothered to check your calendar before you left this morning, you'd already know. A Miss Connors called and said that Deborah Lerner has been located and would be coming over to the Baker's Dozen at 11:00 this morning, or a little later depending on how long her prior interview with the Police lasts. Miss Connors asked her to drop by to discuss making arrangements for disposing of Mayor Porter's personal possessions. You also asked me to set up a meeting with Rachel Deacon after lunch and I have her scheduled for 1:00."

The Police wouldn't be releasing the contents of the hotel room any time soon, so Connors' pretext for interviewing Lerner was a thin one. I decided to try a compliment. "Why would I look at a calendar when I have you, Moira? I'm just leaving the Kremlin right now. I can make it to the Baker's Dozen with time to spare."

"Don't count on it. They're diverting traffic around East Jerusalem again. It's backed up right through the southern part of Moscow and down into Central Park. Delays up to thirty minutes, officially, probably longer in reality."

I swore under my breath. "More fighting?" The Palestinians had more factions than some of the Cities had neighborhoods.

"Worse than ever."

Jerusalem was a very recent addition to the Cities, having materialized just a few weeks earlier between the northern end of Manhattan and unfortunately the eastern edge of Tel Aviv. Its arrival had effectively placed one of my favorite restaurants beyond easy travel distance and on the opposite side of a minor combat zone. Eventually the trouble would be contained even if that meant a total quarantine until they accepted their new situation, and then they would be allowed to elect or appoint a Mayor to represent their interests. But for the moment, they were an island of utter chaos in a sea of minor chaos.

Manhattan was the first and is still the largest segment of the Cities. It was created, or copied, or whatever the proper term is during the early 1950s, followed later by large portions of Brooklyn. The other boroughs had been snubbed, or maybe they were coming along later. The million or so people who woke up here that first day thought they'd been snatched from Earth by space aliens, but that theory had to be revised pretty quickly when chunks of other cities started showing up and magic started to work. London and Paris were the next two, then Sao Paolo, Moscow, Adelaide, and the others. None of the Cities were complete, of course. The selected sites would just miraculously appear, not replacing existing areas but inserted among them, instantaneously spreading their neighbors further apart. There was no discernible pattern to the choices, although it was quite common for significant landmarks to be included, though not always properly situated. So we had Big Ben and the Kremlin and the Taj Mahal and underground Seattle, but on the other hand we have parts of the Chicago stockyards, the unremarkable Nha Trang fishing port, and Swann Point Cemetery from Providence, Rhode Island. And the Berlin Wall is here, neatly cutting our piece of Central Park into two roughly equal portions.

Significantly, none of the residents of any of the Cities had heard of the other disappearances, which presumably means the segments are being copied rather than stolen from the original world. But by whom and for what purpose is as much a mystery now as ever.

Nor does anyone understand why magic works here or why we have trolls and demons and other supernatural creatures like zombies and ghouls but no vampires, werewolves, or ghosts. They'd just started showing up a few years after the first translation, insisting that they'd been here all along. And then there were the lattice weavers and the monstrous kudzu that was swallowing the Golden Gate Bridge. Could these have come from some future city back on the original Earth? No one knew, but one popular theory was that the lattice weavers were responsible for it all. They were obviously intelligent but they ignored every effort to communicate with them, living mostly concealed in the eaves of buildings during the day, spinning their elaborate but apparently functionless lattices during the hours of darkness.

I retrieved the Studebaker and headed for Boston, detouring through Washington and Paris to avoid the disturbances. Clouds of sooty black smoke were rising from Jerusalem and I heard the sound of automatic weapons firing in the distance. There was a short delay early on when I ran into a column of ambulances, apparently sent from as far away as Athens, but once I was past them things went smoothly and I made it to Beacon Street with a few minutes to spare.

The desk clerk called Connors' office and told me an escort was on the way. It was my old friend Douglas, who looked more cordial this time but who still responded to my overtures with monosyllables. I didn't know if it was his nature or if Connors trained her people to be tight lipped. She struck me as a bit of a hard-ass, though admittedly she was better equipped in that area than most security officers I'd met.

Her office was as neat and austere as Sheri Connors herself. The picture frames on the walls all contained certificates and citations rather than artwork, and the paraphernalia on her desk was of high quality, but strictly functional. No stuffed animals in the corner, no live plants, no photographs of family or lovers. I was particularly surprised to notice the absence of magical items – most offices had at least an air freshening mobile, but then I remembered that magic didn't work at the Baker's Dozen. Still, there was nothing at all to personalize the office. This was clearly her job and not her life. Unless her job was her life.

She was sitting behind her desk facing another woman of about the same age, who sat with her legs crossed, gesturing with one hand as she spoke with considerable animation. This, presumably, was Deborah Lerner, Mayor Porter's executive assistant. Her blonde hair was wound into a modified beehive, not a strand out of place, and her nails were painted with an iridescent scarlet polish that caught my eye even through the office window. Douglas ushered me inside, but closed the door without entering himself.

"Oh, there you are. Deborah Lerner, this is Mr. Dash. He's helping with the investigation of Mayor Porter's death."

I shook her hand, noting that it was trembling violently. Deborah Lerner's face was outwardly composed but I could see something in her eyes. Was it grief? Had her relationship with Mayor Porter been more than simply professional?

"I'm sorry to be meeting you under these circumstances, Miss Lerner." I slipped into the remaining empty chair without waiting for an invitation.

"It's Mrs. Lerner, actually, although John, my husband, died this past year. I'm still not quite sure I believe that the Mayor is gone too." Her voice quavered only a little and I decided she wasn't grieving for her boss. Possibly for the loss of her job though.

"Deborah was just explaining to me why she's been so hard to find." Connors was using Lerner's familiar name, probably in an effort to put her at ease. I was pretty sure it was a tactic rather than a reflection of any actual sympathy and wondered if I was supposed to play the bad cop. If so, Connors was going to be disappointed. I don't like being manipulated.

"I'm sure there was a good reason," I replied, smiling as warmly as I thought I could without overdoing it. Connors gave me a quick, dirty look that confirmed my suspicion.

"It's a little embarrassing, but I've been staying with a friend.

The Mayor closed her office for the rest of the week and said she

wouldn't need me once I took care of a few last minute errands.

That's why I came here that night. To tell her everything was set and

that she needn't worry about anything. I explained all of this to the

officers."

"The police will probably speak to your friend," said Connors. "Just to confirm your alibi."

Lerner grew even more agitated. "But she was perfectly all right when I left, and I checked out with the desk clerk." She looked back and forth between Connors and I. "Why would I need an alibi?"

Connors hesitated and I confess I enjoyed having provoked her a little. She was much more human when she showed some emotion, even anger. Another little prod wouldn't hurt. "Unfortunately, the security here at the hotel isn't very tight. It wouldn't have been difficult for you to check out, then return to the guest area without the desk clerk or anyone else knowing you were there. Not that I think you had anything to do with the murder."

"But I couldn't come back! Mr. Garner was in the lobby

when I left and he would know if I'd gone upstairs again. You can

ask him. He'll tell you I didn't come back. And he would have been

here for a while, longer than I was." A sly look found a brief home on her face, then was gone. "He and the Mayor were, you know,

involved."

"No one seems to know where Mr. Garner is," said Connors.
"And the Police would very much like to speak to him. He's not at
home and he's not at his studio. Can you suggest any place else we
might look?"

Lerner shook her head. "I only met him a few times and he

never said much to me. The Mayor told me he was preoccupied with

his work but I think he just wasn't interested in people who weren't

of use to him." She bit her lip. "Sorry, that came out harsher than I

intended. I just meant that he wasn't much of a people person. He

was polite, but you could always tell it was habit rather than

thoughtfulness."

"Had they been together long?" I asked.

"Just a few weeks. The Mayor mentioned once that he was
coming out of a bad relationship."

"Did she ever say anything about this other woman?" asked
Connors quickly.

"No, nothing much. They probably didn't know each other. I
don't think Mr. Garner liked talking about her. Or anything else in
his private life. That's part of the reason why they met here." She
glanced around to indicate the Baker's Dozen in general. "The first
time, he checked in and she came to visit, but this time it was the
other way around."

"How often did this happen?" Connors beat me to the punch
again.

"Oh, I don't know for certain. The Mayor stayed here twice
since they started seeing each other, but I don't know how often she
visited him. I only found out about their…relationship…a short
while ago."

Connors nodded but seemed momentarily at a loss, so I stepped up to the plate. "Other than getting together with Garner, had anything else changed in the Mayor's life recently? Anything significant, I mean."

Lerner hesitated. "Well, she hadn't made a public announcement, but she'd pretty much decided against running for re-election. The polls weren't going her way and I don't think she really liked the job."

No surprise there. "So what was she going to do? Retire? Move in with Garner?"

"Nothing like that. She had a movie role lined up."

Connors, who had just hung up her phone, looked as surprised as I felt. "I thought her film career was over," I said. The critics had not been kind.

Lerner nodded. "So did almost everyone, I think, but as Mayor she pulled a few strings for some friends back in Hollywood. They owe her and she was planning to collect. You know they're going to start filming the Eve Dallas books?"

I had heard but Connors looked puzzled. "It's a series of detective novels," I explained. "But I can't see her as Eve Dallas."

Lerner shook her head. "No, Sandra Bullock got the part. The Mayor was going to be cast as her sidekick."

I hesitated, pondering that possibility, and Connors spoke up, changing the subject. "Garner has stayed here four times in the past two months. But that's not unusual. He's been with us at least twice a month for the past three years."

I was about to ask a rhetorical question when Lerner answered it for me. "That's because he used to meet his last lady friend here as well. I overheard him mention it once when he came to our office."

We talked to Lerner for a few more minutes, but she was

either a better actress than her former boss or she really didn't know

anything else. Connors thanked her for taking the time to stop by and

summoned Douglas to escort her out.

"So what do you think?" she asked me, almost as soon as the

door closed behind our guest.

I shrugged. "Offhand, I'd say she sounds like she's telling the truth. Unless she's wearing a plausibility charm."

Connors shook her head. "Wouldn't work in here, remember?"

"Doesn't give us much, unless there's something of interest

with the earlier girlfriend. Jealousy is a pretty strong motive."

She looked skeptical. "It doesn't sound right to me. I'm supposed to be discrete about our guests, but between you and me, I've seen Garner with at least half a dozen different women during his visits here. I don't think he ever let emotion or affection get in the way of enthusiastic, sweaty sex. He might be able to fool someone for a few hours, maybe even days, but not longer than that."

"You don't sound as if you approve of Mr. Garner."

She hesitated, looked as though she might be about to respond angrily, then actually smiled. "Sorry. I guess I am a bit of a prude."

"No apology necessary, Miss Connors."

"We should probably stay strictly professional whenever anyone else is around, Mr. Dash, but when we're alone, you can call me Sheri. Sometimes I go so long without hearing my first name that I almost forget what it is." She sat back in her chair, looking suddenly very tired.

"Then Sheri it is," I answered smoothly. "And you can call me Dash."

For a second I thought she was going to take offense, but then she laughed and waved it off. "You're an odd person, Dash."

"No," I said lightly. "I just hate my first name."

She considered that, seemed to accept it. "So what's our next step?"

I wasn't sure how to react to having her invite herself into my investigation, but the crime had happened under her watch and I suppose it was fair that she be involved. It also occurred to me to wonder if her interest might be more personal. I'm not a Hollywood

Hunk by any means, but I'm not without my good points, and the fact that I'd been celibate since Katrina called it quits was not through necessity. I looked her over as surreptitiously as I could, but I'm sure she picked up on it. Sheri Connors was a bit lean but not unpleasantly so, had a nice face when she dropped the professional mask, and I suspected she was too smart to stay in hotel security very long.

"I'd like a list of dates when Porter or Garner stayed here, for at least two years back. And I'd like to talk to the busboy again, the one who delivered the food to the Mayor's suite the night she was killed."

"Peter Robertson," she replied, nodding her head. "Today is his day off, I'm afraid."

I glanced at my watch and stood up. "I don't have time right now anyway. Another appointment beckons."

"Anything I should know about?"

"Different case. Hopefully not as complicated as this one."

She looked thoughtful for a moment. "Maybe we could get together later and compare notes."

"As much as I'd like to, I can't promise anything right now. Besides, until something provocative turns up, we wouldn't have anything to talk about."

"I'm sure we could find something." It was almost painful to watch her awkward attempt at flirtation, but I was flattered. This was clearly not something she did every day. Or possibly any day. It was tempting. Very tempting. But my dance card was really full just at the moment. "I'd like to, but I'm afraid I'll have to take a rain check this time."

I was expecting a return of her previous coolness in the face of what must appear to be a brush-off, and she didn't disappoint me. "All right, another time." I couldn't interpret her tone. She didn't seem angry, just resigned.

"I meant what I said, Sheri. This just isn't the right time."

"All right. I understand. I'll have that information sent to your office as soon as I get it."

On the way back to my car, I realized that I was ready at last to leave Katrina behind me.

CHAPTER FOUR

Moira had arranged for me to meet Rachel Deacon in front of her sister's apartment building in Paris, only a block away from the border with Conakry. Actually this neighborhood was Paris in name only. Language and social barriers had inhibited migration across the Cities' segments in many areas, but some of that resistance had eroded over the years and a few places – Paris, Manhattan, London, and Toronto in particular – have attracted large numbers of immigrants. Not surprisingly, artistic types were drawn toward Paris and this particular section had become one of the most internationalized areas anywhere in the Cities. During the one block walk from where I parked the Studebaker, I heard English, German, Portuguese, and an African dialect I couldn't identify. The ever present falafel vendors were supplemented here by a hot dog stand, a portable stall offering hummus and fufu, and a dilapidated ice cream truck.

The buildings were all well maintained and the sidewalks were clean, but there were peddlers everywhere, competing for space with a handful of street artists. Any pedestrian who hesitated or showed any sign of weakening resolve would soon be surrounded by importuning entrepreneurs hawking their wares, or shouting at one another. Technically the neighborhood was still under the authority of the Mayor of Paris, but in practical terms it functioned almost autonomously and there were no signs of the gendarmes which were quietly ubiquitous elsewhere.

I had arrived on time despite some minor delays en route and had fortuitously spotted a parking space directly across from the newly renamed Wilde Palms, presumably a nod to Oscar. There was moderate foot traffic in the area and the vendors were enjoying a steady flow of business. A tattoo artist working out of a van was inscribing a dolphin on a young woman's ankle, a mime was entertaining a small but attentive audience on the far corner, and a rather pretty young woman was playing a fairy harp in a small inset garden while several children competed with each other to capture the semi-solid musical notes that drifted like bubbles just above their heads.

Rachel Deacon showed up about ten minutes later, a delay just long enough to be irritating but not long enough for me to say anything about it. There was an air of distance about her and although a few of the peddlers glanced in her direction, no one approached. She apologized perfunctorily, blamed it on the bus she'd taken from London, and led the way to the recessed entrance, narrow doors inset with stained glass, the interior concealed by heavy curtains. The building guardian must have sensed and approved of us because the doors opened autonomously and we stepped inside. The doorman greeted us with an almost friendly grunt; he was a troll, but less ugly than most. It was the first time I'd seen a troll wearing a neat, professional looking suit and I almost mistook him for a human. The spiky ears and pale green complexion gave him away, of course.

"Is that you, Miss Deacon?" He sounded suspicious. A suspicious troll is by definition angry, and an angry troll is by definition dangerous. I surreptitiously checked my escape route.

My companion apparently wasn't the least bit nervous. "I'm Rachel Deacon, Pegrus. We met a few days ago. My sister is still missing as far as I know. Mr. Dash here is helping me to find her."

Pegrus regarded me with mild animosity and not so mild skepticism. "I suppose it's all right since he's with you." His eyes said that it wasn't all right and that if I stepped out of line, he'd show me out as violently as possible.

We passed through a small, but well maintained lobby. Ruth Deacon clearly was not a starving artist struggling to survive until her work found its audience. The elevator was carpeted, the levitation spell worked flawlessly, and we were silently and efficiently whisked up to the fifteen floor. I couldn't help noticing that there was no thirteenth floor and I wondered if it was part of the Baker's Dozen.

The corridor into which we emerged was empty except for a potted but artificial plant facing the elevator well and a handful of paintings along the walls, mostly abstracts, some aggressively ugly. Rachel led the way to our right.

"How did you get them to give you access? I know you two were twins, but the hotel guardian reads auras not faces."

"Ruth and I had our souls bonded when we very young. There's a part of her in me and vice versa and it shows in our auras.

The guardian was ambivalent and summoned the manager the first time I came and I had to explain the situation. They were quite cooperative and discrete."

It wouldn't do to have it get out that one of their residents disappeared inside the building, so naturally they were discrete. I had forgotten about the bonding, and I understood very little about the process anyway. I didn't want her to know I had talked to Marie Dussaud so I played dumb. "Isn't that some kind of psychic linking?"

We stopped in front of Room 1520 and Rachel turned to face me. "The ceremony extracts portions of the souls of the participants and exchanges them. In one sense, Ruth and I are the same person. That's how I know that she's still alive. If she weren't, a part of me would also have died at the very same moment." She hesitated. "And the rest of me would have followed soon afterward."

She grasped the doorknob and turned it, overcoming what appeared to be mild resistance. Then it was open and she was leading me inside.

The lights came on spontaneously, illuminating a much larger space than I had anticipated. The room immediately facing us had what appeared to be an inset tile floor, chalk white under a handful of symmetrically arranged beige scatter rugs. It was furnished with an oversized couch, two expensive looking chairs, and a rectangular, glass topped table. A very large, very black abstract sculpture loomed over the couch. To my left I could see down a short corridor to what must be the kitchen. Opposite us were two doorways, both obscured by hanging curtains. To the right was a more conventional door, currently closed. The walls were decorated with framed photographs, all of them black and white. There was in fact very little color in the room at all.

"Your sister was obviously successful."

"I believe so. She worked with at least two of the big advertising agencies and she sold to private collectors as well."

"Are these her work?" I moved to examine the closest photograph, which was obviously the Flatiron Building. The automobiles parked adjacent to it answered my question for me; the picture had been taken long before Ruth Deacon had been born, before the transition that brought Manhattan to this place.

"I don't know," Rachel answered distractedly. "We didn't talk much about photography. Ruth was the artistic one. I'm afraid I've always preferred less colorful ways of making a living." Her choice of the word "colorful" struck me as funny given our surroundings but I didn't smile. Moira had done some checking around. Rachel Deacon was an investment counselor working for Merrill-Trump. The bill for our services would probably be less than what she spent on caviar.

I walked over to the conventional door and opened it. Closet. Cleaning supplies, ironing board, all arranged very neatly.

"Her bedroom and studio are both in the back." Rachel had crossed the room and was standing in front of the rightmost curtain, looking impatient.

I took my time, pausing to glance at each of the photographs along the way. I had waited for her; now she could return the favor. Most of the pictures were of architectural subjects – buildings, bridges, an aqueduct – but in one of them three young men were mounted on horses and in another uniformed soldiers stood next to an antique cannon. "All of these pictures were taken in the original world."

"If you say so." Rachel's voice was tinged with annoyance. "That's one of Ruth's obsessions. When we were kids, she was always asking people if they remembered things from before we were brought here. I never understood her interest. The world is what it is. Everything else is fantasy."

"What were the others?"

"I beg your pardon?"

"You said your sister had obsessions. Plural. What else?"

"Is there a reason why you're so interested in this, Mr. Dash?"

It was my turn to feel impatient. "You're paying me to find your sister, Miss Deacon. If I'm to do that, I need to know what she might have been involved in, who she might have associated with, and what she might have been doing with her time, particularly recently."

"All right." She sounded at least partly mollified, but her voice was still brittle. "Photography, of course. And Ruth was a charter member of the SCA, the Society for Credible Anachronisms."

"She was a Victorian?" I glanced around the apartment, at the obviously modern furnishings. The SCA was a social group whose members mimicked a Victorian lifestyle. They met regularly in London and had chapters scattered throughout the Cities. That might explain the selection of photographs.

"Ruth wasn't one of the nutcases, Mr. Dash. She led a modern lifestyle except when she attended Society events. We both enjoy the finer things in life, and we can both afford to indulge ourselves."

"I'd like to talk to some of her friends in that group."

"There are two names in the file I left with you. They're the only ones whose names I recall."

"Is there anything else, something you've remembered since we met?"

"No, that's it, as far as I know." I sensed that Rachel was holding something back, but I didn't press. I didn't have enough leverage yet.

The first curtain led to a surprisingly small bedroom. Not unexpectedly, it was absolutely neat and orderly. Lacking outside windows, it seemed too much like a cave for my taste. I could have bounced a coin on the bedspread, and the dressing table and closet looked like they'd been staged by an interior decorator. The small adjoining bathroom was spotless and oddly impersonal. The bed and bathrooms would have looked like part of a motel if Ruth Deacon's collection of historical photographs hadn't covered the walls here as well. There was a row of clothbound journals on a shelf in one corner of the bedroom. A quick look told me that they were diaries of a sort, although the entries were almost exclusively related to her work, descriptions of sites she'd visited, sales she'd made, all very impersonal. The journals went back more than twenty years and the most recent one had been completed six months ago. I looked around but couldn't find what was should have been the most recent volume. The contents of her dresser and night table were exactly what you'd expect to find.

An arched doorway led from the bedroom into Ruth Deacon's office, which was similarly neat but, unlike the others, filled almost to capacity. There was a large desk in one corner, covered with file folders and envelopes, each hand labeled and, naturally, neatly aligned. Some had dates and locations; others displayed the names of businesses or products. Most of them contained photographic prints. The rear wall was almost completely concealed by a row of filing cabinets, and three tiers of sorting trays were arranged on top of one of them. There was a square wooden work table with an inset glass plate above a fluorescent light, an expensive looking color printer, a fax machine, a computer, and a photographic enlarger. A heavy duty storage rack held several cameras, an adjustable tripod, and an array of lenses and other paraphernalia I couldn't identify. That left barely enough room for the two of us to stand.

The only other exit was through a curtain back into the main room. Rachel hadn't spoken in a while, but when she followed me into the kitchen, she was radiating edginess again. "Well?"

"Did your sister practice any kind of magic? Other than routine charms and wards, I mean."

"I doubt it. Neither of us has much talent in that area. That happens sometimes when you're bonded. When we were kids, Ruth experimented with psychometry for awhile but I always thought it was easier just to hire an experienced adept. Eventually she gave up. I imagine she employs professionals now."

"You don't use a professional service if you don't want anyone else to know what you're doing."

"Are you implying that my sister was involved in something clandestine?" She tried to sound as though the idea offended her, but I sensed that she'd had similar thoughts. You don't mislead a guardian spirit with a low level spell. There was some major mojo going on here.

"That was an observation, not an implication. But we all have secrets we would prefer not to reveal to others, don't we, Miss Deacon?" She gave me a sharp look then turned her head away.

The kitchen proved no more helpful than anything else in the apartment. We returned to the front room and Rachel moved toward the door, but I lagged behind. Something was missing, and it took a moment or two before I realized what it was.

"Where's the darkroom?"

"I beg your pardon?"

I half turned back toward the office. "Where did your sister have her pictures developed?"

"I don't know. Does it matter?"

"It might. I'm no photographer, but I doubt that a professional like your sister would use a commercial developer."

"Well, possibly she has a studio somewhere."

"Don't you know?"

She dropped her eyes. "Look, Mr. Dash. I genuinely love my sister. How could I not? She's a part of me and vice versa. When we were kids, we were devoted to each other, and once we were bonded, we were inseparable for a long time. Too long, to be honest. We started getting on each other's nerves, so several years ago we agreed to go our separate ways. Once or twice a year we get together, but we're not close in conventional terms. I'd never even been to this apartment until Ruth disappeared and she's only been out to London to visit me twice."

"All right. I can see that. But if Ruth has another place somewhere, an office or a studio, we need to know about it. It's entirely possible that she's had some sort of accident." Which wouldn't explain the guardian spirit's insistence that she was present, but I'd cross that metaphysical bridge later.

"I might be able to help with that." She brushed past me and returned to the office, catching me by surprise. By the time I caught up to her, she was waiting for the computer to boot up. "I looked through her files the last time I was here, hoping to find something, but it was all just business stuff." She got a DOS prompt and typed in a command. A menu appeared and she scrolled down and made her selection.

"These are her financial records. If she was renting studio space elsewhere, there'd be an entry, wouldn't there?"

"Bravo, Miss Deacon. Perhaps you've missed your calling." We read the screen together, paging through more than a year of transactions, payments made and received. I wasn't consciously adding things up as we went along, but it was obvious that Ruth Deacon was pulling down a pretty good income. Once a month she moved funds into a money market account in Tehran and there were no records of withdrawals. There was nothing to indicate that she was renting space anywhere else in the Cities.

"I don't understand it." Rachel shut down the computer when we were done. "I suppose she might have paid cash, but I can't imagine why."

"Possibly she's sharing space with someone else and they're paying the actual bills." Briefly I considered the possibility that Rachel was lying to me, but she seemed genuinely puzzled. I wondered if she had noticed the other anomaly. Supposedly her sister had abandoned her efforts to practice magic, but scattered through her accounts were several payments to arcane supply houses and magic dealers, including the Lagos Castle. Some of these could have been for pre-conjured charms or potions, but Aladdin Inc only supplied raw materials and Esoteria catered exclusively to the professional trade. I decided not to say anything. If Rachel Deacon could have her secrets, then I certainly had a right to one or two of my own.

I couldn't think of anything else I could do there at present and said so. Rachel seemed pleased by the prospect of leaving. "I may need to return at some point, Miss Deacon. Is there any way that you could clear it with the management so that I don't need to drag you down here if that's the case?"

"I'm not sure. I can talk to the Miss Appleby. She understands the situation and has been as helpful as possible, given the situation."

"If you could do that, then, and just call my office when it's set up."

I waited with her until Rachel managed to get a cab, then grabbed a sandwich from a street vendor and ate it while I was driving to Dublin. Although I felt hopelessly inadequate to investigate the string of murders that the Mayors were finding so troublesome, I felt obligated to at least make some effort. Ashley O'Brien's apartment was still a sequestered crime scene, but I had a pass issued by the Police tucked into my pocket. She had lived near Glasnevin on the north side, and I had to make a detour around the Botanical Gardens because of roadwork. I lost my bearings in the process and wasted time when I turned the wrong way onto Griffith Avenue. I'm not that familiar with Dublin and it took a while to reverse course and find the right street. Not for the first time I regretted that I could not afford a celestial guidance system for my car. Eventually I gave in and asked a pair of Buddhist monks for directions.

The street I sought was short and quiet, lined with two and three story buildings, mostly shops with apartments above. Not a seedy neighborhood, but clearly lower middle class. I had no trouble finding a place to leave the Studebaker; there were comparatively few vehicles in Dublin. The only obvious access to O'Brien's apartment was an outside staircase, at the base of which a placard advised that the area was sequestered by order of the local Police. I felt the familiar light pressure of a dormant warding spell as I mounted the first step, but it deferred to my pass and the sensation stopped almost immediately.

Her apartment was depressingly small and cheaply furnished. If O'Brien was in fact a prostitute, she was not a prosperous one. There was a single large room with a bed in one corner, accompanied by a chair and dresser, and a heavy dark stained wardrobe whose doors were deeply scarred and pitted. In the opposite corner, a folding table and matching chairs stood close to a tiny refrigerator and even smaller stove with cabinets above. The cabinet doors were smoke stained. The bathroom barely had standing room. Clothing, food containers, and other debris were scattered everywhere, but it was impossible to guess how much of the mess was pre-existing and how much the result of the Police crime scene investigation.

I made a quick pass through the drawers and closets but I didn't really expect to find anything the Police hadn't. I just wanted to get a feel for the first victim and the way she had lived. In a dresser drawer I found a handful of photographs, most of them featuring Ashley, sometimes alone, sometimes with a male companion, never the same partner twice. None of the pictures in the Police handout were very flattering, but when she wasn't trying too hard to pose, she could be mildly pretty. I decided to break one of the rules and borrow one of the latter, almost a portrait shot. She was leaning against the side of a building, one hand on her hip, wearing a lacey blouse and full skirt, with an amulet dangling from a thin chain around her neck. It looked like a love charm, a heart cut diagonally into two pieces, and I wondered who might be wearing the matching half. This was one of the few charms worn outwardly, to announce to people that the wearer was in a committed relationship.

I was back on the street fairly quickly. There was a small pub at the end of a row of shops. Each of the shopkeepers had been interviewed; transcripts were in the packet I'd received. They varied only slightly in detail and tone. Ashley O'Brien entertained men in her apartment, enough different faces to suggest she was not just dating a lot. She worked as a waitress in the corner pub, had been there for two years. The innkeeper was less forthcoming, and the investigating officer's notes indicated that he strongly suspected the man, Brendan Skane, was well aware of his employee's method of supplementing her tips and wages. He might even have been taking a cut of her earnings.

I walked down to the pub, the Black Goat, and stepped inside. It seemed relatively well appointed, with seating for perhaps forty customers, though it was almost empty at the moment. Two older men sat separately at the bar, bent over their drinks, and a young couple whispered together in a booth at the far end. A heavy set and rather ugly man behind the counter looked up when I came in, his expression distinctly wary, but I pretended not to notice and took a seat at one of the tables.

I sensed his arrival before he spoke. He stood just behind my right shoulder. "What'll you have?"

I ordered a pint of bitter and he moved away without comment, returning almost immediately with a full mug. It slopped over the rim when he set it down in front of me.

I turned and handed him a much larger bill than necessary. "Would you be Mr. Skane?"

"That's my name. Will there be anything else?"

"There might be. I'm looking for some information." I glanced at the bill he was still holding.

"I've told all I know, to the Police and to those others who came before you." He reached into his pocket and pulled out a handful of paper money, dollars, pounds, francs, and other denominations. He either had a gift for computation or more likely wore a conversion charm somewhere because he made change without hesitation. "If you're here to drink, you're welcome, but if you bother me or my customers, it's out with you. Understand?" He dropped my change on the table. I hadn't the faintest idea whether or not he'd overcharged.

"Perfectly clear."

I hadn't really expected to find out anything new this easily. The Police and at least some of my entrepreneurial competitors had all been here before me, and Skane undoubtedly had his story down pat by now. I finished my drink and left, feeling at least one pair of eyes follow me out, then went looking for the playground.

Every neighborhood has one. Sometimes they have fences around them, and contain swing sets, slides, and other equipment, sometimes they're just vacant lots filled with unkempt grass and discarded debris. The playground here was more like the latter, a stretch of gravel broken by tufts of weed. I suspected the local kids played soccer or whatever the sport of the moment might be, but I also noticed cigarette butts, beer cans, and the packaging for a popular condom. There were three boys engaged in some variation of kick the can when I arrived, and they stopped when they saw me, watching warily but not retreating from the invader. This was, after all, their turf.

"Hi, guys!" I called. "I'm looking for some help."

It took a little while, and a few bills, before they loosened up. Brian was new to the area, but Sean and Ian had been born in the neighborhood, and they both knew who Ashley O'Brien was. "The lady what got killed, she was," Sean asserted.

"My mum says she weren't no lady," Ian countered. "She went with men for money."

"That's what I wanted to ask you about," I said. "Was there any particular man you remember? Someone who might have acted strangely, or who might have argued with Miss O'Brien? Someone not from around here?"

They exchanged looks and shook their heads. I thought I'd struck out again, but then Sean volunteered something. "She'd been seeing this one bloke pretty regular for a while."

"Can you tell me what he looked like?"

Their response wasn't much help. He was tall and wore his hair longer than the local custom, dressed posh, usually came by cab and left the same way as far as they knew. No, they'd never seen him in the Black Goat or any of the shops and had no idea how he and Ashley had met. "She was never much of a talker. She had airs, she did."

Sean said he could probably identify Ashley's beau if he saw him again but Ian wasn't sure. They hadn't seen him since the murder, but that wasn't suspicious in itself. I had read transcripts of the Police interviews with those of her customers whom they had been able to identify, but none had admitted to anything more than a casual relationship. And they'd all been locals.

I added a few coins to the fee I'd advanced the boys and left them one of my business cards. "If you think of something else, call that number collect. If it helps, I'll be very grateful." I patted the wallet in my hip pocket to indicate the form my gratitude would take.

The shadows were starting to lengthen and I wanted to talk to Moira before she went home for the day, so I found my car and started back.

I had asked Moira to gather some background material on the Lagos Castle. I trusted Morris and I was sure he had told me the truth when he said he had no serious enemies, but any operation that size involves activities about which even the owner must be unaware. He employed several hundred people, dealt with scores of vendors and thousands of customers. A great deal of cash flowed in and out of his doors, and even the most honest people were subject to temptation. My preliminary theory was that this was an inside job. There was too much security, conventional and magical, to have been overcome without highly sophisticated intervention, and if such technology or sorcery existed, it was unlikely it would be used to curdle some cream or destroy a few books.

Which almost certainly meant that someone on the inside was involved, someone who could cook up the necessary magic once they were past the wards and detectors. Usually that meant an employee, although it was possible that it might be a regular customer or a vendor or repair person who had frequent, minimally supervised access. The number of potentials was much too big to be practical, but Moira had a talent for winnowing out the more likely candidates.

The office was technically closed when I arrived, later than expected thanks to a multi-car accident on the Autobahn. I was sure that Moira would have left a summary of her day's work on my desk, but when I unlocked the door the lady was waiting for me in person, half reclining on the visitors' couch. She was wearing a quite fetching low cut top that clashed violently with a billowing, ankle length skirt.

"Sorry, you shouldn't have waited. I was caught in traffic."

"I thought as much. They're still chattering about it on the Police band. You've had some luck?"

Like I said, Moira claimed she couldn't read me, that her psychic sensitivity didn't work with everyone. She was probably telling the truth, but she was also an astute observer and what she couldn't learn from a person's aura she could often pick up from their body language. "Maybe. Found out something that's not in the Police file anyway. Miss O'Brien had a new and unusually steady boyfriend just before she died, and he's not a local."

"You're not going to tell me he discovered her sordid past and killed her in outrage, are you?" She raised a skeptical eyebrow.

I sighed. It didn't sound all that likely to me either. "Clichés are clichés because they really do happen. Although in this case I can't imagine that it would have taken very long to find out the truth. Everyone in the neighborhood knew her reputation, even the kids. But that doesn't mean that it wasn't a contributing factor."

"Ah, it's the children you've been talking to, is it?" Moira usually disapproved when I used kids as sources, but I've found that in general they're more observant than adults, more willing to talk, and in most cases the authorities, and even my more sophisticated competitors, tended to overlook them.

"Don't worry. I left their souls uncorrupted and their pockets filled with cash. So what do you have for me?"

She stood up, deftly avoided tripping over the hem of her skirt, and retrieved a folder from her desk. It was a depressingly thick folder. "I did what you asked, but I doubt it will help you. I identified over a thousand people who have regular access to the Lagos Castle, and there are probably others who pay cash and walk in as guests or under assumed names. And that's just the restaurant. The gift shop is virtually a public place."

My face must have betrayed my dismay because she smiled at me. "There's some good news to dilute the bad. Anyone on the list could have visited the gift shop, obviously, but most of them would have considerable difficulty in gaining access to the food preparation area."

I felt marginally cheered. "None of the customers are allowed back there, and probably relatively few of the vending and service people."

Moira shook her head skeptically. "Not entirely true. Selected customers are invited for tours of the kitchen. Fortunately there are records of who attended the tours. Unfortunately, there are quite a lot of them, almost two hundred who fit the time frame."

I sighed and dropped into a chair. Darke Industries could hire a bunch of interns to follow up on two hundred leads. I couldn't.

"All right, thanks. I'll look through the folder tonight. You should get going. I can't afford to pay you overtime."

She laughed. "You can't afford to pay me straight time, Dash, but I have a pair of cats waiting for their dinner so I'll see you tomorrow." And a moment later she was gone.

At the end of each day, I take stock of what I've done. It's a necessary ritual for me, a way to disengage and clear my mind. It had been a busy day, but in retrospect not a very profitable one. Deborah Lerner's revelation that Mayor Porter had been about to return to the screen was interesting but I couldn't see how it might be relevant to the case. I suppose a disappointed rival might have wished her dead so that she could get the potentially lucrative part as sidekick to Eve Dallas, but I considered that a very low probability. And why lure her into another room and drive a stake through her heart?

Similarly, the visit to Ruth Deacon's apartment had raised more questions than it had answered. The two sisters were not as close as I had thought, in fact, appeared to be somewhat estranged. But Rachel couldn't have killed her sister without putting herself under a similar death sentence, and Rachel was certain that Ruth was still alive. But where? The only time I've ever heard of a guardian spirit being wrong was when they misguidedly tried to use some of them to watch over high volume public places. The sheer number of comings and goings was too great and they broke down under the pressure. A small apartment building wouldn't present that kind of problem. And where was Ruth Deacon's dark room? Might she have rented an additional space somewhere in the same building? If so, the charges could have been covered in the payments for her apartment rather than listed separately. I made a mental note to have Moira check that out in the morning.

I felt a little better about the O'Brien case. At least I had discovered something the police didn't know, and it was possible that none of my competitors had the same lead. I'd have to figure out a way to follow up on that one. On the other hand, solving Morris Ngambe's problem still appeared to require resources I just didn't have. Once again, I didn't have the staff to mount that kind of massive investigation. I picked up the folder Moira had left for me and thumbed through it, but the mass of information she'd gathered was so discouragingly large that I carried it into the office and dropped it on my desk.

Some nights I brought work home with me, but this wasn't going to be one of them.

Like I said, my place is nothing much to look at from the outside, a narrow row house in serious need of a fresh coat of paint and some decreasingly minor exterior repairs, sandwiched between two larger homes, both of which have been subdivided into apartments. I could probably sell it to a developer or renovate it myself and generate enough income to set me up for a few years, but I like having all that space – three full stories plus basement and attic. Not that I need or use it all. The third floor is mostly empty except for some odds and ends meant for the attic that never quite made it there.

One of the few luxuries in my life is that I have an actual garage, sort of. The former owner, an elderly man who was one of my very first clients, converted what was originally an oversized den, knocking down one wall and installing an overhead door. After Mr. Kabler's wife died his only passion was his antique car, a Daimler, which he never dared park on the street. In fact, at least while I knew him, the bright red roadster never strayed from its nest. Anton Kabler had no other family; they hadn't been brought through during the change, and he had left most of his wealth to various charities. The Daimler went to a museum and the house, to my great surprise, had come to me.

I had to stop in the street, unlock the chain link gate and the garage door itself. There was an automatic opener, but it wasn't working when I moved in and I'd never considered it worth the expense to have it repaired. Besides, sometimes opening and closing the garage door was the only exercise I got.

So tonight I paused, left the engine running, and prepared to go through my usual routine. I'm not sure what warned me that I wasn't alone; I don't have any of Moira's fey sensitivity. Probably I heard or saw something that triggered a subliminal response. For whatever reason, I hesitated halfway to the gate and slowly turned around. There was almost no traffic here. The truncation of Brooklyn during the change had turned Yancey into a cul-de-sac and I was fourth from the end. I could hear voices from the next block over, raucous singing, probably originating from Grady's Bar and Grille, and a dog was barking somewhere close at hand.

I had almost decided I was imagining things when the Banshee appeared.

It wasn't a real Banshee, of course. As far as I know, we don't have any of the real thing. But it was possible to conjure up a pretty good imitation, an insubstantial but very visible apparition which could deliver a precisely targeted and quite dramatic message. This was the second one I'd seen and it was impressive. It swept up out of the darkness, glowing so brightly that I raised my hand to shield my eyes. Not an expensive one, obviously. The bright glow made it possible to skimp on details. It was vaguely woman shaped, but featureless. The glow would be visible from quite a distance, but even though it shrieked its message so loudly that my head began to throb, unlike the case with a Summoning Sphere it was completely inaudible to everyone else. That was just as well. I try to stay on good terms with my neighbors.

"DOOM FALLS ON THE HEAD OF THE INTERLOPER!" it screamed, then spread its cloaked arms like an airborne manta ray. "DO NOT RETURN TO THE CASTLE OF THE MOOR!" I didn't know whether to recoil in fear or bend over laughing. Someone had a decided flare for the overly dramatic. The banshee hovered for a second longer, then disintegrated in a shower of sparks. I stepped back instinctively even though I knew it was all illusory.

The castle of the moor? Had to be a reference to Morris Ngambe. Goff had already warned me off. Now this. What I'd initially believed to be a puzzling bit of vandalism was evidently something more significant. And someone was determined to discourage me from investigating.

CHAPTER FIVE

It was one of those rare days when I reached the office first. Moira arrived to find me sitting at my desk, going through the information she'd culled for me the day before. Her clothing was less spectacularly mismatched than usual, a frilly blouse and plain slacks that almost went together, the effect rather spoiled by a garish sash she'd tied around her waist. She raised an eyebrow inquisitively when she came into the office but all she said was that she was going to brew some coffee.

"Nice job with this, Moira." I nodded toward the folder. "I do appreciate all the work you do around here, even if I don't say so often enough."

"Great! Does that mean I get a raise?" She had paused, halfway back to the outer office.

"You certainly deserve one, but you know I can't afford what I'm paying you now," I admitted.

"You can't afford what you're supposed to be paying me now," she corrected me. "You're six weeks behind."

"Maybe I could take you on as my partner. Then we could split the profits." It was an old joke between us, to which she invariably responded that partnership would be a demotion, since half of nothing was nothing. But she surprised me this time.

"McGann and Dash? It doesn't have the right ring."

"Dash and McGann sounds better, don't you think?"

"We could get married. Then it would be Dash and Dash."

"Aren't two dashes as hyphen?"

"The other way around, I think." She sighed. "Nope. Guess I'll have to stay where I am until we can think of something better."

I returned to the file with some reluctance. Moira had indeed done good work, but her research only underscored how big the job was. There were far too many people for me to investigate in any reasonable amount of time, particularly because I owed Morris far too much to ever charge him my expenses, let alone my usual fee. I set aside the list of potential suspects, the summary profiles of the security systems, mystical and mechanical, at the Lagos Castle, and the detailed timelines and descriptions of each incident. If there was a pattern in any of this, it was too faint for me to detect just sitting here looking at colorless numbers and facts.

The last packet was something Moira had done on her own initiative. Morris had supplied copies of the personnel files of half a dozen key people, his accountant, the gift shop manager, the head chef, both assistant managers, and the head of security. To each of these Moira had added a handful of photocopies of clippings, culled from various newspapers and magazines over the course of the past three years. She couldn't have done this thorough a job so quickly on her own, which probably meant she'd used her own money to pay a clairvoyant to do an archival search.

I felt a fresh twinge of guilt. Moira would have starved if she'd been dependent upon her salary for a living, so she obviously had other resources. This wasn't the first time she'd dipped into her own pocket. I actually knew very little about Moira's life outside the office beyond her home address and telephone number and that she owned two cats, or vice versa. Some detective I am. I always insisted on paying her back, at least in those cases I knew about, but I still felt badly even though for all I knew she was a wealthy woman.

Bad conscience aside, the clippings were interesting. I'd met the security man, Oliver. He seemed a good sort, honest and hard working, though perhaps less than imaginative. I couldn't imagine him having an agenda of his own, but I'd been surprised before. Oliver was a former detective with the NYPD, but he'd resigned to go into the private sector. The news stories were innocuous; he'd attended a security conference and was serving on an advisory board for the Cities. I also knew Jacob Tutuola, the head chef. There was a thick wad of magazine articles attached to his folder, awards he'd received, contests he'd won. Jacob lived for his kitchen; it was inconceivable that he would ever do anything to spoil what it produced.

Next was Jessica Crane, the store manager, whom I'd only recently met. Her personnel file was surprising. She had a degree in arcane studies, specializing in charms and amulets. That would have made me particularly suspicious if it wasn't so obvious. Crane had been an instructor at the New School for three years but had never received tenure, had worked as an independent consultant and lecturer for about a year, then went through a radical career change. She spent a year managing a magic shop in Port-Au-Prince and had been working for Morris ever since. The redirection of her career seemed very odd and I made a mental note to check into it as I started through the attached clippings. The first few were trivial, but next was a news story I still remembered.

The Tuilleries had appeared at the same time as the rest of the Paris sector, but not contiguous to it. The portion of Manhattan where it appeared had been consumed, not pushed aside as was the case with all of the other transitions. For the first few days it had been recognizable, although some of the trees seemed to have been bizarrely distorted. Then came the first of the changes. There had been people in the park at the time, and many others in the general area, so there were numerous firsthand accounts. A disturbance like a heat shimmer had begun in the center of the gardens, rapidly expanding like ripples in a pond until they reached the periphery. The vegetation was transformed immediately. It became so dense that it was virtually impassable, and the shapes of the leaves and branches were altered so that much of it was no longer recognizable. No one who had been in the Tuilleries at the time ever emerged, as far as was known. The phenomenon repeated itself six months later, once again changing the appearance of everything visible from outside. It was no longer possible to discern what was happening in the interior. Subsequent events had occurred at intervals ranging from a few days to several years. There had been two within the past month, but they were the first in almost five years.

The area was monitored, but of late little effort had been expended to explore the interior. Billowing mists obscured most of the gardens, and it was always dark there, no matter what time of day it was. No one who had entered the Tuilleries had ever come out, not even the early expeditions mounted by experts armed with high order magical defenses. A few misshapen creatures had emerged, and each and every one of them had been so completely hostile that they had been destroyed quickly, sometimes requiring the application of significant sorcery. After the first few such incidents, the ward system was erected, which had so far proven effective in containing the threat, but we still knew virtually nothing about what was going on inside the barrier.

Three years ago, an effort had been made to over-fly the Tuilleries in a heavily warded helicopter equipped with highly sophisticated surveillance equipment. The mission had been a complete failure and nearly a tragedy. The engine began to malfunction almost as soon as they crossed over the perimeter, and the backup levitation spells didn't last much longer. They had managed to make it back outside the barrier before crashing, but just barely. The pilot had reportedly died of an stroke but no one else had sustained any serious injury, at least nothing physical. Two crew members committed suicide within the next few weeks and there had been rumors that others had developed deep rooted psychological or physical problems.

I was looking at a grainy newspaper photograph in which members of the expedition were being led from the wreckage. A younger Jessica Crane was one of them. Her resume must have understated the case. She would have needed to have displayed considerable talent to have become a member of that ill fated team.

Unfortunately, nothing else stood out. I had met both of Morris' assistants, Jeff Blaine and Kwani Leshoon. They were both ambitious and competent and seemed genuinely loyal. Last was the accountant, Audrey Dalton. We'd been introduced and I hadn't liked her; she seemed almost completely devoid of personality and the only thing she could talk about was numbers and financial strategies, but she was reportedly good at her job. Her clippings surprised me a little; she had lectured on a number of occasions, always about her specialty, of course, but she was also apparently an ardent collector of contemporary art. An expensive hobby, I suspected. Audrey Dalton might be worth a second look.

At some point Moira had brought me a mug of coffee, which seemed to have materialized on my desk without human intervention. It tasted completely substantial, however, and I felt considerably better once it was inside me rather than the mug. Moira hovered, waiting to have my full attention.

I glanced up at her. "I'm going out for awhile. Anything I should know?"

"Probably lots of things. You certainly should know that Miss Deacon called to find out if you've made any progress. She sounded quite distraught." Moira didn't sound excessively sympathetic.

"If she calls back, tell her I'm on the job, and these things take time. Ask her if she's cleared it with the management so that I can search the apartment again if I need to. And see if she can get us a copy of the rental agreement."

"Will do. And you're going out where?"

"Field work. I'll be out of touch for a while. Somewhere in Hyannis."

"You really ought to get a mobile phone," she admonished, not for the first time.

"I'll put it in next year's capital budget. While I'm gone, can you try to get in touch with a couple of people for me? Set up appointments." I had copied out the two SCA names from the Deacon folder.

She glanced at the names. "One of these numbers is in Berlin. Do you want me to ask for a meeting elsewhere?"

Berlin is one of our most obstreperous and dangerous areas. Unless you count the skirmishes between Tel Aviv and Jerusalem, we haven't had anything like an actual war in the Cities, with one exception. Shortly after Berlin joined us, they sent troops and tanks into Addis Ababa, and then moved toward the border with New Delhi. For once the Mayors acted quickly and in near unanimity, raising a small and chaotically inefficient army that prevailed through force of numbers rather than strategic or tactical brilliance. The Berliners were driven back, though never actually conquered, and they continued to make belligerent noises.

"No, I'll go there if necessary. Mayor Himmler has been trying to promote the tourist trade so there should be minimal hassle."

Moira looked dubious. I had barely persuaded her not to volunteer for the Cities Expeditionary Force at the time. "Watch yourself. They're not nice people."

"The people are fine. It's the government that's nasty."

For a change, there was no traffic problem. I bypassed the Hong Kong waterfront and drove into Hyannis from the south, getting a great view of the fishing junks out on the South China Sea. The shops were open but there wasn't much traffic, foot or vehicle, other than a small group of Hindus picketing a hamburger joint, and I had no trouble parking on a convenient side street only a couple of blocks from my destination.

Steven Sandobhal had made a fair living as a cartoonist and illustrator, but one look at the cottage where he'd been killed told me that at least some of his father's considerable wealth had found its way here. The "cottage" had almost as much floor space as my triple-decker, it was set right on the beach, and there was a completely superfluous swimming pool as well as a tennis court directly behind it. A Rolls Royce lived in the detached garage, parked right beside the vintage Lamborghini. The Lamborghini had an empty containment tank and the Rolls ran on gasoline, an obvious indication that its owner had money to burn. The entire property stood inside a glowing Police ring, but once again the token in my pocket satisfied it that I was entitled to enter.

The door was physically locked as well, so I had to resort to my charm key, which left only three more uses before it expired. The interior was as impressive as the outside. Expensive furniture, original art on the walls, a stereo system to die for, and a view out the front window that would have made a great screen saver. I did a preliminary walk through, found the bedroom, a fully equipped kitchen, two guestrooms, three bathrooms, a small den, a large workroom filled with brushes, canvases, paints, and other supplies, and – to my complete surprise – a fully equipped dark room with a closet full of photographic equipment and supplies. Something stirred at the back of my brain.

Sandobhal appeared to be an amateur photographer, and something of a voyeur. Almost all of his photographs were beach scenes, usually including one or more scantily clad young women. Even to my uneducated eye, there was something clumsy about his technique. His subjects were often off center so that the eye tended to wander rather than focusing on a central point, and they were almost exclusively unposed candids. I guessed that at least a portion of them had been taken surreptitiously. Some were out of focus, or the light levels were wrong. When I moved on, I was left with the strong impression that the late Mr. Sandobhal had been more interested in the subject matter of his photographs than in producing artistic work.

None of the women had looked familiar, and I'd examined every photograph closely. No sniggers please. I was looking primarily for Ruth Deacon because I believe in coincidences and I strongly suspected that my two cases were somehow connected. It wouldn't be the first time. The world of the Cities was considerably less random than the old world; that had been proven statistically as well as cosmologically. There was a magical principle called Congruence which suggested that disparate events with common factors were more likely to be related than not. Of course there was also a conflicting principle called Incongruence, which suggested that the creators of this world had a sense of humor and liked to tantalize us with apparent parallels that were actually pure chance.

But this was intriguing. There was a dark room missing in the Ruth Deacon case, and there was a totally superfluous and completely private one here. Could this be where Ruth developed her work? It was a long way from her place, but there might be a reason that justified the inconvenience. On the other hand, it might just be an actual coincidence and I might be getting my hopes up unreasonably.

I searched the house pretty thoroughly after that. The freezer where Sandobhal's body had been found was disconnected and empty. There were several caches of photographs scattered around the cottage, but they followed the same pattern as those I'd already looked at. There were different beaches involved – not all of which required swimsuits – but basically they were all informal shots of semi-dressed women and young girls. Nowhere did I find anything to link Sandobhal to Deacon, nor did I find a single likeness of the dead man. Voyeur he might be, but narcissist he was not.

Frustrated, I sat down at the kitchen table and opened the Sandobhal file, which I had brought with me. I paged through the transcripts and crime scene photographs, looking for something that might register as out of place or inconsistent, something to suggest a new line of inquiry. The only pictures of the victim were taken after his death, either in the freezer or at the morgue, so it was unfair to judge from them, but I guessed that he had had average looks, perhaps a bit gaunt. Not pretty enough to draw a lot of young women, but not ugly enough to scare them off if he had money to spend, and that certainly seemed to be the case.

I was just about to close the folder when something caught my eye and I paused, then slid one of the crime scene photos out where I could see it better. Sandobhal's body was lying on its side in the freezer, arms crossed under his cheek, legs bent awkwardly. His tanned skin was covered with frozen crystals, and the ritual marks carved into his body were almost completely obscured, although they showed clearly in the morgue shots, taken after he'd thawed. What caught my attention was a small detail I hadn't noticed before. Adjacent to his bent left elbow was a small, dark object, connected to a thin line that vanished beneath a forearm. The resolution wasn't good enough for me to be certain, but I was reasonably sure the object was an amulet. More precisely, it was half an amulet, heart shaped, possibly identical to the one I'd seen in the photograph of Ashley O'Brien.

I'm not sure how long I sat there. I had been suspicious of a connection to Ruth Deacon, most likely wishful thinking, but here was an almost definite commonality between two of the victims, and there was no reference to it in any of the Police files. I was reasonably certain that no one else had picked up on it. Of course, it still might be a complete coincidence; odder things have happened. But two coincidences in less than thirty minutes strained my credulity. All of my instincts said that I had stumbled upon that most elusive of objects, a physical clue.

My reverie was finally interrupted when the outer door opened. I glanced up and recognized the newcomer, a short, muscular woman who wore her dark hair in prominent bangs that completely covered her forehead. Michaela Rusk was an operative for Darke Investigations, which suggested they had decided to take up the case after all. Business must be slow. "Good morning, Mickey. I haven't seen you around in a while."

Mickey Rusk was not conventionally attractive but she was a bright, intelligent woman and we'd even gone out together a couple of times. She was also one of the best operatives on Darke's payroll. It would be a stretch to say we were close friends, but we got along all right. She'd tipped me off about a couple of jobs Darke had passed on and I'd helped her out with a couple of her cases when I didn't have enough work of my own to keep me out of trouble.

"You haven't been looking in the right places. Isn't this a little ambitious for you?"

"What can I say? I love a challenge. And I did get here before you, after all."

She shook her head. "Afraid not. This is a follow up."

"Oh? Find anything interesting the first time?" Had I missed something? She ignored the gambit, looking pointedly at the folder in front of me. "It's just the handout, Mickey. I've only been here a few minutes." More like an hour and a half, but she didn't need to know that. Friendship is friendship but this was business. "Want to compare notes?"

"I think I'll pass. Should I come back later?"

She was obviously not going to make a move until I was gone, so I gathered my paperwork and stood up. "No, I'm finished here. I'll leave you to it."

I was almost at the door when she called to me. "You're working for Morris Ngambe, aren't you?"

I paused and turned my head. "Morris is an old friend. I'm helping him out but he's not a client."

She nodded, accepting the distinction. "Just a word of advice. Watch your back."

"Do you know something that I should know, old buddy?"

Mickey looked uncomfortable, perhaps even nervous. "Just be careful. Darke has ears everywhere and someone is passing the word to steer clear."

"I thought Stavros Darke never backed down."

"He hasn't. If Ngambe had approached us, we'd have heard him out. But Darke hasn't called him either, and you know how he goes after high profile cases. Solving a problem at the Lagos Castle would be right up his line. There has to be a reason why he hasn't solicited the job."

I mulled that for a second or two. "All right, thanks for the warning, Mickey."

For a change, I ran into neither traffic nor significant delays on my way home, other than having to wait for a Bollywood film crew to move some scenery across the back road I'd chosen to bypass downtown New Delhi. Moira's pleasant mood had cooled and she greeted me with only the sketch of a smile. "I tried tracking down the two names you gave me. Elliott Shorter's telephone has been disconnected. I could ask Arthur to scry him out, but we haven't paid last month's bill and you know how grouchy he gets. But I did find Gunter Abberlin. He said he'd been at his home all day if you wanted to stop by." Her tone suggested that I'd be foolish to set foot within ten kilometers of Berlin.

"Thanks. I'll see if I can fit him in."

I retrieved my purloined photograph of Ashley O'Brien from the file and asked Moira to find out if Wanda Veil could see me late in the afternoon. Wanda was a sensitive and had lots of contacts among professional spellcasters. She was also a friend and wouldn't charge me for a little unofficial consulting. The amulet in O'Brien's photo was very clear, but the morgue picture was out of focus, poorly lit, and too small. I could tell the two pieces were similar, but that's all. My instincts told me they matched, or perhaps it was again just wishful thinking, but I didn't have anything else to go on. And to follow that lead, I'd need some official support.

My Police contact was Sergeant Delpy from the NYPD, and during our brief introduction over the telephone he made it abundantly clear that he thought I was a nuisance at best. It was no surprise that the Police resented it when the Mayors called for a Public Appeal, and I was expecting minimal cooperation if not outright opposition, but if I had to rely on my own resources, I might as well abandon all hope immediately.

Delpy's voice quickly went from bored to antagonistic. "You're supposed to make an appointment with the front desk when you want to talk to me."

"I know that, Sergeant, but this was such a little thing that I didn't want to take up your valuable time with an actual visit."

"Yeah?" He wasn't buying. "So what do you want?"

"I'm looking at one of the photographs from the Sandobhal crime scene. The victim was either wearing a charm of some kind or there was one lying in the freezer under his body."

"Yeah, that's right. It's mentioned in the investigating officer's summary, if you bothered to read it."

I had read it, but the presence of a piece of unremarkable jewelry hadn't seemed significant at the time. "I need to see that amulet."

Delpy laughed. "Yeah, and I need to win the Irish Sweepstakes. Did you ever hear the term 'chain of custody', Dash?"

"It sounds vaguely familiar," I allowed.

"Well, you aren't in it. If we let people fool around with physical evidence, every case we got to trial would be thrown out of court. So you get a picture in your packet and that's it."

I sighed. I should have known it wouldn't be easy. "All right, how about this? Can you get me a better photograph of the amulet? Something that shows identifying details, front and back."

"That might be possible," he admitted, "if there was a good enough reason for it. If you've found out something that pertains, you're supposed to report it, Dash. Those are the rules."

Yes, those were the rules. But even though there was theoretical confidentiality for each contract investigator, information was valuable and most Police officers, particularly sergeants, were notoriously underpaid. I couldn't afford to bribe Delpy to tell me what my competitors might have turned up, but most of them labored under no such restraint. "I don't have anything concrete. I'm playing a hunch. There's not much to go on here. If there was, you guys would have picked up on it already."

The last was an attempt to placate him and it apparently had some effect.

"We're awfully busy here, Dash. But I'll see what I can do."

"I need it pretty soon, Delpy."

"How soon?"

He wasn't going to like this. "Sometime this afternoon?"

"Yeah, and how about I deliver it to you personally during my lunch break? Who do you think I am, Dash?"

A public servant, I thought, but that's not what I said. "An overworked and underpaid Police officer. Listen, Sergeant, I know this is an imposition, but if it works out for me, I promise I'll return the favor."

Delpy knew better than to talk price over the phone, but I could almost feel the change in his attitude. "I'll leave it at the front desk. But you owe me, Dash."

Moira walked in just as I was hanging up, carrying a small parcel wrapped in cloth. "Wanda says she's free at 3:00 and would be happy to see you."

"Great. Anything else?"

"Miss Connors called to let you know that Evan Garner is still among the missing and the police are very interested in his absence. She wants you to give her a ring or stop by but said it's not an emergency. Hope Leibowitz asked me to remind you that you owe her a dinner. Mr. Pheng called, quite irate, but I explained to him that it was my fault, that I had forgotten to forward the report you prepared."

"But I didn't prepare one. I just haven't had time." And to be honest, I'd forgotten about it.

"No, so I took the liberty of transcribing the notes you left me and sent it over by courier."

I went from feeling guilty about reneging on my promise to Pheng to feeling guilty that I'd put Moira into an awkward position. "Wonderful. Remind me to give you a raise."

She gave me a dirty look. "Two prospective clients called, neither of them emergencies. I scheduled them both for the end of next week."

That left me only a few days to find a missing person, solve a murder mystery, identify a serial killer, and discover how and why and by whom my oldest friend was being magically harassed. Plenty of time. "Anything else?"

"Just this." She offered me the wrapped bundle.

"What is it?"

"It ought to be my letter of resignation, but it's actually two ham and cheese sandwiches, a mango, and some cookies. You're on your own for a drink. You won't have time to stop for lunch today and if you starve to death, I'll never get my back pay."

I took the package. "Thank you from the bottom of my heart, Moira. I'll stop for a fruit drink in Nairobi. You think of everything."

"That's what you don't pay me for." Despite the sarcasm, she smiled, and I noticed, not for the first time, that my secretary was a very attractive woman. If only she had some clothing sense. At least today her blouse and slacks looked as though they might have been meant to share the same body. "You look very nice this morning, incidentally." Maybe some positive feedback would help.

I'd tried it before and her response was invariably flat, but this time she surprised me by her directness. "Did you know that professional aura readers almost always have no sense of style?"

"No, I didn't know that." I felt mildly awkward; I wasn't sure where this was going and it was sufficiently out of character to startle me.

"Would you like to know why?"

"Sure, educate me."

She crossed her arms and pushed the inside of one cheek out with her tongue for a second or two. "The aura is a pale reflection of the soul, but even so, it can be a beautiful thing, or so hideous that it makes the reader physically ill. When you've looked inside a person and seen what they really are, it stops mattering what kind of shell they're wearing."

And with that, she was gone, leaving me to wonder if I'd just missed something important. But I had no time to think about it. I had appointments to keep.

Nairobi was in the midst of another growth spurt – upwards rather than outwards by necessity - but I found a tented concession with genuinely cold drinks and ate the lunch Moira had prepared while sitting at a picnic table and watching a pair of giraffes graze on a stand of trees. I drove through Mecca as quickly as possible because I always felt unwelcome there. It was one of the most insular of the Cities and outsiders were often disconcerted by the silent, disapproving stares they evoked. Berlin had checkpoints on every street, a feature they shared only with Peiping, and the decidedly uncooperative border guard gave me perfunctory, although substantially accurate directions.

Gunter Abberlin lived in a relatively large house on a relatively small piece of land in Blankenburg. He even had a driveway, although it was filled with vehicles, most of them horse drawn. Some of the horses were real; others were homuncular animatrons. The door was opened by an overweight butler who ushered me in to a small waiting room without ever actually meeting my eyes, instructing me to remain there while he "fetched the master." The room was impeccably fitted with vintage furniture including an oversized desk, a functional fireplace, and a glass fronted bookcase containing the works of Charles Dickens, Thomas Hardy, the Bronte sisters, Rudyard Kipling, Robert Louis Stevenson, and many other writers whose names I didn't recognize, most of them German.

Abberlin didn't keep me waiting for long, and seemed genuinely pleased to see me, insisted on shaking my hand vigorously and called me "old man" three times in four sentences, with a heavy German accent. He offered me a brandy, which I declined, and asked how he could help me.

I had barely opened my mouth when three other people burst into the room, a woman whose brittle laughter was like nails on a blackboard, and two tallish men who might have been twins except that one was as fair as the most Nordic purist could desire, while the other had skin so dark that it shone like a polished jewel. The woman wore an expansive pink and white dress that was obviously supported by some sort of hidden apparatus, while the men wore what I assumed were jackets and ties. The black man was clearly dressed as Sherlock Holmes, complete with deer stalker cap and Meerschaum pipe.

"Oh, sorry, old chap," said the fair one. "We thought you were alone in here." His accent was decidedly French.

Abberlin beckoned them over. "Mr. Dash, these are friends of mine. That's Lady Winterbourne, Bertie Cholmondesley, and Mr. Sherlock Holmes."

They were so enthusiastic that I would have felt gauche if I hadn't played along. "It's a pleasure to meet you all. I've followed your exploits closely, Mr. Holmes."

He nodded, accepting his due. "Watson tends to exaggerate a bit, I'm afraid, but it does make for a more entertaining story."

"I assume you're all members of the SCA?"

Abberlin intercedes. "Actually, we're having a joint get together with the Sherlock Holmes Society. Our membership does rather overlap."

"I'm actually here because I'm looking for one of your members who seems to have gone missing. I'm not sure what she calls herself within the society but her real name is Ruth Deacon."

The three newcomers looked blank, but Abbelin nodded. "That's Evelyn, Evelyn Raine. We haven't seen her in months, have we?" He glanced at the others, none of whom contradicted him. "She was rather difficult to get on with. Her research was meticulous and she was constantly calling us out for minor mistakes, an anachronistic turn of phrase, a menu item that wasn't appropriate, that sort of thing. Rather a stickler for detail."

"More like a martinet," added Cholmondesley. I was pretty sure he was Italian.

"It wasn't that we resented her corrections," insisted Lady Winterbourne, who was obviously authentically British. "But you see, the SCA presents the Victorian era as it should have been, not as it actually was. Not even Evelyn would substitute perfumes for bathing, or decline advanced medical treatment. But she would get quite shirty at times about the most trivial of variances."

"I imagine she could have made a lot of enemies with that kind of attitude."

They didn't bite at the bait, insisting that the SCA was just a hobby, not a way of life. "She was irritating and I won't say there weren't members who avoided her company," admitted Abberlin. "But we have hundreds of members and it was easy enough to avoid her. I can't imagine anything happening within our group that would have led to violence."

Which didn't mean it hadn't.

I chatted a bit longer, declined a second offer of a brandy, and took my leave. I made good time through Mecca, which is mostly open land, because for a change there weren't any pilgrims contesting the right of way. There were two adult elephants and a newly born calf walking alongside the road in Nairobi and I stopped until they'd turned away rather than startle them. A group of young boys was following in their wake, mostly local although I spotted a couple of Asians and at least one Nordic type. I wondered if he was a runaway from Berlin.

A thin packet was waiting for me at the Police station. A grizzled looking desk sergeant handed it to me with obvious reluctance. I stopped on the sidewalk outside the building and gave the contents a quick look. They were somewhat grainy faxes, but otherwise exactly what I wanted, front and back close-ups, plus a third shot with the amulet next to a ruler to indicate the scale. Each photo was held in a Hyannis Police Department frame with the name of the case file, the investigating officer's name, and the date and time the photograph had been taken. They were a week old. The handout files had been less than complete. I wasn't surprised.

I was only a couple of minutes late for my appointment with Wanda Veil, whose apartment in Pretoria was also her place of business. Wanda's real name was Lucy Hall, but she had decided that didn't sound mystical enough. A lattice weaver had moved into her eaves two years earlier and she had decided to let it remain, so the top of her house had a furry fringe that moved slightly when a breeze passed through.

Her front room looked like something out of an old fortune teller's shop, mystical symbols inscribed on almost every surface, subdued lighting, curtained alcoves, the smell of incense in the air. She greeted me in what she liked to call her uniform, diaphanous robes inscribed with translucent crescents and stars. A crystal ball sat in the center of a small card table, while another and more substantial table displayed a tarot layout, and still another a Ouija board, the I Ching, a glass bottle full of throwing sticks, and a summoning stone. Wanda catered to every predilection; I had visited her once while her assistant was clearing away the entrails she'd just read for a customer. The air freshening mobile had been overwhelmed.

"Come in, Dash. Let me turn up the lights." Most of the gloom vanished when she touched the switch. Wanda was just under five feet tall and looked like an undernourished child in some ways. There was a touch of gray in her hair, but she still had a strikingly beautiful face. She was dark skinned and when off duty dressed in accordance with local custom, but she was actually born and bred in New Orleans. I found her extremely attractive but, alas, she preferred the company of her own sex. "What do you want from me this time?"

"No keeping secrets from you, is there?" I pulled out the three photographs I'd received from the Police and the one I had stolen from Ashley O'Brien's flat. "Can you tell me something about these?"

We sat next to the crystal ball while she examined one picture, then the next, running through all four, then taking two and placing them side by side.

"I assume they're some kind of love charm," I suggested.

She shook her head noncommittally. "Possibly, even probably. A lot of these symbols are new to me, and the ones I recognize are in unusual combinations. You've noticed that they aren't halves of the same original, I assume?"

I hadn't noticed until just moments before, but I wasn't about to admit it. "Two left sides, no right. I thought at first that it was the same charm in both cases, but when I looked closer, I saw differences in the details."

"They're closely related though. They have a common purpose, and I very much suspect they were inscribed by the same hand. These are hand worked, each is one of a kind, and they would have been very expensive to produce."

"One was owned by a very wealthy man, the other by a bar girl, both recently deceased. But the latter may have received hers as a gift from an unidentified lover."

"If these are love charms of some sort, the other halves should be in the possession of their partners."

I had a sudden thought. "What would happen if one member of each pair died suddenly? How would the survivors be affected?"

"I can't tell you that. If I could physically hold one or both, I might be able to learn something of their purpose but a photograph conveys nothing of the essence. Can you bring them to me?"

"That's not possible, at least for the moment. One is in police custody and the other is apparently missing."

"Well then the best I can say right now is that they represent powerful but unfamiliar magic, and that the couples wearing each pair are linked in some fashion. I assume you're looking for the partners?"

I nodded. "It's the only real lead I have."

"You might check the various Cities morgues. It's possible that this is a form of bonding with which I'm unfamiliar. A lovers' death pact magically enforced, or a link so intense that sundering it results in despondence. They would be suicides in either case. It's not likely, but it's a possibility."

"A charm to cure cold feet. You fall out of love and you die."

Wanda laughed. "It's probably not quite that drastic, but it might well make unfaithfulness impossible or at least very difficult in some fashion. I might be able to find out more if I showed these to a few friends."

I grimaced. "Those are actually the only copies I have."

"Not a problem." She gathered the photos and stood up, went to the nearest alcove and pulled the curtain back. A first class scanner and high quality printer stood on a workbench.

There was one other thing I wanted to ask her, but I waited until she'd done her technological magic and returned the photos to me. "Wanda, what do you know about the Tuilleries? Other than what everyone else knows, I mean."

She didn't answer right away. Instead she opened another curtain, revealing a well stocked bar. She mixed two drinks, and didn't have to ask what I wanted.

"Do you think magic is evil, Dash?"

The question caught me by surprise. "No, not necessarily. It gets used for evil purposes some times. It's not evil to levitate a cinder block into the air, but if you cancel the spell and drop it on someone's head, it was used for an evil purpose."

"And by the same logic, magic isn't good either, right?"

"No, I suppose not."

"That's the understanding we've come to since we've been brought here. Oh, there are a few cultures that consider all magic evil – like the Mennonites and the Scientologists. But generally magic is viewed as just another aspect of the natural world, like gravity and electricity." She paused for a second. "And in most cases, that's true. But not always."

"Are you saying that the magic in the Tuilleries really is evil? It's not just unknowable and dangerous?"

"Deeply evil. The authorities don't want that to get about because it might make us uneasy about all forms of magic. So they play it down and insist that once we understand what's going on there, we'll be able to harness that power and possibly even use it for good. But that's not the case. There really is evil magic and, by extension at least, good magic. We may never be able to use whatever it is that lives in the Tuilleries because it would destroy us."

"Well, at least it's contained."

"Is it?" She shook her head almost imperceptibly. "Mostly you're right. But evil has the power to corrupt. The highest crime rate in the Cities is in the neighborhoods directly adjacent to the Tuilleries. In the years before the barrier went up, several entities escaped into the Cities. Officially, they've all been tracked down and either destroyed or driven back inside, but no one really knows for certain. Attempts have been made to study the area, but no one has ever returned after passing through the barrier. We just don't know enough to make even an informed guess."

"There was an attempt to fly over the Tuilleries a few years ago."

Wanda nodded. "I remember it. Another failure. There was a great deal of opposition to it in advance, and when it ended so disastrously, that effectively put an end to another line of study."

"What happened exactly? The newspaper story was pretty vague."

"Deliberately so, I imagine. The Mayors don't want to stir up the public. They have enough trouble maintaining a semblance of unity in this madhouse as it is."

"But you know more than the official story?"

"Yes, although some of it is conjecture. Officially, the helicopter's engines began to malfunction shortly after they crossed over the outer perimeter. The barrier is dome shaped, so they assumed that if they flew high enough to stay above the curved surface, they could observe the entire area from the air. They were wrong. The expedition was attacked by something evil, something we don't understand."

"Attacked how?"

"This is the part that's guesswork. The consensus is that something tried to get into the helicopter with them. Something from the Tuilleries. It probably didn't take a physical form, but that didn't make it any less dangerous. The newspaper reported that the pilot died of natural causes, but in fact he was boiled alive inside his skin. Several other members of the expedition developed malignant tumors within the first year, and most of them were dead soon after. Two members of the party committed suicide within a month of the crash and only three of the team are still alive today."

That took me by surprise. "I know one of them. Jessica Crane. She works for Morris Ngambe."

"A brilliant young woman. The experience traumatized her and she resigned her research position two days after her release from the hospital. My guess is that long term exposure to magic in the course of her studies helped shield her from the attack. The second survivor is Arthur Wainscott, a talented clairvoyant from Whitechapel. He has been confined under restraints in an asylum for the past two years. The third is an acquaintance of yours. He was there to operate the heavy weaponry if it should prove necessary. As it happened, of course, there was never any opportunity."

I'm not psychic, but I guessed immediately whom she must be talking about, and I was right.

"His name is Herman Goff."

CHAPTER SIX

I ate the last of my lunch in the car. Wanda had given me quite a bit to think about, but I wasn't sure that any of it was really relevant to the cases at hand. I had planned to call Sheri Connors next, but I was close enough that I decided to stop by instead. You never know what might happen when you show up unexpectedly. And I had thought of a question I needed to ask while I was there, one I should have thought of earlier.

The desk clerk recognized me and offered to page Connors, but I told him not to disturb her just yet. I knew the way to food services. He looked very uncomfortable when I turned and walked away, and I was sure he would be on the phone to security the moment I was out of sight, but that couldn't be helped.

Bransky was in his office, shuffling paper, and he looked distinctly irritated, then resigned, when he saw who was rapping at his window.

"Come in Mr. Gash."

"That's Dash, actually." I took a chair without waiting for an invitation.

"What can I do for you today?"

"I'd like to talk to the Robertson boy again, if I may. There are a couple of things I need to clear up."

"Very well." He turned in his seat to examine a chart on the wall. "Peter is on duty, as it happens. I'll have him sent here immediately."

"I could go find him," I suggested.

"No, that wouldn't do at all. We don't want our guests to think that there's some sort of criminal investigation going on here." The fact that the murder was still on the front page of the newspapers sold in the lobby apparently hadn't occurred to him.

We didn't speak while we waited, which fortunately wasn't long. Peter looked nervous when he entered, but relaxed when he saw me. Apparently he was more bothered by the possibility that he was in trouble with the boss than the chance that he might be a suspect in a murder case. That wasn't the reaction I was used to. Most people associate detectives with the Police, and most people have guilty consciences.

"I won't keep you long, Peter. I just had a couple more questions."

"Sure. No problem." He looked as relaxed as it was possible to be in Bransky's presence.

"You told us what you saw in Mayor Porter's room when you delivered the food but what about later? What about when you picked up the dirty dishes? What was going on then?"

Peter looked confused for a moment. "I don't understand, sir. I never went back to her room. I go off duty at 8:00 when I work that shift. Someone else must have brought back the cart."

I turned my head but Bransky was already rustling his paperwork. "That's correct, Mr. Dash. Peter has been with us five years. I believe I told you during your first visit that the busboy who retrieved the cart was new. His name is Christopher Hayden and he has only been with us a few months. And before you ask, no, he is not on the premises at the moment. He works late nights almost exclusively. We give senior personnel preference in choosing their slots. The tips are better in the evenings, you see. Hayden was only called in on that particular night to fill in for an absent employee."

I was angry with myself for having missed this earlier, but there was nothing I could do about it now. "All right, Peter. Thanks again for your help."

I waited until he was gone before turning back to Bransky. "Is there anything I should know about this Hayden kid? Anything out of the ordinary?"

He shook his head. "No, he seems an acceptably reliable young man, though they almost always make a good impression when they're first hired. Shows up on time, does his work well, no complaints from guests that I'm aware of. There have been a few minor mistakes, but we make allowances for the peculiarities of the hotel. I've been watching him a bit closer than usual because of his brother's history, but he seems all right."

"What's wrong with the brother?"

"He used to work for us, but he was arrested last year for improper behavior and is at the moment confined to Alcatraz." He frowned. "His employment was severed as soon as we heard, of course. Fortunately, his indelicacies did not take place at the Baker's Dozen, I am happy to say."

"And what exactly was the nature of those indelicacies?" I asked, not quite idly.

Bransky looked uncomfortable. "He was moonlighting as a part-time maintenance technician at a geisha house in Tokyo. Electrical work mostly, same as he did here. We were aware of his secondary occupation, but there were no complaints about his performance here. One of their employees told his supervisor that Paul had installed hidden cameras in some of the private rooms. I was quite shocked because he always seemed such a discrete, well mannered young man. It caused quite a scandal at the time."

"But you've had no trouble with the brother?"

"None whatsoever."

I estimated that I'd just about exhausted my unescorted time and I was right. Connors ambushed me as I was leaving Bransky's office. She was composed and professional on the surface but I could tell she was seething underneath. With good reason, I admit. This was her turf and she wouldn't be doing her job if she didn't try to keep tabs on everything that happened that pertained to the murder. But no one had told me that I needed to keep her in the loop, and I suspected her presence might inhibit some of the employees from speaking freely.

"I'm surprised to see you here, Mr. Dash. Someone must have forgotten to advise my office that you were coming to interview Mr. Bransky again." Her words were so frosty that they could have turned off the air conditioning for the next half hour.

"Actually I came here to see you, Miss Connors. My secretary said you called. I just happened to think of a question I'd forgotten to ask last time and I didn't want to waste your time on what I thought was a minor point."

She wasn't buying it, but she decided to pretend she was. "What minor point might that be?" She wasn't very good at pretense.

"I wanted to ask the busboy if he'd noticed anything different when he picked up the dirty dishes later that evening. As it happens, he couldn't have because he wasn't here at the time. Mr. Bransky informs me that someone named Hayden took his place." I decided not to mention what I'd learned about Hayden's brother. Connors undoubtedly knew about it already. She'd be a poor excuse for a security officer if she hadn't done a thorough background check on a new employee, particularly one who had regular contact with guests and frequent access to their rooms.

"Hayden is new, but he's proven to be reliable. Do you want to speak to him?"

"Bransky says he's not on duty."

"Personnel would have his home address. I don't want you to think we're not being cooperative here, Mr. Dash." Implying, of course, that this particular sin was mine alone.

I considered her suggestion, but decided to defer the interview. If, as I suspected, Hayden at least knew about the concealed camera, then accosting him at home might tip him off that his secret was out. Better to talk to him at work, make it seem routine, even casual. He was more likely to let his guard down. Peepers tend to be arrogant and sometimes they overplay their hand. "No, I don't think it's that important. Just another line item to check off. I should be able to stop back sometime this evening if that's all right." I also wondered why Connors hadn't made the same connection between the concealed character and the brother's history. Or maybe she had and I wasn't the only one playing the cards close to my chest.

"You'll let me know in advance this time?" She let some of her anger show again. Not that it had been well concealed before.

I pretended not to notice. "Will do. You had some information for me about Evan Garner?"

She shook her head. "Only negative information. He hasn't been home or at his studio since he left here. None of his friends have seen or heard from him. Neither have his sister or his agent. The Police are very interested in talking to him now."

"How about his car?"

She shook her head. "Doesn't have one. He used public transportation only. It's not public knowledge but he was mildly epileptic and didn't trust himself to drive. The desk clerk didn't pay attention the night Porter died. I assume he arrived the same way. As far as I know the Police have had no luck tracking down where it took him. If he wasn't in a hurry he might even have hired a carriage or a rickshaw."

"I imagine the Police are digging into the Mayor's past as well as his. I don't suppose you've heard anything on that front?"

Connors shrugged. "They're not talking to me about that. Actually, they're barely speaking to me at all. Detective Palmerston doesn't return my calls and I only know as much as I do because I have a couple of Police friends. I thought you were the one who had the inside track with them."

She was right, but it looked like I was going to have to exert myself if I wanted to stay current. Mayor Burford had told the Police to cooperate, but that didn't mean they were going to make it easy for me by volunteering anything. "Appearances are sometimes deceiving. If they can't solve this thing themselves, they'd rather it stayed open indefinitely than have someone like me show them up."

She surprised me by laughing softly. "Don't I know it? My dad was NYPD, a lifer. He wouldn't tolerate any suggestion that the Police were not up to the job."

I welcomed the mild thaw. Things would be much easier if Connors was on my side, or at least neutral. And I was suddenly thirsty. "Got time for a drink?"

"As long as it's coffee. I'm working."

"So am I. But I think better with alcohol in my system." So we both had coffee, but mine was Irish.

I had planned to visit the Gudanoff crime scene next, but I had to pass very close to the Lagos Castle on my way to Gorky Park, and I stopped there first on impulse. Morris was in a meeting so I didn't intrude, but Lily let me use the phone to call my office. As usual Moira picked up before the first ring, a talent I still found unsettling.

"Just checking in. Were you able to reach Rachel Deacon?"

"Yes, she was very cooperative once she realized what I wanted. I still think she's hiding something. Anyway, I've already received a fax of Ruth Deacon's monthly statement and her original rental agreement."

"And..."

"And it's for a standard five room apartment with bath. It's exempt from rent controls but there's been almost no change since she originally moved in. I suppose it's possible she's subletting space from another tenant on an informal basis, but it isn't reflected in anything I've seen."

"There were no unidentified payments in her check register. At least no regular ones."

"She might have paid in cash."

"Why would she do that?"

"You're the detective. You answer questions. I just ask them."

"And that's why I bring home the big bucks."

"And that's why I don't bring home any bucks at all."

I had asked for that, so I couldn't very well resent it. "Okay, thanks for the update. I probably won't make it back to the office before closing. If not, I'll see you in the morning."

Since I was being impulsive, I decided to stop and say hello to Jessica Crane, if she was at work. I'd learned a good deal about her since the first time we'd met and I expected to see her with fresh eyes.

Business seemed brisk, but I'd only been in the shop a couple of times before so I didn't have much basis to judge by. Crane was there, working one of two registers, while a harried looking younger woman with straw colored hair and an overcrowded charm bracelet that hampered her movement tried to keep pace on the other. I looked around for a while, noticed nothing amiss with the stock. A few of the books showed signs of deterioration, but it all appeared to be normal aging. I browsed through a primer on magical theory for a while, but even this layman's presentation lost me from time to time. When I put it back on the shelf, the crowd had thinned noticeably and a few minutes later, Crane closed down her register and left the straw haired girl on her own.

"Are you waiting to see me, Mr. Dash?" She must have spotted me and correctly interpreted my reason for being there.

"If you could spare me a few minutes, Miss Crane."

"Jessie, please. If you don't suffer from claustrophobia, we could use my tiny little office."

She wasn't exaggerating. The room was small enough in the first place, but the closeness was exacerbated by the clutter. Boxes and boxes of promotional samples, advertising circulars, and other materials lined the walls. More were piled on the floor and filled several utility racks to overflowing. I removed a stack of catalogs from a folding chair while Crane sidled around her narrow desk.

"Any more incidents?" I asked.

She shook her head. "Nothing significant that I know of. We did receive one customer complaint but it was for a purchase made ten days ago. I understand there was some spoiled lamb in the kitchen, but it wasn't served to a customer and there's a possibility it was normal carelessness this time rather than a deliberate act." She let a couple of beats pass. "Why are you here, Mr. Dash?"

"Morris is a friend of mine and he asked for my help."

"No, I mean why are you here to see me, specifically? You didn't spend almost an hour browsing through the gift shop to ask me how things were going. You could have called and asked Morris or his secretary if that's all you were after."

"I thought you might have some ideas of your own."

Our eyes met, hers disconcertingly intense, and I surprised myself by looking away first. "You should tell Morris to give you a better office."

"He offered. I like it here just fine. The clutter discourages visitors so I get some privacy. You've checked into my background, haven't you?"

The non sequitur took me by surprise. "It's part of the job. I know you used to be a rising star in the magic world and that you changed careers suddenly a few years back."

"I nearly died, Mr. Dash. Experiences like that tend to generate life altering decisions. Charms and curses were my specialty. I can't imagine any way that a conversion or corruption spell could have penetrated or been carried through our defensive barrier. But I've been out of touch for two years and magic theory is an evolving science. I'm not the person to ask. You might want to talk to Madame Griselda or the Cho triplets."

"There's an alternative explanation. As you say, it would take a considerable effort to cause so much trouble from the outside. But what if the spellcasting was being done right here or in the restaurant? Someone could be conjuring inside the shield."

Crane shook her head. "Unless someone's made a breakthrough, that's not possible either. The benevolence field we generate inhibits all forms of unsanctioned conjuration. All of our charms are created off site and have to be brought in through a single entrance where they are thoroughly screened. It is impossible to create any new magic within the restaurant or gift shop."

"But pre-existing magic still functions?"

She nodded. "Theoretically, a corruption source could have been introduced before the barrier was erected and it might not have been identified by the installation team when the barrier was upgraded. But Morris has had the entire complex swept three times since the trouble started. If there was any cursed object inside the containment field, it would have been detected."

I grunted. "You do recognize that there has to be a flaw somewhere?"

"Obviously. Either our screening procedure has a loophole or it's being subverted."

"There's another possibility. Who erected the shield?"

"Masters and Wardwell."

I grunted again. "They're supposed to be the best."

"They are the best. Morris doesn't compromise on security. And they audited the entire system two weeks ago."

"And how long has the barrier been in place?"

"The original was already here when I started almost three years ago. It's been upgraded several times since, about every six months. The last upgrade was in April, not counting any adjustments that might have been made during the audit."

"You've just made my job that much harder, Miss Crane."

"Jessie," she repeated. "And it is what it is, Mr. Dash."

I started to get up, hesitated. "One more thing, Jessie."

She was already on her feet. "Anything I can do help."

"I believe you know a gentleman named Herman Goff."

She flinched. "Yes, I know him slightly. I haven't spoken to him in years."

"Not since the expedition, I imagine."

Crane shook her head. "Not once. We have no reason to get together. Our common experience is not the kind of thing you celebrate. He was just hired muscle. I didn't even know his name until after the crash. We barely talked back then and once the debriefings were over with I lost track of him. I think he works for a security company or something similar. Locks and alarms, not magic."

"Have you ever seen him here? In the store or the restaurant, I mean?"

"No, not that I know of. He never struck me as a fan of fine dining." She suddenly grew impatient, or let simmering impatience boil over. Obviously this wasn't a subject she liked to talk about. "Are we done? I don't like to leave Carly alone for very long. She has a tendency to panic."

"Yeah, I guess so. Thanks for taking the time to talk to me." I got to my feet. "Oh, one more thing." I removed the clearest photograph I had of Sandobhal's amulet and held it out. "Could you just take a quick look at that and tell me if you can identify it?"

She accepted it hesitantly, examined it for a few seconds, then handed it back. "Not offhand. It's probably a love charm of some sort. It looks custom made. We have some similar ones in the store, pre-scored so that they can be broken into two equal parts. This one is a bit more elaborate than ours, and I don't recognize all of the inscribed characters, but it's probably just a variation."

"Thanks. That's pretty much what I thought."

There is a disparity in time between ours and the original world as well as in space. When Manhattan arrived to begin the process, the residents believed it was 1952. Madrid arrived next, only a few weeks later by local time, but they insisted that it was 1971. Forty years later, Brooklyn appeared, copied from the 1980s. But the progression wasn't linear. Berlin had manifested itself less than twenty years back, but they came from 1937. British dominated Hong Kong was from 1911 and London and Peiping were still arguing about who had jurisdiction there, although the local government seemed to be getting along just fine on their own. Moscow was from 2001, reeling already from the collapse of communism, and they fought a short lived civil war between the allies of Boris Yeltsin and Vladimir Putin, before Goncharev rose to power and became their first Mayor.

Gudanoff had lived on the tenth floor of a modern high rise at the northern edge of Gorky Park. It took me a few minutes to talk myself past the security officer in the lobby, who insisted that I be escorted to and from the apartment, and summoned a uniformed and armed woman with closely cropped hair to accompany me. We didn't speak on the ride up and she quietly took her station outside the door when I passed through the barrier.

Aram Gudanoff had been a professional lobbyist, and his list of contacts included everything from public interest groups to manufacturers to labor unions. As far as I could tell from his profile, he had no real political beliefs of his own. He advocated what he was paid to tout and railed against what he was paid to contest. Judging by his apartment, the wages of pragmatism were not niggardly. I had thought that Sandobhal was living in luxury, but Gudanoff made him look bush league. Some of the Mayors had more opulent residences, but only a few of them.

His living quarters took up fully a third of the tenth floor. He was actually renting two adjacent units rather than a single apartment; the wall between them had been partially removed. There were paintings scattered along the walls, most if not all of them originals, and some were by artists I recognized, including enchanted canvases whose subjects actually moved through predetermined routines. There was a miniature waterfall, currently inactive and custom made furniture. I found high end stereo equipment in one room, a small home theater in another, and the kitchen was better equipped than some restaurants. The bedroom was enormous, and you could almost have played soccer on the bed itself, which was circular, covered with silk pillows, and conveniently close to a fully stocked bar. I glanced up automatically and was not surprised to find an oversized mirror on the ceiling.

It was impossible not to make the connection to Mayor Porter's demise, and further conjectures crowded at the gate, waiting for me to acknowledge them. As a lobbyist, Gudanoff had obviously dealt with many of the Mayors on a very personal level. Porter might well be one of them. I inscribed a mental note to ask Moira to make some inquiries. Deborah Lerner should certainly be able to help if there were contacts that weren't a matter of public record. Every meeting with lobbyists, official or otherwise, was supposed to be reported, but in practice the law was rarely followed.

I was conducting a general sweep but I was also looking for something specific this time, some evidence that Gudanoff had owned half of a heart shaped amulet. Two such instances might, against all of my instincts, have been coincidence. Like I said, coincidences aren't as rare here as they were in the original world. Three, however, would definitely establish a link, a connection among all of the victims, and it would be something that the Police hadn't discovered. Although all of the various subsidiary Police forces were supposedly integrated into a unified system of law enforcement, in practice petty rivalries and personal attitudes often diluted the free flow of information from one to the other.

I really hoped to find something to confirm my suspicion, but in the end I was disappointed. There was no mention of any jewelry on Gudanoff's body in the files I'd been given. In fact, they stated quite clearly that the victim was found naked in an otherwise empty bath tub, wearing no jewelry at all, not even a ring. I had already gone over every photograph from the crime scene with a magnifying glass and assured myself there were no amulets in any of them, heart shaped or otherwise. Gudanoff did in fact have considerable personal jewelry, more than most women. I searched an entire cabinet full of watches, rings, silver and gold chains, studs and cuff links and tie tacks. I even found a considerable variety of amulets, some of them clearly ornamental, others likely designed for magical purposes – luck, energy, self-confidence. There were so many that some of them almost certainly had expired. Gudanoff clearly believed in grabbing every possible advantage.

I also found a fairly extensive collection of photographs. Gudanoff was apparently a narcissist because he appeared in nearly every one. There were pictures of him with a number of public figures, mostly but not exclusively political. One showed him with his arm around Mayor Burford, who looked pleased with himself. There was even one with Mayor Porter, but it was a large group shot and they were not standing close together. In several of the photographs, he wore pendants or charms around his neck, and I studied these very closely, but none of them were what I was looking for.

Frustrated, I did another pass through each of the rooms, forcing myself to be thorough even though I knew that the Police, to say nothing of the other independent investigators, would have gleaned everything useful already. And at the very last minute, just as I was about to leave, I got lucky.

I was in the kitchen, opening cabinets, pushing their contents around. Nothing seemed out of place. One narrow drawer proved to be the only island of disorder in an ocean of neatness. Here Gudanoff apparently threw everything that he didn't have a place for. There were paperclips and pencil stubs, a small screwdriver, a ball of twine, a handful of mismatched coins, and other debris, including several packets of matches.

I took the matches out and looked at them. Most were from restaurants and hotels, although there were none from the Lagos Castle or the Baker's Dozen. A few advertised products, and one was inscribed with Chinese characters. Three had no markings at all, just colorful patterns, and one of these looked familiar. I held it in my hand for several seconds before I realized where I had seen it before.

The pub near Ashley O'Brien's apartment.

It might not mean anything. They were probably mass produced and not peculiar to that bar, and I had no proof that Gudanoff had ever patronized the place. On the other hand, he would have had to have met her somewhere, and what was more likely than a bar? I decided to make time to look up my young friends in Dublin and show them a picture of Aram Gudanoff. I had a strong feeling that he was O'Brien's last boyfriend.

It was getting toward dusk when I left Gudanoff's, but still too early to go to the Baker's Dozen. I ate a light supper at a little diner I knew in Toronto. When I came out, I discovered that someone had broken into the Studebaker while I was gone. Thankfully it was someone skilled enough to use a lockpick or an unlocking spell. I had replaced broken windows twice in the past two years. One of the drawbacks of my job is that I have to park in bad neighborhoods. My intruder had opened the glove box and made a mess, but nothing appeared to be missing. Since there had been nothing valuable in the car in the first place except the radio, that wasn't surprising. I was surprised to find the radio intact, but maybe the market for poorly made, barely functioning electronics had bottomed out.

There was no point in reporting the incident. I straightened up the mess and headed for the Baker's Dozen.

It was full dark when I got there. There were heavy storm clouds over Boston and a brisk breeze was stirring the street trash. I didn't recognize the desk clerk, but when I told him my name he immediately picked up the phone and dialed Connors' office. The ubiquitous Douglas materialized less than a minute later.

"Miss Connors will meet you in food services," he said politely.

"I know the way."

He nodded his understanding, but he accompanied me anyway.

Hayden was a good looking youngster in his early twenties, blonde, clean shaven, well built but not muscle-bound, and transparently nervous. His hair was unstylishly short and he had one of those trendy vampire clan tattoos under his left ear. He looked so ill at ease that I let him sit and stew for a minute or two before saying anything because I knew he was sitting on something he didn't want to reveal. Connors stood by the door; she had greeted me with a thin smile but hadn't spoken a word since I'd arrived.

I decided to try to sound professional this time. "I understand you're new here at the Baker's Dozen."

"Yes, sir, I am." His voice was thready and he spoke too fast.

"Sort of following in your brother's footsteps, I gather."

He frowned. "I don't understand what you mean, sir."

"Well, didn't your brother used to work here a while back? That's what Mr. Bransky here told me." I glanced at Bransky for confirmation and he nodded.

"Yes, sir, he did. He worked in building maintenance, but he was gone before I started."

"Found himself a better job, I imagine."

"No, he had some trouble and had to go away for a while." His glance at Bransky was mildly hostile. I could tell he wondered how much I knew.

"You were on duty the night Mayor Porter was killed, is that right?"

"Yes, sir."

"In fact you picked up the cart from Mayor Porter's room, didn't you?"

"Yes, sir. It was a mistake, actually. She was done with it but she hadn't called for room service. I'm still having trouble telling one floor from another and I went to the wrong room. I apologized for the error even though she didn't seem particularly upset."

"Was she alone at the time?"

"She had company, a man. I only caught a glimpse of him; he was lying on the bed with his face turned away."

"Did you recognize who he was? Had you ever seen him with the Mayor before?"

"No. I mean, that was the first time I'd ever waited on her, so I don't know if she'd had men in her room before. And like I said, I never saw his face. Even if he had been turned toward me, I was so surprised to see who had answered the door that I might not have noticed."

"You returned the cart the same as you always do."

"Yes, sir."

"Tell me, were there any champagne bottles on the cart? Empty ones, I mean."

"Yes, there were three, I think. I dropped them in the recycling bin on my way."

Bransky spoke up for the first time. "We usually do the recycling in the food services area, Mr. Dash, but sometimes the busboys drop them off to save time."

I nodded and stared at Hayden for a few seconds. I could tell he was making a conscious effort not to squirm in his seat. He was afraid he was going to make a mistake but it was too late - he already had. "How did you know the lady was Mayor Porter? Did she identify herself?"

"No, I recognized her as soon as she opened the door." His admission was transparently reluctant.

"You follow politics then?"

He shook his head. "No, I remember her from the movies. *Bikini Assassin* and *Scream V*."

"She wasn't much of an actress."

He smiled. "No, I guess not. But she really looked good in a bikini."

"So when did you decide to cast her in your own movie?"

He tried to look puzzled but succeeded only in looking guilty. "I don't understand. What are you talking about?"

"We found the camera, Chris. Either your brother installed it and told you where to find it or he taught you how to do it. What time did you go off shift that night?"

"Just after 9:00. I was filling in; it wasn't my regular time." He glanced toward the door, but Connors was blocking the exit. "Look, I didn't do anything wrong. Not really. I mean, I didn't force her to do anything. Part of it was her idea even!" He was almost pleading.

"Why don't you tell us what happened, right from the beginning?"

It was almost exactly what I expected, right up until the end. I think he only lied once, when he claimed that he had never used the hidden camera before, but I wasn't interested in a small time voyeur. He had recognized Porter just as he had said. But he had understated her condition. She had opened the door almost completely naked and had tried to convince him to join her and Garner in bed. The boyfriend had objected and separated them, handed Hayden an unusually large tip, and asked him to take special care to make sure the champagne bottles and glasses were recycled. "He told me to forget that he'd been there, but she winked at me and when she was closing the door she whispered that I should come back later and I said I would."

"There must have been an aphrodisiac in the champagne," said Connors. "One of the non-magical ones. Something that dampened her inhibitions."

I nodded. "Porter wasn't called the Ice Maiden just because she played Princess Leia in *The Empire Strikes Out*. Garner must have gotten tired of the coy act." I turned back to Hayden. "So what time did you go back to her room?"

"A few minutes after nine. I bought another bottle of champagne and then clocked out and used the employee exit, but I came back through the loading area. I'd unlocked one of the service doors and there's no guard down there." I heard Connors shift position and knew she'd just taken a mental note. "When I knocked, she didn't answer for a while and I thought she'd passed out or changed her mind, but then the door opened. She was, you know, really friendly and said she was glad I had decided to come back. Look, she was a famous actress. I was never going to get another chance like that in my life. I had to go for it."

"So why did you talk her into switching rooms?" asked Connors.

"I knew the camera was there, but I'd never used it before. Honest! Anyway, no one would ever have believed me unless I had proof. I mean, how many guys can say they had sex with the Ice Princess?" He looked at Bransky and I, sure that we at least would understand. "I rolled back the rug and showed her how we could climb down to the bed in the other room. I let her think I was still on duty and that someone might come looking for me, so it was better if we were someplace where no one would think to look. It was thin, but she was pretty wasted and a little nervous about climbing down but I went first and showed her how easy it was."

"So then the two of you had some more to drink."

"Yeah, but it was just champagne. No drugs. And I drank most of it. She was too...ummm...busy to drink." He gave us a sheepish grin that vanished when he saw Connors' expression.

"So what went wrong? Why did you kill her?" I kept my voice neutral, watching closely to see how he reacted to the charge.

"I didn't do it! I wouldn't!" He looked so horrified that I knew instinctively this onion had one more layer. At least one more. I had thought Hayden might be the killer, that the Mayor might have done something to drive him into a thoughtless fury. It was still possible, but I couldn't see him in the part.

"We were both lying there on the bed and she told me to get on top and so that's what I did and then something hit me from behind. Feel the back of my head," he turned and rubbed at his scalp. "There's still a big bump there. The next thing I knew, I'm on the bed all alone, with a splitting headache. She's nowhere in sight, the room is freezing cold, and I thought she must have climbed back up to her own room."

"How would she have done that?" asked Connors.

"There's a rollup ladder hidden behind the camera. I dropped it before we jumped down so we could climb back up when we were done. "

"So what happened next?"

"Well, like I said, I thought she'd gone back up to her own room so I figured that she'd sobered up and hit me with something and that was the end of it. I went in to take a pee and almost fell over her." He looked at each of us in turn. "I swear I had nothing to do with it. She was already dead when I found her."

"So you just left her there?"

"What else was I supposed to do? At best I'd lose my job and more likely I'd be arrested for killing her. The door was bolted from the inside and her room above us was locked. I dressed and cleaned the place up and closed the hatch. Then I went home."

"What about the camera? Did you take the film?"

"No, there wasn't a cassette in it. I must have forgotten to put one in the last time I used it." His mouth clamped shut as he realized what he'd just admitted.

"You're lying," said Connors with absolute conviction.

I sighed. She was right. Hayden would not have forgotten to put a cassette in the camera. But I was pretty sure that the tape of Mayor Porter's final moments was now in the possession of whoever had knocked the boy unconscious and put a stake through the heart of the late Mayor of Hollywood.

CHAPTER SEVEN

"So if Hayden didn't do it, who did?"

Connors and I were back in Room 1313, the one where the body had been found. My Police pass hadn't worked on the barrier here, but Connors had one of her own.

I shook my head. "I think we're asking the wrong question. Maybe we should be trying to figure out why the killer used a wooden stake."

"Hayden has clan tattoos. It might have helped to build a case against him and divert our attention from the real murderer. Or maybe the Mayor was just in the wrong place at the wrong time and this is all about Hayden. Maybe one of his undead wannabe friends is behind this."

"Maybe." It didn't sound promising, but it wasn't a

possibility I could dismiss out of hand. Logic said that Porter had

been the target, but humans aren't always logical. "What did you

find when you checked up on him?"

She frowned, but her puzzled look was patently assumed. Her eyes skittered away from mine. "What do you mean?"

I made an impatient sound. "I thought we were cooperating

on this, Sheri. You checked on Hayden as soon as his name came up.

Even a mediocre security chief would have done that, and I know

you're better than that."

She dropped the pretense right away, but I could tell she was still on edge. "All right, I made a few calls. Hayden is a dabbler not a convert. He joined a clan because it was the thing to do a while back, at least in his age group. They're into group sex and fancy costumes, but none of the hardcore stuff. The blood they drink is tomato juice. He's a dilettante. Nothing twisted. Probably joined to meet girls."

"And you didn't find anything that seemed odd? Other than his brother's interesting hobby, I mean. Some of those clans people are into some really shady sidelines."

"I looked pretty closely." She was visibly uncomfortable and I still felt she wasn't saying everything she knew. "But I don't think that's what we're dealing with here. A dedicated clan member would have brought the weapon with him. The stake was improvised, an afterthought. "

"Yeah, you're probably right. I think the Mayor was the intended victim and the busboy was just a convenient scapegoat. If the Police had stumbled onto the connection, they'd have him locked up by now."

"They're apparently betting on Evan Garner. His disappearance is certainly suspicious."

"There are other reasons why the killer might have used the stake."

She thought about it for a few seconds. "There'd be no intimate connection. If the killer used a personal weapon, a knife or a gun, there might have been physical evidence pointing to him, or her. A good seer might have picked something up from a sliver of metal or a bullet once it was outside the building."

I nodded. "Very good. Leaving aside the vampire connection for the moment, there's still something we can deduce from the murder weapon. If this was a premeditated killing, why take the time to fashion the stake here? Why not prepare it beforehand?"

"Well, a wooden stake wouldn't have shown up on our metal detectors if he'd carried it in, and it would be small enough to be easily concealed from sight, so that can't be the reason."

"Which suggests that when the killer entered the hotel, he or she hadn't yet decided to commit a murder."

"A crime of opportunity then."

"It looks that way. But nothing was stolen. Her jewelry and cash were still in her room. So it probably wasn't a robbery gone wrong either."

"Her door was locked, Dash. Both rooms were locked from the inside."

"We'll worry about that later. The killer managed to get in, so obviously there was a way to circumvent the lock. A good master spell key would have done the trick." She shook her head and I realized the flaw immediately. "Okay, okay! Magic doesn't work in here. But a conventional lock pick would have done the job just as effectively. Or a master key. You do have master keys to all the rooms, don't you?"

She nodded. "I have one, and there's another in the security office. All of the senior maids have them as well, although theirs only work on the floors they're assigned to."

"The point is probably moot anyway. Since nothing was stolen, nothing that we know about anyway, I'm not inclined to believe that was the motive either. And since she wasn't running for re-election, I think we can rule out political intrigue."

"Which leaves a crime of passion." Connors shook her head. "But you said you don't think Hayden killed her. I suppose the Police might be right, that Garner came back later, sneaked up to her room, gained access somehow, became enraged when he saw her screwing around with the hired help, and snapped."

"That's one possibility." A thought occurred to me. "What do you suppose the Mayor's mood would have been in the morning, if she hadn't died, I mean?"

"I don't imagine she'd have been too happy. Drugged and seduced twice in a single evening." Connors surprised me by letting a wicked little smile show. "I would have liked to have been there to see that."

"You didn't care for her Honor, I gather?"

She gave me an appraising look, then shook her head. "We've crossed paths a couple of times. The Mayor didn't think much of the security arrangements at the Baker's Dozen and she was pretty vocal about it." Connors gave a self conscious laugh. "I guess now she'd have some justification for feeling that way."

"So she'd have wakened in her bedroom with a pounding headache, and murky but undeniable memories of having had sex with not only her current boyfriend but also one of the busboys. If she hadn't had such a calm, gentle disposition, she might have created quite an uproar."

Connors looked at me as though I'd grown a second head. "You have to be kidding. She was a petty minded, vindictive snob, and she was a Mayor. If she was in a forgiving mood she'd have been satisfied with public humiliation for Hayden and the loss of his job, with a lengthy prison term for Garner. More likely she'd have tried to press charges against them both for dispensing illegal drugs, sexual enslavement, rape, and abduction, and she would have sued the hotel. I suppose you could make a case that I had a motive, since she would almost certainly have demanded that I be discharged. She might even have hired the Gestapo to abduct Garner and subject him to a lengthy and bloody interrogation." She ran out of steam. "I get your point," she said quietly. "But that only strengthens the case against Hayden and Garner."

"Hayden took advantage of the situation, but he didn't give her the drug." And why, I wondered, would her reputed current lover have needed to drug her? Was she in fact drugged at all? I made a note to find time to read the autopsy report.

"But Garner left the building before Hayden showed up. Why leave and then come back later?" She shook her head, dismissing her own question. "To establish an alibi, of course."

"Garner went downstairs to the desk and told them he was leaving, but we both know that it wouldn't be difficult to evade detection, particularly if you're already inside the building and if you're a frequent guest who knows the layout and at least some of the security procedure. He probably just went back up to her room instead of leaving."

"I keep telling management that we need to have security cameras on the thirteenth floors. All of them." She made an exasperated sound.

I was thinking out loud now. Connors was a good sounding board, almost as good as Moira. "When Hayden showed up at Porter's room the first time, she tried to entice him to stay, didn't she?"

"Yes." She was hesitant, not getting my point.

"He was being invited to participate in a threesome, remember? With Garner as the third leg. Let's say that Garner had already decided to kill her at that point, that he'd begun to realize that there were going to be unpleasant consequences when the drug wore off. Porter might have told him that Hayden was coming back later and that's when Garner saw his way out. He would pretend to leave the hotel, then sneak back and knock on the door. He tells Porter he forgot something, or can't stand the thought of leaving her, or whatever. She lets him in and maybe he pretends to go when she isn't looking, closes the door hard or something, and hides someplace. Then it's just a matter of waiting until Hayden showed up."

"Just in time to be framed for her murder."

"That may have been Garner's plan from the outset. If so, it must have come as a considerable shock when Hayden opened the trapdoor to the other room. Garner probably stayed out of sight until the two of them were preoccupied, then followed them down, armed with whatever he used to knock out Hayden."

"And Porter. There was heavy bruising on the side of her skull, according to the autopsy. She was almost certainly unconscious when he staked her."

"And with both of them out cold, he would have had plenty of time to fashion his makeshift stake, finish off the mayor, retrieve the cassette from the hidden camera, and then exit through the Mayor's room. If he had a master key, he could have relocked the door behind him."

"It all sounds plausible."

"Yes, it does." But I didn't like it.

We played with a few more increasingly unlikely scenarios, but my heart wasn't in it. I needed more information. I lapsed into what was apparently an awkwardly long reverie, looked up to find Sheri offering me a mug of coffee. She even smiled. "Hope I'm not interrupting a productive line of thought."

I took the coffee. "No such luck. I was trying to think of a way Porter could have committed suicide in order to implicate Garner after a lovers' quarrel. Something in the back of my mind keeps insisting that things aren't what they appear to be, but the something isn't forthcoming about alternative answers." I sipped at the coffee. It was quite good.

Sheri settled into her chair and for the first time in my experience, she seemed almost relaxed. The key word there is "almost." I don't think I'd ever met anyone who maintained such an unremitting, intense awareness.

"Why are you here, Sheri?" The words came out unbidden.

She frowned. "What, now you're getting existential on me?"

"You know what I mean. Why are you working at the Baker's Dozen?"

She shrugged, sat back in her chair. "This isn't such a bad place. The pay is decent and most of the time there's no one looking over my shoulder."

"It's a deathtrap for security professionals. There's almost no market for non-magical security skills anywhere else in the Cities. You're underfunded, obviously frustrated, and there's no place for you to go within the organization. Do you want to be monitoring security cameras and supervising a staff of half a dozen underpaid guards for the rest of your life?"

She looked offended, but only mildly. "I have ten full time employees and I bring in extra help for special occasions." Her posture changed, acknowledging the accuracy of my description. "But you're right. I'm trapped here, but not the way you think. Not entirely."

I waited to see if I needed to prompt her further. She had turned away, was staring at a wall, her eyes not really focused there. "I'm sensitive to magic, Dash."

"How sensitive?"

"Very." She turned and met my eyes. "I can't use even simple charms. They get amplified. If I touch a good luck charm, everything goes my way. Big time. I win lotteries, get marriage proposals from multi-millionaires, draw royal flushes on every hand."

"Sounds great." But I knew there was a catch.

"Sure, until the Council of Mages detect the anomaly and undo things. A minor enhancement of luck is perfectly all right because the effects cancel each other out. A sensitive – I'm not the only one but we're rare – upsets the entire arcane balance. Give me a good weather charm and bright, sunny days follow me around, disturbing the normal weather patterns. If I worked at, say, the Ritz in London, the security charms would be so effective that they'd exclude guests or visitors who wore knockoff clothing, had a single joint in their possession or even remnants of pot in their bodies, maybe even if they had an illicit thought. Most definitely they wouldn't allow anyone to enter who was planning any marital infidelity. The management would not be pleased."

"Can't you get the condition treated?"

She laughed, but there was no humor in it. "Right. I once paid a conjurer to reduce my ability to exaggerate magical devices.

But the conjuration itself was amplified and I became a mobile Baker's Dozen. Nothing magic would work within twenty meters of me. I had the devil of a time getting that reversed, and it cost me six months pay. And the reversal left me right back where I started."

"I'm sorry. I've never met a sensitive before."

"Most of us are recluses or we live with the Mennonites. They don't like magic so we fit right in. I've thought of going myself, but I like it here. I'm not the country girl type."

I made an effort to change the subject, but there was an awkward space between us and we were both relieved when I used the press of time as an excuse to leave.

It was already dark when I emerged from the Baker's Dozen. I retrieved the Studebaker, which was intact this time, and pulled out into traffic. A panel truck immediately turned out of a side street, its headlights glaring in my mirror. My paranoia kicked in immediately, but the truck veered off at the first intersection. It was Friday night, I realized, and vehicles were pouring into Manhattan from every direction. I had planned to stop at the office before going home, but that now seemed impractical, and there was nothing there that wouldn't wait until morning in any case. Normally, my shortest route back to Brooklyn was through the northeast corner of Tehran and into lower Manhattan, then directly across to the Golden Gate Bridge, but I figured I'd do better today if I headed east through Rabat and then north to Brooklyn by way of the anomalous land connection through Rio de Janeiro.

Things started to go awry as I was exiting onto the moderately well maintained secondary road that skirted Rabat's commercial district. I'd been increasingly aware of a clicking sound, vaguely electrical, that seemed to be originating from inside the dashboard. Like I said, my car is pretty old, not quite in the antique class, and I try to take good care of it, but only when I can afford to. It runs pretty well, but I've grown accustomed to mysterious noises and unless they're really insistent, I can ignore them without much effort.

The clicks became louder and started to come closer together as I exited the highway, and the rhythmic pattern I thought I'd heard earlier had now given way to multiple random patterns, almost like Morse code. After another two miles, I stopped pretending that nothing was wrong. It was no longer possible to separate the individual clicks, which now sounded like a crackling fire or popcorn exploding in a pan. The disturbance was clearly coming from the glove compartment, the same glove compartment that had been rifled earlier in the day. Perhaps it hadn't been an act of random vandalism after all.

Fortunately it was easy to pull off the road here. There were low adobe style houses on either side, most of them deserted. With Nairobi and Adelaide sharing a border, the citizens of Rabat had too many better paying jobs and more luxurious living accommodations within reach for them to stay in such comparatively primitive quarters. I pulled up in front of one of the less dilapidated buildings. It was some kind of leather goods shop but it had closed for the day and only a single security light showed, glowing above the entrance. I stopped the engine, hoping that would bring things to a halt, but if anything the seething, clicking sounds accelerated. Turning in the seat, I flicked on the dome light and started to reach for the glove compartment latch, then hesitated, thinking better of it. My intervention proved to be unnecessary because the door dropped open all by itself and something dark and agitated dropped out.

Scarab beetles. Large scarab beetles. Dozens of them. They scurried about as they fell onto the seat and the floor, some disappearing from sight, others swarming up the backrest or the passenger side door. I pulled my hand back, surprised rather than frightened, as more of them emerged. The outflow showed no sign of slowing and genuine fear began to replace my initial astonishment.

Reaching behind my back, I opened the car door, planning to step out of the car, but my uninvited passengers decided that was the moment to make our acquaintance more personal. They surged toward me in a body and I recoiled rather than withdrew, falling awkwardly, banging my elbow against the door handle and landing heavily on my back. Fortunately the ground was soft sand and I was startled more than hurt.

They followed, spilling out of the car in a dark wave, darker even than the night. I rolled to my right and got to my feet, half stumbling as I retreated to what I thought was a safe distance. The moons were both close to full and the night sky was clear so I had a pretty good view once my eyes adjusted.

It looked like my car was melting. The scarabs came out of the open door in unabated strength, scattering in every direction. They coated the roof and the near side and were spreading out across the ground like an oil spill. I backed away slowly, keeping at least a meter distance between myself and the forward skirmishers, and I must have taken at least a dozen steps before the volume finally seemed to peak. Fortunately, they didn't act as though they were attracted to me specifically, and their frantic activity level started to decline once they were spread out in a semi-circle extending several meters from my car, overlapping the pavement. I was too stunned to even think at first, but eventually my brain started to function again and I realized that I'd been targeted by a curse. The scarabs weren't real, but they would function as though they were for as long as the magic empowered them.

The next sign that the curse had crested was a gradual slowdown. The scarabs continued to move, but less purposefully. A few minutes after that I could tell that their numbers were declining. I never actually saw any of them wink out of existence, but patches of bare sand began to appear where before there had been nothing but carapaces and skittering legs. They evaporated into the darkness, and after another few minutes there was no sign of any of them.

I was sure they were gone, but there was no way that I was getting back into my car until daylight. I dusted myself off as best I could, kicked the car door shut, and started toward the center of Rabat, watching for a cab.

Unfortunately, the scarab beetles might have been an illusion but they had been solid enough to chew up the wiring and make it impossible to start the engine the following morning. I suppose I should have been happy that it was still there in the first place, but I guess the Studebaker was old and disreputable enough that it hadn't been worth stripping for parts. Terry Grieco owed me a favor so he agreed to tow it in for me and fix the wiring for his cost.

I was not in an optimistic mood. The two leads I'd developed in the multiple murder case were looking thinner by the moment, I still had no idea how to find Ruth Deacon, and Morris Ngambe's magical vandalism was more of a mystery than ever. Even my advances in the Porter murder had led to an apparent dead end. Evan Garner still seemed the most probable suspect, and the Police were far more likely to find him and close the case than I was. And now, on top of everything else, someone was trying to kill me. Or at the very least, scare me away. But from which case? Was this Goff's follow up on his warning to stay away from the Lagos Castle? Goff was more likely to have ambushed me in a dark alley and broken a limb or two. This seemed a bit subtle for him, but then again he'd probably be following instructions, not developing his own strategy.

I went back to the office to finish updating my case files. Fictional detectives never seem to have time, or the inclination, to do their paperwork, but fictional detectives also have the author on their side, ready to throw them a clue just when they need it. Maybe I should have brought in the Sherlock Holmes impersonator I'd met in Berlin as a consultant. I don't trust my memories, particularly when there are so many ways that they can be tampered with. So I try to write down everything that I've discovered, been told, suspected, or dreamed up. Sometimes it helps.

Moira interprets my idiosyncratic handwriting and types up my notes when she has a chance, and usually we talk about the cases when she's done. She was the one who first noticed the disparity in the testimony of the Carcieri brothers, one of my more lucrative jobs, and she'd suggested new lines of inquiry more than once. I don't know how much of it was her fey gift and how much simple intelligence, but I always paid attention to her comments. So when I finally made it to Manhattan and she told me she'd found something that might help I told her to bring two cups of coffee and come into my office.

"So what have you got?"

Moira had brought the coffee in on a tray, and with a file folder tucked under one arm. The latter was in her lap now, and she opened it without speaking, took out a slim magazine with a slick cover, and handed it to me. It was a recent issue of *The Broken Frame*, an ambitious but to date unsuccessful theater related magazine.

"You'll want to look at page twenty-four." She was sounding smug, which meant she'd found something interesting. I opened the magazine and flipped through to a two page spread of small photographs. They showed various people arriving and departing from theaters in Manhattan, Athens, Piccadilly, and a few places I couldn't identify. The photographs were small and grainy.

"What am I looking for?" But even as I scanned the page I recognized the profile of Aram Gudanoff. He appeared to be speaking to Algernon Stewart, a well known stage actor. It was a night shot, taken from close at hand, and even though the reproduction wasn't all that great, it wasn't hard to find what Moira wanted me to see. Gudanoff wore an ascot, which almost concealed the fact that there was a thin, metallic chain around his neck. I had to squint to make it out but tucked into a fold in the ascot was a dark object which looked very much like half of a heart.

My face must have lit up like a basilisk because Moira sat back in her chair, obviously satisfied. "I guess I earned my pay today."

"You earn your pay every day, Moira. In fact, your efforts are so valuable that they're beyond price. It would be so hard to reward you in proportion to your contribution that I dare not even try. How in the world did you find this?"

"Propinquity. I was babysitting for my sister last night and this was right there on her coffee table."

I looked at the picture again. "It's not very clear. It might be something else."

She cocked her head to one side. "If you want to be certain, you could probably run down the photographer and look at the original. She's credited at the bottom of the page."

"Good idea." My eyes trailed down to the credits and, for several seconds, I stopped breathing. When I looked up, Moira was smiling broadly, looking more pleased with herself than ever.

The photograph was credited to Ruth Deacon.

"So there's a common element in all three killings that the police don't know about," said Moira at last. "Are you going to tell them about the amulets?"

"Of course I am. At some point anyway. Right now, it's the only edge I have."

"But you haven't been able to find out anything about them, where they came from or what purpose they serve. How are they going to help?"

I shook my head. "I don't know yet, but it's one piece of the puzzle that the other players haven't seen."

"Has it occurred to you that someone might know you're on this particular trail? If you're getting too close to something, maybe that's why they sent the scarabs to discourage you."

I'd already thought about that. "The only person to actually warn me off was Goff, and he was talking about Morris' problems. I haven't made any headway there at all. Mayor Porter was probably killed by Evan Garner, and the police are chasing him for that one, so there's no reason for him to pick on me. But I'm starting to think that Ruth Deacon's disappearance is connected to our serial killer somehow, so maybe I'm getting close to something that links both of those cases."

"You think she's lying dead some place with a half heart hanging around her neck?"

"Her sister insists that's not possible, that her sister is still alive. But she and Sandobhal were both into photography, and she took a picture of Aram Gudanoff."

"And Gudanoff appeared in a picture with Mayor Porter."

"Let's not go there just yet. Gudanoff appears in pictures with practically everybody. There is such a thing as coincidence."

"But he was a professional lobbyist. He almost certainly saw the Mayor during the course of his work. There might be a stronger link there."

"I'm not ruling out the possibility. I suppose I could talk to Deborah Lerner about it, find out how well acquainted they were. But she wasn't wearing an amulet when she died." Or anything else for that matter.

"Neither was O'Brien."

"But we know that she had one in her possession earlier. There's no indication of that in the Mayor's case." At least not yet. I was beginning to wonder just how many cases I was investigating. Were there really four, or only two? Could Ruth Deacon and Mayor Porter just be two more victims of the amulet killer? If so, why wasn't Porter's body mutilated the way the others had been? My head was starting to hurt.

The phone rang in the outer office. Moira stood up and went to answer it, while I leaned back in my chair. Moira had nudged me into a whole new frame of reference and I was having trouble focusing. Then she was back at the doorway. "It's Wanda, and she wants to talk to you."

I picked up the phone. "Dash? I need to see you right away. Can you come over here?"

"My car is in the shop. Can it wait for a couple of hours?"

She hesitated. "I'd feel better if you didn't. I'm going away for a while and I might be hard to reach."

I didn't have to be psychic to know that Wanda was upset. Her voice crackled with tension, and the fact that she was "going away" implied that she was in trouble. Anything that scared Wanda Veil by definition scared me. "All right, I'll take the subway. Give me half an hour."

It actually took longer than that. There had been a cave in and a team of kobolds was at work trying to clear the tracks. I got off three stops earlier than I had planned and walked the rest of the way to the bus terminal, then stood holding a strap on the very crowded bus to New Delhi. A lattice weaver had built a nest in the rearmost seat but traditional Hindus believed that they were sacred creatures and wouldn't allow them to be disturbed. I had the oddest sense that this particular one was looking at me, which was very odd since they had no discernible organs of vision, or any other sense for that matter.

Wanda was cordial but I noticed the way her eyes swept the area outside while the door was open and once I was inside, she bolted the door and muttered what I assumed was a locking spell.

"What's going on, Wanda?"

She waved at one of the chairs, not watching to see if I took it. "I've had a visitor, Dash. A very unpleasant visitor. I think you've already made his acquaintance."

"Goff." It wasn't a question.

"Yes, Mr. Goff came to see me. He made a regular appointment, but once he was here, he informed me that he wasn't interested in a look into his future because he already knew what was there. He told me he was here to tell my fortune rather than the reverse."

"Did he threaten you?"

"Not specifically. He just implied that if I continued to help you look into matters at the Lagos Castle, I might discover that my lifeline had been shortened."

"That's an actionable magical threat, isn't it?" I was furious. Wanda was one of my oldest friends and I couldn't stand the thought that she might be in danger because of me.

"Not really. He was careful to stay on the right side of the fence, but he made his meaning clear."

"What do you want me to do about it?"

She shook her head. "Nothing. I don't know why he bothered, frankly. I told you everything I thought might be useful, and there was little enough of that. But I've always preferred to err on the side of caution, so I'm going on an unscheduled vacation until things settle down."

"I'm really sorry about this, Wanda. I had no idea."

"Not your fault, Dash. And to be honest, he pissed me off enough that I'd go out of my way to help you if I thought there was anything I could do. But my talents aren't going to be useful, at least not with that case."

I raised an eyebrow. "All of my cases seem to be running together at the moment, Wanda."

"Then maybe this will do some good after all. It's not much. Don't get your hopes up. But I showed that scan around to a few friends."

"And someone recognized it?"

"Sort of." She looked uncomfortable. "No one had actually seen one of them, at least not with their eyes. But Ed...no, let's not use names. One of my friends is a dreamwalker and he's seen images of amulets very much like these. Sometimes artifacts with unusually high power concentrations resonate on the dream plane. They show up like reflections of the waking world."

"Did your friend know what their purpose is? Or where they come from?"

"No, nothing like that. He only recognized the image. But everything in the dream plane exposes its true name. He knows what the amulets are called."

"All right. Anything might help."

"I hope so. Anyway, they're called Heart's Desire."

"I've thought right along that they were love charms. The name seems to confirm that."

"It might be so. But they're powerful, Dash, more powerful than any love charm I've ever heard of. Amulets aren't designed to contain that kind of power. This is on a scale you'd find in a lodestone or a scepter. I didn't think it was possible to concentrate it in such a small vessel."

"Well, apparently it is now."

It took a while to get a ride back. The Shah was visiting Pretoria and he'd brought his entire entourage with him, which congested the streets and disrupted the bus schedules. I eventually found a cabbie who was willing to risk crossing part of Jerusalem to get me back to Manhattan, but I didn't have enough money to pay the premium he was demanding so I ended up taking a long and uncomfortable rickshaw ride.

When I got back to the office, Moira had more bad news for me. The Studebaker wouldn't be ready until the next day. "The damage was more extensive than they originally thought."

"Great. Any more rays of sunshine to brighten my day?"

She gave me an odd look. "I don't know whether this will help, but Miss Connors called again."

"Did she say what she wanted?"

"No. I don't think she likes me very much." I gathered the feeling was mutual.

"She's never even met you, Moira. She's just not a very social person."

But apparently I was wrong about her sociability because when I called her, she wanted to invite me for supper, at her apartment. "I'm afraid I haven't been as cordial as I could have been. Consider this an awkward, overdue, but genuine apology."

When she heard about my car, Connors offered to pick me up but I insisted on making my own way. I pulled out my wallet and did a quick inventory. "I can take a cab. Traffic is horrible around here in the evenings."

Her address surprised me. It was in Manhattan, not Boston, which was what I'd expected, and not in the low rent district either. The Baker's Dozen must pay its staff considerably more than I would have expected.

I spent the rest of the afternoon sharing grunt work with Moira. We called photographic supply houses first, but no one could suggest any possible location for Ruth Deacon's dark room that we hadn't anticipated. Then we tried studios, large and small. Several of the people we talked to were familiar with Ruth Deacon's work. She did occasional spreads for magazines and newspapers, but it was only a sideline. Her artistic compositions generated most of her income. On impulse, I dropped Sandobhal's name a couple of times, but no one I talked to had ever heard of him.

When we ran out of names, I tried calling Deborah Lerner, and ended up talking to her machine. I told her I wanted to ask her a couple of questions but that I'd be out during the evening, so if she didn't call back before five, we'd have to speak in the morning. Then I called back and gave her Connors' number. "You might be able to reach me there if you don't call too late."

Moira hadn't fared much better. She did find one person who remembered that Ruth Deacon had shown up at a reception in the company of a tall, Hispanic type who sounded like Sandobhal, but the woman insisted that she wouldn't recognize him again if he walked into the room and she had never heard his name. Moira pressed and the woman agreed to look at some photographs if Moira stopped by her apartment the following morning.

"If I do field work, do I get a bonus?" she asked.

"Of course."

We wrote up our notes for the day. I was exhausted. I get much less tired when I'm out and about than when I'm working the phones or shuffling paper. I told Moira to take the rest of the afternoon off, not the most generous of gestures since she'd have been gone in another half hour anyway, then used the tiny bathroom adjoining my office to try to clean up a little. I didn't want to think of this as any kind of date, just two colleagues getting together to discuss a case, but for all I knew Sheri Connors was an entirely different person once she was away from the job. And it had been a long time since Katrina had moved out.

I walked three blocks to the nearest liquor store and picked out two bottles of medium priced wine, one red and one white. They all taste the same to me but the clerk told me they were both quite suitable for a quiet dinner. Then I hailed a cab, this one driven by a thin Scotsman who spoke very heavily accented English and who had a picture of a heavy set woman and five light haired children, presumably his family, dangling from the rear view mirror. He didn't seem to spend a lot of time watching the road in front of him but he delivered me to the right place and managed the forty block trip with only three near collisions.

And just before I got out, he told me that I was being followed.

Tailing someone in the Cities is much easier than it was in the original world. Morphing spells are relatively inexpensive for inanimate objects; I'd used them more than once myself. Once the spell was invoked, a vehicle changed its appearance – color, plates, even model – at a preset interval. The transition was instantaneous and masked so that an observer would be incapable of noticing that anything unusual had happened. So even if the quarry was watching constantly, he or she would never detect the pursuer.

Unless one had other resources.

"I have the second sight, sir. He went on by when I pulled over, but I doubt he's far away."

"Just one man?" I asked.

"That he was. I didna see his face, but he was a bull of a man."

It had to be Goff. I was already furious about his treatment of Wanda Veil, and I hadn't liked him to start with. As the cab drove off, I glanced at my watch. I was still a few minutes early so I walked around the block, glancing into every parked or passing vehicle, hoping to catch sight of Goff, but either I'd missed him, he'd driven off, or I was wrong and someone else was following me.

The troll guarding the door scowled but let me pass. Obviously I didn't measure up to the class of clientele he was used to serving. I get that a lot. "Ninth floor," he said grudgingly.

It was an old fashioned elevator, completely mechanical, no levitation runes inscribed on floor or ceiling, but it carried me up smoothly and silently, the door whispering open. The hallway was carpeted and well lit, but there were no numbers on the doors and I had to walk slowly, reading the names, until I found Connors' apartment. There was a bell, no recognition glyph, so I pressed the button and waited for a full twenty seconds before the lock clicked and the door opened.

Sheri Connors smiled at me as she stepped to one side, inviting me in, but I almost didn't recognize her. She was very definitely not wearing her professional clothing this evening.

CHAPTER EIGHT

Connors' apartment was exactly what I should have expected. Although it was large, almost the equivalent of two floors of my house, it was so sparsely furnished that it looked as though she had just started to move in. Everything I saw was of good quality, but none of it was showy. She obviously favored the plain and practical, nothing frilly or overstuffed or highly decorated. Her colors were black and white and various shades of gray, with occasional bits of very dark blue providing a limited contrast; it reminded me of Ruth Deacon's apartment, but more tastefully done and somehow more cheerful, if a bit clinical. The chairs and tables were all rectangular, her shelves were brushed steel assembled with hexagonal bolts, and the half dozen small paintings sprinkled through the apartment were abstracts dominated by straight lines and recognizable geometric shapes. There was an impressive but fake marble fireplace with several small sculptures arranged on the mantle. They looked like shapeless blobs to me, but what did I know about art? There were, as expected, no charms, freshening mobiles, or other magical items. Her drapes were black but were partly open, revealing a better than average view of night time Manhattan.

She had met me at the door wearing what I assume was for her casual attire, a Chinese style sarong, white silk with an ebony trim, and slippers. I handed her the wine I'd brought and she made appropriate but unenthusiastic sounds of gratitude. "I actually just opened a very good wine right over there," she gestured toward a glass topped table arranged to face two chairs and a couch. "Why don't you pour us a couple of drinks while I check on dinner?"

The decanter and goblets were cut glass, square not round, and I was exaggeratedly careful handling them even though they were quite hefty and not at all delicate. She was back almost immediately and sat in the chair that I hadn't taken. "It will just be a few minutes more. Try the wine. It's very good."

It was in fact quite good. I recognized that this was an appropriate time for small talk, but I've never been very skillful at it. "Why did you invite me over tonight, Connors?"

"I told you on the phone. Look, this is hard for me, Dash. I like my job. It's highly structured and the lines of authority are clear and unambiguous. You're like an extra piece in a jigsaw puzzle. There's no place to fit you in. You're from an entirely different context and frankly, you make me uneasy because you're so unpredictable."

"That's some apology."

She bowed her head and massaged her forehead with her free hand. "This isn't how I had planned to open our conversation. What I'm trying to say is that I reacted badly when I found out about you because it seemed to imply that I wasn't competent. It took me a while to realize that I shouldn't resent you because we're both being manipulated. We're looking for the same results and we're more likely to get what we want if we work together."

Actually, I was pretty sure that we weren't looking for the same thing. I wanted to identify Porter's killer so that Mayor Burford would be in my debt. Connors wanted to protect her job and the reputation of the Baker's Dozen. If that meant identifying the killer, that would be her goal. But if she decided it would be better just to let things fade into background noise, she'd have no problem with that.

"I would be happy to work with you, Connors." With reservations. "We're not in a competition."

"Great. And outside of work, my friends call me Sheri."

Dinner was quite nice. She served it on square plates, milk white with a very subdued black and silver pattern around the edges. We ate in a good sized dining room adjacent to the kitchen, seated across from one another at a table so small that it seemed lost in the available space. I suspected that Sheri did very little entertaining. By mutual agreement, we didn't discuss the Porter case while we ate. She told me a little about her previous jobs, and then asked what it was like to run my own agency.

"You'd like it," I told her. She would have too. As her own boss, she could set up any system of rules she liked and enforce them absolutely. I used magical consultants but didn't practice myself. It would be a little more awkward in her case, but I thought she could probably manage. I was warming to her a little, or perhaps that was the wine, but I could also see where she would be a very difficult person to get close to. Even when she was "relaxed," her guard wasn't entirely down. "On the other hand, it doesn't pay very well." I glanced at her sideboard and hutch cabinet, both of which were filled with cut glass, leaded crystal, and other expensive items. "Obviously security chiefs do a lot better."

She laughed. "Not that much. I come from money. My parents died a few years back and left me the proverbial bundle. This was their apartment, in fact. I redecorated a bit. Mom was a Victorian and Dad indulged her."

"Sorry."

"Don't worry about it. We weren't close. So what kind of cases do you handle when you're not investigating murders?"

I described a few, leaving out names and muddling things when necessary to protect my clients' privacy. On an impulse, I reached into my jacket pocket and took out the photograph of Sandobhal's amulet and handed it to her across the table. "I don't suppose you've ever seen anything like this at the hotel?" I still didn't believe the Porter case was related to the others, but it couldn't hurt to ask.

She studied it for several seconds before answering in slow, deliberate tones. "It's some kind of binding charm, isn't it? Two lovers split the heart and each wears half?"

"Probably. It hasn't been determined yet just what the amulet's purpose is."

"A forensic sorcerer probably could tell you. If they had the amulet itself, I mean, not just a photo."

She was right, but I doubted the Police would go to that expense, since they didn't appear to be aware that the other two victims had owned the same type of charm. I could tell them, of course, and they'd call someone in, but doing so would be to reveal the only advantage I had in the investigation. I wasn't ready to do that yet.

"Does this have something to do with Mayor Porter?"

I shook my head. "Not that I know of. But three people have died recently while wearing, or at least owning, one of these."

Her eyebrows rose. "The ritual killings? I've heard a little bit through the grapevine."

"Yes, but keep this to yourself for now, all right?" The alcohol had muddled my judgment and I'd already said more than I had intended.

By the time we finished dinner and most of a second bottle of wine, Connors had loosened up considerably and I was beginning to think of her as a woman and not just a colleague. There was still enough stiffness between us to rule out romance, at least for now, but I thought it might just be possible to move from coolness to friendship. I followed her out to the kitchen while she made coffee and she even laughed at one of my jokes.

The pot was percolating happily when the telephone rang. Connors answered somewhat shortly, listened for a few seconds. "Just a moment." She turned to me with some of the warmth evaporated from her manner. "It's for you. Deborah Lerner."

I had forgotten to mention the possibility she might call. I took the phone and identified myself.

"I got your message. Sorry it's so late, but I just got in."

"That's all right." My head was so foggy that I almost forgot why I had asked her to call. "Do you by chance know Aram Gudanoff?"

"Aram? He's dead." She paused. "Is this related to Mayor Porter's murder?" Her voice was suddenly breathless.

"I was hoping that you could tell me. Did the Mayor know Gudanoff?"

"Oh, everybody knew Aram. I've had dinner with him a few times myself. Purely professionally, of course."

"How well did they know each other?"

There was a long pause and I could almost feel Deborah Lerner struggling to balance discretion with her civic duty, or more likely with her desire to gossip. "Pretty well," she admitted. "They were lovers. But it didn't last long, only a few weeks. The Mayor had intimacy problems. But Aram couldn't have killed the Mayor. He was already dead by then."

"What about the other way around?"

"No, that doesn't make any sense. It was the Mayor who broke it off. She was already interested in Evan Garner by then."

"Was the breakup messy?"

"Not at all. I don't think Aram cared. It was just another part of the job for him. He had at least one other woman in his life even when he and the Mayor were still going strong. And the Mayor preferred things more cerebral, if you know what I mean."

"She didn't like sex?"

Lerner sounded uncomfortable. "She wasn't primarily interested in the physical aspects of a relationship, but she wasn't a prude, if that's what you're asking, despite the rumors. And she did recognize that the offering or withholding of sexual favors could be a source of personal power."

"Would you have any pictures of them together? Gudanoff and the Mayor?"

"I don't know. I could look around tomorrow."

"Please do, and if you find anything, call my office. They might be very helpful."

It took a few minutes to mollify Connors, but once I had summarized the conversation, she caught on to the implications right away. "So the two cases really are related?"

"Well, it could still just be coincidence, but I don't believe it. And there's also a connection to another case I'm handling, just as tenuous but stretching the laws of probability even further."

"So tell me about it."

I wanted to, but I'd already recovered my sense of discretion, and Rachel Deacon was paying for that as well as my putative skill at investigation. "All I can say right now is that it involves a missing person. I'd rather not go any further until the link is more definite."

"Another victim?"

"I don't think so. I have reason to believe that the subject is still alive, possibly in hiding, possibly being held against her will."

"You know, your job sounds a lot more interesting than mine. All my cases involve fights between drunken guests, petty theft, false alarms, vandalism, and stuff like that."

"Just at the moment, my job is a little too interesting. And most of the time I'm tracking down juvenile vandals, embezzlers, bail jumpers, teenaged runaways, and petty blackmailers. I do more paperwork than fieldwork."

I stayed a little longer but the wine was starting to make me sleepy and my instinctive caution kicked in. Connors didn't try too hard to discourage me and we shook hands as I left, although I don't think she'd have objected if I'd tried a kiss. I thought about it too, but decided it needed further consideration before I committed.

Connors had offered to call me a cab but I insisted that I wanted to walk for a while first, partly to clear my head. I wished I'd brought my alcohol inhibiting charm with me but I'd left it home deliberately. Chances are it would have prevented Sheri from enjoying her drinks at all. She was the first person I'd ever known more than casually who didn't incorporate magic into her everyday life. Even I had a kitchen witch mounted above the sink, a spoiling retardant in the refrigerator, a dream sieve above my bed, and a few other odds and ends sprinkled through the house. Most of these used such low order magic that their effectiveness was questionable, but I had acquired them almost without thinking about it. Everyone else had them, so who was I to buck the trend?

I had just enough left in my wallet to pay cab fare back to Brooklyn, but I walked most of the way across Manhattan before hailing one. At one point I was convinced that I was being followed and I circled a block and lurked in a doorway for a while, but nothing happened and it was probably just my normal paranoia.

It was late by the time I got home. The Manhattan cabbie had balked at taking me to Brooklyn, insisting that he wouldn't be able to get a return customer at that time of the night. I finally convinced him to drop me off on my side of the bridge; I could have walked the rest of the way, but I was nervous about being that close to the kudzu alone and at night. There were no cabs on the Brooklyn side so I walked the rest of the way.

The message light was blinking on my phone, but I was too tired to deal with it, and fell asleep half dressed, sprawled across my bed.

I woke up clear headed but stiff limbed, having slept in an unusually uncomfortable position, but a shower and coffee helped. The blinking light told me I had three messages waiting, but I ignored them again, cooked myself a sinful quantity of bacon and ate most of it before deciding I'd put things off long enough. The first message was a welcome one. The Studebaker was back in running condition. The price was more than I had expected, but they'd let me take my time paying it. The second was less welcome, a call from Mayor Burford's administrative assistant. His Honor would like an update at the earliest possible opportunity.

The third call was the most intriguing, and it was from Moira. "Hey, Dash, I'm going to be late this morning. I'm going to stop by Mrs. Dietrich's house on the way in and show her that picture of Sandobhal. Rachel Deacon called. I told her that we were making some progress but that we really wanted to find out where her sister had her pictures developed. She suggested some of the things we've already tried, but then she caught me by surprise. There's an exhibition of Ruth Deacon's photography at the Anderson Studio in Houston. Might be worth a visit but you'll have to hurry. It closes tomorrow. That's Sunday, in case you don't check your messages tonight, and you probably won't."

Tomorrow had become today.

I glanced at the wall clock. It was unlikely that Moira would be in yet, but I called anyway and left a message on the answering machine telling her that I'd be late. Then I raided my emergency cash fund under the linoleum in the bathroom, taking most of what was left. The handful of crumpled bills barely filled my wallet. It was a short walk to the garage and my car was standing right out front, just inside the anti-theft barrier. They weren't open yet either, but I knew the passcharm and was soon on my way.

Traffic was lighter than usual and I made good time. Houston is quite a drive, all the way down past Peiping. There were a lot fewer oil refineries than there had been the last time I'd visited the area. We have very limited oil reserves in the Cities, at least so far, and several of the installations had been cannibalized for equipment and metals. Unfortunately, oil supplies don't magically regenerate the way most foodstuffs do. When it's gone, it's gone. Houston's proven reserves are the largest we know of, but they've ratcheted down their output and driven the price up to generate a steady, mildly outrageous profit. Which is why most powered vehicular traffic makes use of harnessed demonic power, electricity, or other arcane energy sources.

Once past the industrial district, the city proper loomed ahead. Houston isn't much of an arts town, but there has been a growing homogeneity among many of the various parts of the Cities these past few years, excluding those few who remained so insular that outsiders were regarded with suspicion and freewheeling entrepreneurship with outright horror. They had finally dropped the tolls on the Sam Houston Parkway so I used that to skirt around to the exit I wanted.

The Anderson galley looked like an interloper with its ornate front and windows filled with abstract sculpture. Many of the items inside were far more conventional, however, including what I thought was a pretty good selection of landscape paintings. At least I could tell what they were supposed to be, and in a couple of cases I even recognized the setting. An easel stood just inside the front doors, listing seven different exhibits with arrows pointing in the appropriate directions. There were no guidespells and I almost got lost. The studio was much larger than I had realized, the building having originally been some kind of warehouse or distribution center.

The Deacon exhibit was in the rear, one of the smaller rooms. Each of the photographs had been professionally matted and framed and they were arranged on the interior walls and on panels erected within the room. A fluorescing sign just inside the door indicated that this was the "FINAL DAY!", and perhaps half a dozen people milled around the room. I turned to my left and began scanning the pictures, about a third of which had "Sold" stickers affixed to the identifying placards, not sure exactly what I was looking for but increasingly disappointed when I found nothing. The subject matter varied – everything from architecture to animals to odd shots of the sky or close-ups of familiar objects from unfamiliar angles and all of them black and white. I didn't quite see the point. None of them had a human face, identifiable or otherwise, but one was a wide angle view of an ornate table covered with pieces of jewelry. I leaned closer, trying to find a heart shaped amulet among them.

"That's one of her best, isn't it?"

The voice came from close behind me and took me completely by surprise. I turned to see a short, rather portly man in a tailored suit standing at my elbow. His pink face almost seemed to glow under the artificial lights.

"I don't believe we've seen you here before." His voice projected absolute certainty. "I'm Oliver Anderson. I own this studio, Mister...?"

"Dash. Yes it is. And no, you haven't. This is my first time here. I wanted to see the Deacon exhibit before it closed."

"Why, precisely? I don't mean to be abrupt, Mr. Dash, but you don't strike me as a collector of fine photography."

"No, I'm not. Have you spoken to Miss Deacon recently?"

His expression became guarded. "Not for some time, I'm afraid. Might I inquire what your interest is, exactly?"

I took out my identification and showed it to him. "I've been hired by Rachel Deacon to find out what happened to her sister. No one has seen or heard from her for several days and she's worried."

Anderson relaxed, but not much. "I sympathize, Mr. Dash, but I'm afraid I can't help you. This exhibit was all arranged last fall and the work itself has been here for some time. I haven't seen Ruth Deacon since opening night, and that was three weeks ago."

"She didn't say anything to you about going on a trip or having any unusual problems?'

"Nothing at all. Miss Deacon was never very communicative, frankly." He glanced at the photograph behind me. "Might I ask what was so interesting about this particular piece?"

"I was looking for an unusual piece of jewelry that she might have had in her possession. I thought it might be in the picture."

"You must be talking about that horrid thing she wore around her neck all the time."

My heart raced for a few seconds, but only long enough for Anderson to describe an amulet that was almost certainly a duplicate of the one her sister wore. "No, that's not what I'm looking for. I think that has something to do with the bonding between herself and her twin. They both have one. What I'm interested in is a love charm of some sort."

Anderson's face twitched. "Oh, I very much doubt that."

My instincts stirred. "Why would you say that?" He looked increasingly uncomfortable. "Mr. Anderson, my client is very much worried about her sister's welfare. If you know anything that might help us to find her, I really need for you to tell me."

I thought he was going to resist, but instead he nodded, more to himself than to me. "Please understand, Mr. Dash, that I do not gossip about my clients. Miss Deacon is a very talented person and a valued contributor to this studio's success. Can I trust that anything I might say to you will be held in confidence?"

"Absolutely."

"Well then, let's just say that the last thing I would expect to see Ruth Deacon involved in is romance of any sort. Part of my job here is to arrange social events where artists can get together with prospective buyers. Ruth's work sold steadily but she could have done much better if she'd attended our little get-togethers. But she would have no part of it, and she made it quite clear to me that she had no interest in meeting clients in an informal setting."

I interpreted his roundabout speech. "Are you saying that Ruth Deacon was gay?"

"Oh no," he shook his head. "She felt an equal distaste for women. Ruth was absolutely asexual. She even called herself the Ice Queen."

I had a moment of deja vu. Mayor Porter was known as the Ice Princess. Another connection? Maybe so, but if the amulets were love charms, particularly powerful love charms, then perhaps Ruth Deacon had found a way to overcome her natural disinclination. Or perhaps someone had given it to her, subverting her nature without her knowledge. "I don't suppose you've ever seen this?" I took the photograph of the amulet out of my pocket and showed it to him. He held it quite close to his eyes, then handed it back.

"Actually, I have. Ruth Deacon was wearing it, or something very much like it, on opening night. But it wasn't a love charm, Mr. Dash. It was a kind of joke. She told me she wore it on that occasion to indicate her lack of enthusiasm for the event. Half-hearted, you see." He handed the photograph back to me. "Ruth liked her little jokes and she didn't care if no one else understood them."

I was so lost in my own thoughts on the way back to Manhattan that I absentmindedly missed my turn and wasted an uncomfortable half hour in Peiping. Theoretically the Communist Chinese are fully integrated into the Cities, but they remain insular and defensive about their economic system, and casual visitors are not welcomed.

Three of my four active cases were now intertwined. Mayor Porter had known Gudanoff rather more intimately than I had expected, and Ruth Deacon was tied to the three ritual deaths by the amulets. Porter's body had not been mutilated, however, which suggested that she was killed for different reasons than the other three. If Rachel Deacon was truthful, and correct, then her sister was still alive, somewhere, which suggested that she wasn't one of the victims. Could she be the killer? She and Sandobhal were both photographers. They might have met somehow. I considered showing his picture to her sister, but decided it was low priority. The

Deacons were not close and probably knew virtually nothing about each other's friends.

And what were the amulets? Ruth Deacon's suggestion that they were symbolic of her half hearted lack of enthusiasm for the public appearance was probably a lie to conceal their real nature, but if they were some kind of powerful love charm, who wore the other half of hers? Moira had a list of visitors provided by the apartment building manager, but they were mostly service technicians and there was not one other repeated name over the course of the past two years. Not conclusive but certainly suggestive.

There were too many questions buzzing around inside my head. I needed to think about something else for a while, which reminded me that I hadn't done much of anything toward solving the mystery at the Lagos Castle. It was close enough to my route back that I decided to stop off there, just so Morris would know that I hadn't forgotten about him.

The moment I stepped inside the door, Lily came over to me. "Go right up, Mr. Dash. He's expecting you."

I hadn't seen that coming. Had Morris hired a prescient? It didn't sound like him. He might sell charms in his gift shop but he was still old fashioned enough to prefer relying on more conventional ways of learning things. I climbed up to his office and found him at his desk, the phone pressed to one ear.

"Never mind. He just walked in. Thanks again, Moira." He hung up. "That was your secretary. I was looking for you."

"So I gather. What's up?"

"We've had another rash of incidents this morning."

"The same as before?"

"More or less."

It had started very early. Once a month Morris invited all of his senior staff to a fancy Sunday breakfast in one of the private dining rooms. Sometimes they talked about business but it was meant primarily so that the restaurant, gift shop, and behind the scenes people could meet one another, attach faces to the names. Morris felt that it helped prevent friction. Sunday mornings were best because the gift shop was closed until noon and the restaurant didn't open until 10:00 AM. That morning had seemed perfectly ordinary for the first half hour or so, but then things deteriorated very quickly.

"The cream was curdled in the pitcher. Some of the eggs were spoiled and the sausages tasted wrong. The same kind of things that happened before, but this time it was targeted directly at my staff."

"Why do you say that? Someone may have put a spell on your kitchen, but they wouldn't necessarily have known who was going to be served the bad food."

Morris clenched his fist and slammed it down on his desk. "But that's just it! Everything in the kitchen was untouched. It was only the food served to us that was bad. And more than that." He leaned forward, speaking slowly and clearly so that I wouldn't miss a word. "The food was perfectly good when it was brought in. I drank a cup of coffee before anyone else arrived and the cream was fine. Some of us had eaten sausage and eggs. It was only after we'd all been there for ten or fifteen minutes that the problems started."

That did seem interesting. "Who was the last to arrive?"

"Denning. He works in advertising. But if you're suggesting he brought something in with him, something that spoiled the food, I think you're wrong."

"Why is that?"

"Because I only hired him a week ago, and that was after the earlier incidents."

Well, I hadn't really expected it to be that easy. "Do you suppose you could come up with the order in which people showed up?"

He shook his head. "No. I was back and forth to the kitchen a couple of times and most of the others were in and out. I only remember Denning because I had to introduce him around the table."

"So what else happened?"

"Jessica called about an hour later to tell me one of her customers had been bitten by a good luck charm."

"Bitten?"

He opened a desk drawer and gingerly lifted out a shamrock shaped pewter charm, placing it carefully down on the desk. It was a dangle, designed to be worn on a bracelet. I leaned forward to examine it closely and Morris gave me a warning look. "I've had it deactivated, but be careful anyway. Here, use this." He handed me a pencil.

I used the pencil to flip the shamrock over and my eyes widened when I saw its underside. What should have been smooth metal was instead a shallow lamprey mouth, rimmed with a jagged border that looked disturbingly like teeth. "Ugly little critter," I said as I poked at it.

"There was another one just like this. I sent it to a scryer for analysis, but transformation curses are so simple that they don't leave much of any trace. I doubt we'll learn anything that way."

"Anything else?"

"A copy of *The Book of Household Spells* crumbled to dust on a shelf, and all of the wolfsbane in the apothecary has withered. Jessica was quite upset about that because it's one of her best sellers and we're completely out of stock. We also had a wraith in the lobby, thankfully only for a few seconds, and the levitation spells all need to be redone. The elevators were taking people to the wrong floors."

"How about the perimeter spells? Have they been breached?"

Morris shook his head. "I don't know. Probably not. I have security going over them right now and before you ask, yes, I brought in an independent contractor to monitor their work."

I shook my head wearily. "I have to tell you Morris that this is beyond me. This kind of sophisticated magical attack is out of my league. Maybe you should petition the Arcane Council to look into things." Theoretically, the Council had the final say on all things magical, but they were disinclined to involve themselves in anything other than theoretical matters. Much of their time was spent trying, unsuccessfully, to unravel the problem of the Tuilleries.

"My request is pending a decision, but I'm not hopeful. Why would someone go to so much effort just to commit petty vandalism? If I have an enemy that powerful, why hasn't he done something really serious?"

The same thought had occurred to me. "Maybe this isn't an attack against you."

Morris blinked. "Someone else then? Someone who works here? The same question applies then. Why such random, petty attacks?"

"Maybe they're not attacks at all. Maybe they're test runs, or accidents."

I felt rather guilty leaving Morris even more befuddled than when I arrived, but I had nothing reassuring to offer him at the moment. The possibility that the incidents had not been directed against him or his business might have cheered him a bit if it hadn't also emphasized the fact that we were no closer to finding the source, or preventing future recurrences. I told him that I wasn't going to forget about his problems, but I couldn't do much to bolster his confidence when I had just finished telling him that I was at a complete loss to explain what was going on.

Moira was on the phone when I arrived at the office and she waved a greeting. Today she'd chosen to wear a quite attractive red silk sarong, whose slinky effects were somewhat offset by the cowboy boots and the bandanna in her hair. I collected my working files and took them into my office, spreading them out on the desk. Maybe if I reviewed each one in relation to the others, something that hadn't stood out earlier would be more obvious now.

Moira came in a few minutes later, smiling secretively. "I've got something for you."

I wasn't in a cheery mood. "Thrill me."

"Barbara Dietrich recognized the picture of Steven Sandobhal."

"Remind me. Who is Barbara Dietrich?"

"She sells picture frames and matting supplies. Ruth Deacon was one of her regular customers."

That got my attention. "And she recognized Sandobhal?"

Moira nodded. "She seems quite certain. Says he came in with Deacon once or twice."

"So they did know each other. Did you ask about the amulet?"

"No luck there. She doesn't remember how they were dressed. They seemed friendly, but not too friendly. Mrs. Dietrich didn't think they were a couple. Does that help?"

"It doesn't hurt, but I'm not sure what it means yet, frankly. I need to sort this all out in my head."

"Well then, I'll leave you to it."

Moira returned some time later to bring me a sandwich, correctly interpreted my mood and said nothing. I ate it mechanically, and when she came back and took the plate away I realized that I hadn't the slightest idea what I had just eaten. I read the same notes over and over again. I drew diagrams linking all of the victims, and then all of the living people I'd spoken to. I even took out a map of the city and plotted the locations of the murders. No patterns or connections emerged, other than the obvious ones.

I had given up and was sorting the materials back into their respective folders when one oddity suddenly caught my attention. I picked up a sheet of paper, a photocopy, and read it through from start to finish, then went back and read it again. Moira had missed something. No, that wasn't fair. Moira had not been in Ruth Deacon's apartment, so she couldn't have noticed the disparity. But I had been, and I'd read this before, and I should have spotted it right away.

Moira could tell something was up the moment I stepped into the outer office. "I'm going to Paris, Moira. And I need a tape measure."

She nodded slowly. "The toolbox is in the closet by the door. Are you going to Ruth Deacon's apartment building?"

"That's right." I suspected my smile looked a bit silly but I was feeling optimistic for the first time all day. "There's a discrepancy in her lease." I opened the closet door, discovered that Moira had once again rearranged my chaos into order. The tape measure was right where it should have been instead of where I expected it to be.

"I didn't notice anything wrong with the contract." She actually sounded defensive. I found the idea that Moira might have a weak spot vaguely unsettling.

"It's nothing you would have seen. But I was there. Ruth Deacon leased a five room suite, and she's been in the same apartment ever since she moved in."

"So?"

"So Rachel Deacon and I were there and we searched it. We searched quite thoroughly through all four rooms."

Moira blinked, and the defensive look was replaced by sudden comprehension. "Four rooms, but she was renting five."

I nodded. "There must be a concealed room we missed. I'm headed right over there." Something else occurred to me. "Call Rachel Deacon and tell her where I've gone and ask her if it's at all possible for her to join me. I think there's a good chance that we'll find her sister in that room. If we can find the room itself, that is."

CHAPTER NINE

Rachel Deacon showed up about fifteen minutes after I'd arrived, and by then I was already scratching my head. I had measured the width of the front room and kitchen as accurately as possible and it came to just a shade under thirty meters. The two rear rooms, bedroom and office/studio, were much easier and they came to a total of twenty two meters, an eight meter discrepancy.

I was standing in the front room, considerably perplexed, when Rachel arrived, looking put out and vaguely wary.

"Your secretary said I should meet you here, that it was important."

I decided to ignore her tone. "I think so. I think I know where your sister is, sort of."

She gave me a sarcastic look. "You inspire me with confidence, Mr. Dash. I think I'll have to write you a check for your fee, sort of."

"I'm pretty sure that your sister is in her dark room, Miss Deacon."

She nodded. "All right, but we don't know where her dark room is."

"Yes, we do. It's in this apartment. It didn't make sense for her to have rented space elsewhere. Her office and equipment are here. The building's guardian says that she never left the building and guardians are never wrong." At least as far as I knew.

Rachel glanced around, her expression uncertain. "Do you mean there's some kind of hidden room?"

"The back wall of this apartment is eight meters shorter than the front wall."

Without speaking, she walked out into the kitchen and back, then went into the bedroom, emerging a moment later from the office. "I don't understand. The walls all look perfectly straight and the corners are square."

"They are square. It's not an optical illusion. It's some kind of magic. All of the apartments on this floor were built to the same pattern and they all have two rooms in front, three in back. I think the darkroom is situated directly between your sister's bedroom and her office."

"But how can that be?"

"I don't know. Some kind of expansion spell that collapsed, possibly. Your sister might have wanted a larger dark room and used magic to increase its size. If the spell failed, it might have collapsed the original space around it as well." I'd never heard of such a thing happening, but then there were a lot of things going on lately that I'd never heard of before.

But Rachel Deacon was shaking her head. "No, that can't be it. If Ruth was caught when it failed, she'd be dead. And I know that she's alive."

"Are you absolutely certain of that? Could something have happened to sever the bond between you?"

"No, definitely not. I mean, I suppose that the bond could be broken by some higher order of magic, although it's not supposed to be possible. That would mean that I could survive her death, or vice versa. But that wouldn't explain why I can still feel her. She is alive, Mr. Dash. If the part of me that is with her had died or been returned to me, I would know it."

So that was that. I was closer to a solution but it was still just beyond my reach. Ruth Deacon was probably alive and, somehow, inside her empty apartment in a room that was inaccessible to us. But was she hiding or trapped or a prisoner? And could she stay alive there indefinitely without a fresh supply of food, water, and air? Did time run the same where she was as it did for the rest of us? Was there a way of reversing the spell from outside? I had lots of questions. Maybe I should have hired a private investigator.

"There's one other thing." I reached into my pocket and produced the amulet photograph. "Have you ever seen your sister wearing one of these?"

Rachel looked at it closely while I watched her face. If she was concealing recognition, she was doing a good job. "It doesn't look familiar, but as I told you, my sister and I haven't spent much time together recently. Is it significant?"

I shrugged. "Probably not. Just being thorough. She was apparently wearing it at her last public appearance. It's some kind of love charm. I was hoping to find out who has been wearing the matching half."

Rachel surprised me by laughing. She raised one hand to cover her mouth. "I'm sorry, but I think I can promise you that Ruth wasn't involved with anyone."

"Why is that? She is certainly attractive enough..." I stumbled verbally. "You're both attractive women." Daunting, but attractive.

She laughed again, but it was without humor this time, almost sad. "Do you know why people are bonded together, Mr. Dash?"

I knew that each partner could draw on the other's strength, but little else. "Not really," I admitted.

"How old would you say I am?"

I would have guessed thirty or a little more, but I said late twenties.

"Making allowance for your attempt to be gallant, I'll add about five years to that. So at the most, I'm what, thirty-five?" She didn't wait for an answer. "Next week Ruth and I will be fifty-eight years old."

My skepticism must have been written all over my face. "That's rather hard to believe, Miss Deacon."

"The bonding process has several benefits – unusually good health, strength of character, and a substantial increase in life expectancy. Barring accident, we should live twice as long as we would if we'd been left unbonded."

"If that's the case, why isn't the procedure more common?"

"Because it is extremely difficult to perform and entails some risk. We might have been crippled, physically or mentally, if things hadn't gone perfectly. It is also very expensive. But the greatest deterrent is that it has certain drawbacks. You already know one of them. If either of us dies, accidentally or otherwise, the other will follow within days. You can't get something for nothing, Mr. Dash, not even with magic. In return for our gifts, my sister and I had to make certain concessions. One of the things we gave up was the capacity to feel affection for others. We're incapable of love, Mr. Dash. Love potions and charms can't change that."

But perhaps one could pretend to be affected, I thought to myself. If Ruth Deacon had wanted to manipulate someone, she might well have faked susceptibility to a love charm. I hadn't a clue about the identity of the other party, but that didn't mean he, or she, didn't exist.

Rachel Deacon seemed somewhat mollified by the discovery of the anomaly in her sister's apartment, but she made it quite clear that she did not consider it entirely adequate. After all, we didn't know for certain that Ruth was in the missing room, and even if she was, we still hadn't actually found her. I was forced to concede that she was right.

"If that's all you have for me, Mr. Dash, I have work to do."

I stayed after she took her leave, elated and deflated simultaneously. I hadn't found her sister, not exactly, but I was sure that I knew where she was. Sort of. It was just a case of finding a way to get there from here. I walked back and forth between the bedroom and office several times, wondering if I was somehow passing right through her. The thought was unsettling and I returned to the front room. The revelation that the heart shaped amulets were probably not love charms after all didn't help my mood either. If they were, it made no sense for Ruth Deacon to wear one. I understood enough magical theory to know that the outward appearance of an enchanted object didn't necessarily reflect its purpose. Theoretically you could turn a cockroach into a love potion or a rose into a curse of leprosy. But why bother? If it was part of an elaborate deception of some kind, who was being deceived?

I used Ruth Deacon's phone to call my office. As usual, Moira picked up before the first ring. "I wish you wouldn't do that all the time. It's very annoying."

"So dock my pay. You have messages."

"I figured. Anything I want to hear?"

"That depends, I suppose. Miss Connors called to thank you for an entertaining evening. She wanted me to be sure to tell you that she'll pass along anything she hears as quickly as possible."

"So she said last night." I still wasn't sure how I felt about Sheri Connors. She'd made a very obvious effort to be pleasant at her apartment even though it was crystal clear that she wasn't entirely comfortable stepping out of her professional persona. It might be possible for something to develop between us, but there wasn't enough room in my life for a complicated relationship just now. And I knew Sheri would be complicated.

"Miss Crane called from the Lagos Castle gift shop. She asked me to tell you that she found two more charms that had gone bad and an entire batch of potion had to be thrown out."

"Did she say when this all happened?"

"She wasn't sure about the charms because they were in storage, but the potion soured sometime early in the morning."

Which put it at approximately the same time as the incidents at the staff breakfast. I was sure that Morris' problems originated with an intruder or a disgruntled employee, but I wasn't any closer to identifying the party responsible than I had been to start with.

"Anything else?"

"One more. Someone named Mark Keller called from Mayor Burford's office and asked that you call him as soon as possible." She read me the number, which I wrote down on the pad of paper Ruth Deacon had conveniently located next to the phone. "He said he'd be there until he received your call."

"Drawing overtime at the taxpayer's expense."

"Are you coming back to the office today, Dash?"

"I'm not sure." I was restless, felt the need to do something physical. Sometimes there's so much data that the best course is to sit at a desk and play analyst. This wasn't one of those times. "Why do you ask?" Moira is glib and sarcastic most of the time, at least when she's talking to me, but she'd been my secretary for almost three years now, and I could sense when something was wrong.

"I just have a feeling that it might be better if you stayed away." Moira's feelings on such matters generally had good cause.

"There are only a couple of hours left today. Maybe you should just close up and go home if you think there's any danger."

"No, I don't feel any sense of personal danger. At least not for me. It's probably nothing. There was another change in the Tuilleries this morning and every psychic in the city has a headache."

"Take care anyway. I'll check in when I can."

I called Burford's office immediately, was put on hold for a minute or two, then found myself listening to an enthusiastic young man who spoke so fast I had to ask him to slow down and repeat himself. The gist of it was that Evan Garner had been found, that he was dead, but the police were keeping things very quiet until they'd finished their own investigation. "The Mayor wanted you to know that we've made it clear to the local authorities that he would appreciate their cooperation and that you will exercise discretion with any privileged information you receive. They'll be expecting you."

But not happily, I was sure. "All right, thanks. Give me the address."

The sun was dropping rapidly toward the west, which meant it would rise there the following morning. The world of the Cities is flat, say the savants, and the sun doesn't rotate around it. Instead, it travels across the sky from west to east and east to west on alternate days. The moons, on the other hand, are fixed in place, although for some reason they DO rotate, presenting us with differing faces at different times of the month. Science is not my strong point, but as I understand it, the sun dictates the tides here, where the moon was responsible in the original world. We have people who try to read the future in the stars, but they're fixed as well, and it's pretty well accepted that astrology is just nonsense.

Evan Garner's body had turned up in Toronto, behind a small bookstore three blocks from Bloor Street, a quiet, less than thriving neighborhood. It had been snowing on and off for the past several hours and it was almost painfully cold, particularly since I'd come from Manhattan, which was in the middle of summer, and across Moscow, which was experiencing an unusually warm early autumn. Mercifully the air was dead calm so the snow hadn't drifted, but it still came halfway up to my knees. The Police had cordoned off the entire shop and the adjacent alley, and it took me a few minutes to talk my way through the cordon despite Keller's efforts on my behalf.

There was a narrow accessway behind the store, so narrow that the mobile crime lab and ambulance were unable to negotiate the turn. Both were parked in the alley, filling it so completely that I had to turn sideways to edge past. At the corner, another officer questioned my presence, held me until his superior arrived. Fortunately, Detective Colby had a mobile phone and deigned to confirm my right to be present. He wasn't cordial but he nodded me through.

A tall, ugly looking storage shed stood at the end of a short row of trash cans. It was made of corrugated steel panels, bolted together securely. The door was open and a shiny new padlock dangled from the hasp. The crime scene people had set up portable lights inside so Evan Garner's almost nude body was perfectly visible when I reached the doorway. He was lying on his back over a pile of decaying cardboard cartons. He looked surprised as well as dead, but there were no obvious wounds and no blood. For clothing he wore a pair of jockey shorts and, around his neck, a silver chain from which dangled half of a heart. Bingo! All three of my cases were now connected. Garner's body had not been mutilated like the first three victims, which was puzzling, but then again, neither had Porter's.

The shed was tightly constructed and the snow hadn't penetrated except right at the threshold, although there were traces of it near the body, possibly tracked in by one of the investigators. "Sloppy work," I muttered under my breath.

Colby had come up behind me. "The tracks were already there when we arrived." He sounded offended rather than defensive.

"Who discovered the body?"

"The bookstore owner. He keeps supplies out here, cash register tapes, plastic bags, things like that. He came out at lunch time for some light bulbs and got the shock of his life."

"Not so big a shock that he didn't grab himself a closer look."

Colby shrugged. "He claims he didn't. Never set a foot inside once he saw what was there, or so he says."

I frowned. "Do you believe him?"

"Yeah." Colby didn't sound happy. There was a flurry of flashbulbs as the photographers finished their preliminary work. We both retreated a couple of steps, blinking.

"Then someone else has been visiting the body. How did they get past the lock?"

Colby gave me a long, appraising look, and apparently decided that I was at least partly colleague and not entirely irritating. "Doesn't take much magic to get past an ordinary padlock. But the owner, Watson, admits he usually doesn't bother to secure the shed."

"The body has been there a while." The lividity was visible even from the doorway.

"Hard to estimate given how cold it's been here, but I'd guess three or four days minimum, maybe longer. The owner says he hasn't been out here in more than a week."

I nodded as though he'd confirmed what I already knew, although I hadn't had the foggiest notion. "So who tracked in the snow?"

"Might be a homeless person hoping for a sheltered place to sleep. Or a kid looking for something to steal. The snow started at six this morning so it could have been any time today."

A technician approached us deferentially. "You can go in now, Detective. Just don't disturb anything you don't have to."

Colby glanced at me and gave a barely perceptible nod. "You coming?"

"Right behind you."

The body was just a body. I've seen dead people before and never much cared for the experience. At least Garner didn't smell. Colby crouched on one side, running his eyes over the dead man's skin, looking for some trace evidence that would probably have been meaningless to me even if I'd seen it. I was more interested in the amulet. It looked exactly like the other, but it was the first time I'd actually seen one physically. It was a bit larger than I expected, and darker. In the photographs it had looked rust colored, but this was a deeper, rich color – almost that of blood.

I was reluctant to take out the photograph in Colby's presence because that would alert him to the fact that this was not an isolated crime, but he probably knew that already. Mayor Porter's death had made most of the major newspapers, and there had been follow up articles that mentioned her relationship with Garner. He'd been relatively cordial up until now, so I decided to show him that I could be generous as well.

I expected the photograph to show the matching half of the amulet, which was now in the custody of the Hyannis Police. But even though the inscriptions seemed identical, there was one major discrepancy. Both of them were the left sides of hearts. They were not a matched pair. Which meant there were two more half hearted amulets out there somewhere. Or were there even more?

Colby leaned across the body to glance at the photograph. "Was that found on Porter?" he asked quietly. "A lover's quarrel?"

I shook my head. "Afraid not. That would be too easy. And they don't match anyway. It might just be coincidence." I made the photograph disappear back into my pocket, trying to look nonchalant. "Any sign of the cause of death?"

Colby didn't deign to pursue the matter, just shook his head. "Nothing obvious. No blood."

"Not here anyway."

That got me a direct look. "You don't think he was killed here?"

"Do you?"

He shook his head. "No, not really. The body was dumped, but not recently. There would have been more snow if he was dragged in here today."

"I don't suppose you found a copy of a videotape in the area?"

Colby frowned at me. "Should I?"

"I honestly don't know. Probably not. But if you do, it might explain a few things. Can I get a copy of the autopsy report?" I knew I could, but it never hurts to act humble. Besides, Colby had been decent enough and I didn't want to get his back up.

"I'll see that you do. Was this other amulet of yours involved in the Porter murder?" His cop radar was probably beeping like crazy.

"No," I admitted. "It's part of another case."

He considered that. "Then there's a connection between Porter and Garner and this other matter?"

"Like I said, it might be just a very big coincidence, but yes, I think there might be. But I'm damned if I can figure out how. And I haven't a clue who killed Garner and dumped him in your backyard."

"If you unravel any of this, I'd appreciate a heads up."

"Give me your card. If I come up with anything more definite, I'll call you."

It was dusk by the time I left Toronto and I probably wouldn't have gone back to the office even if Moira hadn't warned me off. I was close enough to Dublin to run over and confirm at least one small part of my theory, although it took longer than I expected. I found young Ian relatively quickly, but he was unwilling or unable to confirm that the man in the photograph I showed him, Aram Gudanoff, was Ashley O'Brien's last boyfriend.

His friend Sean wasn't at home. It took the two of us almost an hour to find him, and even then it was more by accident than design. Ian spotted him as we were taking a shortcut through a small, badly maintained and poorly lit park, and hailed him. For a second I thought the other boy might bolt, and something that looked suspiciously like a pack of cigarettes disappeared inside his sweater, but I pretended not to have seen anything, and Sean enthusiastically identified Gudanoff. "That's him, right enough. He drove his own car one time and he paid me to watch it while he went inside to fetch her." Alas, Sean was one of those rare boys who had no interest in motor vehicles. He couldn't even remember what color it had been.

"Thanks boys." I rewarded them both and returned to the Studebaker just as darkness stole all the color out of the world.

I stopped at a bar I liked right at the edge of Boston, ordered a sandwich and a beer and used the pay phone to call Moira at home while I was waiting. She'd been quite sure that her presentiment posed no threat to herself, but I was still a bit anxious about it and wanted to reassure myself that she all right. It was the first time I'd ever called her apartment and I had to look up the number on the contact card I kept in my wallet, but I was immediately reassured when she picked up, just before the first ring.

"Dash? Is that you?" Her voice was tense, excited.

"Yes, it's me. I wanted to check to see if you had any messages for me," I lied.

"Just one. Abe Chertoff called. He wants you to get in touch with him right away."

Chertoff owned the building where I rented my office. "Did he say why?" I was only one month behind in my rent. He'd carried me a lot longer than that in the past.

"No, but he didn't sound happy."

His number was in my wallet, so I hung up and called again, although I ate a bite of my sandwich and washed it down with some Sam Adams before dialing.

"Dash? Where the hell are you?" Chertoff had a squeaky little voice that was almost painful to hear when he was agitated.

"Boston. What's the problem, Abe?"

"I try to be easy to get along with, Dash, but I have other tenants, you understand? I can't have things like this going on in the building."

"Things like what, Abe?"

"Your office! The stuff coming out of your office!" He was shouting now.

It took a couple of minutes to calm him down, and he still wouldn't tell me what was wrong. "Just go down there and look for yourself, Dash. And fix it by tomorrow morning or you're going to be looking for a new place to hang your hat."

Actually, I never wear a hat, but I got the general idea.

I got lucky traffic wise, and even found a parking space less than a block away. Nothing seemed out of the ordinary at the building. The guard glanced up, recognized me with a nod, and looked back at his security monitor. The elevator was working again although the new levitation spell was less than perfect and the ride up was jerky. I got out on my floor and turned toward the office, and even before I was in sight of the door, I began to understand why Chertoff was so upset.

The ceiling was moving. More precisely, the things crawling on the ceiling were moving. They looked a little like slugs, except that they were so translucent they were almost ghostly. There was no sound either, and it didn't take much of a detective, mundane or magical, to realize that, unlike the scarabs, these were chimaeras with no physical presence. That didn't make them any less disgusting.

When I turned the corner, I saw where they were coming from. Not surprisingly they were squeezing out from around the edges of the door to my office. They were much more numerous here, two and even three layers deep in places, and they had begun to cover the walls and floor as well as the ceiling. I actually had to step through some of them to reach the door and unlock it. They were just as immaterial as I expected, but my skin still crawled as though I'd touched something physical and slimy.

It was much worse inside. The phantom creatures covered the floor and the furnishings, piled as high as my waist. They writhed and wiggled and undulated in a perpetual, disgusting frenzy. As far as I could see, there was no physical damage anywhere, but my stomach began to churn and I finally closed my eyes, groping my way across the office to the inner door. At first it was easier now that I couldn't see them, because as far as the rest of my senses were concerned, they didn't exist. But then my imagination got the better of me. I pictured myself covered from head to foot with giant, transparent maggots, and the image made me gag and open my eyes to reassure myself that it wasn't true.

It wasn't. They were only up to my armpits.

I turned and ran, without shame, back into the corridor, and I had to sit on the floor at the far end for several minutes before I could muster the courage to return and lock the door.

I expected the arcane infestation to have ended by morning, but when Moira and I showed up, almost simultaneously, we found an angry group of tenants in the lobby. Abe Chertoff was there and my attempt to slip past unobserved failed. He had already called Shadow Extermination. "I'll be adding their charges to your bill, Dash! And I expect to be paid on time this month!"

Moira insisted on trying to get into the office, but even she recoiled when she saw what was waiting for her. That entire floor of the building was affected now, and a few of the discorporate creatures had even made their way into the elevator shaft. "This wasn't cheap, Dash. Someone really wants you to drop a case."

"Yeah, but which one?" But I was pretty sure I knew which one. I don't know why the petty crimes at the Lagos Castle were so important, more important apparently than murder or missing persons, but someone was sparing no expense to discourage me from pursuing it.

I told Moira to let the exterminators in when they arrived, then avoided the still furious Abe Chertoff and sneaked out of the building. I wasn't going to get any work done there for at least the next few hours, and I was so angry that I was restless. I retrieved my car and drove to the Lagos Castle, but Morris wasn't in, and the frazzled young woman in the gift shop, whose name I had already managed to forget, told me that it was Jessica Crane's day off.

Frustrated, I decided to take a random drive, but my subconscious mind must have taken control because when I finally calmed down enough to care where I was, I found myself only three blocks from the Baker's Dozen. I decided to go where my instincts had led me and a few minutes later I was standing in the lobby.

The desk clerk told me that Connors was in a meeting and could not be disturbed, but I hadn't really wanted to talk to her anyway. To be perfectly frank, now that I was inside, I wasn't sure exactly what to do next. "Has the crime scene been released yet?"

The clerk looked more than slightly uncomfortable and answered in hushed tones. "We're trying to move to past that incident here, Mr. Dash."

"Has it been cleared or not?"

He wasn't sure, so I took the elevator to the 13th floor and discovered that it did matter which button one pushed, because I ended up in the wrong place and found myself wandering through one level after another before I finally found the right room. The Police barrier had been downgraded to a warning, and I pushed through it with gritted teeth. The interior was just as I had last seen it, except that the hatch to the lower level was closed now and the rug back in place. Presumably the hotel would have it removed before either of the rooms were rented again.

I forced myself to spend half an hour going through Porter's personal items one final time, with no more success than on the previous occasion. Angry at myself for wasting time, I returned to the lobby, waved at the desk clerk, and returned to my car. I had just started the engine when something moved in the back seat.

"I need to talk to you."

The voice wasn't threatening, and when I glanced into the rear view mirror I immediately recognized Chris Hayden. "Shouldn't you be at work? You could lose your job."

"I already did. Connors had me fired right after I told you what happened that night." He sounded angry.

"Well, you did screw one of the guests without letting the hotel charge for the service. And you knew about the hidden camera."

"That was the first time I ever used that camera, and I didn't even get the tape. And if they fired everyone who slept with the guests, they wouldn't have enough people left to run the hotel. It's not exactly a secret why so many bigwigs stay with us. Since magic doesn't work inside, chastity and fidelity spells vanish, so you can cheat if you want. And since love charms don't work either, you can be sure about exactly what you're getting and what you're feeling."

As much as you ever could, I amended silently. "But in your case, the guest died, and you knew it and didn't tell anyone."

Hayden was suddenly more subdued. "Yeah, I suppose. But Connors could have stood up for me a little. They didn't even give me severance. And she owes me."

My ears perked up. "Why is that?"

I had tried to sound casual, but Hayden closed down, speaking more carefully now. "She knew about my brother before he got caught and she never said anything, even when he was working at the hotel."

"Connors knew your brother well then?"

He laughed humorlessly. "Pretty damn well, I'd say. She was sleeping with him."

It was almost too incongruous to be true, but Hayden didn't sound as though he was making any of this up. This, then, was a side of Sheri Connors I hadn't seen. "And she knew about his peeping tom habit?"

"He showed her some of the tapes he'd made."

"From the hotel, or from the geisha house?"

"The geisha house. I don't think she knew about the other camera. I don't think she'd have been happy about having it here. Anyway, if I'd told people about her and my brother, it would have caused trouble."

"Why didn't you?"

"Because she promised she'd get me a job at the Dozen later on, and she did."

"Have you said anything to her about all of this? Since they fired you, I mean?"

He let a few seconds pass before answering. "No."

"Why not?"

"Because she has a temper. If I piss her off now, she can have me blackballed. I'll never clear security to work at a good job anywhere in the Cities. You know how that works."

"So why tell me? What do you expect me to do about it?"

"She won't talk to me, but the guys tell me she likes you, treats you like a real person. I thought maybe you could ask her to keep the reason why I was fired off my official record, maybe even give me a letter of recommendation. I really didn't do anything the hotel didn't want me to do, did I? Why should I suffer because of it?"

"And why would I bother to act on your behalf?"

"Because if you do, I'll tell you something you don't know. Something about the murder."

CHAPTER TEN

Hayden demanded that I do what he wanted before he'd say anything, but I refused. He was stubborn, but when I finally ordered him out of my car, he wilted. "All right! All right! I'll tell you. But you've got to speak to Connors for me."

"If what you have to tell me is useful, I'll see what I can do. That's as much as I can promise." I would do it too, if only for an excuse to talk to Sheri again.

According to Hayden, Porter was still both drunk and drugged when he was with her, and she had sometimes confused him with other people, sometimes forgot where she was or what she was doing. During these lapses, she talked about things that he neither cared about nor understood, but at least one sequence had caught his interest. The Mayor had been bragging about her imminent return to the screen but had spoken disparagingly of her announced role as Peabody in the first Eve Dallas movie.

"She said she was going to be a leading actress again, not second fiddle. Any part she wanted would be hers for the asking."

"Not with her track record." Even so, I made a mental note to have Moira give a call to an old friend of mine in Hollywood.

"Maybe not, but she claimed she had an edge, something that no one else had. Magic, powerful magic, something that could give her whatever she wanted, her heart's desire." I stiffened when I heard the last two words, and even though I have never displayed even the faintest hint of prescience or any other psychic power, I knew almost exactly what Hayden was going to say before the words came out of his mouth.

"She was wearing this charm on a chain around her neck, absolutely refused to take it off. She said it was going to solve all of her problems. But this is the thing, Mr. Dash. When I came to, you know, after she'd been killed and I found her body, the charm and the necklace were gone. I looked all around for it and it wasn't there."

Apparently finding a dead body hadn't upset Hayden so much that he couldn't spend some time looking for a potentially valuable artifact before scampering. I thought I already knew the answer that was coming, but I had to ask the question. "What did this charm look like?"

"It was heart shaped and had lots of writing on it, runes or something, nothing I could read."

Then came the surprise. "Do you remember which side of the heart it was? Left or right?"

Hayden sounded puzzled, but he answered directly. "I don't understand, Mr. Dash. It was a heart, like I said."

"A complete heart? Both sides?"

"Yeah. Of course. Why wouldn't it be?"

Why indeed?

I did a quick mental inventory. I had three dead bodies each of which were ritually mutilated, two more that hadn't been, and one – Ruth Deacon – whose status was uncertain. There were at least two sets of heart shaped amulets which appeared to be linked to all five murders. O'Brien's was missing, as was half of the one Porter had worn the night she died, the other half presumably having ended up around Garner's throat. That one and Sandobhal's were now in Police custody, in two different locations.

I got rid of Hayden by promising to try to intercede on his behalf, then locked the car and went back inside to use the lobby telephone. I made a quick call to the office and asked Moira to get in touch with Saul Rubens, but I had a second quarter in my hand. I had known for a while that the amulets were important to this case – or these cases – but now it seemed to me that they were the key to all the answers. Pictures wouldn't do. I needed to see one up close.

I knew it would do no good to contact Delpy, my Police contact, so I called Keller at Burford's office and told him what I wanted. He sounded uncertain but promised to speak to the Mayor on my behalf. "I'll call you back."

"No," I countered. "I'll call you back in an hour."

"I don't know if I can get in to see him that quickly."

"One hour from now. It's important."

Then back to my car and down to the six block slice of Port-au-Prince to visit a little magic shop where my credit was still good. Twenty minutes later, I was back on the road, headed toward Hyannis with an inscribed, triangular coin in one pocket and a brief incantation engraved in my memory.

It took a few minutes to find the Hyannis Police station, which had been designed to blend in with the tourist traps in the area. I called Keller from a public phone booth and heard what I wanted, then entered. I identified myself to the officer at the front desk, who went from suspicious to hostile, but who deigned to call his superior. Another officer appeared in due course, and since he never introduced himself I assumed he'd skipped the preliminaries and gone directly to hostile. He acknowledged that Mayor Burford's office had requested that the ordinary rules be waived in this particular case, implying by tone if not words that there was something distasteful if not actually improper about all this. He then led me through a series of doors and down a set of stairs to a locked room, spoke briefly to another uniformed officer who unlocked the door. The inside was dark, murky even, with no windows, the walls lined with overstuffed shelves, a single security light burning in the ceiling.

When he followed me inside, I glanced at his name tag. "If you'll just let me begin my examination of the exhibit, I'll let you know when I'm done, Sergeant Kennedy. I don't need to take up any more of your time."

But he wasn't having any of that. "Mayor Burford's office says you're a duly licensed consultant, Mr. Dash, but the rules of custody require that you conduct your examination in the presence of an authorized individual. I'm sure you understand."

That would make what I wanted to do more difficult, but not impossible. I sat down at a plain, rectangular table while Kennedy ran his eyes along the shelves, found what he was looking for, and lifted down an evidence bag. He dumped the contents into a white enamel tray and set it down in front of me.

It was the left hand side of a heart shaped amulet, delicately inscribed. I had half expected it to be the right side. It was entirely possible that the photograph provided to me had been reversed, by intent or by accident, but that wasn't the case. So there definitely were two amulets. I picked it up, somewhat gingerly I must admit, but it felt perfectly ordinary, perhaps a bit light for its size. The chain was in the tray as well, but the amulet itself had been detached.

For the first few minutes, I was honestly studying the charm. No matter how closely I looked, however, it betrayed no more of its nature than had the photographs. It felt perfectly ordinary, but I've never been sensitive to magic so that didn't mean anything. The workmanship was superb. The fracture line was so smooth and perfect that it was hard to believe it had ever been part of a greater whole.

Kennedy had been watching me closely and was starting to stir impatiently. I realized I had to act quickly if I was going to do this at all. My free hand slipped into my pocket and felt for the triangular coin. "Would it be possible to get a little more light, Sergeant? I just want to be sure I haven't missed anything before I leave."

He made an exasperated noise, but mention of my imminent departure seemed to have softened his resolve. He stood up and walked toward the door to turn on the rest of the lights and as soon as he had turned away I brought out the coin, pressed it against the amulet, spoke the brief incantation under my breath, and slipped the amulet itself into my other pocket. The coin immediately became an exact duplicate of the object it had just touched. I set it down in the tray.

To keep Kennedy from suspecting anything, I had to study the fake amulet for a minute or two longer. As soon as I thought I could safely disengage, I pushed the tray away. "All right, Sergeant. I'm done. I apologize for having taken up so much of your time, but you know the Mayors. These murders have the public in an uproar and they want to give the impression that they're looking at every possible angle."

Kennedy seemed somewhat mollified, but he wasted no time returning the evidence bag to the shelf and ushering me out. The chameleon spell would only last about an hour, but I didn't think it likely that anyone else would be interested in the amulet for some time. At least not the Police.

So now I had half of one of the two amulets in my possession, one fourth of the puzzle. Would I be any the wiser if I had all four? I had no idea.

I called my office, not sure if anyone would answer, but Moira did her usual magic act. "It's safe to come home, dear. The wigglies are gone."

"How's Chertoff?"

"Less incensed than the nice law firm next door. They're going to sue you for everything you own."

"Which wouldn't even cover their costs. I'll be there in a few."

As promised, there was nothing disgusting in the corridor or even in my waiting room, but I still felt a thrill of revulsion. I kept expecting a blind, formless head to peep out from behind the desk. Moira greeted me with a strained smile and pointed to the fax machine in the corner. The power was off and an entire roll of fax paper had overflowed the out box and fallen into an unruly pile on the floor.

"I saved that for you."

Puzzled, I crossed the office and looked at the mess. It was the same message, over and over again, filling the entire roll. THIS WAS YOUR LAST WARNING!

"Any idea who sent it?" I felt anger, in fact, positive fury.

Moira shrugged. "The phone line was disconnected and the power was off. I don't think we're going to have any luck tracing it through the ether. So how was your morning?"

"Long. I'm starving. Why don't we order some sandwiches? What's this?" I picked up a magazine from the corner of her desk, *Form and Function*.

"I was curious about Evan Garner. There's an article about him in there."

I glanced at the table of contents and began paging through.

Moira looked subdued. "There's almost no text, and it's all about his work, nothing personal."

I found the right page and grimaced. Garner's sculptures looked vaguely familiar but then again, all of these non-realistic formless blobs look the same to me.

Moira waited until I set the magazine down. "I also made some calls to Hollywood like you asked. Saul was pretty offended when I asked if he'd cast Mayor Porter as Peabody under pressure." Saul Rubens was an old friend. He'd been Morris' business partner for a while, then went to Hollywood to make his fortune. "He insists he decided on his own. But Edna in casting says they never even scheduled any auditions and that he came up with her name out of the blue and wouldn't listen to any other suggestions."

"He's probably not lying. He probably thinks it was his idea."

"I figured, but that's not the most interesting part. The part was recast just a few days ago."

That surprised me. "Did she back out at the last minute? That doesn't fit with what we already know."

Moira was shaking her head. "SHE didn't back out. Sandra Bullock did. So Porter was upgraded to the Eve Dallas role. Now that she's dead, the whole project is on hold."

I could just barely see Porter in the supporting part. As the lead, she'd be a disaster. Saul was a shrewd and successful producer. He wouldn't have made decisions like that unless his judgment was being affected by external causes.

While we were waiting for the sandwiches to arrive, I told Moira most of what I'd been doing and thinking, but didn't mention that I'd stolen Police evidence. I trusted her not to tell anyone, but there was no point in making her an accessory unless it was absolutely necessary.

"So there are two amulets, not one?"

"That's obvious, isn't it?" I snapped. "Sorry. Gudanoff and O'Brien shared one of them, and both of them ended up dead, their bodies mutilated. Sandobhal and Ruth Deacon appear to have shared the second, unless there's a third one, which so far seems unlikely. Sandobhal was also mutilated. Deacon is still alive, according to her sister, and presumably unscarred but something very odd has happened to her as well."

"And Mayor Porter ended up with a complete heart, at least for a while, until she shared it with Evan Garner. Which one was it?"

"Well, since Sandobhal's half was in Police custody at the time, it couldn't be that one. So again, unless there is a third, she somehow recovered the halves formerly held by Gudanoff and O'Brien."

"And what happened to Ruth Deacon's half?"

"I don't know. Probably she still has it, wherever she is." I ran my fingers through my hair and took a deep breath. "And I'm still no closer to understanding what the amulets are supposed to do. Since Ruth Deacon is supposedly incapable of feeling emotion, and everyone else who has worn one has died, I'm thinking maybe they're not love charms after all."

The delivery boy arrived from the deli on the first floor, gave me a dirty look when I added his tip to my tab. I almost told him to forget the tip, but he was gone before I could say anything.

"It's too bad we can't get hold of one of the amulets." Moira was looking at me intently. I don't think she actually knew what was in my pocket, but she was psychic enough to sense that I was holding out on her.

"What good would that do?" I temporized. Was she suggesting that she knew what I had done? My hand crept into my pocket and closed around the amulet.

"You never know until you try."

I decided she must know that I was lying. "I thought you said you couldn't read me." Irritably, I pulled out the truncated heart and put it on the desk in front of her. "I acquired it by means of unconventional investigatory procedures. Don't ask."

"You stole it." Moira gave me an odd look, reached out tentatively with her right hand. The moment her fingers touched the charm, she recoiled, drawing back. For the first time since I'd know her, she looked frightened.

"What's wrong?"

"I don't know exactly. It's like nothing I've ever felt before." She shook her head slightly. "I don't think it's actively dangerous, but it's very powerful. I don't know how to explain this. It's like hearing a composition for harp played on bagpipes."

I shook my head at her. "Come again?"

"Anything touched by magic picks up a kind of current. People who are sufficiently sensitive can feel that current even if they can't manipulate what it does or even understand how it's flowing." She shook her head, obviously irritated that she couldn't express herself better. "This isn't a very good metaphor but it's the best I can come up with on short notice. I can feel the magic in this; it's powerful and it's in constant, rapid motion. Most magic is passive; it sits there until a mind directs it to do something. This is active; it has volition and it doesn't have to wait for instructions before it acts. But there's something thick and cloying about it as well, like a river of oil or sewage rather than water. I'm sorry, that's the best I can do." She looked away from the charm. "I'd rather not touch it. And there's something else."

She paused and I fidgeted, waiting for her to continue. "What is it?" I asked at last. "We don't have all night."

"It has a bad feeling. When I was touching it, I felt frustrated, angry. I wanted to break something."

"Not much left in this office to break," I said quietly as I made the amulet disappear back into my pocket. "Wanda said something similar. She didn't know what it was either but she said it was something new, that it wasn't like familiar magic."

Moira still looked uneasy and she made an obvious effort to change the subject. "So what about Morris' problems? Any progress there? I visited his gift shop last night and everything seemed okay. He's got quite an operation there. I've eaten at the restaurant and I knew about the gift shop, but I just never got around to checking it out."

"He was selling charms and falafel when I first met him, and the combination hasn't changed much since, although his offerings are more elaborate. And no, I'm not making any progress. That's why these warnings don't make any sense. I don't even have a next step to not take. A team of experts far more qualified than I am has re-certified the defensive spells, which means the cause of the vandalism is probably internal. Unfortunately, all of the incidents have been in areas that are accessible to scores of people and we have no way of pinpointing the exact time any of them were set in motion. Morris has already installed more surveillance equipment, but anyone with the talent to elude detection so far isn't going to going to have any difficulty fooling a few cameras and monitor spells."

"What about the staff breakfast? Didn't you say that there were only a limited number of people in the room?"

I nodded. "There were just over a dozen people, not counting those who prepared and served the food. But that doesn't necessarily mean anything."

Her shoulders slumped. "Because the food might have been cursed in advance anyway. It wouldn't be hard to add a time delay to a simple curdling spell."

"Which is why I decided not to get fixated on that particular time frame."

"So what are you going to do? You can't tell Morris you're giving up."

"No, I can't. Particularly since I'm close to something."

She gave me a quizzical look. "What do you mean? You just finished telling me that you're at a complete loss."

"And so I am. Or so I think I am. But someone else thinks I might know more than I think I know, so maybe I do. They wouldn't be going to this much trouble if they thought it was as hopeless as we do."

"I see what you're saying, but how does that help?"

I was spared answering that because Moira suddenly turned and picked up the still silent phone. "Dash Investigations. May I help you?" She listened for a moment. "Oh, sorry, Miss Deacon. I didn't recognize your voice at first." Which was almost certainly a lie. "Yes, he's right here. Just a moment."

She handed the phone to me. "It's Rachel Deacon. She says she's found something."

Ruth Deacon had rented a safety deposit box. She had paid cash for it so the charge hadn't shown up in her financial records. Her sister's voice betrayed the closest to actual animation I'd ever heard. "She opened it less than two weeks ago. I only found out about it because the bank just got around to mailing her a copy of the contract and receipt."

"Have you been there yet?"

"No, I wasn't sure if they'd let me open it. Ruth is still alive, legally as well as physically."

"What bank is it?"

"Something called *Le Troisieme Parisien.*"

"Great." If it had been one of the larger banks, they'd have extensive magical protection for their depositors. I knew the *Parisien.* It was barely solvent. "I don't think we'll have any problem if we can find her copy of the key."

"I don't remember seeing one at her apartment."

"We weren't looking for one at the time. Can you meet me there if I head over right now?"

There was a longer pause than usual. "I suppose so. Are you sure this isn't just another blind alley, Mr. Dash?"

"I'm not sure of anything, Miss Deacon. But the fact that your sister disappeared only days after opening a deposit box is suggestive."

"All right, but it will take me at least half an hour to get there."

For a change, things went my way. Rachel was waiting in front of the building when I arrived, though her mood had edged toward stormy. We barely spoke on the ride up in the levitator. Once inside, I started on the bedroom while she went through the office, and I found the key almost immediately, tucked into an envelope marked "LTP" in the dresser of her night table. I frowned at it for a while before calling Rachel. "Let's go," I said, holding the key up so that she could see it.

It was only two blocks to *Le Troisiemme Parisienne* so we walked. Rachel's mood had changed and she seemed almost eager now, but we still had a bad moment at the bank. The middle aged woman who presided over the safety deposit boxes asked to see identification and I wasn't sure if Rachel had the nerve to try to pass off the difference in first names as a mistake. But just then one of the clerks came by and greeted her by name. "Oh, hello, Miss Deacon."

"Do you know this woman, Alice?" asked the keeper of the keys.

"Oh yes. I waited on her twice while you were away, Maxine. Hers is box number 404."

That seemed to have done the trick. We were ushered into a small, poorly lit room with tawdry furniture after retrieving our box, then left alone to examine its contents. There were very few. A packet of photographs caught my attention and I began looking through them while Rachel started scanning an assortment of envelopes and loose papers. The first several pictures were long distance photographs, necessarily, of the Tuilleries. In most cases it was impossible to determine what the specific subjects of the photographs were, since they contained the usual riotous mix of distorted plant life, with the occasional animal limb or completely unidentifiable object interposed among them. There were two exceptions, both of the same artifact, a crumbling stone monument. Several of these structures were periodically visible through the chaos that ruled there, but I had never seen such clear images before. In the first, a stone pillar, almost phallic, protruded up through a mass of what were probably wildly threshing vines. The second was of the same monument, from a slightly different angle. In this instance, some of the vegetative wildlife had subsided, enough that I could see a portion of the markings on one side of the pillar.

There were several lines of unreadable text. Just above it was the unmistakable shape of a heart.

The remaining photographs were a mixed lot, and I had the impression that Ruth Deacon had simply used up what remained of a roll of film and hadn't bothered to separate them. They were innocuous shots of buildings and occasionally people, and I had almost set them aside before something clicked and I flipped back through them. In the picture in question, a half dozen people stood on a street corner, apparently engaged in an animated conversation. I recognized one of the faces, and that with considerable difficulty. But after several seconds, I was quite certain that it was indeed Steven Sandobhal. I finally had definite physical evidence connecting Sandobhal to Ruth Deacon. This had to be more than coincidence. I sat staring at the photograph for a long time, and only gradually became aware that the setting was also familiar. One of the buildings behind them was the Lagos Castle.

"You look like you've found something." Rachel had looked up from her pile of paper.

I pushed the photograph in her direction. "Do you recognize any of these people?"

She picked it up and studied it for several seconds before handing it back. "The young woman in the skirt looks vaguely familiar but I don't really recognize her."

I looked at the picture again. She looked familiar to me as well, but she was gesturing with one arm and half of her face was hidden. "I'm going to take this with me if you don't mind."

"By all means. I'm not finding much of anything in this lot."

We traded piles and I started going through the material she'd already examined. Some of it was what you might expect – a copy of the contract for her apartment, sales receipts for some expensive photographic equipment, a handful of negotiable bonds with pretty significant face values. Another group of receipts covered the purchase of historical artifacts from a number of sources, galleries, collectors, and antique shops. Two of them were from the Lagos Castle gift shop, one for a book, the other for some jewelry. All had been paid for with cash. There was also a diary, which looked promising until I opened it. It read "My First Diary" on the title page and the last entry had been made before I was born. There was no sign of the missing last volume of her working journal, but there was a chance that Ruth had it with her when she went wherever it was that she'd gone. Her last will and testament was short and clear; in the event of her death, all of her assets were to be liquidated except for her photographs and the proceeds donated to the New School's photography department. Her photographs were willed to the Metropolitan Museum of Art. At first I thought it odd that there was no mention of her sister, but then I remembered that if one of them died, the other would soon follow.

There was a small box of jewelry, but nothing even remotely resembling a heart, broken or otherwise. A small envelope marked "Rachel's apartment" held a key. "I gave that to her years ago," Rachel explained. "I'm surprised she still has it." In another envelope I found a dozen postage stamps, shrink wrapped to a card. They were more than a century old and presumably valuable. The last envelope I opened contained a piece of stiff cardboard covered with glyphs.

"I missed that," said Rachel. "What is it?"

I was almost certain that I recognized the characters, but I wasn't going to admit that right now. The reverse side was commercially printed. It was a gift card for a free dessert at the Lagos Castle, and it expired in two days. "I don't know. I'll take it with me and check around." Unless I was very much mistaken, however, the swirls and icons on the card were the same as those that had been carved into the bodies of Ashley O'Brien, Aram Gudanoff, and Steven Sandobhal.

Rachel put the remaining items back in the box and a few minutes later we were standing outside the bank. She seemed preoccupied and barely acknowledged me when I thanked her for coming on such short notice. As soon as I was inside my car, I pulled out the inscribed card and the photograph of the amulet, comparing the characters. Some of them matched, but not the others. Was that significant?

I was still carrying several photographs in my jacket pocket and I took them out, thumbing through until I found the one Rachel Deacon had provided the day she hired me. Ruth Deacon had made purchases at the Lagos Castle, and I had a photograph of Steven Sandobhal in the same general area, which had probably been taken by Ruth herself. If I could find someone who had seen them together, it would be further proof that they knew one another. That might give me enough leverage to push the Police into looking into Deacon's disappearance. I have no problem taking credit, and being paid, for their work.

Jessica Crane was alone in the gift shop, but there were only a couple of potential customers in the store, and they looked more like browsers than buyers. She smiled and waved briefly when she saw me come in. "Not exactly mobbed today, is it?"

She shook her head. "This is usually a slow time, and I think word is starting to get around that we're having problems. A couple of people have asked about it. Our official position is that we received a tainted lot and that we've sorted it out now. At least it gives me a chance to have Carly spend some time rearranging the store room. So what can I do for you today?"

I took out the photograph of Rachel Deacon. It had snagged the catch on the back of the charm which popped out as well, falling to the floor and bouncing away. I picked it up quickly. I wasn't ready to show it to Crane yet. "Do you recognize this woman? She's one of your customers."

She frowned down at the picture. "I don't think so. But an awful lot of people come through here during the course of a day. Not a regular or I'd know her."

"Would you have a record of her purchases if I gave you her name?"

Jessica pushed out one cheek with her tongue to signify deep thought. "If she had an account with us, I sure could, but not otherwise." I took out the receipt and handed it to her. She studied it for a few seconds. "The mark down here means Carly waited on her. This is a nice piece she bought. Expensive though."

"Any magical properties?"

"No. It's an older item, from before the Transition."

"All right, how about this guy?" I put down the photograph with Sandobhal standing on the street corner.

She examined this one intently and thought I saw a flicker of recognition, but she shook her head. "No, sorry. He's a complete stranger. Another customer?"

"Not that I know of." I hadn't really expected much, but it was still disappointing. Now that I thought about it, there were much better ways that I could have spent the last hour. I started putting the photographs back in my pocket, managed to drop the amulet again.

"What is that?" Crane was peering over the counter as I recovered it.

There really wasn't any reason not to show her. She wouldn't know that I had stolen it from the Hyannis Police. And besides, she was more of an expert on magical items than I would ever be. It couldn't hurt. I put the amulet on the counter so that she could see it clearly. "Odd looking, isn't it? Any idea what it might be?"

She let it sit where it was for a few seconds, then picked it up gingerly and held it close to her face so that she could see the markings clearly. "Where did you get this?"

"It turned up in the course of an investigation. Have you seen it before?"

"Nothing like this appears in any of the texts I'm familiar with," she said thoughtfully, slowly turning it back and forth. "But I don't keep up with the current research. Do you have any idea what it's supposed to do?"

I shook my head. "It looks like a love charm."

She shook her head. "Too complex. There are multiple levels of enchantment in the inscription."

"You can read it?" I felt a sudden thrill of excitement.

Which she quickly dampened. "No, sorry. I don't recognize most of the glyphs, but they're arranged in a nested pattern. That means that elements of the main spell are reinforced by other castings. Only a very skilled conjurer could keep this many subsidiary magics in the proper balance."

"Is there anything else you can tell me about it?"

It was almost as though she hadn't heard me. She was studying the amulet so closely that the rest of the world might not have existed. I felt a surge of irritation and was on the verge of speaking again when she finally shook her head and put the amulet down on the counter. "Not offhand. If you'd like to leave it with me a while, I still have some of my old textbooks in the back. Carly asked me to bring them in for her. She wants to take an apprenticeship as a thaumaturgist."

I barely remembered the girl but she hadn't seemed the assertive type. Thaumaturgy required a pretty secure ego. "Does she have any talent for it?"

"Hard to say. She has a touch of prescience, just enough to know when we're going to be busy and when not. And she learns quickly."

"I imagine you're a good teacher."

If Wanda Veil and her friends weren't able to help, it was unlikely that Crane could find anything on her own. I reached down and retrieved the amulet, tucking it away in my pocket. "I think I'll keep this with me for now. There are a few more people I need to show it to."

"Well, don't forget about me. A mystery like that is almost enough to make me regret deciding to leave the field."

Someone was sitting on the hood of my car. I could see him from two blocks away and recognized him before I'd closed half the distance. It was Herman Goff. Just what I needed to perk up my day.

"What do you want, Goff? Decide to deliver your latest threat in person?"

"I don't know what you're talking about, Dash. I was just out taking a walk and spotted your car." He reached down and patted the hood. "It's not like there's a lot of Studebakers in good condition in the Cities."

"I'd like to keep it that way. Get off." I waited as he slowly slid down onto his feet. Goff was a big man, very big, but for some reason he didn't look as imposing today. There was something in the way he held himself. The arrogance looked more like a pose than a conviction. It made him look smaller. And for some reason I felt better about myself. I wasn't about to let him push me around.

"I told you to stay away from this place, Dash. I meant it as a professional courtesy."

"And you had nothing to do with the scarab beetles or the banshee or phantom slugs, I suppose?"

Goff laughed. "Sounds like you've been having an interesting time, Dash. Maybe you should have listened to me."

"Maybe I should have done a lot of things. You're wasting my time, Goff. If you don't have anything to tell me, get out of the way. I have places to go." I started toward the car door but slowly, giving his Neanderthal brain time to function. Goff knew something. I was sure of it. I couldn't bully him into talking; I half suspected he was too stupid to be frightened even when there was good reason to be. Neither was he subtle, and he might well be vulnerable to a play on his own fears.

"What was it like, Goff? Flying over the Tuilleries, I mean."

Whatever Goff had expected me to say, that wasn't it. He'd never been quick on his feet to start with, but it took even longer than usual for him to come up with a response. "What's it to you?" Was that a tremble in his voice?

"Just curious. Did you know that almost everyone who went with you is dead now?"

"People die. It's nothing to do with me." He looked uncomfortable.

"Aren't you afraid that whatever got them is going to get you too?" I stepped toward him, invading his personal space, and my hands curled into fists. I hadn't realized how much I despised this man until now. Goff retreated a half step, looking increasingly uneasy. I discovered that I was enjoying myself.

"I don't talk about that place. It's bad luck." His face suddenly hardened.

"All right, so let's talk about why you don't want me to work for Morris Ngambe. He doesn't know you so it's not personal. Someone hired you to chase me off. Someone who's obviously not getting what he paid for."

"You get rich, you make enemies. Some enemies play fair; some make up their own rules. Ngambe's hurting, but he's not losing a lot of blood. Leave things alone and maybe they'll stay that way. Stir things up and you might not like where it leads."

Goff wasn't handy with metaphors either, apparently. "You need to find a better class of client, Goff."

Maybe I could have poked and prodded and enticed some more out of him, but he was looking stubborn now and I just didn't have the patience for it. So I gave him a disgusted look and opened the car door. He stood where he was and watched me drive away.

CHAPTER ELEVEN

It had been a wearing day and I headed for home rather than the office almost without making a conscious decision to do so. My head was spinning. On the one hand I had too much information – five dead bodies and one still missing, four magical artifacts only one of which I could definitely account for, and three clients waiting for me to solve their problems. On the other hand, I had too little. I didn't know what the amulets were meant to do, the problems at the Lagos Castle were a complete mystery to me, and even though I'd made progress finding Ruth Deacon and uncovering the links among the three ritual murders, I didn't feel as though I was even close to identifying the party or parties responsible. And now Evan Garner, prime suspect in the Porter murder, was dead. Had he killed Porter and been silenced for some other reason, or was he just another victim?

Darla greeted me at the door, complaining that once again I had forgotten to feed her. I'd bought a bottomless water bowl a while back so she always had something to drink, but the food ones were rare and way out of my budget. I suppressed a flash of anger; I was tired and even such a petty annoyance as having to feed the cat was blown out of proportion.

The bag of food I'd been using was empty. I tossed it aside angrily and started for the pantry, where I knew I had another. Impatiently, not understanding the delay, Darla pressed against my ankles at just the wrong moment. I didn't fall exactly, but I lurched to one side and banged my elbow against the door jamb. The pain was like a bolt of fire in my brain. I whirled to the knife rack, grabbed the cleaver, and raised it above my shoulder, blind with fury. Darla's back arched and she hissed at me for the very first time since we had known one another. It was that single realization that brought me back to myself.

I very deliberately put the cleaver back, located the unopened bag of cat food, and refilled Darla's dish. She had gone to hide somewhere else in the house by then, and I couldn't blame her. Then I took a can of beer and walked into the living room, dropped into the couch, and thought about it. I took the amulet out of my pocket, placed it on the coffee table in front of me, and thought about it some more.

Despite my profession, I'm not a violent person. And I have a pretty even temper, all things considered. But a few minutes earlier, I had nearly killed Darla over a trivial matter. Something was wrong. The more I thought about it, the more wrong it felt. I had snapped at Moira earlier in the day, and I'd been unusually aggressive with Goff. Admittedly I was under a lot of pressure, but that's nothing new and I'd never reacted this way before. Something was different.

The only thing that had changed about me was that I was carrying half of a magical artifact which had been involved in a rather unpleasant murder. I hadn't done anything to activate its powers – not that I knew of. Was it still functioning under the influence of its former owner? Or the killer? Or under its own power? I wasn't sure, and until I knew better, I decided that it might be best not to carry it with me unless I absolutely had to.

I hung it inside a lampshade where it couldn't easily be seen.

I had vowed not to check my messages until morning, but there was only one and it blinked at me accusingly until I played it. "Dash. Give me a call, will you?' It's important. You have my number." The caller hadn't identified herself, but I would have known that husky voice anywhere. Mickey Rusk from Darke Investigations. She wasn't prone to exaggeration.

I drank most of the beer very quickly, and began to feel a little better, but I'm not sure if it was the alcohol or the separation from the amulet. When my pulse had returned to something like normal, I looked up Mickey's number in my Rolodex. I got to actually hear a phone ring before it was answered. "Yes?"

"Mickey, it's me. Dash. I just heard your message."

"No, you didn't. I never called you and this conversation is just a figment of your overactive imagination. And you're going to erase your tape as soon as you hang up. Are we clear on that?"

I'd been geared up for banter but I shifted down to serious. "I haven't had a call all day and this is just a dream. What's up, Mickey?"

"I want to pass on a little bit of information and I don't want it to get back to the agency. You've always been square with me and I haven't forgotten that you talked Darke into giving me a chance."

"That was a long time ago."

"Don't talk. Just listen. You and I both know that Darke has ears everywhere. Well, your name came up and I just happened to hear part of it, enough to know you've got trouble. Someone is very unhappy with you and wants you to drop one of your cases."

"I know. Herman Goff has been trying to chase me off all week."

"Goff is an errand boy, an irritation. He'll get in your face and make vague threats, but he won't follow through. Goff lost his courage a couple of years back and now he just gets by on his looks and reputation."

"Still, someone must have hired him. He wouldn't come after me just for the practice."

"I don't know who's paying him, but I think Darke suspects someone powerful. And he wants nothing to do with it. I've never seen him this way." For a moment, Mickey sounded almost awed. "Forget Goff. There's a major player in the game and whoever it is has raised the stakes. They want you out of the way bad enough to pay for a Berserker."

That got my attention. The term "tank demon" is a misnomer. They're actually imps rather than demons, they don't have any actual ego or self awareness and they're technically not even evil. They're just very powerful, very dangerous natural forces that don't happen to have physical bodies. We don't have "real" demons, unless that's what's living in the Tuilleries. Human ingenuity being what it is, however, it was possible to conjure up a pretty fair substitute, fortunately only if you were very, very skilled. The ceremony involved a human sacrifice, which obviously made it illegal right from the outset. The victim's body would be preserved as a zombie while it was being infused with the spirit of an imp, which would likewise perish in the process, but its essence became concentrated and biddable. The resulting Berserker had limited intelligence leftover fom its human origin and could be compelled to follow simple instructions from its maker.

"I don't suppose you could give me a hint about where this information comes from?"

"I've told you everything I know. Darke was poking around a little because he thinks it might have something to do with the ritual killings, but he dropped both investigations today, told me he was

reassigning me. I think something's going on that has him nervous.
I've never known him to be this passive when there's trouble
brewing. He's usually right there mapping out ways to turn a profit
from it."

"Great. Anything else you'd like to share?"

"Isn't that enough?"

"Yeah, I guess it is. Thanks, Mickey. I owe you."

So much for my plans to go to bed early. I went back to my
Rolodex and found Marie Dussaud's number. She let it ring a couple
of times before answering, but greeted me by name before I'd had a
chance to speak. I hate it when they do that.

"What can I do for you?"

"I'm sorry to disturb you at home, Marie, but it's kind of an
emergency."

"I don't need to be psychic to know that, Dash. You never
call me except when it's an emergency. What is it this time?"

I gave her an edited version of what Mickey had just told me.
She was silent for so long that I wondered if the connection had been
broken.

"You certainly do know how to make enemies," she said at
last. "You'd better come right over. And be careful. If there's a
Berserker after you, it won't necessarily wait to catch you alone. The
only thing they see is their target."

I risked a ticket on the way to Paris, but I figured speed was
more important than caution. Marie had a small chateau in a very
exclusive part of the city, with a winding driveway flanked by trees
so nearly identical that they looked artificial. She opened the door as
I came up the short staircase and gestured me inside.

"You're safe in here. The whole house is warded. I've made a
few enemies myself, I'm afraid."

Most of the interior was dark and Marie ushered me
immediately into what she called her reading room, although it
looked more like a small library. There was a heavy, oversized
mahogany table in the center of the room, at one end of which a
dark, octagonal disc lay on a rectangular silver platter.

"I don't suppose you wear a chain of your own?"

I followed her to the table. "No, I've never trusted good luck
charms. It's too easy to get around them. I've always preferred to rely
on my wits when there's trouble."

"I'm amazed you've survived this long." She wasn't looking at me. She had picked up the octagonal charm and was rubbing it between her thumb and forefinger. "You can carry this in your breast pocket if you prefer. The closer it is to your heart the better. Its protective power only lasts for a limited amount of time but you can extend that by letting it take a little of your life force."

She handed the charm to me and I almost dropped it. Although it looked like a piece of flint or quartz, the texture was softer, yielding, and it was warm to the touch. It felt almost like living flesh."

"What is it?"

"When a zombie is created, the body's heart stops beating. It is commonly believed that the soul is gone, but that's partly a misconception. Until the body itself dies, the soul can never be completely free. It is anchored to it by what you might think of as a spiritual thread. Part of the source of a Berserker's rage is jealousy of the living, and a beating heart is the most obvious symbol of what has been lost."

"So how do I kill it?"

She shook her head. "The Berserker is limited by the zombie body, but zombies themselves are hard to destroy. You can't poison them or shoot them or make them bleed, they can't drown and they don't need to breathe. "

"How about fire?"

"That might work, but you'd have to burn the brain to ash before it would stop sending signals to the body. Your best bet would be to cut its head off. The body should just stop then and eventually the life force will run out. You'd still have to be careful of the head though. It will remain alive until the brain stops functioning or the term of the incantation expires. A zombie bite will become infected, almost by definition."

I turned the charm over in my hand. It looked the same on the reverse as the front. "Can I use this to destroy it?"

"No. If the Berserker finds you - make that when the Berserker finds you - just show it the charm. If I've imbued it properly, it should capture the full attention of the remaining conscious mind almost instantly and mesmerize it. Just keep it in close proximity. Your best bet would be to put it inside the zombie's mouth."

Just what I wanted to do. Stick my hand between the jaws of an animated corpse. "And what if you haven't imbued it properly?"

She shrugged. "Then you'll be dead. But don't worry. My charms almost always work."

"That makes me feel much better."

"One possible alternative is to find the person responsible and get them to call it off."

"That'd be fine if I had any idea who that person might be. There are probably twenty or thirty in Port-Au-Prince alone who could create a zombie in their sleep."

Marie shook her head. "This isn't an ordinary zombie, remember? It's carrying a Berserker. That means that whoever created it is someone with unusual talent even for an adept. It also requires a lot of effort so this isn't just a casual enemy. Whoever it is doesn't like you very much."

"That narrows the field from humungous to simply colossal."

"One other thing. If you do manage to cut off its head, bring it back here to me. The head I mean."

"And I'd be doing this why?"

"Because if it's intact and animate, I should be able to talk to it."

"You must really be lonely, Marie."

"I know the wiseacre stuff is your defense against fear, Dash, but it's really annoying."

"All right. But why do you want to talk to the head?" There's a sentence you don't say every day.

"Because there's a good chance I can get it to tell us something about why it was created."

"And who was responsible?" That sounded promising, assuming I could accomplish the simple task of cutting off the head of a zombie possessed by a demon while it was presumably attempting to rip mine off for reasons of its own.

Marie was shaking her head. "It's very unlikely the conjurer would confide their identity to a Berserker. But it might give us a hint or two."

"I'll see what I can do."

I actually did feel somewhat more at ease on the way home. I had forgotten to put the outside lights on, so I parked as close to the door as possible. I usually keep a flashlight in the glove compartment but I hadn't replaced the one that the scarabs had eaten, so I left the headlights on for a minute or so and studied the shadows.

One of them moved. I almost jumped out of my skin and I was shifting into gear and preparing to burn rubber getting away when a familiar figure stepped into the cone of light in front of the Studebaker. It was Sheri Connors.

I killed the lights and the engine and got out. "Hello, Dash," she said softly, then swayed. I thought she was going to fall and jumped forward to catch her but she straightened up and shook her head. "I'm okay. I had a few drinks earlier and I'm not used to it."

"What are you doing here, Sheri?"

"I don't know exactly, but I needed to talk to someone and your name came up. Could we go inside?"

What do you say when an attractive woman shows up at your house in the middle of the night acting vulnerable, even if you do have a killer zombie on your trail? I invited her in. "Can I get you some coffee?"

"That would be nice."

I put the pot on and prowled the house, double checking that the windows were still bolted, the back door locked. I was under no illusion that my precautions would prevent a Berserker from entering, but at least it would have to make a lot of noise and give us a chance to run.

The coffee was ready and I carried two cups on a tray with sugar and milk. "I don't have any cream," I explained.

Sheri took one of the cups. "It's okay. I prefer it black." She proved it by drinking half a cup immediately, even though it was scalding hot.

"Are you ready to talk about it?" I asked. Whatever "it" was.

"I'm sorry. I have no right to unload on you like this. Maybe I should just go." She made no move to rise though.

"How did you get here anyway?"

"My car is parked at the corner."

"No, I mean how did you find me? I don't advertise my address." Not that it prevented the banshee from finding me.

She smiled tentatively. "I told you my father used to be a cop. I still have some connections."

"Okay, that covers the how. What about the why?"

All trace of the smile evaporated and she suddenly looked much younger. "My mom died while I was just a kid and Dad never remarried. He raised me as best he could, and considering his situation, I think he did a pretty good job. One thing he always told me was that I had to be tough if I was going to get anywhere. The whole never let them see you sweat thing."

I nodded sympathetically. "You're working in a field where appearances are important. But you have to be able to separate your job from your private life."

She laughed unpleasantly. "What private life? When I'm not at work, I'm on call. I have no time for hobbies, I haven't taken a vacation since I started at the Baker's Dozen, and the last guy I dated was months ago. That ended badly."

I could sympathize with that. Katrina was the third woman to live with me, and she'd lasted the longest, almost six months. "Maybe you need to put some space between yourself and your job. You're an intelligent and attractive woman, Sheri. You probably just need to let people see who you really are."

She had been sitting with her head bowed forward over the coffee, but now she turned to face me, her eyes glittering. "That's just it, Dash. I don't know who I am. I thought I did, but I was wrong. My first lover turned out to be a peeping Tom and my second dumped me for a woman who treated him like dirt." She had begun to cry.

I'm not good at this sort of thing, but I couldn't just sit there. I moved over to the couch and sat beside her. "That's not even three strikes, kid. I've been made a fool of that many times in a single day."

Although I have a pretty clear memory of what happened after that, I'm not going to share it with you. Suffice it to say that she broke down a little, I comforted her, we didn't talk much, and a few minutes later I was shoving all the magazines off one side of the bed to make room for her. Not that she used that side very much.

When I woke up in the morning, she was already gone. I was blissfully replaying the previous night's encounter in my mind when I realized she couldn't have reset the locks when she left. A moment later, completely naked, I was securing the bolt and doing a hasty check to make certain that I was alone in the house. Darla, apparently having forgiven me, demanded to be fed.

During the drive to the office, I briefly considered not telling Moira about the Berserker in order to avoid alarming her. I ultimately rejected the idea because if a lumbering corpse showed up at the office looking for me, it was probably a good idea that she be aware of the situation. Besides, I'd gotten in the habit of confiding in her and it would have felt dishonest to do otherwise now.

As it turned out, I wouldn't have been able to carry off a deception if I'd tried. Moira sensed the protective charm the moment I arrived. "What in the world have you done to your aura?" Without waiting for an answer, she walked right up to me and reached inside my jacket, fumbling around in my pocket until she found what she was looking for. "Aha! And what is this supposed to do, boss?"

I didn't mention Mickey's name, but I told her about the late night tip and my visit to Marie Dussaud.

"What have you gotten us into this time, Dash?"

"I really don't know. It doesn't look to me as though I've accomplished enough to deserve this kind of attention. Maybe I'm closer to a solution than I think."

"But which solution?"

"An excellent question."

I poured my own cup of coffee for a change and perched myself on the corner of Moira's desk. "I thought I had a jump on the Porter murder, but now that Evan Garner is dead, I don't know much more than the Police, maybe even less. I'm certainly not close to finding the killer. Everything I know about Ruth Deacon has been passed on to her sister, and I still have no more idea what is going on at the Lagos Castle or why than I did when Morris first called."

"Which leaves just the ritual killings."

I nodded. "If I'm the only one who knows about the amulets, then it might make sense to eliminate me before I pass the information along."

"Who knows that you're interested in them?"

"Too many people to be useful. There's Sergeant Kennedy in Hyannis, the guy in Burford's office, the owner of the studio where Ruth Deacon sold her work, Jessica Crane, Ruth Deacon, Morris Ngambe, and Wanda Veil, to name a few. And Wanda showed it to some of her friends."

"You could let it be known that you're no longer interested in the case."

"I think we're past the point where that would help. There's something else I should tell you." I repeated what Mickey had told me about Goff. "So if he's working for someone else, that's two different cases I'm supposed to drop."

"Or two different people want you to drop the same case, maybe for different reasons."

"My brain hurts. Let's not worry about this right now."

Half an hour later the telephone rang. It was Detective Colby of the Toronto Police. "You wanted to know how Evan Garner died, Mr. Dash. I have the autopsy results in front of me right now."

"I appreciate your taking the time to call me, Detective." I was actually mildly surprised. It was highly unusual for the authorities to volunteer information to private operatives.

"Let's just say that I'm a man of my word. And I hope the same is true in your case. We do have an agreement, don't we? About sharing information?"

"Absolutely."

"Well then, the victim died as the result of asphyxiation."

"He was smothered?"

"No, his windpipe was crushed. It wasn't a manual strangulation. The coroner believes that he received one blow across the throat, possibly a padded weapon of some sort. Someone trained in martial arts could have done it bare handed."

"I don't remember seeing any restraint marks on his wrists or ankles. No defensive injuries either."

"The coroner didn't find anything suggesting a struggle. But he did confirm that Garner was not killed in the shed, as we suspected."

"So Garner was just dumped in your backyard."

"That's how it looks to us."

"How about the scryopsy?"

"The body was too far gone. Not even a glimmer."

"Did our mysterious visitor ever get identified? The one who tracked snow on your crime scene?"

"No, we're not done canvassing the area, but I still think it was a vagrant or a kid who stumbled onto the body and took off. There wouldn't be any reason for the killer to make a second trip."

"Might have lost something and come back looking for it."

"Maybe." He didn't sound enthusiastic. I didn't blame him. "Anything else?"

"No, it's your turn. What's the significance of the amulet he was wearing? Our experts tell us that it's nothing they've ever seen before."

I had to give him something, but if I told him that Steven Sandobhal had a similar one, they'd want to look at it, and they'd find a completely spent and now innocuous charm in the evidence bag where it should have been resting in Hyannis.

"You know that Garner was hooked up with Mayor Porter?"

"Old news. We're already assuming that the two murders are connected."

"Someone planted a hidden camera in one of the rooms at the Baker's Dozen. It was in use the night she died, but the cassette is missing."

"Which is why you asked about one the night we found the body."

"Right. I think the killer, possibly the murder itself, was recorded on that tape."

He digested that for a few seconds. "You didn't answer my question about the amulet?"

"I don't know what they're for either, Detective, but I think it would be very interesting to find out who has the other half of that heart."

"All right, thanks. If you find out anything..."

"I'll let you know. I promise. Oh, one more thing. What was the time of death on Garner."

He told me and I blinked but I just thanked him and hung up. The medical examiner hadn't been able to establish an accurate TOD because of the freezing weather conditions, but the scryopsy had determined that Evan Garner's death had occurred with a few hours of Mayor Porter's demise. I wasn't really surprised but it still left me thoughtful.

The next item on my agenda for the day was not something I was looking forward to. I called the Baker's Dozen myself, asked to speak to Sheri Connors. She answered in cool, professional tones that thawed slightly when I identified myself.

"We need to talk."

"All right. Do you want to meet someplace else?"

"No, I'll be there in an hour or so."

Moira had only heard my side of the conversation but she'd picked up on my mood. "Is something wrong? I thought you liked her."

"Let's just say we need to clarify a few things." My problems with Sheri Connors were personal and I didn't feel any temptation to discuss them with Moira. Particularly after last night. But sympathetic as I might be toward Sheri, she hadn't been entirely honest with me and I had to confront her with what I knew now, before my emotions became so involved that my judgment might be suspect.

A water main had broken in Manhattan and a bunch of kids who must have come up from the Raj were playing in the spray, but this time the delay worked to my advantage, reducing the inflow of traffic from the south. I made much better time to Boston and arrived with half an hour to spare even though I had to detour around a demonstration by the ayatollahs on the border with Tehran. The Shah's troops looked very frustrated because they couldn't arrest the demonstrators, who were very careful to remain on the Boston side of the line of demarcation. Eventually the Boston Police would chase them back to Paris, and the Shah would lodge a pro forma protest that would be ignored by the rest of the Mayors.

The young man on duty at the front desk was the same one who'd been there during my first visit, and since he'd been helpful then I decided to see if he might be willing to talk freely again.

I waited until he was done assisting an elderly couple, then approached casually, waiting for him to notice me. "Good morning, Mr. Dash. I was told to watch for you. Let me call." He reached for the desk phone but I put a hand on his wrist.

"No, hold off for a minute. I'm early and I don't want to disturb her. I need some background for my report though and I wondered if you could help."

He managed to look flustered and pleased simultaneously. "Well if there's anything I can do, of course, I'll be glad to."

I hadn't caught his name before but he was wearing a tag on his jacket pocket. "Thank you, Dennis. Have you worked here long?"

"Almost five years now, but only at this desk for the past two. I was in Special Services before that."

"So you must know Sheri Connors pretty well."

He looked a bit less certain now. "She came to us three years ago. But I don't have much to do with her department in the normal course of things."

"No, but I'm sure you've heard a lot about her from your fellow workers."

"I prefer not to listen to casual gossip, Mr. Dash." His face hardened slightly and I realized that I wasn't going to get very far this way.

"And you shouldn't. I'm sorry if that's what you thought I was getting at, Dennis. I just wanted to know if she was well thought of, whether or not people would be inclined to be cooperative when she asked. She's a very professional person and sometimes people misinterpret that as unfriendliness."

He relaxed, but not all the way. "She is rather cool a times. But I imagine she's under a lot of stress. It's no secret that she has to walk the line between providing security and not inconveniencing guests who, well, who aren't always living up to the standards they might elsewhere."

"Exactly. So is she popular among the staff?"

I thought he was going to balk because he was silent for so long, but apparently he'd just been thinking. "I find it very difficult to say, Mr. Dash. I've never heard any serious criticism of her, and she appears to treat her people fairly. But I've also never heard anyone say they particularly liked her either. She's distant, never quite connects with you. But I imagine that's an asset in her position."

"Yes, it probably is." This wasn't going anywhere, so I switched directions. "I suppose you get a lot of repeat customers."

"Oh yes, we have a very loyal clientele. We offer something that is available no place else in the Cities, you see."

"Immunity from magic."

He nodded. "Our meeting rooms are booked months in advance. It's so reassuring to know that there aren't any spirit walkers listening in. No one can use persuasiveness spells or luck charms or anything else that might affect negotiations."

It was also a perfect location for clandestine trysts, but the hotel would hardly advertise that. At least publicly. "Evan Garner was one of your regulars, wasn't he?"

"Oh yes. We'll miss him here. He stayed with us once or twice a month without fail. The staff was very sorry to hear of his death. He was a very generous person." Big tipper, I translated.

"Quite the ladies' man, I understand." I winked to indicate this was just talk among us guys, but Dennis surprised me.

"Not really. We do have a number of gentlemen who value discretion, of course, but Mr. Garner was a quiet man who kept to himself most of the time. As far as I know he never entertained lady guests in his room until just recently, when he met Mayor Porter."

"How long ago was that?"

"Only a few weeks. At least that's the first time we saw them together here. They had separate rooms, of course, but it was common knowledge that they were involved. If it had been anywhere else, I would have been convinced that she'd used a love potion on him. I don't think I've ever seen a man so captivated by a woman."

I would have continued the conversation, but just then I was hailed by Sheri Connors, who had emerged from an elevator.

"Dash! You're early. I was coming down to wait for you."

Her voice was pleasant but she was clearly suspicious. My first inclination was to make some offhand comment about having just asked the clerk to call her office, but then I remembered why I had come here and I decided not to bother. Last night notwithstanding, it was her turn to be on the defensive.

"Why don't we go up to your office? I need to talk to you about a few things."

Neither of us spoke on the way and something of my mood must have translated itself subliminally, because when she closed the door behind us, I could tell that she was going to play this cool and professional. Or at least that's what she thought she was going to do. I had other plans for the nature of our conversation.

"You left without saying goodbye."

She didn't smile. "It was very early. I needed to shower and change before first shift today and I figured you needed your sleep."

"I'm sorry to have to be so blunt this morning, but I've been doing a little checking into the Hayden kid's background and I have some questions we need to deal with."

She blinked but her expression was otherwise unaltered. "I thought you'd decided he was just in the wrong place at the wrong time."

"Oh, I don't think he murdered Mayor Porter. I gather he's no longer employed here."

"No. Under the circumstances, there was no way we could keep him on."

"I understand you helped him get his job here in the first place."

For just a second, I thought I saw a hint of apprehension if not actual fear. Connors was too savvy to miss the fact that I was laying the groundwork for something. "I didn't think he should suffer just because his brother was a criminal. If I'd had any idea that they shared this particular common interest, I would never have approved his application."

"You knew his brother personally, didn't you?"

Connors was silent and her lips had thinned. There was no hint of friendliness in her face or her voice now. "I wasn't aware that I was part of your investigation, Mr. Dash." I could see that we weren't going to be sharing another bed any time soon. It bothered me a little, but I had to push on.

"Everyone is part of my investigation until I'm satisfied they shouldn't be. And you didn't answer my question."

I'll give her credit. She was obviously fuming under the surface, but she let very little of it show. There was an awkwardly long pause. "I was Paul Hayden's lover for about three months. He was my first, the peeping Tom. I was inexperienced and vulnerable and blind to just about everything else in the world. We met here in the hotel, when he was working on the electrical upgrade. He was very charming, very good looking, and I guess I was ripe for the picking. I suppose I should have suspected something right from the start because he was always asking questions about my job, how things worked in security, that sort of thing. But I was in love, or thought I was, and I probably wasn't paying as much attention as I should have been."

"So you looked the other way."

"No! Never! If I had had any idea what he was up to, I would have done something about it."

"Did Paul show you the tapes from the geisha house?"

I had wanted to catch her off balance but if I had, she wasn't going to give me the satisfaction of seeing it. "You've been talking to his brother, haven't you?"

"He came to me. He seemed to think that you owed him better treatment, since he was concealing the fact that you were his brother's de facto accomplice."

That blow did strike home. She actually flinched. When she finally answered, her voice dripped ice. "Did it ever occur to you to ask how the geisha house found out about the cameras?"

I had the sudden sinking feeling that I'd just missed a step on the staircase and was about to lose my balance. Although I only hesitated for a second, Connors quickly regained the initiative. "If you had bothered, you would have found out that they were tipped off anonymously. When Paul showed me those tapes, he caught be completely by surprise. I thought I was in love with him and here was this entirely new personality revealing itself to me. It was only afterwards, when I was alone, that I realized that he'd shown me the tape precisely so that he would have something to hold over my head. So I called my counterpart at the geisha house and told him where to look for the cameras."

"Does Hayden – either of them – know you turned Paul in?"

She shook her head. "I doubt it. Paul might have suspected, but probably not. He's got quite an ego. I don't think it would ever occur to him that a woman he had charmed could turn on him. If it's necessary to clear my name, I'll go public. I taped the telephone conversation, and I'm sure Marimoto at the geisha house will confirm my story."

"But despite that, you helped his brother get a job at the Baker's Dozen?"

"I had no reason to think it was a family business. Chris had a clean record and he's good at what he was hired to do."

"You might have told me this sooner." I was trying to find an anchor spot on a slippery slope now. In my line of business, I often feel like a bully. Sometimes it's the only way to get the information I need. Few people die because of hurt feelings. It's not my favorite part of the job.

"If I had known it was relevant, I might have." Some of the anger had subsided, but I could still see my metaphorical breath in the room. I was pretty sure I wasn't going to be getting any more dinner invitations from Sheri Connors, let alone secretive night time visits. I felt a pang of regret. A big one. "Why the interest in the Hayden brothers anyway? You don't think Chris knows more than he's told us, do you?"

"I haven't ruled that out. I told you that I was thorough. You should have anticipated that this would come out eventually." It sounded defensive even as I said it, but I couldn't think of anything better. "It always seems worse when someone else brings it up."

"Then are you satisfied now?"

I might have mended fences a little then, but someone had conjured a demonically possessed zombie to chase after me, I wasn't making much progress in figuring out what was going on, and I'd just had yet another potential break prove useless. If Connors wanted to stay mad, then so be it.

"For the time being."

I wasn't there much longer. We talked about Evan Garner's murder for a while, but she had no suggestions to make that hadn't already occurred to me, and it was pretty obvious she wanted me to leave. The Police hadn't spoken to her during the past two days, but she didn't seem to care. "At this point, management would be happy if the case was never solved. An arrest and a high profile trial would just remind people of what happened."

"And what about you?"

She gave me a measured, almost clinically neutral look. "I wouldn't mind at all if you told me you were dropping the case and walked out the door."

I stood up. "Well, I can satisfy half of that." And I left.

The hotel had a bar and I stopped for a drink. There was a woman on duty, a tall Hispanic from Sao Paolo who looked as though she could have filled in for the bouncer, although her expression was pleasant and her voice surprisingly soft and low. She spoke good English and she told me she'd left Sao Paolo because of the depressed economy. "The best jobs are all reserved for the wealthy families." Apparently it didn't occur to her that a hotel bartending position didn't have much upward mobility either. I sat at the extreme end of the bar and ordered a beer, glancing around by habit to check out the other patrons. It was early, but there were several couples seated at tables, one group of whom were making a disproportionate amount of noise, and about half of the seats at the bar were filled, mostly by men.

The bartender returned with my drink, the mug looking almost dainty in her oversized hand. Incongruously, she was wearing a very delicate charm bracelet decorated with the signs of the zodiac. A memory stirred but when I tried to focus, it slipped away, so I drank some of the beer instead. Either the alcohol helped, or the memory wasn't as thoroughly buried as it might have been, because a minute later I was pulling my collection of photographs out of my pocket and shuffling through them. When I found the one I wanted, I brought it up close to my face.

There was Steven Sandobhal, looking as though he might be listening to an important conversation. Across from him was the woman I'd been unable to identify. Her hair was done up in a bun so I couldn't tell how long it was and the photograph was black and white, so I couldn't be positive about its color, but it was clearly light, probably blonde or a very fair brunette. Her raised arm obscured almost her entire face and there was nothing in her clothes or posture to suggest that I'd ever seen her before.

But her other hand, the one that dangled near her hip, was visible as well, and she was wearing something on her wrist. It was a charm bracelet, a heavy one. I had seen it before, or one very much like it. Unless I was very much mistaken, the young woman talking to Steven Sandobhal was Carly, Jessica Crane's assistant at the Lagos Castle gift shop.

Whenever a surprising new element appears in a puzzle, it casts doubt on the previous arrangement of the pieces, even those that seemed to fit together nicely. I'm not sure just how long I sat there thinking furiously, but when I finally got around to drinking some more beer, it was almost at room temperature. I had forgotten that magic didn't work at the Baker's Dozen. The mugs didn't stay chilled indefinitely.

I left a generous tip and stood up, still unsettled. There was always the chance that this meant nothing, of course. They were standing in front of the Lagos Castle and Carly worked there. This might have been a casual encounter between strangers. But it didn't feel right. My first impulse was to talk to Carly, but I would need to be circumspect. It might be better right now if she didn't know just yet that I was aware of the connection.

CHAPTER TWELVE

My first impulse was to rush directly to the Lagos Castle and I even drove partway there before I decided not to be so hasty. I took the next right and made my way back across town to the office. The door was locked and a little bird materialized and perched on my shoulder, chirping its message into my ear, then vanished in a puff of smoke. Moira had gone out to run an errand and would be back soon.

I let myself in and spent several minutes paging through the case files in the outer office, looking for some connection that might not already have occurred to me. When Moira returned a few minutes later she found me sitting at her desk.

"You aren't messing up those files I just put in order, are you?"

I shook my head, too preoccupied for the usual banter. "I just had a little epiphany. I'm hoping for a bigger one."

She dropped down into one of the visitor's chairs and crossed her legs. Quite nice legs as a matter of fact. "Anything you'd care to share?"

I pushed the photograph across the desk. "The woman in that picture works for Morris Ngambe."

Moira leaned forward, peering down at the picture. "And you know this how?"

"The bracelet. I saw her wearing it in the gift shop the other day. She runs the cash register and she's been studying magic."

"And I gather she knows, or knew Sandobhal."

"So it appears. I've used up my quota of coincidences on this case, Moira. This has to be significant."

"Could she be the person causing Morris' problems as well?"

"It's not impossible. She's not senior staff and I'm not sure how easy it would be for her to gain access to the kitchens, for example, but it's the closest I've come to having a genuine suspect. If she's as clever as I think she is, she'd find a way around most obstacles. Maybe they were practice for something more powerful."

"Does she have a connection to the ritual murders?"

"I haven't found one yet, but that doesn't mean it isn't there. And if I find one, it might also suggest that she's involved with the

Porter and Garner murders and Ruth Deacon's disappearance. Which could mean that she's the one who's been warning me off." I didn't add that she might also be responsible for creating the Berserker which was presumably somewhere out there looking for me. Nor did I mention the one flaw in my argument. Mickey Rusk had said that Darke knew or suspected who was harassing me and that it had given him pause. I couldn't see him worrying about a would-be sorceress, no matter how gifted she might be. "Where are my notes on the Deacon case, incidentally? They weren't in the file cabinet."

"Aren't they still on your desk? You told me to leave them when I took the others away."

"Right!" I stood up. "I kept your seat warm for you."

The moment I opened the inner door separating our offices, I knew something was wrong. I'm not the neatest guy in the world, but Moira picks up after me and my clients never recoil in shock when they see my desk. But that's exactly what I did.

The floor was covered with debris, torn papers mostly, but torn furniture as well. My swivel chair was lying against the right wall and the left wall as well. Part of it was also sitting on the desk. I had put up some framed pictures, inexpensive prints, and they'd been replaced by jagged cracks where something had struck with enough force to split the paneling and shatter plaster. My desk was in its usual place, but it was upside down and three of the four legs had been broken off. I kept a small but rugged safe in one corner; it was lying on its side with the door so misshapen that I knew I would need an acetylene torch to get to the contents, which unfortunately included my revolver and ammunition.

"What's wrong?"

Moira had come in behind me and she gasped in shock when she saw the carnage.

"Stay back," I ordered, slowly inching forward so that I could look around. There really wasn't any place for an assailant to hide unless he was crouched in the small corridor that led to my private entrance. "How long were you gone?"

"Twenty minutes or so. It wasn't like this then. I looked in here just before I left."

"Stay where you are and if you hear anything funny, I want you to head right to the stairwell. Don't use the levitators."

"What are you going to do?"

"I'm going to find out if our guest is still here."

The last thing in the world I wanted to do just then was walk across the wreckage of my office and look around the corner into the corridor. If this was the Berserker's work, and it sure looked like it, then my charm was supposed to protect me. I knew that intellectually, but my gut told me I was going to end up in as many pieces as my desk if I didn't turn and run away right now. Even if I was willing to do that in front of Moira, and I wasn't, I was beginning to feel as much anger as fear. This was my place, after all.

The corridor proved to be empty. At the far end, the door to the hall hung oddly from its nearly severed hinges. I'd need to get that fixed before Abe Chertoff found out about it. There was currently a shortage of office space in this part of Manhattan and he could find a new tenant effortlessly. The plague of squirmy illusions had used up most of the tenuous good will I had accumulated.

Despite what I'd said, Moira was in my office, sifting through the scattered papers, sorting them into stacks. "I think most of this is salvageable," she said quietly. "But you're going to need new furniture."

"And a new door."

"What happened here, Dash? What were they looking for?"

"Me, most likely." But it might have been Moira who would have borne the brunt of the attack. The Berserker concentrated on the target it had been assigned, but no one who got in the way, intentionally or otherwise, was safe. "I think it might be a good idea for you to go home for a while. Call Isaac and ask him to fix the door. The rest can wait until we have things resolved. I'll use your office for the time being."

Moira stood up and turned to face me, her hands on her hips, her expression grim. "I won't be run off any more than you will, Dash."

I recognized that tone. Although I was still determined to keep Moira out of the way, I knew it would do no good to press the issue now. Better perhaps that I just stay away from her for the next day or two. Berserkers were psychically drawn toward their prey but since the higher functions of the brain were displaced by a mystical compulsion, the clarity of its perceptions would come and go. "All right, but be careful." I looked around at the wreckage. "I can't do much useful here right now. I'll call you as soon as I know anything."

"Where are you going?"

"To the Lagos Castle. I think it's time that Carly and I got better acquainted."

I approached the Studebaker cautiously. Like my office, it would reek of my aura and was a potential lure for the Berserker. A news vendor's cubicle half a block away provided a good vantage point, and I pretended to be reading the latest issue of the *London Times* while surreptitiously watching to see if anyone else was lurking in the area. The vendor, a dour looking Sikh, glanced at me suspiciously a couple of times but didn't say anything.

Zombies are dead, but if they are fresh enough and if you don't look too closely, they can pass for the living. Once I was satisfied that no one was lurking in the immediate vicinity, I walked briskly to the car, checked the back seat, and then unlocked the door, half expecting to find the steering wheel wrenched off and the brand new wiring ripped out. Everything seemed fine though, and a moment later I was on my way downtown.

The gift shop was moderately busy when I arrived. There'd been brief resistance when I tried to enter through the main door. Apparently my protective charm was unusual enough that it had taken a few seconds for the security system to recognize it as non-malevolent. Jessica Crane was running the cash register and a tall, skinny young man with a plastic smile stood at her side, unenthusiastically stuffing purchases into bags. I pretended to be browsing as I checked out the rest of the shop, but Carly was nowhere to be seen, although she might well be in the stockroom. Jessica noticed me and waved a greeting, but it was obvious that she couldn't talk immediately.

I was getting impatient when the tide finally ebbed a bit. Jessica spoke briefly to her companion, whose smile slipped a little when they changed places, then walked around the end of the counter and came toward me.

"Sorry. We've been very busy today."

"So I see. I guess the rumors have died down."

She shook her head. "No, actually they were mentioned in one of the newspapers yesterday. Now we have thrill seekers wondering if they'll buy one of the contaminated charms." Her shoulders rose and fell dramatically. "I can't figure people sometimes. So what can I do for you today?"

"I was actually looking for Carly. Is she in the back?"

Jessica raised her eyebrows but otherwise showed no surprise. Then she shook her head. "No, in fact she called in sick today. That's why Frank there is helping. Or pretending to, anyway." She gestured toward the register. "Why the sudden interest in Carly?"

I wasn't sure how much I wanted to say, so I said as little as possible. "I have to start somewhere and since she works around magic, that makes her a logical suspect."

"Then I suppose I'm a suspect as well."

"Everyone who works here is a suspect," I said. "But some are more suspect than others. Can you tell me a little about her?"

She didn't appear to be amused, but she wasn't obviously offended either. "All right, what do you want to know?"

"Well first of all, could you tell me her full name and as much as you know about her background?"

"Yes, but there's not much to tell. Carlotta Pride, no middle. Twenty-two years old. Political science major at CCNY, dropped out after two years even though she had a generous scholarship. She told me she lost interest in mundane studies after taking an elective course in arcane theory, but the scholarship was major specific and untransferable. Parents deceased, no siblings. She inherited their house in Toronto but I'm pretty sure it's closed up. She lives here in the city. Has a good sized nest egg tucked away, enough that she probably doesn't need to work, but she's hoping to resume her schooling and become a licensed thaumaturgist, and that's not cheap. I hired her about a year back and I've had no complaints. This is the first time she's ever missed work. Fast learner, a bit socially awkward, sometimes quick tempered although she's never lost it around a customer."

"Where does she live locally?"

"Upper Manhattan, near the Washington border. Second floor flat, I believe. I haven't been there. I can give you the address."

"Outside interests? Friends? Hobbies?"

She shook her head. "I can't help you with any of that. Other than her fascination with thaumaturgy, I know very little about her private life. She's not secretive but she doesn't volunteer anything. I'm pretty sure she doesn't have a current boyfriend, but she was seeing someone regularly up until a month ago. I think they had a fight and broke it off."

"Would she have occasion to go into the restaurant? The restricted areas, I mean."

Jessica suddenly turned irritable. "Do you seriously think Carly is responsible for our recent problems?"

"I'm just doing my job. Even if I do nothing but eliminate her from consideration, that would be helpful."

"Carly is just a clerk. I think she may have gone on one of the new employee tours when she was first hired, but I very much doubt she's been in the restaurant since, unless she eats there. And she certainly didn't come to the infamous staff breakfast." Which didn't mean anything, since the spoiling spell could have included a time lapse.

She was starting to get defensive about her subordinate, an attitude I could understand. "She might have had a confederate." I shook my head as though dismissing the idea, although I wasn't. "Jessie, I'm just trying to be thorough."

She considered that for a few seconds. "I guess I understand. But you're wrong, Dash. Carly is a good person. She's been a great help to me, in more ways than one. I didn't tell you the whole story a while back."

No surprise that. At this point I didn't think anyone had been completely frank with me for quite some time. "About what specifically?"

"The Tuilleries. I told you the truth, but not all of it. There are buried memories that I never want to remember. I was sick for a long time after we crashed. The doctors couldn't find anything physically wrong and the spiritual healers talked about bruised auras and the other catch phrases they use when they don't understand exactly what's happening. For the first few months, I couldn't be around anything magic. Even a simple good luck charm could make me feverish. That wore off eventually, but I couldn't return to arcane research. It was just too wearing."

"But now you're selling charms and other incunabula."

"It was a compromise. I've never had any arcane talents myself, but there was no way to avoid all contact with magic short of

moving to a Scientologist stockade or the Baker's Dozen or a
Mennonite community. And I'd studied the subject for eight years. It
was the thing I knew best. So when a psychic counselor
recommended that I find a way to face my problem without letting it
overwhelm me, magical retailing seemed ideal."

"Has it helped?"

"It didn't, not at first. For a long time I felt a constant sense of
dread, as though something internal was disturbed by the benevolent
magic that surrounded me." She turned away from me, blinking
rapidly. "I think I know why so many others on that expedition died
or killed themselves. Everyone else except Goff and the pilot had
some kind of magical talent. Maybe the effects were stronger for
them, so strong that they couldn't stand to live with it any longer.
Even someone as impervious as Goff must have been affected."

It was hard to imagine Herman Goff being tormented by self
doubt, but I suppose it was possible. "Are you still seeing a
counselor?"

"I was, until a little less than a year ago. That's when Carly
started working here. She was a godsend. I didn't think we were
going to get along at first because all she could talk about was the
practice of magic. Carly knew about my academic work and
whenever business was slow she'd ask me questions she'd been
saving up. I tried to put her off at first, but her enthusiasm was
contagious and I found it easier and easier to talk about things I
hadn't even been able to think about a few weeks earlier."

"Didn't you say she had some talent of her own?"

Crane nodded. "She's a natural born thaumaturgist and she
has lesser talent in other areas. With the proper training, I think she
could develop into a pretty good sorceress." She must have realized
what she was saying because her face changed and she continued
hastily. "But only with training. I can't believe she'd be capable of
anything very sophisticated on her own."

"Could she have been receiving additional instruction? From
someone else I mean?"

"I suppose it's possible." She looked as though she regretted
having been so forthcoming. "But I can't believe she'd misuse her
talent. About six weeks after she started here, she asked me to watch
her perform an incantation. Nothing fancy, just a Shining Path
charm, something like a guidespell. I was really nervous about it

because I hadn't been present at a conjuring since the accident and I didn't know how I would react. But right in the middle of the ceremony, I felt this surge of elation, as though something heavy and dark and unpleasant had been lifted from my shoulders and taken away. And ever since then, I've been at peace with myself and with magic. I've even been helping her with her studies."

I have a pretty good poker face and I didn't think Crane had any idea how her recital had affected my theories. Had something ethereal passed between the two women that night? Something not necessarily benevolent? Jessie seemed to have run out of story by then so I decided to shift gears, at least for the time being. I had some serious rethinking to do when I could steal a moment.

"I mentioned once that I was interested in one of your customers. A woman named Ruth Deacon."

"I remember the name because you asked about her, but I still have no recollection of the person herself."

"Is there any way that I could see a list of her purchases?"

She shook her head. "We don't take the names of people who pay in cash. If she had an account with us, it would be easy enough, but I checked last time and she doesn't."

"How about credit card purchases? She had a Cities Express card."

Jessica looked uncertain. "We do process all card purchases electronically. I suppose it's possible. Let's go back to my office."

We spent thirty minutes determining that it was not. Jessica knew even less about computers than I did, and neither of us was able to figure out a way to retrieve the information we wanted. "There's one other possibility. We could look at special orders."

"Is there likely to be much of anything there? I thought you sold most of your stuff right off the shelf."

She nodded. "That's true for most of the stock, but the more expensive charms and things have to be coded before use. If that wasn't the case, a prankster could activate everything we have on display and they'd be useless to anyone else. For the simpler charms, we activate the key at the register, but most of the expensive items require a more complicated initialization. That takes at least a day."

"Ruth Deacon had expensive tastes. It's worth a try."

I expected her to bring up a new file on the computer, but instead she brought me back out front. Frank was waiting on a customer, behind whom stood three more, and he flashed us a harried, hurt look that Jessica ignored. I tried to look supportive while she fished under the counter and took out a shoebox.

"Here it is."

"High tech, I gather."

"Not all information is worth computerizing," she replied. "Let's go over there."

"There" was a glass topped display case. Jessica took the lid off the box, revealing a row of index cards that nearly filled the interior. "We make up a card when the customer places the order, and we file it here when the merchandise is picked up. Carly is a compulsive organizer and she told me she was going to straighten these out, but I don't know if she ever got around to it." She began flipping through the cards too quickly for me to read them. "Great! She has them arranged by customer."

It only took a few more seconds to find what I wanted. Jessica took out a packet of about a dozen cards, each of which had "Deacon, R" printed in the upper left hand corner. She spread them out on the counter and I saw that they were indeed for a selection of magical charms, invocations, potions, and other incunabula. There was an odd symbol in the bottom right hand corner of each and every card.

"What's that?" I pointed.

"Carly's symbol. She calls it her totem. It looks like she waited on Miss Deacon every time she came in. No wonder I didn't recognize the name."

"Anything special about any of these?"

Jessica glanced through them again. "No. Most of them are weather charms. Didn't you say she was a photographer? That's not uncommon for them. And two of these are for short term luck, and this last one is designed to help augment natural persuasiveness. She must have wanted to talk someone into doing something."

There was something else very odd about that particular purchase, something that I didn't mention to Jessica. Each card bore two transaction dates, the date the item was ordered and the date it was picked up. The most recent purchase had been picked up the day before Ruth Deacon's sister came to see me, and two days after she had supposedly disappeared.

Ten minutes later, I was sitting in the Studebaker, with my head back and my eyes closed. Jessica had given me an index card with Carly's particulars on it, including her cell phone number and the addresses of both her apartment and her parents' house. There was considerable evidence of her involvement, but it was mostly superficial, nothing I could take to the authorities or my clients. I had a nagging feeling that even now things were not what they appeared to be and that someone had been lying to me. I was even pretty sure that I knew who it was. I'm not one for subtlety and my first inclination was direct confrontation, but my case was weak. There were other possible explanations, although they were moving from farfetched to are-you-kidding-me very quickly. I needed some more information, something that would keep the fish firmly on the hook.

The metaphor was an appropriate one, because in a manner of speaking I was about to go fishing. Traffic was heavy and it was mid-afternoon by the time I reached Paris, and once there I had trouble finding a parking space. The banks close early so I was getting mildly frantic when I spotted a Citroen easing away from a spot and slipped in behind it.

There were very few people in the bank. I recognized the young woman who came out to assure me that someone would be with me shortly. I searched my memory and for a change it was cooperative. "Excuse me. Aren't you Alice?"

She blinked and smiled. "Why yes, I am. Oh, I remember you. You were with Miss Deacon the last time she came, weren't you?"

"Yes, I was. She told me to ask for you if I needed help."

Alice looked vaguely uncertain now. "I actually don't work in that area any more. I was only filling in while Maxine was on holiday."

"That's all right. I just wanted to ask you a question about Miss Deacon's box."

She looked even more ill at ease. "We have to protect our client's confidentiality, sir. I'm sure you understand that I can't talk about our clients' business. And I really don't know anything anyway."

"Of course not. It's nothing like that. But Miss Deacon was trying to remember something that she thought you might be able to help her with, and since I was going to be in the area, I told her that I'd stop by and ask."

Alice relaxed, but only slightly. "I'll help if I can."

I smiled broadly, trying to keep things light and friendly. "Miss Deacon has a terrible memory, you see, and the previous time she came in, the time before I was with her I mean, she arranged to meet a friend exactly a week later. But she forgot what day that was and the friend is out of touch. She was hoping you might remember the date for us."

"Oh, is that all?" Alice was clearly greatly relieved. "That's no problem at all. I know because Maxine came back to work the very next morning, which means it was three days before the two of you came in."

"You're sure of that?" The words came out much more intensely than I had planned.

"Yes, of course I am." Alice had retreated a half step and was looking mildly offended.

I forced myself to relax and smiled at her. "Sorry. I had a bet with myself and I just lost. I was sure it was earlier than that."

We were friends again. Alice returned my smile and shook her head. "No, I'm quite positive. She was only there once before that, the day she rented the box in the first place, and that was more than a week ago. I believe she said she was moving her papers there from another bank."

"Well, thank you very much." I shook her hand. "Miss Deacon will be very pleased."

So either Ruth Deacon was not as disappeared as she seemed to be, or someone was indeed lying to me. Or both.

I reached into my pocket, pulled out the card of symbols I'd taken from Ruth Deacon's safety deposit box, flipped it over and looked again at the expiration date. Another little suspicion crept out of its hiding place. I didn't have all the answers yet, but the pattern was becoming increasingly clear. The ritual killings, Ruth's disappearance, Mayor Porter's murder, the disturbances at the Lagos Castle, they were all ripples spreading out from a single source, and they were all interconnected. I was filling in the blank spots pretty quickly now, but one element still eluded me. I didn't know from whence they were all radiating. But I had a suspect.

The day had gotten away from me. The streets were already layered with shadows and I saw a lattice weaver across the street as it crept out from beneath a sidewalk awning and began building its intricate web. I'd spent an hour once peering into the intricate patterns of one of those diaphanous constructions. Much of it consisted of swirling, interconnected patterns, but every so often you could find a remarkably accurate reproduction of something real, a street corner, a person, a building, all rendered in multi-colored thread so fine that the individual strands were not visible to the naked eye. The detail work was incredible. Some studies had suggested that these images were original creations, while others indicated they might be recreations of events the lattice weaver in question had witnessed. It was one of the many unanswered questions in our world. I wouldn't mind at all if one of the mysterious creatures showed me a tapestry that would answer even one of my many questions.

Moira would have closed up the office and gone home by now, unless she'd decided to stay late while the broken door was replaced. I felt a twinge of theoretical guilt. If that was the case, I'd owe her overtime on top of her back pay. I might as well give her a bonus as well, since I couldn't afford to pay anything, at least until Andrew Loing finally sent a check for the right amount. Then I could square things with her, more or less, with Chertoff and my other creditors, and maybe even have some left to replenish my seriously depleted emergency stash back at the house.

I headed uptown in moderate traffic, but I wasn't going to the office to check on Moira just now, no matter how guilty my conscience. I still needed answers and Carly Pride might have some of them. Jessica had given me her home address and sick or not, she was going to entertain a visitor.

I hadn't recognized the street name and wasn't impressed with the neighborhood. If Carly had a nest egg, it wasn't as sizeable as Jessica had implied, or she was hanging onto it at the expense of comfortable living. There was trash in the street, gang signs spray painted on the walls of her building, and a few windows were broken and taped. The rest were covered by shutters. I parked under a street light, the only one working on the entire block, and walked across to the lobby door. There was a buzzer, but it was out of order. No doorman, not even a troll. When I tried the door, it opened easily and I was inside a moment later.

The elevators were mechanical, not levitational, and they weren't working either. A row of small mailboxes was set into one wall, about half with the doors hanging open, displaying broken locks. Someone had urinated in one corner and there was debris everywhere. It took a few seconds to find the staircase, which wasn't marked. Someone had had a small party on the first landing, leaving behind empty bottles and used condoms. I exited on the second floor and found her room, which also had a broken buzzer. I knocked.

There was no answer and I knocked again, more forcefully. I pressed my ear against the door, but there was no sound from inside. I was the only one in the corridor, which was dimly lit and continued the trash and debris decor from the lobby. The lock was an old fashioned one; my charm key would open it unless she had a magical countercharm at work. Was it worth the risk? Probably not. But I was tired of being kept in the dark, figuratively as well as, at the moment, literally.

The door clicked open obediently and I was inside.

It took a few seconds to get used to the darkness. The curtains were drawn and the light switch just inside the door clicked cooperatively but with no effect. Once my eyes had adjusted, I saw that I was standing in what was probably intended to be a living room, but which was so filled with boxes and bags that it blocked my view of the rest of the apartment. The nearest contained books and scrolls, and beyond that I could see what appeared to be a professional quality seer's globe nested among other incunabula.

I sidled around the pile and crossed to the nearest window, pulling the curtain back. It was close to full dark outside, but a neon sign across the street helped. A perfunctory search confirmed that no one was home. The bed was neatly made and the kitchen was sanitary and orderly, but the rest of the apartment was a disaster area, so overcrowded that effective cleaning was virtually impossible. Most of the clutter was arcane related, and there was even a shelf full of codices – paperback reprints - in the bathroom. There was no sign of foul play or a hasty departure. Two battered suitcases sat in the closet, and nearly all the hangers were in use. There was fresh food in the refrigerator, along with an interesting variety of preserved animal parts, and a handful of loose change on her dresser.

Carly wasn't home, but I didn't think she'd gone far.

I had done a cursory search, but I didn't have a flashlight with me and didn't want to risk lighting the candles that were apparently her primary source of illumination. I was really more interested in talking to her than going through her belongings, which clearly tallied with Jessica's description of her obsession with magic. With a last look around to see if I'd missed anything obvious, I slipped back into the corridor.

Although my first instinct was to call it a night, I was still feeling guilty about Moira so I took a short detour so that I could stop by the office. The levitator was working today, so I rode up smoothly and without companionship. The security lights had come on but our building pretty much emptied out by five in the evening. Our floor was even quieter. The lawyers were often gone by three.

When I reached the office, I had a moment of complete disorientation. When I'd left, the private entrance door was mangled and off its hinges, but the front was fine. Now the back way in was secured by a shiny new door that didn't quite match the color of the hallway, but the front door was splintered and hanging open. I closed my hand over the charm Marie had given me and cautiously stepped inside.

I half expected to see a repeat of the chaos my private office had suffered earlier in the day, and half was about right. Two of the chairs were overturned, a floor lamp lay shattered, and Moira's desktop had been swept clean. Her inbox, pencil stand, telephone, and phone log were scattered across the floor. So was her shoulderbag.

Barely daring to breathe, I checked my office. Some order had been restored there, probably Moira's handiwork, but there was no sign of her. She would not have left without her bag, so I was forced to draw the worst possible conclusion. The Berserker had returned, still searching for me, and this time Moira had not been out running an errand. It shouldn't have hurt her if she'd just stayed out of its way, and the best possible scenario had her pursuing it to see if it would lead her back to its creator. But that wasn't Moira's style.

The Berserker must have taken her. But why?

CHAPTER THIRTEEN

You wouldn't think that it would be possible for a zombie, no matter how natural he looked, to carry a presumably unconscious or struggling woman out of an office building located on a major street and then disappear without attracting some attention, but that's apparently what happened. There was a nomadic news vendor from Adelaide right across from our entrance, and he seemed genuinely unaware that any such thing had happened near him. There was a back entrance, but it had both a conventional alarm and a magical one. I checked there as well, but couldn't see anything that suggested that either security system had been broached or circumvented, and in any case I doubted that a Berserker would have been subtle. That left the loading dock, which was also supposed to be secure, but which I found wide open, unguarded, and providing easy access to a quiet alley.

I was trying to decide what to do next when a shimmering, spherical object dropped down from overhead. I stepped back, expecting the raucous cry of a Summoning Sphere, but this one had been modified and delivered its message in emotionless, characterless tones. "If you ever want to see Miss McGann alive again, then stay away from the Lagos Castle."

The sphere then imploded with a little pop.

I'd been angry a time or two during the past ten days. I don't like being lied to, I resent having my office trashed, and someone had messed with my Studebaker. Anger can be a useful tool; it burns away the debilitating effects of irritability, it gets the adrenaline pumping and clears the mind. As a tool, I've found it to be very effective, in small doses, applied at the appropriate time. Fury is an extreme form of anger, but it edges over into another category entirely. Fury is uncontrolled and unproductive and of no use to a rational mind. Nonetheless, for the next several minutes, I understood the term "blind with rage". I hope the boxes stacked on the dock contained nothing fragile because I threw several of them around, and kicked a few more. When I finally ran out of steam, my clothes were sticky with sweat and I had a pounding headache. I think it was that pain that finally brought me back to myself.

I went back to the office and retrieved Moira's purse. Then I went to the antique shop a block away. The owner was an ex-client but he wasn't willing to extend credit to me until I let some of the fury seep back and then he was so happy to get me out of his store that he even gave me a discount. He'd offered to wrap my purchase, but I'd declined. The sword felt good in my hand, just the right weight. The edge could have been sharper, but I didn't think I'd have any trouble lopping off the zombie's head. Assuming that I could find it and orchestrate an opportunity.

I probably should have called first, but I was so focused on what I needed to do that I forgot the niceties. At least two alarms went off when I pounded on Marie Dussaud's door, but she quieted them and let me in. She was wearing a nightgown and looked only half awake.

"What's the matter, Dash? You look terrible."

"They've taken Moira." I held up my hands, shoulderbag in one, sword in the other. "It wasn't after me. It wanted her."

"Oh my God! How? When?" She opened the door wider and I pushed inside.

I filled her in. Marie was closer to Moira than she was to me. They went to lunch together regularly and in fact it was Moira who had introduced me to Marie back when I was first looking for a psychic consultant.

"Why would they go after Moira? Why not me?"

Marie gave me an odd look, then shook her head. "It doesn't matter. What matters is that we need to get her back."

"You think she's still alive then?"

"Probably. If someone wanted her dead, the zombie could have killed her in your office. As a hostage, they know they have something to hold over your head."

"Yeah, I get that. So what do I do?"

"Let me have her bag there." I did so and she emptied it out on the table top. It felt like I was invading Moira's privacy looking through her things, but I suppressed the feeling. This was an emergency and I would be only too happy to have the opportunity to apologize. Marie was examining what seemed to me a completely innocuous and unhelpful assortment – hair brush, mirror, lipstick, pens and pencils, tissues, some loose change, a pocket calendar and appointment book, a pair of ear-rings, a chocolate bar, a shamrock shaped locket that was probably a good luck charm, three or four barrettes, a folding umbrella, a crossword puzzle magazine, a pillbox, a paperback copy of *The Dali Code*, and a few small items that I didn't recognize.

"What are you looking for?" I asked.

"This!" Her face lit up as she found what at first appeared to be a piece of ivory but what was in fact a length of polished bone. Runes were inscribed along its length. "It's a scrimshaw charm. I gave it to her ages ago and I wasn't sure if she was still keeping it with her."

"Will that help us to find her?"

Some of her enthusiasm evaporated. "Maybe. That's not what it was intended for, but it might help. Come with me."

We sat down at another table, this one in a small alcove. There was a crystal bowl in the center and Marie dropped the piece of bone into it. Then she went to a cupboard, opened a narrow drawer, and returned with a second, virtually a twin of the first. "You know that Moira is fey, don't you?" She dropped the second piece of scrimshaw into the bowl.

I nodded. "But not enough for her to work professionally in that area. She can only read about half the people she meets, and gets only surface impressions even from them. And sometimes she can sense things before they happen."

"She's a latent. There's a lot of talent in her family. I've always thought she had the potential to be more than that, but I don't think she ever cared enough about it to be tested. About a year after we met, I talked her into trying an experiment. These are called Secret Sharers. The two pieces of bone are taken from the same specimen – in this case a Rhesus monkey – and marked with matching inscriptions. If you look closely, you'll see that one is the mirror image of the other, not a direct copy."

Marie was slipping into lecture mode and I made an impatient sound.

"Don't try to rush me, Dash. We need to let them get reacquainted. They've been separated for years."

"What are we trying to do here, Marie?"

"Moira can skim the minds of certain people, almost literally read their thoughts. The Sharers amplify that process, but only between the bearers of each half of the matched pair. She and I experimented on and off for several months but we had very limited success. I still think it's because she wasn't trying hard enough, but that's just the way she is. Anyway, there's a possibility that I might still be able to communicate with her this way."

"Even though she doesn't have her half any longer?"

She nodded. "The link will start to fade, of course, but distance in the physical world doesn't work the same way on the psychic plane."

"And then she can tell us where she is!"

"Exactly. But there's a problem. I said distance wasn't the same but I didn't say it didn't matter. If she's too far from us, or more precisely from her Sharer, then we won't be able to reach her."

That didn't sound good. "How close does she have to be?"

Marie turned away from me. "If she's still in Manhattan, then she's probably in range. Any further than that," she sighed, "and the chances are much less promising."

If this had been a Hollywood script, we would have made contact, Moira would have told us where she was, and I'd have ridden to the rescue. Unfortunately, it wasn't a script. Marie did manage to make a kind of phantom contact, enough to feel certain that Moira was still alive, but that's all. "I can't get through to her, Dash. I think I could read her if she responded, but she can't feel my presence."

"Can you read her thoughts at all?"

"Only impressions. She's a little bit frightened and a whole lot of angry."

"Has she been hurt?"

Marie shook her head. "I don't think so. She's uncomfortable but I don't read any pain. And this might help. She doesn't seem to be moving."

"So she's somewhere in Manhattan or close by, probably locked up someplace. All I have to do is search every building on the island until I find the right one." I stood up, anxious to do something even though I hadn't the faintest idea what to try next.

"No, she's outdoors, I think." Marie was holding one of the Sharers in each hand and staring off into a place invisible to me. "There's a breeze, and some kind of plant with funny leaves."

I blinked. "Marie, is there any way I can see what you're seeing?"

She shook her head. "No, the Sharers are very specific to their carriers."

"Well then, can you draw me a picture? Of the leaves, I mean, and anything else you can see."

"Sure, I suppose so." She set the Sharers back in the bowl. "How is that going to help?"

"I don't know that it is, but I can't think of anything else to do."

She sketched what she'd seen on the back of an advertising circular. Marie was no artist but the three-lobed leaves were unmistakable and my heart leaped. Moira was being held somewhere near the unnatural kudzu that dominated the Golden Gate Bridge.

I promised Marie that I would check in with her as soon as I knew something and then drove across Manhattan rather more recklessly than usual. Traffic was moderate both coming and going on the Golden Gate Bridge as I parked, illegally, behind a power station on the Manhattan side. It was a warm night but there was almost always a stiff breeze on the bridge, so I zipped up my jacket and started along the pedestrian walkway.

Five minutes later I reached the outer perimeter of the kudzu. By then I'd discovered that carrying a sword in one hand was both awkward and wearing, but I had no sheath. With the flashlight I'd borrowed from Marie, I compared the leaves on the vines to those in Marie's sketch. Close enough.

The kudzu isn't actively malevolent, or at least no one has seriously suggested that it is. But it undeniably does not function the way it did back in the ordinary world. When it first started to appear on the Golden Gate, maintenance crews were sent to clear the upper tresses. On each occasion, they swore that they had eradicated it, but within days it was back, originally just on the Manhattan side tower, later on both. Eventually the bridge authority decided that more drastic steps were necessary, and they suspended the periodic clearings while they tried to decide what those steps would be. That gave the kudzu the opportunity to expand dramatically, and across the span of only a very few weeks it covered both towers all the way down to the caissons and by stretching from one set of cables to the next, it provided a reasonably complete roof for almost the entire roadbed.

Various herbicides had been sprayed from above and below, with no discernible effect. Botanists were finally called in, and they made the immediate observation that the kudzu was not rooted in the soil, that it was free standing on the bridge. There was an immediate panic because it was feared that the vines were drawing their sustenance from the bridge itself, weakening the structure, but that proved to be a false alarm. Clearly then the kudzu was drawing its substance from some arcane source. Ordinary kudzu could grow as much as a foot in a single day, but the variety resident on the Golden Gate expanded at nearly ten times that rate. Further efforts to destroy it were made intermittently and ineffectively while a series of studies – botanical and magical - were undertaken, and eventually it had taken over the bridge so completely that there was no realistic hope of clearing it away. Basilisks were brought in once a week to keep the lower tresses and roadbed free of obstruction, successfully limiting its expansion, but no effort was made to drive back the main body, which had continued to thicken until it reached its present scale, looming overhead like an oversized zeppelin. Some of the branches were as large as the thirty-six inch cables, but paradoxically engineers reported no detectible change in the load despite its massive presence. The Scientologists insisted that it was all a mass hallucination.

Fortunately, the kudzu never flowered and therefore produced no seed. It seemed to be content with its single conquest and had turned inward. Although not actively malevolent, it did not welcome visitors. Researchers, maintenance workers, homeless people, and nutcases had all climbed up inside, and their accounts – though varied – had suggested that something very bizarre was happening there. The kudzu reacted differently to different invaders. For some the vines reconfigured themselves into ramps and ladders, facilitating progress through the hidden interior. Visitors welcomed in this fashion reported hollow spaces analogous to rooms, clusters of vine configured to mimic animals or inanimate objects from the human world, mazes, rolling hills, even miniature tropical rain forests caused by concentrated condensation. Others found their way barred, and were forced to hack and slash their way if they wished to penetrate further. Rumor had it that many of the latter had never been seen again, but there were no authenticated cases of anyone actually disappearing. Stories about people being carried off when they walked across the bridge appeared to be equally untrue, but few people were willing to take the chance and pedestrian traffic had become extremely sparse.

I wasn't feeling particularly peaceful when I approached the first tower, but my anger wasn't directed toward the kudzu. I hoped that it was sophisticated enough to sense the difference. It was less active once the sun was down, which I hoped might also work in my favor. The first few minutes were likely to be the most difficult because the bridge authority had erected barricades around the bases of each tower, to prevent just such foolishness as that in which I was about to engage. The barricade was heavy duty hurricane fencing with barbed wire around the top, but I was spared the necessity of climbing over. One section had been ripped away and dangled over the side of the bridge, suspended by the twisted strands of barbed wire that still snaked back to the original structure.

I hadn't notice the damage when I'd come across the bridge that morning, so it was probably new. It looked exactly what you might expect to see if an enraged zombie had come this way.

I started to climb.

It was easier after that, carrying the sword in one hand and with the flashlight stuck through my belt. I had planned to use the former as a machete and cut my way through, but once I was a few meters up into the body of the overgrowth, I was able to rest it against my shoulder and continue with the other arm thrust forward to feel the way when I couldn't see clearly. Although the vines were smaller this low, they were so numerous that it was like walking across a plaited foot bridge. The mass of it swayed beneath my feet and occasionally sagged, but I never felt as though I was in imminent danger of falling.

I did, however, feel that I was being watched, that I wasn't alone. There was constant movement around me, some of it caused by the wind cutting through the vines, some of it quite clearly not. The kudzu was aware of me and adjusted itself to my presence. Fearing that other eyes, unliving eyes, were also watching, I fumbled in my pocket and brought out Marie's charm, just to reassure myself that I hadn't lost it. And naturally I stumbled and dropped it. I paused and searched with the light for a minute or two, but it must have fallen between some of the loose vines and dropped further down. Once I had resigned myself to its loss, I looked back the way I had come just in time to see a wall of vines slowly closing across my escape route. It was difficult to suppress a surge of panic, but then I thought about Moira, trapped here by an undead thing powered by a Berserker, and I let anger wash away the fear.

Although I had been gradually ascending, there had been so many turns and twists that I was unable to orient myself in relation to the outside world, which I could no longer see. The wall of kudzu blocked all external views, fortunately also shielding me from the wind. It even became warmer somehow, and at times it was as though I was climbing through an artificial structure rather than a natural one. The vines grew thicker here, and I was able to walk at a natural pace along level stretches, but then the path would lead upward again, sometimes so steeply that I had to use my free hand to find handholds and pull myself forward.

Suddenly, the temperature began to drop quickly and the darkness changed character. The walls receded on either side and I realized that I had emerged from the kudzu and now stood in the open air. The very top of one of the towers was visible a few meters away and a quick look around told me that I was now on the Brooklyn side of the bridge.

"All right, you've brought me here. So where is she?"

I'm not sure if I was talking to the Berserker or the kudzu, but it was the latter that answered. There was a rustling between me and the near tower and the vines peeled back to form a loose frame around the shape that stood facing me.

I played the flashlight up and down the figure. He seemed to be an ordinary man, not much taller than me, a tad heavier, particularly in the shoulders and upper body. He was bare-chested above corduroy slacks, his hair was cut short, and he stood with his hands on his hips, almost completely motionless. It was his face that gave him away though. Even in the poor light I recognized the fixed expression, the eyes staring into the unseeable, the slack mouth.

"Where is she?" I called, not knowing if I should expect an answer. Some zombies could speak, although their vocabularies were limited. They could be used to convey simple messages. In this case, the message had already been delivered non-verbally. I took a step forward, my free hand tightening around the hilt of my sword.

There was no reaction so I continued my slow advance, extending the sword in front of me and switching hands so that the flashlight was in my left. I halved the distance before I saw her. Moira was lying on a bed of vine just past the zombie, facing away. Her mismatched clothing was unmistakable. I called out her name twice but there was no response. She was motionless, but I couldn't tell whether she was unconscious or dead. The possibility that I had arrived too late fueled my anger and I quickened my pace.

The Berserker didn't move until the very last moment. I was close enough to strike by then and I raised the sword over my head, determined to deliver a single killing blow to the side of the Berserker's neck. I doubted I was strong enough to sever the head completely with one stroke, but I hoped to disable it long enough for a follow up. I think I even yelled something inarticulate as my arm came forward, a shout of primitive blood lust, but I was premature. Just before the blade would have struck, the Berserker raised its arm. The demonic force gave it alacrity beyond that of the usual lumbering zombie shambler. The edge of the blade struck its hand, splitting it all the way to the wrist. When I tried to pull back, I discovered that it was firmly wedged in the bone.

The other arm swung toward me and I stepped back, stumbled, and lost my grip on the sword hilt. I retreated another few steps, wondering how much support the kudzu would provide me if it pursued, but that turned out to be irrelevant. The Berserker returned to its previous position, somewhat awkwardly now because the sword remained lodged in its left wrist.

It didn't require a degree in arcane studies to figure out what was going on. The Berserker was tasked with protecting its hostage rather than killing me. Its creator either wanted me alive or, more likely, hadn't expected a rescue mission and hadn't provided contingency instructions to the Berserker. That took some of the immediate pressure off, but how could I take advantage of the situation?

I approached a second time, and was completely ignored until I was within reach. The hilt of the sword nearly clipped me in the jaw as I danced back away from its swinging arms and I grabbed at it wildly, but ineffectively. As soon as I was beyond its grasp, the Berserker once again resumed its original position.

There was enough room to sidle around and I did so, but when I tried to close the gap, the Berserker interposed itself, re-establishing the standoff. I tried twice more with the same results. I wasn't getting anywhere and I was starting to get cold. I thought I saw Moira stir slightly once but I couldn't be sure. Clouds were scudding across the sky and shadows danced all around me.

There had to be a way around this impasse. The kudzu had led me to this spot for a reason. Was it in league with the Berserker? Was it trying to help me? Or was it just curious to see how things would turn out? Even if it was on my side, how would that help? If it was capable of handling the Berserker on its own, it presumably would already have done so.

I tried a sudden lunge, hoping to grab the sword and pull it free. It was as if the Berserker had read my thoughts. The uninjured hand knotted into a fist and came rushing toward my head. This time I did lose my balance as I tried to avoid the blow, which brushed my shoulder and sent me rolling across the bed of vines. I stood up quickly, half expecting it to have come after me, but it was back on guard, apparently oblivious to my presence as soon as I was out of range.

One of the thinner vines had tangled itself around my legs as I rolled and I untwisted it now as I considered ways to end the stalemate. I was probably nearly as strong as the Berserker, but I felt pain. It didn't. Advantage Berserker. The vine resisted my efforts to free myself, but not very effectively, and when I was done one end deliberately wrapped itself around my left ankle again, just tight enough to make its presence known.

And just like that I knew what I had to do. What the kudzu wanted me to do.

Crouching, I caught hold of the vine and began pulling on it, drawing more and more of its length out of the mass of similar strands that made up the floor here. There was almost no resistance, and I felt a surge of confidence. The kudzu might not be a product of the original, natural world, but it was a living creature and it sided with the living against the dead. The Berserker was mostly dead. I just needed to take care of what was left.

Once I had a long enough piece of the vine free, I fashioned the end into a loop. "I hope this doesn't hurt," I whispered nonsensically as I tightened the knot. If it did, the kudzu made no detectible complaint. Prepared as best I could be, I started toward the Berserker, stopping just short of the point where it would react to my presence.

"Okay, friend, it's time to end this." I slipped the flashlight into my pocket and prepared to cast.

I'd like to say that I threw the lasso over its head on the very first try, but in fact I'd never tossed one before, and I was well off target. Not that it would have mattered. The Berserker swatted it away with an almost casual gesture, never turning its head, never acknowledging my presence. I tried four more times with the exact same results whether I stood directly in front of the creature or to either side. It was too dark to tell whether or not its expression changed, but I had the distinct feeling that it was, if anything, bored.

Eventually I figured out what my mistake was, but more by accident than design. My foot had slipped on my last cast and I'd nearly snared the hilt of my sword instead of its head. I was trying to decide whether that might not be a more viable target when the flashlight slipped out of my pocket. It was still on and the beam startled me as it fell. I reached for it with both hands, catching it just before it rolled out of reach.

That's when I had the inspiration. I spread the lasso, this time with the flashlight back in my left hand. I came as close to the Berserker as possible without tripping its defenses, because I wasn't sure how accurate I would be as a southpaw. I was staring directly into its eyes by then, but it was looking at something else and I don't think it even knew I was there except when I was attacking. Taking a deep breath, I jerked my left arm up and let the flashlight fly, more or less accurately, toward its face.

The left arm came up automatically, brushing the flashlight away as though it was nothing more than an insect. But by then the lasso was already flying through the air. For a moment I thought I'd failed again, but the loop settled down over its shoulders. I'm not sure what it might have done next because I didn't give it a chance to react. I backed away quickly, drawing up the slack, and tugged, hoping to pull it off its feet.

It wasn't an entirely successful maneuver, but the Berserker did drop to one knee, grabbing the vine and pulling me up short. I reversed course immediately and ran past it, hopping over Moira's still inert body, breaking left, pulling the vine as taut as possible as I ran completely around it. I had a bad moment when it swung at me as I rushed by because the sword became dislodged and hit me on the shoulder as it was thrown clear, fortunately with the flat of the blade. Then I started another circuit and managed to pin one arm against its side, the uninjured one, and it flailed at me with its mangled but unbloody hand. I completed one more circuit, using up the last of my slack, then planted my feet and used both arms to draw the vine toward me.

The Berserker staggered, then fell heavily.

I dropped the vine and ran toward where the sword had fallen, having a bad moment when I couldn't find it among the vines, but then it was there, hard and cold against my hand, and I picked it up and ran back to where the Berserker was kneeling, slowly and mechanically freeing itself. It had already pulled most of the vine from its body but the advantage was mine now. I swung the sword.

It's harder to lop off a human head than you might think, particularly with a dull sword. It took eight cuts before it was completely severed, and only then did the thing that had once been a man stop trying to get to its feet.

Moira was still out of it when I reached her, but she was breathing normally and by the time I had removed the ropes from her wrists and ankles, her eyes were open.

"Dash? Is that you?"

"Yeah, kid. It's me. How are you feeling?"

"I've been better." She sat up, shivering. "Where in the world are we? And how soon can we leave?"

"We're leaving in just a minute. I'll be right back."

"Where are you going?"

"To pick up a little souvenir."

CHAPTER FOURTEEN

I left the sword where it lay and picked up the zombie's head by the hair, pretending that it was just some neutral but interesting object. The climb down was uneventful and rather awkward, not just because I'd lost the flashlight and we had to feel our way, but also because Moira's mood changed quickly. She replied to anything I said tersely and volunteered nothing herself. I figured out that she was mad pretty quickly. I am a detective, after all. It took a little longer to determine that she was mad at me.

"I'm sorry about all this," I offered meekly. "I have no idea why it came after you instead of me."

"Don't worry about it."

"Are you all right?"

"Yes."

"You don't sound all right. You sound upset."

"Sorry." Clearly she was not.

We had almost reached street level before I realized why she was mad, or at least part of the reason. While I'm sure she was grateful that I'd rescued her, she wasn't at all happy with the fact that she had required rescuing. I don't think it was me, exactly, that she was mad at, but I was the person who'd seen her helpless. This changed the dynamic between us and I was going to have to think of some way to ameliorate the situation. But not just now.

When we reached the Studebaker, I offered to take Moira to the hospital but she insisted that she was fine. When I offered to take her home she proved it by yelling at me. "Do you think after everything I've just gone through I'm going to let you send me home without an explanation of just what's going on?"

I chose discretion over valor and took her with me to see Marie.

She was obviously greatly relieved to see me and even happier to see Moira, deeply insulted but comparatively unscathed. "And you've brought me the head as well. Wonderful!"

Moira disappeared into the bathroom while Marie was taking care of the preparations, which consisted of situating the severed head – whose eyes were still blinking – in the middle of a circular plate into which a pentagram had been inscribed. She then sprinkled it with a variety of ointments, most of them distinctly pungent, then lit four candles, one at each corner of the table. Moira returned at that point, looking considerably more like herself, although she glared at me on the few occasions when she actually allowed herself to look at me. She regarded the severed head with only marginally less approval.

"How charming," she said sarcastically.

"I doubt we'll learn much useful," Marie cautioned us. "Anyone with the skill to invoke a Berserker would certainly be able to ensure that we couldn't identify its creator. Berserkers are like animals, essentially, guided in this case by the residual human intelligence of the zombie. But unless its creator was a personal acquaintance, there's no chance at all, and there's little enough even in the best possible case. We can only try."

There was some chanting after that, and Moira and I sat away from the table, feeling temporarily useless. At least I did. We didn't talk. Then there was a long pause and Marie's voice changed, became more authoritarian. "Do you acknowledge my power over you?"

The dead lips moved for a few seconds, but no sound emerged. Marie continued, apparently not at all disappointed. "Tell me your name." More writhing lips, more silence. "What is your purpose, Leonard?"

Leonard the Zombie? I laughed nervously.

"SSSHHHH!" Marie gave me a cross look. "It's hard enough to hear without you drowning it out."

"Hear what?" I asked, but I kept my voice low. "It hasn't said a thing."

"It doesn't have lungs any more, Dash. It can't speak normally. But until its life force is completely dissipated, it can still communicate. You just have to listen with your inner ear." That conjured an image that almost made me laugh again, but I stifled it.

She repeated her question, waited, then gave me a strange look, but she didn't repeat its answer. "Tell me who gave you your purpose." This time the lips remained motionless and I thought our time might have run out, but Marie shook her head. "As I expected, it won't answer that one. But we may be able to find out something indirectly."

She questioned the head for another twenty minutes, asking it when it had received its instructions, where it had been at the time, when it had stopped breathing, what it was supposed to do next, and so forth. Sometimes the lips moved and sometimes they didn't. I stopped paying attention after a while. Listening to one side of a cryptic conversation is not my favorite pastime.

But finally she pushed her chair away from the table and let her head fall back. "That's it. It's just dead meat now. I did manage to preserve a sliver of its essence, just enough that it might react in some way if it is returned to the presence of its creator."

I glanced at its face, which was now relaxed, mouth and eyes closed. "Great. I'll just carry a severed head around with me until it moans. Did you learn anything useful?"

"It won't moan. No vocal cords or lungs. I'm not sure just what it will do. It's not very precise magic." Marie sat forward and rested her arms on the table. "I do know that it was sent by an adept who provided very sophisticated instructions. The details aren't important just now but the result is that it was compelled to take Moira to some hidden place and hold her there until it received further instructions. I'm not sure that they would ever have come. If Dash hadn't found you, you might have died of exposure up there, Moira."

"He does have his uses," she admitted grudgingly.

"We'll discuss my heroics some other time, ladies. Right now I want information so that I don't have to risk my neck fighting the undead again tomorrow night."

"Well, I'm afraid I can't tell you much. I tried to get some kind of description of the place where it received its instructions, but what little intelligence and memory it retained started to deteriorate as soon as you cut off its head. It just kept saying 'dark' over and over again, and something about a needle piercing the sky."

"That might be a tower of some kind." A very large tower, like the Canadian National tower in Toronto. I reached into my pocket and extracted the card with Carly Pride's personal information on it. She had inherited her parents' house, and it was in Toronto. Another coincidence? Not likely. "I think you should stay with Marie until morning, Moira. Just to be safe."

Her expression turned stubborn. "I'm perfectly capable of taking care of myself, thank you, when I'm kept informed."

I exerted myself not to sigh. "I told you everything I knew about the Berserker, Moira. I still don't know why it didn't come after me directly."

She didn't appear mollified. "What are you going to do?"

"Follow a lead. Don't worry. I'll be careful." I would too, but that wouldn't stop me from making life very difficult for Carly if she was in fact responsible for Moira's abduction.

"You're going after the conjurer, aren't you? You know who's responsible for all of this."

"I think I know someone who's involved anyway, and I'm going to check things out. You know me, Moira. Despite present appearances, I'm not the hero type. I'll be all right. I'm more concerned about your safety now." That was the wrong thing to say, since it reminded her of her recent vulnerability, and I saw her lips thin and back straighten.

Thankfully, Marie took my side and Moira grudgingly agreed to stay, but I could tell she was worried that I was tackling something beyond my capabilities. I wasn't sure that I disagreed, but I knew that I had to see this through.

It was a pretty long drive to Toronto, which was just past Khartoum and just short of the periphery of small communities that lined our northern coast. Fortunately, traffic was light at this hour and I made good time, delayed only by some kind of midnight procession near the Vatican, and of course the roads through Khartoum still haven't been entirely restored since the damage they suffered during the revolution. I wasn't familiar with Toronto except for the downtown proper but I had a good idea where the neighborhood was in relation to Eaton Center and I headed that way. The clerk at an all night convenience store didn't recognize the address, but he had a street map and helped me figure out the fastest route there.

Cavor Street was quite short, a dead end in fact, and it functioned almost as an extended driveway leading to the Pride house. From the intersection, I could look back the way I had come. The CN Tower's lights were clearly visible. The closest streetlight was out but the sky was lighter here than it had been in Manhattan, and it had finally stopped snowing, replaced by freezing drizzle. In fact, most of what had fallen was already melted except where the plows had piled it up. I reprimanded myself for not thinking to bring along another flashlight, but there was nothing I could do about it now. I parked a block short of the house, hoping that my headlights hadn't alerted anyone who might be inside. There were no lights in the house that I could see from this vantage point.

A chill breeze sprang up out of nowhere, adding to my woes. I zipped my jacket up, found a pair of gloves under the seat, and slipped out of the Studebaker into the night. There was considerable background noise, vehicular traffic headed toward the foreshortened QEW, mostly trucks passing through or making late night deliveries. The closest working streetlight was hissing angrily and flickering. There were no lights on inside the adjacent house either and when I reached the property line, I had to stop until my eyes adjusted to the even thicker darkness that snuggled up against the building. It was larger than I had first thought, stretching deep into the lot. There were thick, low evergreens all around the visible perimeter, crowding against the walls, and it was obvious even in darkness that they hadn't been tended to in years.

I stepped onto the grass, similarly unkempt but plastered to the ground by a thin layer of ice, and started along the near wall, headed toward the rear. If I was going to break in, and I probably would have to, then I preferred as much privacy as possible. There was a fenced enclosure ahead of me which turned out to be a tennis court, and I slipped between that and the house, continuing for another several meters before reaching the corner. I hesitated there because there was a faint light source ahead and to the left, and when I peered around, I saw a single small bulb glowing over the rear entrance. Just beyond it stood two large trash cans and a trellis covered with some kind of climbing vine. Not kudzu.

It was almost an invitation, so I instinctively mistrusted it. There was a window close at hand, but the curtains were closed and I couldn't see anything. I tried to lift it ever so slightly, but it was either locked or stuck, and it wouldn't help to break the glass because the window was barred. It didn't require psychic talent to guess that the rest of the windows would be similarly secured. The house might well be empty, but if so, why was the rear entrance lighted while the front was completely dark? A convenient oversight? Perhaps a little too convenient.

But I went over to the door anyway, as quietly as possible. If there were magical alarms set up, I'd already tripped them.

A faint, unpleasant smell hovered in the air near the door. Something decomposing. I lifted the cover off the nearest trashcan, already anticipating what I was going to find. I wasn't disappointed. Even in the dim light, I could see the carcass of a recently slaughtered chicken and the stubs of at least two black candles. Voodoo? Was this where my zombie had come from? It looked very much as if that was the case. This was way too easy and something told me to go back to the Studebaker and drive away.

I never listen to that something. I still wanted to get into the house.

Very cautiously, I tried the screen door. It opened with the faintest of squeaks. The inner door, however, was not so easy. I tried my charm key but there was no reaction from the lock. I wasn't surprised. If Carly was actively interested in magic, it would have presented no great difficulty to purchase a spell to safeguard the locks against charm keys and similar burglar tools. She might even be talented enough to create her own security charms. On the other hand, she hadn't bothered to secure her apartment. Why take extra pains for a presumably empty house? Unless it wasn't really empty after all.

Most security charms were reactive rather than proactive. Magic responded to magic, but it might not respond to a more mundane approach. I had a lock pick on my key chain, poorly disguised as a good luck charm. It had been a long time since I'd had to use such primitive means for a clandestine entry, but I hadn't lost my touch. The lock was elderly but well oiled and whatever security spell was in effect interpreted the disengagement of the lock as an authorized entry. That's one of the problems when one gets too dependent on magic. You forget to make allowances for less sophisticated approaches. I slipped inside without making too much noise.

It was dark, but not so dark that I couldn't tell that I was in a narrow hallway. To my right was a large room filled with furniture, most of it covered with sheets or blankets. It was almost certainly the dining room, dominated by a long, waist high table in the center of the room, with chairs stacked in one corner between two enormous sideboards. Straight ahead was the front door, barely visible in the distance. There was a lighter glow where the faint streetlight filtered through the beveled glass inset in the door. There was a large closet to my left, the door slightly ajar, and it appeared to be empty.

I stepped into the dining room and saw that it connected directly to a large front hall, adjacent to which was an even larger living area. More shrouded furniture stood there, chairs, couches, and end tables, judging by size and shape. There was a fireplace large enough that two people could have comfortably stood inside it. The walls were bare, but as I came closer, I could see outlines where large paintings had formerly been hung.

From the hallway, a wide staircase led up to the second floor, reaching it only after a sharp twist to the left that made it look out of balance. The upper landing was shielded by a waist high barrier, solid rather than fenced. Presumably the landing led to bedrooms, but it was so dark there that I couldn't see anything else. I decided to explore the rest of the ground floor first, and the second room I looked into turned out to be a moderately well appointed library, although I couldn't see that until I decided to take a chance and turned on the lights.

It was also the first room I had seen in which the furniture was uncovered. The walls were, as you might expect, pretty well covered by books except in one place where a very large shield and crossed swords broke the pattern. The shield bore an elaborate embossing, a dragon and lion fighting one another. There was a roll top desk in one corner, and three small couches arranged in a circle facing one another in the very center of the room. Judging by the scrape marks on the hard wood floor, they had formerly been in closer proximity, but had been moved back. The reason for the move was even more obvious.

Someone had drawn a series of symbols on the floor, spiraling outward from a single focus. A small mahogany table straddled the central point, its top covered with dried blood and chicken feathers. An ugly looking, serrated knife with a long, heavy blade had been set down in the middle of the mess. I didn't need Marie Dussaud to tell me that this was where the zombie had been made, and presumably also infused with the Berserker.

Somewhere in the house, wood creaked.

I froze where I was, hardly daring to breathe. Was it just normal settling noise or was there someone else in the house? I wasn't armed, although if Carly was as accomplished a sorceress as the evidence suggested, mundane weapons wouldn't have been of much help if it came to a fight.

I turned off the light and backed out of the library, alert to any further disturbance. There was a sudden soft clattering sound and I flinched, but then realized the light rain had intensified. The sky had looked like it might clear earlier, but storms moved in fast in Toronto, which still had lake effect snow even though the lake wasn't there. The sound of the rain grew even louder, drumming against the roof and awnings, and I cursed silently. But if it masked the sound of my theoretical opponent, it would also cover any small noises I might make.

I returned to the main hallway and glanced toward the staircase. The upper landing was still cloaked in shadows, almost featureless. I really didn't want to go up there. Was there any reason that I should? The evidence I was looking for was in the library and I'd already seen it. What more could I hope to accomplish? If Carly was in the house, I was in deep trouble. Like I said, I have no magical talents at all and I had brought nothing with me to offset her obvious advantage. Even my handgun was still caught inside my mangled safe. My best choice was to leave now. On the other hand, if she was in the house, she was almost certainly aware of my presence and presumably prepared to stop me from leaving and exposing her secret. It wouldn't appreciably increase my risk to search the second floor, and it was possible that there was something else here, some additional revelation that would lock the puzzle pieces even more tightly together.

What the hell, I said to myself. And started toward the stairs.

No sooner had I done so than one of the shadows above separated itself from the others and moved to the edge of the landing. I stopped immediately, trying to focus on the figure, but then I was diving for my life as a spear of flame shot down toward me. I lost my footing and landed hard on my side, but not hard enough to keep me from rolling purposefully away from the staircase and around the near corner where I was shielded from view.

The rug was burning where the bolt had struck and acrid smoke was spiraling up. I could see more clearly now, but I was already nostalgic for the concealing darkness. There was no reason to remain silent and as I stood up, I called out to her. "Carly! Hold your fire!" Under other circumstances, I might have enjoyed the pun. "Why don't we talk about this?"

There was no answer. I considered my options and figured my best bet was the front door since all of the windows on this floor were barred. But I had to get there, work the lock, and leave without getting fried in the process. I didn't like the odds. Then I had an inspiration and retraced my steps to the library. This was apparently my day to use primitive weaponry.

The shield was much heavier than I expected. If it was authentic and not just a prop, I can't imagine how in the world anyone would manage both it and a sword without collapsing from exhaustion. Even with both hands grasping the arm-piece on the reverse side, I found it difficult to manage, and I'm not a small man. I returned to the corridor, peering about nervously, but there was no sign that Carly had descended from the landing.

The carpet was still smoldering but the flames were guttering. I paused at the corner, stuck my head out, and looked the situation over. There was a flash and I jumped back, my eyebrows singed. The wallpaper was on fire and a chunk of the plaster wall had almost disintegrated.

"This isn't going to help, Carly!" I called. "People know where I am and why I came here." A lie, but I doubted she'd take the time to use a truth spell. She didn't answer this time either, but I heard footsteps. She was moving but not down the stairs. Along the landing then? Looking for a better angle?'

There was no way she could get a clear shot at me unless she descended or I moved, but I still held the shield in front of me, just in case. My best plan, and it was not a good one, was to move carefully across the end of the hallway until I reached the door, sheltering behind the shield. I was less confident now than I had been. If the impact of one of Carly's fire bolts could blow a hole in a wall, it would certainly knock me over even if it didn't penetrate the shield.

Another possibility occurred to me.

If I could somehow manage to cross the open space moving toward the stairs rather than the door, I should be able to get under the landing, which would then screen my escape into the dining room and down the other end of the corridor to the back door. It meant exposing myself for about fifteen or twenty steps though.

Even at a sprint and unencumbered by the heavy shield, I doubted I could make it.

I peered around the corner for another look. The fire was out near me; it hadn't taken hold in the plaster, but it was spreading away along the wall, feeding on the elderly, dry wallpaper. Decorative cords ending with oversized tassels dangled beneath the landing, and one of these was alight now, the flames climbing hungrily. Maybe luck was going to favor me after all. If the fire spread quickly enough, Carly might have to abandon her commanding position. My enthusiasm for that scenario lessened when I realized it might provoke her into coming down to deal with me from close at hand.

I crouched in hiding for what seemed an endless length of time, but which was probably only a couple of minutes, then took another peek. The dark figure above me hadn't changed position, and another bolt sped my way. I retreated hastily as another section of the wall exploded in a shower of plaster and sparks. The carpet was on fire again as well.

The flames had spread dramatically. There were tapestries on the far wall and they were ablaze, the flames licking at the underside of the landing. Alas, it was not the side where Carly stood that was in jeopardy and she still held her vantage point. Should I wait her out? Sooner or later the fire would reach her. What would she do then?

But my opponent was wilier than I expected. I was taken completely by surprise when the front door opened of its own volition, letting in a blast of chill, fast moving air. My first thought was that it was bait and that she was waiting for me to bolt for freedom, ready to kill me the moment I broke cover. But then something entered the room, something which shimmered unnaturally. I had trouble focusing on it because the dancing flames and smoke were playing havoc with visibility, but the fire flared up just then and I saw more clearly.

The rain falling outside had stopped in to visit. It wriggled in like some oversized worm, the front end weaving back and forth as though it too was trying to see through the gloom. It completely filled the doorway, so there was no escape that way unless I could push my way through its substance, and somehow I doubted that Carly would have made such a simple mistake. She had summoned the water to douse the fire, obviously, and unless I did something fast, my thin excuse for a plan was going to become as insubstantial as smoke.

I picked up the shield and waited until the column of water had advanced well into the hall. Then I ran for it.

No, let's be honest here. I more or less stumbled for it. The charred rug offered less than perfect footing, the shield was really too heavy for me, and I breathed in some smoke and started to choke before I'd taken three steps. I had a moment to see that the flames had spread all across the bottom of the landing, and in several places were creeping up the sides. The wallpaper on the opposite side of the room was burning in a few places, probably sparks blown about when the door opened. The stairs themselves were starting to smolder.

I ran directly toward the water worm. Above me, my assailant stepped forward and one arm jerked in my direction. A ball of fire hurtled toward me, but I had only a distorted view of it because I was behind the column of water now. I still held the shield but it was already slipping from my grip. I closed my eyes and slid to my knees, ducking behind the shield, and even through closed lids I saw the flash. But I didn't burst into flame. In fact, I never even felt the heat.

What I did feel was wet and cold.

I dropped the shield and got to my feet. The water worm, or at least the forward end of it, had been splashed all over the hall. The fire bolt had hit it squarely. I was a bit stunned and I lost my grip on the shield, which fell with a loud clang. The figure above me raised its arm and I jumped forward in desperation. The sheltering overhang was only half the distance it had been before, and I made it with a split second to spare, just as another blast of flame slammed into the floor directly behind me.

The impact knocked me from my feet, but I fell forward. There was fire on every side and a virtual ceiling of it above me. Sparks and small burning pieces were dropping everywhere. I was winded, but I got to my knees. She would come after me now, I was certain. She couldn't let me escape.

There was the sudden, frightening sound of wood and nails and plaster surrendering to the force of gravity and I realized that the landing was collapsing. My left knee hurt badly enough that I think I cried out, but I started moving and I kept going until I was out from under it, through the dining room, and back in the corridor that led to the back door.

That's where I was when I heard the scream. The entire landing had come crashing down behind me, and in the middle of it was a moving figure, its cloak – which I now saw was decorated with occult symbols – already half consumed. Human nature being what it is, I actually took a few steps back, but there was no possible way that I could have reached that struggling figure without being overwhelmed by the flames. Mercifully, the screaming stopped very quickly. I hoped that she was dead then and hadn't just inhaled enough flame to char her lungs.

The fire was spreading even more rapidly now, hungrily devouring everything in sight. Nursing my sore knee, I made my way out of the house and around the side, and I was sitting beside the Studebaker, watching, when the sirens started.

I felt glad to be alive, but I also knew there was no way that I should have survived. I should be dead. Why wasn't I? What other force had been at work tonight, and why had it decided to save me and not Carly Pride? And then the answers began to come to me and I knew what I had to do.

The fire department arrived before I could leave and they had a lot of questions. More questions than I had answers. I insisted that I'd been driving by and had spotted the flames and drove up to the house only to see if there was anyone in need of assistance. I claimed to have forced the front door open only to retreat without entering, receiving minor burns in the process. I have an honest face, I guess, because when the Toronto Police arrived they accepted the story at face value and let me go.

The sun was coming up by the time I got to Brooklyn, but as soon as I called Marie's house to reassure the ladies that I was still alive, I went to bed anyway. I couldn't be certain because my mind was so addled with fatigue, but I was pretty sure that I had all the pieces of the puzzle that I needed now. It was only a matter of fitting them together.

There was a message from Moira on the answering machine. Marie was driving her home and she'd be in to work, but not until mid-morning. Since it was already past that time, I called the office. She was stiff and formal but not actively hostile. I assured her that I was fine, and asked her to look up Mayor Burford's phone number for me.

Keller seemed to be in a better mood today, and even more so when I told him that I was pretty sure I was close to winding up the project I was doing for the Mayor. "I just need to confirm a couple of things. And I need the Mayor to call his counterpart in Toronto, Mayor Curtis." I explained what I wanted to know and hung up, took a long shower, and was toweling myself off when the telephone rang again.

It was Keller and he had my information. "There was a single victim found after the fire on Cavor Street. The body was unrecognizable, but dental records match those of Carlotta Pride. Her identity was confirmed during the scryopsy. DNA confirmation will take another day or two if you need that as well."

"No, that's just fine."

"Should I set up an appointment with the Mayor for you? He's quite anxious to hear what you've found out."

"Yes, you should. But not at his office. We need more space." And then I told him what I wanted and he listened to the end.

"Are you sure all that is necessary?"

"Oh, yes. I only hope it's enough."

When I hung up, I felt as though I had finally passed the last obstacle and come to the end of the road.

Boy, was I wrong!

CHAPTER FIFTEEN

I guess I was still being a little bit naïve. On some level I expected Burford to call me back within minutes, bubbling over with gratitude, to tell me I could have whatever I wanted. Well, it was Keller who called me back, it wasn't until the next day, and he pretty much told me that what I was asking for was out of the question.

"You have to understand, the Mayors have very full schedules. We can't just tell a half dozen of them that they need to drop everything, come to a meeting to which we've summoned a considerable number of private citizens – who have obligations of their own – on the word of some relatively unknown investigator."

"Did you tell Burford that I'd solved the Porter murder?"

"Yes." Keller was very patient but even through the telephone I could feel his eyes rolling. "And if that's true, he's very pleased to hear the news. If you'd like, I could set up an appointment and you can come in and tell him all about it."

Well, I could, but since the case had wider ranging implications, and since it was entirely possible that forces existed which would not hesitate about eliminating one person with dangerous information – whether that person was a detective or even a Mayor – I didn't like the idea of a private meeting with a man whose discretion I could only speculate about. I figured I was safe at the moment, because I had appeared to fall for the hoax that had been prepared for me. Once the truth was out, I needed some powerful protection or I might end up some morning with odd runes carved into my skin. Or worse.

"Let me think about it. I'll get back to you." I hung up.

Moira read my face if not my aura. "That didn't sound as though it went well."

"Bureaucrats." I made a disgusted noise, and hoped I was right.

I tried again the next day, and the day after that. Keller was sympathetic but unhelpful the first time, and irritated and unhelpful the next. I considered accosting Burford some place in public, since I couldn't get past security at the Kremlin without his cooperation, but

Keller wouldn't tell me his schedule, and I wasn't sure that it was a good idea anyway.

The next day I couldn't even reach Keller. A woman with a nasal whine told me that he was unavailable but that she would be glad to take a message. I didn't leave one. When I complained to Moira she suggested an alternate approach. "If Burford won't talk to you, why not try someone else?"

I don't have any connections on that level, but Morris does. I called and gave him a very abstract summary of the situation. No reason why I should put him at risk. He promised to do what he could and a few hours later I had an appointment with Mayor Bencolin of Paris, except that when I showed up, the Mayor had been called away for an unexplained emergency. "He might be unavailable for some time," according to the secretary.

Morris tried again. When he called me back, he sounded deeply worried.

"What have you gotten yourself into this time, Dash?"

"What do you mean?" I was pretty sure I knew what he meant.

"No one will talk to you. They all have different reasons – a busy schedule, a temporarily debilitating illness, a political crisis, a family problem – but everyone's saying the same thing. They don't want to talk to you about the Porter murder, or anything else."

"Any idea why?"

"Someone's pulling strings behind the scenes, obviously. Someone with a lot of power. I'd press further if I thought it would do any good, but the only Mayor I ever knew well enough to push for the truth was Shackleton, and he died last year."

"Okay, thanks for trying Morris."

"What are you going to do, Dash? It sounds to me like you're skating at the edge of a very deep hole."

"I'll just have to improvise."

When I recounted this conversation to Moira, she was uncharacteristically silent, obviously troubled. I even felt a bit guilty and made a disparaging comment about the Mayors that was meant to be funny but came out sounding bitter.

"I think we should go see Marie."

"Why? Does she have pull with one of the Mayors?"

"No, not exactly. But we might be able to find a way around them. But I need to talk to her first."

I glanced at my watch. It was late in the afternoon and I was emotionally if not physically exhausted. Rachel Deacon had sent in her final payment that morning, advising me formally that she was terminating our agreement and would pursue other means to locate her sister. It had covered most of the more pressing bills, with enough left over to pay Moira a couple of weeks' worth of back pay and line, if not fill, my own wallet.

"I'll try anything at this point but..." I stopped because Moira had turned and picked up the telephone.

"Dash Investigations. May I help you?" She listened for a moment. "One moment please."

She shrugged to indicate that she didn't know who it was as I took the phone. It was Keller. "Just listen and don't say anything, not even my name. Understand?"

"Whatever you say."

"Do you know the Treasure Island Bar?"

"The one in South Hollywood?"

"That's it. Meet me there."

"When?"

"As soon as you can get there." And the line went dead.

"What was all that about?" Moira was sitting on my desk with her legs crossed. Have I mentioned that she has very nice legs?

"That was Keller. He wants to meet with me. Now."

"Are you going?"

"What have I got to lose?"

"Your life, among other things. People are dead, Dash. Don't join them."

I was touched by her obvious concern. "It's the furthest thing from my mind. And we're meeting in a very public place." I roused myself. "I need to get going. It's way over in Hollywood."

She followed me to the door. "Watch your back, Dash. You never know. I might get carried off by another zombie. Who'd come to rescue me if you weren't around?"

I did actually know where the Treasure Island Bar was, although I'd never been inside. There was a ratty looking, mock pirate ship mounted on the roof with neon sails that tried to look as though they were billowing in the wind. Not very successfully. They had a tiny parking lot, and the streets within two blocks were lined with cars so I had to walk a bit after finding a spot for the Studebaker. I could hear the music and crowd noises from a block away, even though it was barely dusk. I wondered how high the noise level rose when they were really rocking.

I was greeted inside the door by an animated caricature of a pirate, complete with wooden leg, patched eye, and a parrot on the shoulder. It was mechanical rather than magical and roared, "SHIVER ME TIMBERS AND WELCOME TO TREASURE ISLAND!" The bar was large and dimly lit, mercifully. The decorations ran from garish to outlandishly garish. Streamers of fake gold doubloons dangled everywhere and every bit of furniture – bar, tables, chairs, even the phone booth – were encrusted with improbably large, bright, and varicolored fake jewels. The walls were covered with fake cutlasses, skull and crossbone flags, and artlessly draped cargo nets. The inappropriate rock music had been turned up so loud I was surprised conversation was possible at all, but then I don't suppose most people come to bars to enjoy scintillating social intercourse.

There were several dozen people gathered in noisy little clusters and I wondered how I'd ever find Keller, since I had never met him and had no idea what he looked like. Fortunately, Keller found me instead, tapping me on the arm. "Let's go to the back. There are empty booths there."

Keller was short, a bit on the heavy side, with mutton chop sideburns and unruly hair. He was wearing a decent suit, which meant he made a lot more money than I did, but it sat uneasily on his body. He already had a drink but he gestured and a waiter showed up, dressed in pirate garb of course.

"Another of these."

The waiter turned to me and I shook my head. He ignored me and waited. "I'll have whatever my friend's having."

He nodded. "Two Flaming Volcanoes, coming right up."

Keller was staring into the dregs of his drink and not looking at me. "So why am I here?" I asked.

He glanced up. "What'd you say?" His words were ever so slightly slurred.

I repeated myself, raising my voice.

"You can't ever tell anybody about this, you understand?" He reached across and grabbed my sleeve. I moved my arm away.

"Confidentiality and discretion are my middle names."

"Someone doesn't like you." He settled back in the booth and finished his drink. It wasn't his first, obviously.

"There are lots of people who don't like me. Did you have someone in particular in mind?"

"Yes, of course I do. Except that I don't know who he is. Or she is."

Obviously this was going to be one of those conversations. "Suppose you start at the beginning. Does this have anything to do with Mayor Burford?"

Keller nodded. "He's a good man, the Mayor. No one ever expected him to be Mayor, you know."

I did know. He was a deputy Mayor appointed because no one really disliked him, but when Halloran drowned, he got the job. "I know. Why won't he see me?"

At first I thought Keller hadn't heard the question, but maybe he was just trying to decide how much he wanted to say. "Something very strange is going on, Mr. Dash. The first time you called and asked us to get a bunch of the Mayors together, Burford was real enthusiastic. He went off to talk to some of them himself. But when he came back, he didn't say anything about it and when I asked if I could help with the arrangements, he didn't know what I was talking about."

The waiter returned with our drinks. I tasted mine automatically. It was vile.

"I thought he'd just changed his mind, but then you called again and it seemed to come back to him, but this time he wasn't as excited. He told me he'd talk to a couple of people and see if they thought it was a good idea. I don't know if he followed through or not, but he never got back to me. Then you called again and I gave him your message and he seemed confused and angry, both at the same time. I thought he was just preoccupied so I tried again the next morning, and he didn't know what I was talking about."

"Are you saying he forgot that you'd spoken to him?"

"No, I'm saying he forgot the whole thing. He didn't even recognize your name at first. I told him you were working on the Porter murder and that seemed to help, but he thought you were working for the Boston Police as a consultant." Keller shook his head. "I don't know what this is all about and I don't want to know, but someone messed around with Mayor Burford's memories, and the Mayors are all supposed to be protected by an anti-lobbying spell. Whoever is behind this is using some powerful magic. Burford can't help you. I can't help you. But I thought you should know."

I probably should have picked up Keller's tab, but my wallet was still anemic. And he could afford it.

I was in the office early the following morning. Moira hadn't even brewed coffee yet. She gave me a quizzical look but knew better than to talk to me until the first jolt of caffeine hit my system. She brought me a cup as soon as it was ready.

"How did it go last night?"

I recounted the conversation with Keller. "Something's going on behind the scenes, Dash. Something bad."

"I'm with you, but I don't see how I can do anything about it." Some of the frustration must have been audible in my voice.

"I asked Marie if we could come over this morning."

"I still don't see how that will help anything."

"Humor me, Dash. There's something that you don't know yet that might help us." She looked distinctly uncomfortable.

"Are you holding out on me, Moira?" I wasn't angry, not quite, but I was fully prepared to be mortally offended if she knew something about the case and hadn't told me.

"Just wait until we talk to Marie."

Marie looked just as puzzled as I felt when we arrived. She ushered us in, offered us refreshments which I declined, but Moira asked for herbal tea and somehow I found myself sipping the same from a dainty little cup that I was terrified of breaking.

The amenities satisfied, Marie made me very happy by coming directly to the point. "You said it was very important for us to get together, Moira. What exactly did you have in mind?"

"I need to get in touch with my sister."

"Your sister?" I blurted.

"Your sister!" Marie echoed, looking stunned.

"Yes, I need to talk to her, or at least get a message to her. It's important, Marie. You know I wouldn't do this if that wasn't true."

"You have a sister?" I still hadn't gotten my mind around that. Moira wasn't supposed to have a family. She was complete unto herself.

"I know you can get a message to her," said Moira, ignoring me.

"Wait a minute! Why didn't you ever tell me you had a sister?" I felt offended but I wasn't sure why.

"You never asked," she replied without looking at me. "And we're not close."

"Not anymore," corrected Marie, and I knew there was a story there, but a story that would have to wait until another time. "But there was a time when you and Molly were inseparable."

"We both grew up, in different directions. Can you reach her?"

"I don't understand," I interposed. "Why can't you call her yourself, Moira?"

She didn't answer, looked away from me. Marie hesitated as well. "He has to know, Moira."

"So tell him." It was barely a whisper.

Marie drew a conscious breath. "Molly McGann is Moira's older sister. She's also a member of the Collegium."

I don't think I've mentioned the Collegium. It's not entirely inadvertent. People don't talk about the Collegium much. The Mayors pretty much run everything in the Cities, as much as the residents let them run things anyway, but there's also the Arcane Council which rules on magical questions. They're sort of like the Supreme Court back in the original world. They're the ones who determine what kinds of magic are legitimate, how powerful a love charm can be, and they establish precedents when magic causes anomalies that were not anticipated by civil law. The members of the Council are pretty formidable practitioners themselves, of course.

But there's formidable and then there's formidable. The Collegium Arcanum was formed way back when Manhattan was the only City. We were fortunate – unless it was designed that way – that we had three very knowledgeable experts on magical theory who were prepared, as much as anyone could be, when they discovered that the theoretical knowledge they'd accumulated now had a practical application. It was the Collegium who figured out how to create the bottomless food stores that averted mass starvation during those first few years, and it was the Collegium who created the wards that kept the Tuilleries within bounds. Mostly.

Somewhere along the way they faded from public scrutiny. Oh, we still knew they were around, but they dropped off the radar and somehow it became gauche even to talk about them. Conspiracy theorists believed that the Arcanum had cast a mass spell on everyone else to prevent anyone from being too curious about what they were doing, and there might even be some truth to the story. No one knew exactly how many people were members, or what they spent their time doing, although presumably they were plumbing the depths of the magical system that surrounded the Cities. If they'd found answers, they weren't saying anything. Several people were rumored to be members, but they never acknowledged their status if it was true and no one ever pressed them on the issue. They hovered somewhere ambiguously between feared and respected.

And Moira's sister was one of them.

"I know I never asked," I said quietly. "But this kind of thing qualifies as a Big Deal. You might have volunteered the information."

"I don't like to talk about it." Moira's voice was low and threshed with emotion.

I forced myself to set aside the many new, unanswered and perhaps unanswerable questions that were popping up all over the landscape of my mind. "All right. How does this help us?"

"Someone doesn't want you to talk to the Mayors. Someone using powerful magic. We need a counterbalance."

"Your sister. A member of the Collegium." I was still having trouble with the concept.

"Do you have any better ideas?"

I didn't, of course, but I thought I should have. Appealing to the Collegium seemed wrong, somehow, like I was playing a game of chess and was asking a referee to move a piece. Except that this wasn't a game. The pieces that were lost really died.

"All right, I give up. How do we do it?"

"We don't," said Marie, breaking a long silence. "I do." She sat back in her chair and closed her eyes.

"Then how do you reach her?"

"Ssshhh!" Moira shushed me. "She's doing it now."

I opened my mouth, thought better of it, and sipped some more herbal tea. It wasn't bad, actually, once you got over the strangeness.

The tea hadn't even cooled when I sensed that we were no longer alone in the room. There was no physical sign at first, no odd odors, mysterious sighing, ectoplasmic optical effects, or anything like that. At first I dismissed it as paranoia, but the sensation became too powerful to ignore. Moira fidgeted in her chair and looked unhappy.

Then there was a fleeting shimmer in the air, and something that wasn't there one moment was very much there the next.

It didn't look very much like anyone who could be Moira's sister. In fact, it didn't look very much like a human. Which makes sense, since it wasn't. It looked vaguely like a naked, gnarly man except that he only stood as high as my knee, his upper body was round like a gourd, and he stood on two bowed legs that ended with clawed feet. In one hand he held a handful of earthworms and he was chewing on one of them. I could tell because he was dribbling from one corner of his mouth. It was a homunculus. I'd read about them, but I'd never seen one in the flesh, or quasi-flesh I suppose.

"We need to speak to your mistress," said Marie, her face impassive.

"Busy mistress. Shouldn't be bothered." It's voice was a reverberating croak, if you can imagine such a thing.

"This is important. We need to speak to her now."

The homunculus shrugged what should have been shoulders, except that I'm not sure there was a collarbone in there anywhere. "Mistress tells Sferoi that she does not wish to speak to anyone, not even you Mistress Dussaud. Sorry."

He didn't sound sorry.

Moira stirred in her seat. Her voice was deliberate, level, almost matter of fact. It didn't sound at all like her.

"Tell her that her sister wants to speak to her."

Sferoi froze, looking more like a carved figure than ever. I opened my mouth to speak after a minute had passed, but Moira and Marie both flashed me warning looks and I subsided. A few more endless seconds passed and finally the diminutive figure shook itself and its skin began to glow all over, so brightly at first that I had to avert my eyes. And then it faded and a perfectly ordinary looking woman was standing in its place.

Well, perfectly ordinary except that she was only about eighteen inches tall, was dressed in a swirling, gauzy costume that didn't seem entirely separate from her skin, and radiated such a powerful sense of presence that I felt no temptation to speak. She also looked a little like Moira.

"Well, little sister. It's been a long time. To what do I owe the gift of your presence?" I thought I heard just the faintest hint of malice.

"I wouldn't have bothered you if it hadn't been important, Molly. You know that."

"Indeed I do. I can hardly wait to hear what disastrous situation you've gotten yourself into."

"It's not that. It's, well, complicated."

Molly, or the image of Molly since I was quite sure she wasn't really present, sighed. "It always is with you." If I'd said something like that, Moira would have blistered my skin, but she held her tongue. Molly seemed impressed by her restraint and her voice softened. "Why don't you tell me what's wrong?"

Moira provided a brief summary and then turned to me to fill in the details. I felt extremely uncomfortable at first, but once I'd gotten started, it came more easily than I expected. The very act of describing my discoveries and theories out loud helped clarify them in my mind and I was more convinced than ever that I was right. I'm not sure how long I talked, but eventually I ran out of words, and it was only then that I realized again to whom I was speaking. "Sorry, I got a bit carried away."

I had a horrible feeling that this wasn't going to work either, but Molly didn't leave me hanging long. She asked a couple of questions to which, thankfully, I had answers.

"I see flaws, but on the whole I think your solution is the right one. We will arrange your meeting." And her image grew suddenly fuzzy.

"Wait!" I leaned forward anxiously. "When? Where?"

"In due course." Her voice was low and distant, as though she were calling to me from the opposite end of a very long tunnel. Then she was gone and Sferoi was there, stuffing wriggling earthworms into his cavernous mouth. He winked at me and then he was gone too and the three of us were alone again.

"Now you'll understand why I don't talk about my sister," said Moira.

CHAPTER SIXTEEN

Things moved very quickly the next day, so quickly that I felt a twinge of alarm. Up until now I had at least enjoyed the illusion of control. Now I was just a passenger on a runaway trolley, carried away with the rest of the passengers. Even worse, I was one of the few that knew we were headed toward a solid brick wall.

The invitations were in the morning mail. Never on its best day has the Cities mail, even in Manhattan, been that efficient. The postmark was two days earlier, but the contents had obviously been composed more recently. Moira and I were both invited to a private performance of an unusual entertainment at the National Opera House in Oslo that same afternoon. I didn't need any encouragement but I felt a sudden rush of enthusiasm for the encounter which must have been the byproduct of some kind of compulsion spell. I had revealed all of my aces during the conversation with Molly McGann, named all the players by name, and there was no doubt in my mind that each and every one of them would have received something very similar this morning.

There might be a way to resist the compulsion, but it would require the use of very powerful magic, and anyone who failed to attend today would be as good as admitting his or her involvement in dark, forbidden magic.

I was impatient to have this all over with, and my neck out of the noose I felt tightening around it.

I'd never been to Oslo before except to pass through and it took a while to find the right street. There were no guards of any kind posted outside when we arrived, at least not that I could see. A harried looking stagehand met me inside and gave me the grand tour. Moira was coming separately, with Marie Dussaud, but I wanted to arrive well in advance and get a feel for the place. The auditorium was large enough to have accommodated several hundred people easily, but it was well contained. There were exits at all four corners, and there was another door backstage, but the most direct way in was through the front. The curtain was drawn and someone had set up two mismatched card tables and some folding chairs on the stage. To one side, under a canvas tarp, was a little surprise I planned to unveil later. The stagehand told me it had been delivered at the crack of dawn. There were quite a few extra chairs scattered about the stage, but I didn't think I'd be making much use of any of them. I like to move around when I talk. And I planned to do a lot of talking. I'd spent a lot of time during the last ten days listening to other people, listening to a lot of lies, and I was relishing the opportunity to reverse things. It was time for the truth.

In a roped off area behind the stage, several Norwegian Police officers were quietly eating donuts or drinking coffee. Someone had conjured a bottomless pot in one corner. They had no idea why they'd been assigned to the theater but they weren't complaining.

Our guests started arriving twenty minutes before the announced show time. Morris Ngambe came first, with Jessica Crane at his side, looking calm and slightly bored. She raised one hand to acknowledge my presence, then turned back to listen to Morris. Moira and Marie came in next and took seats in the row directly behind them. Marie was carrying a fair sized wicker basket in lieu of a purse. Moira introduced her to Jessica; she and Morris were old friends. Several people arrived fairly quickly after that. Sheri Connors came alone and sat near the back. She had a puzzled look on her face, as though she couldn't understand why she had come. Christopher Hayden showed up a moment later, obviously feeling even more out of place. He hesitated in the doorway, and it looked like he might bolt when he noticed Connors. The compulsion was inescapable though and he came inside, but moved to the opposite corner of the room and took an aisle seat.

Deborah Lerner and Oliver Anderson appeared simultaneously, although they were not together, and right behind them was Alice from the Paris bank and Detective Colby from Toronto. I didn't think I'd mentioned Colby and wondered how Molly had known to invite him. I nodded to each person as they arrived but remained on the stage, not wanting to say anything until everyone was present. Wanda Veil appeared at the entrance and waved cheerily, but sat near the back. She was followed almost immediately by Herman Goff, who looked like his dentist had just told him he was out of both novacaine and analgesic potions. The last to arrive was Rachel Deacon. She came to a sudden stop when she saw me, frowned heavily before taking a seat. I ticked each name off against my mental list, satisfied myself that everyone was present, except for the Mayors, who had yet to make an appearance. I was going to look like a real fool if they didn't show. Moira assured me that even if the Mayors were immune to compulsion, they would hardly refuse a request from the Collegium, but until I actually saw them arrive, I wasn't going to feel easy about this.

There was a minor commotion at the door and a clot of people entered, most of them bodyguards. Mayor Curtis was the first to enter, and I wondered how much pressure had been brought to bear to secure his presence. He'd just been elected Speaker of the Mayoral Council. Even Moira liked him. She'd met him once at some social function. Behind him came Mayor Chang of Hong Kong, with Burford, who looked flustered and uncomfortable, bringing up the rear. The combined party of Mayors moved directly to the stage and the threesome seated themselves behind the card tables while their bodyguards moved ostentatiously to strategic locations throughout the auditorium. No one looked at me except Curtis, who gave me a brief this-had-better-be-good glare.

Curtis took charge so smoothly that you would have thought this had all been his idea. "Thank you all for coming on such short notice, particularly any of you who might be here voluntarily. I'm sure the rest of you know by now that your presence has been compelled under the emergency provision of the Cities charter and at the request of the Collegium Arcanum, which has determined that the subject we will address today is sufficiently serious to justify a transient infringement on your individual civil and magical rights. We appreciate your cooperation in this matter and we will not prolong things any longer than is absolutely necessary."

I started forward to say my peace, but like most Mayors, Curtis liked to hear himself talk. "As most of you already know," he continued, "there have been several brutal murders committed in recent weeks, all presently unsolved crimes. Although our various Police have been tireless in their investigation, the large number of matters requiring their attention has made it very difficult for them to devote their full effort to solving these heinous crimes. Although we are confident that the established authorities would bring the perpetrators to justice in due course, it was thought expedient to enlist several of our more talented citizens to help speed things up. Acting cooperatively with the Police, Mr. Dash is now in a position to throw light on these horrendous murders and," he consulted a piece of paper, "and certain other matters which are of interest to some of those present here today."

Curtis was either done or pausing for breath. I stepped forward immediately, to forestall any extension of his speech. "Thank you, Mayor Curtis. Ladies and gentlemen, thank you all for coming." I deliberately kept my voice relatively low so that they had to strain to hear. I get better results when my opponents are on edge. "As his honor has already told you, I was one of those who chose to respond to the Public Appeal following the deaths of Aram Gudanoff, Ashley O'Brien, and Steven Sandobhal. I was reluctant to do so because at the time I was also involved with three other clients. Under normal circumstances, I would be unable to tell you about the specifics of these because of client confidentiality, however, it turns out that they are all interconnected, although they don't all have the same solution."

There was some stirring in the audience, but not much. "One of those cases involved the disappearance of Miss Ruth Deacon, whose sister is here with us today." Rachel squirmed in her seat, effectively identifying herself. "Another involved an apparently separate murder, that of Mayor Porter of Hollywood, while she was staying at the Baker's Dozen Hotel." Sheri Connors met my eyes squarely and looked as relaxed as she ever did, which wasn't very. "And finally, there was a series of unexplained acts of magical vandalism at the Lagos Castle in Manhattan, presumably directed at the owner, Morris Ngambe." Morris nodded, his face solemn.

I started pacing back and forth on the stage, not looking directly at the audience any longer although I was acutely aware of them. I could almost feel their eyes following me. "The explanations for all of these various events are intertwined so tightly that it is impossible to deal with one in the absence of the others. Even now there are elements that I can only guess at, although I hope that by bringing you all together like this, we might be able to answer some of those questions as well. But the broad outline of what has been happening is very clear, and the identities of the parties responsible for these various crimes, not all of whom are in this room, have been firmly established."

That last did result in some nervous stirring, but no one spoke. I gave them a few seconds to think about what I'd just said.

"Let's begin with the three ritual murders. Most of you have been told only that the police believe the three murders to be linked. What very few of you know is that they based this belief on the fact that each of the three bodies was mutilated in the same fashion. Specific symbols were cut into the flesh of the victims, symbols identical in all three instances. This led to the obvious conclusion that they were the work of a single individual, or multiple individuals working cooperatively. Unfortunately, in this particular instance, that logical assumption by the Police was incorrect, or at best only a partial truth."

I had turned to the audience, watching to see if anyone would betray themselves by moving nervously. I hadn't expected this to be the case and I wasn't disappointed.

"The chain of events which led to their deaths started with the creation of two very unique pieces of jewelry." I reached into my jacket pocket and brought out the half heart I had stolen from the Hyannis Police and retrieved from its hiding place this morning. "You can't see this clearly from a distance, so I'll describe it to you. It's one half of a heart, a charmed heart. The two original charms, each known as the Heart's Desire, were both split into two pieces. We'll discuss their creation a bit later, but for now let's just accept their existence. I don't know exactly what the Heart's Desire does. I'll leave that to the experts to determine later. But I can venture a pretty good guess. They grant their owners one or more wishes, and they're powerful enough to overcome any contravening magic, perhaps even the underlying arcane structure of our world."

"That's not possible," protested Jessica Crane. "All magic derives its power from the Arcanum. A noncompliant charm is a contradiction in terms."

"Not necessarily, but we'll address that later also if you don't mind. For now, let's just accept that the amulets are extremely powerful and valuable to those who understand how to make use of them. As far as I know, and I sincerely hope I'm right, only two of them exist. One of them was sold to or given to or maybe even stolen by Aram Gudanoff. The other went to Ruth Deacon."

I was watching Rachel Deacon when I said this and, to my great satisfaction, she showed no reaction at all.

"It's very likely that neither of these individuals understood the power of the amulets, or their more sinister aspects. They are not passive objects subject to the wishes of their owners. They have a purpose of their own, and their relationship with those who possess them is symbiotic at best. I don't know the mechanics of how to invoke the power of the Heart's Desire, not in detail, but I've got a pretty good idea and it clearly requires a human sacrifice. The owner splits the amulet into two pieces, giving the second half to the proposed victim. It looks very much like a love charm and it's possible that some form of sexual bonding is necessary, although given Ruth Deacon's aversion to physical intimacy that might not be the case. It does appear to be essential that the victim wear or carry the amulet for some period of time before the ceremony - which involves ritual mutilation - can be performed."

Rachel Deacon was on her feet, her face red. The sisters might not have the capacity for human affection, but they certainly could feel anger. "Are you accusing my sister of committing murder, Mr. Dash?"

"Yes, I am, Miss Deacon. Your sister killed Steven Sandobhal, whom she knew casually through her photography business. They were not close friends before that, and he was not a part of her professional circle so he was unaware of her lack of interest in a physical relationship. Somehow she talked him into wearing the amulet and when the time came, she killed him and mutilated his body."

I hurried on to prevent her from protesting further. "Aram Gudanoff had a different problem. He was far from averse to having a sexual relationship with his victim. Unfortunately his social circle consisted of public figures, including Mayor Porter incidentally, and it might have been awkward if one of them turned up dead, particularly after having been seen in his company. So he looked elsewhere, found a pliable young waitress in Dublin, romanced her a bit, and murdered her when the requirements of the amulet had been fulfilled. He then reclaimed the second half of his amulet and prepared to reap his reward. Ruth Deacon, incidentally, was less thorough. She failed to retrieve the amulet worn by Sandobhal," I raised my hand to show them the half heart again, "which was subsequently recovered by the Hyannis Police." I set the amulet down on one of the card tables. I didn't want it on my person any longer than necessary. Neither Mayor touched it.

"I have no idea what Gudanoff was planning to wish for, or whether or not he actually got what he wanted. He was certainly killed before he could reap much benefit from his effort, so I imagine he hadn't asked for a long and happy life. We'll talk about that also after a bit. Ruth Deacon did, however, use her wish, but things didn't work out quite the way she had planned." I turned and looked squarely at Rachel. "Your sister was obsessed with the original world, wasn't she?"

Rachel looked uncertain, but she nodded. "Even as a child, she couldn't stop asking questions about it. That was the first thing that separated us. I wanted to live in the present. Ruth had this bizarre notion that everything was better in the old world, that we were just living some kind of shadow existence and had no idea what life was really like. I couldn't talk her out of it."

"Did she ever say she wished she could return there?"

"Yes, many times, but..." And her eyes widened and she fell silent.

"Exactly." I clasped my hands behind my back and resumed pacing. "Ruth Deacon wished herself back into the original world, and I think that's where she is. But she was careless. Unlike Gudanoff, she failed to retrieve the second half of the amulet. Maybe she forgot it, maybe she panicked, maybe she misunderstood its significance. My guess is that she made her wish, and got half of what she asked for. She and her dark room were somehow shifted back into the original world, but I think she's imprisoned there, trapped in a room that doesn't exist. That's why the guardian spirit believes that she's still in her apartment. Since you're still alive," I looked directly at Rachel, "she must be also, most likely suspended in some kind of timeless limbo where she doesn't need food or fresh air. Despite her crime, I sincerely hope that she's not conscious."

"This is all guesswork," Rachel answered angrily. "You have no proof that my sister killed anyone."

"No, I suppose not. Nor do I have any proof about your own little crime spree."

That took the wind out of her. Her expression went from furious to guarded in an eye blink. "What are you talking about?"

"You hired me to find your sister, but you've known for some time now what kind of dark magic she was involved with, and I'm pretty sure you came to pretty much the same conclusion I did."

"That's nonsense!"

"Is it?" I turned to Alice, the clerk from the bank. "You recognize Miss Deacon, don't you?"

"Yes. I mean I think so." Her voice was so faint that I could barely hear her. "But I don't understand any of this. I thought her name was Ruth."

"They're identical twins," I said quietly. "You've waited on this woman, or her sister, at your bank in Paris, haven't you?"

She nodded.

"How many times did she access her safety deposit box?"

"Why, I don't know how many times she came in. I waited on her once, when she opened the box originally, and twice since then. But she could have come in again while Maxine was there."

"Thank you, Alice." I turned to Rachel. "When you and I opened that box, you already knew what was inside. You had found the key in her apartment the first time you visited and impersonated her. I assume that Ruth's most recent diary was in the box, and in that diary were the details about how the Heart's Desire worked. So you removed it, hoping to make use of the amulet for yourself, but you needed me on the case because you had no idea where the two halves had gone. You were clumsy, though. When you and I searched her apartment together that first time, you hadn't returned the key. It wasn't until you wanted me to look at the contents of the safe deposit box that you planted it where I would find it. I searched that drawer very thoroughly, Miss Deacon. There was no envelope and no key in it until my second visit. And you made a second mistake, one which I admit I didn't realize myself until just recently."

"What are you talking about?" She looked suddenly uncertain.

I took out the Lagos Castle gift card with the runes on the back and handed it to Morris. "Do you recognize this?"

"Of course. We use them to lure customers in."

"How do you hand them out?"

"It varies. Sometimes we give them to people as they leave the restaurant, sometimes we do mass mailings. Whatever occurs to us."

"Do you recognize this particular one?"

"Not this single piece, no. But it's recent. We arrange it so they have to be used within a week at the most."

"And when did this one expire?"

"Today is the last day." He sounded puzzled. "What's the point of this, Dash?"

"Bear with me just a second longer. If it expires today, it was printed exactly one week ago, correct?"

"Most likely the day before."

"But no longer than eight days. And I found it in Ruth Deacon's safety deposit box, which supposedly had not been opened for the previous ten days. Which means that it was left there by Rachel Deacon when she extracted the diary." I turned to her. "You wanted to provide something to keep me looking for the amulets. So you copied some characters out of Ruth's diary onto a random piece of paper, but you deliberately changed several of them, leaving just enough to establish a link, but not enough to reveal anything if I showed it to an expert."

I clasped my hands behind my back and began to pace again, organizing my thoughts. "Ruth Deacon's half of the amulet is still with her. So now we only have to account for the other one, the one Aram Gudanoff owned. One half of that set has reappeared, around the neck of Evan Garner, deceased, former lover of Natalie Porter, Mayor of Hollywood, also deceased. The other half was found with the body of Carlotta Pride." I glanced around the room, and one person was looking very uncomfortable. It was the person I had suspected, but I still wasn't happy about it.

"But who killed Gudanoff and why?" The question came from behind me, from Mayor Chang.

I didn't turn to look at him, but I addressed his question. "The why is simple. Gudanoff let slip something about the power of the amulets to someone who decided to make use of them herself. He was romantically involved with another woman and perhaps for the first time he actually thought he was in love. We'll never know exactly how it happened, but his lover discovered the truth, and she killed him in order to steal the amulet."

"But who was she?" It was Dubois this time.

"Who else but Mayor Natalie Porter?"

Some of the sudden whispering was behind me but several members of the audience seemed surprised as well. I waited until the worst of it had subsided before continuing. "Porter killed Gudanoff and performed the ritual. It's obvious what she wished for, a resumption of her film career with a boost to super stardom. The next day, a prominent actress backed out of a major new film and the producer cast Porter in the part, even though far more talented actresses would have jumped at the chance. Unfortunately, she didn't live long enough to see her dream come true. The amulets work, you see, just as they're supposed to. But they use evil magic, and evil magic always has a way of getting back at you. No one who has performed the ritual and made their wish has managed to enjoy the fruits of their labors, and presumably no one ever will." I looked straight at Rachel Deacon. "A fact which might make some of us reconsider our priorities."

Detective Colby stirred in his seat. "If Porter killed Gudanoff to get the amulet, who killed her and took it?"

"That's an interesting question, and proof if we needed it that the amulets are not powered by neutral magic. They're positively evil. After killing Gudanoff, Porter found herself a new boyfriend, or perhaps she'd been keeping more than one iron in the fire all along despite her icy reputation. It was no secret that she was involved with Evan Garner, the sculptor, that he'd fallen for her suddenly and deeply. He was a regular guest at the Baker's Dozen, where he was well liked. He also kept very much to himself, successfully concealing from the hotel staff that he had a lover who visited him there regularly until Porter enchanted him. It was this woman, hurt and angry, who killed both Porter and Garner, when she discovered that he was sleeping with both of them."

"Then she wasn't after the amulet?" It was the Chief again.

"No, but I suspect that the amulet compelled her to commit the crime. She was extraordinary vulnerable to magic, easily influenced, and she must have been exposed to it during her last few trysts with Garner, might even have tried wearing it. I'm not unusually sensitive to magic, but after carrying this on my person for a few hours," I picked up the half heart, then dropped it again, "I became irritable and had disproportionate violent urges. In her case, natural outrage about Garner's apparent unfaithfulness would have been amplified until it was too strong to resist. Resentment and embarrassment were inflated into overpowering rage. She murdered Porter, arranging things to implicate one of the busboys, and stole the amulet on what must have seemed at the time to be an impulse. The amulet isn't passive, remember? It wants to be used. She returned to Toronto several days later and planted one half of the amulet on the dead body to muddy the trail. If she had known about the symbolic mutilations, she might have added those as well, although they would have been ineffective in invoking its magic. She and Garner had never worn the split heart."

I had reached one end of the elevated stage and I turned to face the audience directly, and one person in particular. "What I don't understand is how the other half of that amulet ended up with Carly Pride. How did you manage that, Sheri?"

Connors sat where she was, absolutely motionless, her expression neutral. I thought at first that she would refuse to answer, to acknowledge my accusation, but then she broke the silence. "I brought it to her to try to find out more about it. You mentioned that the woman who worked at the Lagos Castle was an expert on charms but you didn't tell me her name. I thought she seemed awfully young, but she might have been a prodigy. She said she'd ask around but I never heard from her again."

"But you did kill Mayor Porter."

She nodded. "It seems like a dream even now, like I had stepped outside of my body to watch while it acted on its own. I loved him and I wanted to marry him and he dumped me for that piece of trash. He was obsessed with her even though she was just playing with him." Connors sounded calm, completely under control, almost clinical. "I thought I'd never feel any emotion as strongly as I did when we were making love, but I was wrong. Hate is much stronger."

"I wondered why you seemed so disapproving of Garner right from the outset. Later, when I looked at some of his sculptures, they looked familiar, but it was only yesterday that I remembered where I had seen similar ones before. In your apartment." She dropped her eyes and remained silent. "When I told you that the amulets were connected to the other murders, you went back to where you had dumped his body and planted the amulet, didn't you?"

She nodded, her eyes no longer focused on anything in the room. "I thought it would confuse things, convince you that they'd been murdered by whoever killed the others. If I'd known what the amulet could do, I might have wished that Evan and I were together again." She looked up at me with a wry smile. "But that wouldn't have worked out either, would it? He'd have come back as a corpse, or something worse, wouldn't he?"

"Something like that, yes." Actually, I didn't know what might have happened, but she obviously needed to know she hadn't thrown away her one chance at happiness. I tried to gentle my voice, knowing it was a useless gesture. "You're sensitive to magic, Sheri. You weren't in control of your actions. If you plead temporary magical influence, I'm sure the jury will be sympathetic."

She shrugged her shoulders. "I don't really care. Can you imagine what it's like to watch someone you love die, and to know that you're responsible? I really don't care what happens now."

It was Wanda who broke the awkward silence that followed. "So who tried to warn you off the case and sent the Berserker after Moira?"

"That's not a simple question either." I looked toward Herman Goff. "I don't suppose you'd like to tell us who hired you, Goff?"

"Client confidentiality, Dash. And I didn't do anything illegal so you can't truth spell me."

"Not necessary. It must have been Carly Pride who paid for the banshee. She thought she was responsible for the problems at the Lagos Castle, that some of her conjuring had misfired. She was experimenting with things well in advance of her abilities, things even her sometimes mentor, Miss Crane there, may not have known about. But she only wanted to scare me, didn't she? Someone else hired you later, someone requesting a similar service."

Goff didn't respond this time, just crossed his arms and looked stubborn.

"Your second client was Rachel Deacon. Rachel was also determined to keep me away from the Lagos Castle." I turned in her direction and she actually flinched. "She paid for the beetles and the ghost slugs, didn't she?"

"That's a lie!" Rachel's voice shook. "I never did any such thing."

Goff looked stubborn.

"Attempted murder is a serious enough charge that they'll subject you to a truth spell, Goff."

For a moment, I didn't think he'd crack, but he did. Just not the way I expected. "She paid me for the slugs, but I had nothing to do with any beetles. I don't know what you're talking about."

That made me miss a beat. There was no reason for him to lie. Was there another player in the game?

"Why would I do such a thing? It's ridiculous!" Rachel was agitated and obviously wanted to leave, but the compulsion that had brought her here would not allow her to go until its purpose had been fulfilled.

"You had your reasons. Suffice it to say that you wanted to scare me off.

I turned to address the group in general. "A few days ago, a rather hyperactive zombie attacked Miss McGann here, but it wasn't Miss Deacon who was responsible. It had been infused with a Berserker, a deadly creature commissioned by someone else entirely, someone working at adept level. But before I tell you who was responsible, I need to explain how the amulets came into being in the first place. And to do that I have to go back even further, back three years."

I briefly recapped the story of the failed expedition to study the Tuilleries. "Only three people from that group survive today and two of them are currently in this room. That's more than just coincidence. The truth is that something did come out of the Tuilleries when they flew over it, something unknown to either science or even the Collegium, something evil. I suspect that whatever that force was, it lodged a bit of itself in each and every person who was exposed. The experience was too much for most of them, and they died or killed themselves or went insane. I'm not sure what happened to those evil fragments, but I think they're still out there somewhere. Goff was too tough or too stubborn to give in. The other survivor was Jessica Crane."

Jessica stirred in her seat, looking confused and anxious. "What are you suggesting?" Her voice was hoarse.

In the row behind her, Marie Dussaud was opening the wicker basket.

"Just hear me out. Miss Crane here suffered from physical, psychological, and spiritual problems for a considerable time after the expedition. She was forced to abandon her work in arcane studies and eventually took a job running the Lagos Castle gift shop. Her problems reportedly continued until shortly after she hired a young assistant named Carlotta Pride, who was an avid student of magic. Crane has informed me that she began to regain her former peace of mind and even experienced a reawakened interest in magic in the months after she met Miss Pride. It was as though some burden had been lifted from her shoulders and shifted elsewhere. The logical conclusion is that this dark presence relocated to a more suitable host, the force that infected Crane was passed on to the younger woman, who was known to have had a powerful though undeveloped magical gift."

"Powerful enough to create the amulets?" asked Mayor Burford from behind me.

"Actually, I don't think so," I admitted. " If Carly Pride was capable of conjuring evil magic inside the Lagos Castle, magic over which she still had less than perfect control, then some of that corrupt power might have spilled over, affecting other items, spoiling food, disrupting beneficial charms, even causing deterioration of physical objects. But she was a relative novice despite her talent. One incident might have been a lucky casting, but she couldn't possibly be responsible for the constant stream of problems."

I turned to Rachel Deacon. "When you went to the gift shop and picked up the charm you'd ordered to make yourself more persuasive when you came to see me, Carly mistook you for your sister, didn't she?"

I hadn't expected her to answer, but Rachel finally seemed to have accepted defeat and discovery. She nodded slowly. "She called me Miss Deacon the first time I ever went there. It took a few seconds for me to realize that she'd confused me with Ruth, and by then she'd said some very interesting things about a special order my sister had placed so I played along and she said enough about the amulets that I guessed about their power to grant wishes. But she never said anything about the human sacrifices, I swear! I went to see Ruth right afterwards, but she was already gone by then. That's when I decided to hire you."

"Carly didn't know that the amulets required the life of a human being before they'd work. But you really weren't interested in Ruth, were you? You wanted the amulet for yourself."

She shook her head, her voice stronger. "I wanted both, Mr. Dash. The amulet wouldn't be of much use if my sister died before I could invoke its power. I'd follow her within hours, remember? And I only wanted the amulet to get free of the bonding. There's no other way to do it."

"I'll take you at your word. So that's where the evidence points, ladies and gentlemen. I was supposed to believe that Carly Pride, corrupted by the presence that had transferred to her from Jessica Crane, created the two amulets that started this entire chain of events. When I started to get close, she conjured up a Berserker to stop me, but it failed, and when she tried something even more dangerous to protect herself, it backfired and she died. So all of the guilty parties would have been either dead or identified."

There was a stirring behind me and I turned to find Mayor Curtis scratching his head and looking unhappy. "I assume you're about to tell us that's not the case."

"I'm afraid so, your Honor." I let my eyes trail slowly across the auditorium. I liked having an audience, even if it was captive. "You will remember that I said that it appeared that Carly Pride was the prime mover behind the amulets. Appearances are sometimes misleading. Carly was really just another victim."

I turned toward Moira. "When you went to the Lagos Castle gift shop for the first time, did you meet Carly Pride?"

Moira shook her head. "No, I never met her."

I looked at Marie. "Could the Berserker that abducted Moira have done so if its creator had never been in her physical presence?"

"Absolutely not."

"And Carly had never met Moira." I let that sink in. "We are supposed to believe that Carly knew about the amulets, that she was talented enough to create them with the help of the evil force that possessed her. But we also know that she was trying to earn enough money to study thaumaturgy. That's rather an odd ambition for someone who used some pretty sophisticated sorcery when she was trying to kill me." I started pacing again. "At the time, I thought I was lucky to have escaped with my life. But was it luck? Perhaps I was meant to live because by surviving I became the only witness to Carly's guilt and the manner of her death."

Marie reached into the wicker basket and pulled out the now inanimate head of the zombie I'd killed. She placed it on the seat directly behind Jessica Crane. The moment she released her grip, its eyes popped open, then slowly closed again. Marie smiled. She had hoped the head would react in some fashion when exposed to the presence of its creator, and it had.

Which confirmed what I already knew. "It was you throwing fire balls at me in Toronto, Miss Crane. You overplayed your hand, I'm afraid. Once I had time to think, I realized that any adept with that much power could have killed me easily. I was meant to escape. Carly was innocent and she was a convenient pawn to expend in order to protect your secret. I'm guessing you had her in a binding spell until it was time to throw her from the balcony just before you escaped, so that I could hear her screams as she burned to death."

Her face was absolutely expressionless, betraying neither fear nor anger, and her voice was almost placid. "You have quite an imagination, Mr. Dash."

"I should really have guessed the truth earlier. When I came to see you with this the other day," I picked up the half heart, "it fell out of my pocket twice. It has an affinity for you, I imagine. I'm not that clumsy." She didn't answer. "And the problems at the Lagos Castle were your fault as well, although they were unintentional. I made a couple of calls this morning. There have been three transformations in the Tuileries recently. Each of them coincides with an outburst of trouble in the restaurant, the gift shop, or both. A piece of whatever lives in the Tuilleries is in you, and what affects the whole also affects the part."

"Can you prove any of this?" asked Mayor Curtis.

"I think so." I walked to the edge of the stage and pulled the canvas tarp off the object concealed there. It was an aura reader, one of the mechanical ones used in the barrier around the Tuilleries. A large red indicator light was blinking rapidly. "It senses you even from up here," I said quietly. "Should I prove the point by having you brought up onto the stage?"

She stood up slowly, looking completely unconcerned. "You were wrong about the scarabs, Dash. I did that myself in a moment of pique. And that's not the only mistake you've made."

She raised her arm and I felt an electric tension in the room. She was drawing the magic latent in her surroundings, sucking it in like a vacuum cleaner. There were five soft pops, so close together they were hard to distinguish from one another. Five smallish bodies materializing in a circle around Jessica Crane. No, not a circle. A pentagram. The nearest to me was Sferoi. The others were about his size, but there was no other resemblance. One was vaguely feline, one was covered with purple scales, the fourth had wings, and the last could almost have been human, if it hadn't been for the second pair of arms.

None of the five homunculi made a sound and there was no physical evidence of the struggle that ensued. Crane stood rigid, apparently concentrating her energies, and the five minions of the Collegium held their position. Surprisingly, no one in the audience moved except that Sheri Connors slumped over in a faint, overwhelmed by the flux of magical power that surrounded her. We could all feel it. All of the hair on my body alternate wriggled and stiffened and for some reason I had a blinding sinus headache. It might have gone on for hours – it certainly seemed that way. But it couldn't have been more than a minute or two before Crane relaxed and settled back into her seat.

Her voice was steady, almost amused. "Very impressive, Dash. I underestimated you. I was sure you'd taken the bait. Carly was a child. She even helped me create the amulets, though she never guessed their purpose."

"And just what was their purpose?"

Jessica ignored the question. "I misjudged my clients, I'm afraid. They failed to follow directions. Each of the bodies should have been destroyed immediately following the ceremony. The Deacon woman even forgot to reunite the heart before making her wish. Not even I know what kind of limbo she's made for herself."

The homunculi were moving now, slowly closing in on her without breaking the regularity of the pentagram. "I'll make you a gift, Dash. Not much, but something you didn't figure out on your own."

The homunculi were very close to her now, and she still hadn't shown any inclination to resist further. That bothered me a little. What happened next bothered me even more.

Crane looked at me with obvious amusement. "You're not as clever as you think you are, Dash. You made one significant mistake."

"That's always a possibility." I couldn't think of any holes in my reconstruction, and she hadn't denied anything I'd said.

"I didn't send the Berserker after you," she said quietly.

I thought about it. "You're not going to try to convince me that Carly was in league with you after all?"

She looked offended. "That child? Talent is an overrated quality. Knowledge and discipline and devotion are all more important. With those three virtues, I could make even you into an adept."

"Are you suggesting that you had another confederate?" Why would she volunteer this information, if it was true?

Her face changed, became almost unrecognizable, but it was rage and fanaticism that transformed her features, not magic. Even so, I felt as though I was no longer listening to Jessica Crane but another entity entirely, something that lived within her body and mind. "I'm just an apprentice, you fools. Did it never occur to anyone to wonder how the barrier at the Tuilleries was pierced? There's a greater power at work than any of you can possible conceive of, and it's out here among you, not locked up in the gardens." She had been gesturing to include everyone in the room, but now she turned back to face me directly. "And what you've done here today will not be forgiven, or forgotten. Do you understand?"

And then the homunculi were very close to her and a second later they had blinked out of existence, at least in the here and now. So had Jessica Crane.

The Oslo Police took charge of Sheri Connors.

There was one other revelation which I haven't mentioned yet and said nothing about while we were at the Opera House. In order to send the Berserker after Moira, Crane had to have been in her physical presence at least once. Sendings won't work without firsthand knowledge of the aura of the target. Unfortunately, Moira had made it easy for her by visiting the gift shop and identifying herself to Crane at precisely the wrong time. So it was only logical for me to assume that Crane had sent the Berserker after a target of opportunity.

But Crane had denied creating the Berserker. She might well be lying just to make me uneasy, but that seemed rather petty, not at all her style. It bothered me and I planned to think about it some more after a while, but not just now. I told myself to worry about it later. But then Marie Dussaud tugged on my elbow.

"Could I speak to you for a moment, Dash?"

"Of course."

"Alone?"

I glanced around, then ushered her into a small vestibule backstage where it was unlikely that anyone could overhear us. "What's up?"

"Do you remember my saying that there was something odd about the way the Berserker went after Moira instead of you?"

"Sure. Why?"

"You let me believe that Carly Pride was its creator, that she'd met Moira at the gift shop."

"I hadn't actually figured everything out yet but yes, even then I suspected that she couldn't have done it, at least not alone. I didn't work out the rest until later."

"Well, I held something back too. I wasn't sure if it was my place to say anything."

Now she had my attention. Had I missed something relevant?

"Evil magic is all about perverting human aspirations. It's an essential element, what makes it so seductive. That's why things like the amulets are called the Heart's Desire or something similarly innocuous. It's also an important element in the invocation of a Berserker."

"How so?"

"It didn't really matter if its creator had met Moira. The Berserker would have found her anyway."

I could feel my face creasing into a frown. "But that contradicts what you told me earlier."

But she was shaking her head even before I finished speaking. "No, it doesn't. The Berserker was targeted at you, not Moira, so whoever was responsible only had to have met you, and that could be almost anyone connected to the case. To be precise, it was ordered to steal the single thing which you valued most in the world. And that's what it did."

She let the words sit there while I tried to wrap my brain around them. "Are you trying to tell me...?" My voice trailed off.

"Yes," she said composedly. "And now that you know, I think it's time you told her as well."

And then she was gone, and I thought about it for a while. Once when Katrina and I were still together, she told me that our problem was that she was a hopeless romantic and I was hopeless at romance. "Even you don't know what you feel, so how am I supposed to guess?"

   She was probably right, but I am what I am, and I do the best I can with what I have. So I went and found Moira and took her someplace where we could be alone and did exactly that.

THE END...but Dash will be back.

www.ingramcontent.com/pod-product-compliance
Lightning Source LLC
Chambersburg PA
CBHW072213170626
46813CB00003B/918